Marius' Mules VI:
Caesar's Vow

by S. J. A. Turney

1st Edition

"Marius' Mules: nickname acquired by the legions after the general Marius made it standard practice for the soldier to carry all of his kit about his person."

For Dave & Lisa.

I would like to thank those people instrumental in bringing Marius' Mules 6 to fruition and making it the book it is. Jenny and Lilian for their initial editing, Tracey for support, love and a steady stream of bacon sandwiches. Leni, Barry, Paul, Robin, Glynn, Alun, Neil & Stu for their beta reading and catching a few eye-watering bloopers – you saved me some real trouble there.

Thanks also to Garry, Paul and Dave for the cover work. Prue, Gordon, Robin, Nick, Kate, Mike and innumerable other fab folk for their support.

Cover photos courtesy of Paul and Garry of the Deva Victrix Legio XX. Visit http://www.romantoursuk.com/ to see their excellent work.

Cover design by Dave Slaney.

Many thanks to all three for their skill and generosity.

All internal maps are copyright the author of this work.

Also by S. J. A. Turney:

Dramatis Personae

*For ease of reference, the most commonly used name in the text is **emboldened**. Not all characters in the story are here referenced, but the principle ones carried forward from previous volumes are, as well as a few new characters of import. Other names will be introduced in the text appropriately.*

<u>The Command Staff:</u>

Gaius Julius **Caesar:** Politician, General and Governor.
Aulus **Ingenuus:** Commander of Caesar's Praetorian Cohort.
Quintus Atius **Varus:** Commander of the Cavalry.
Gnaeus Vinicius **Priscus:** Camp Prefect of Caesar's army.
Decimus Junius **Brutus** Albinus: Legate and favourite of Caesar's family.
Marcus Vitruvius **Mamurra**: One of Rome's most famous engineers.
Lucius Minucius **Basilus:** Lesser staff officer.
Gaius **Rufio:** Staff officer.

<u>Seventh Legion:</u>

Lucius Munatius **Plancus:** Legate.

<u>Eighth Legion:</u>

Gaius **Fabius** Pictor: Legate.

<u>Ninth Legion:</u>

Gaius **Trebonius:** Legate.
Grattius: Primus Pilus, once in sole command of the Ninth.
Ianuarius: Senior artillerist.
Petreius: Senior artillerist.
Marcius: Junior artillerist.

<u>Tenth Legion:</u>

Marcus **Crassus 'The Younger':** Legate, younger son of the triumvir.
Lucius **Fabius:** Tribune, former Centurion & friend of Priscus & Fronto.

Tullus **Furius:** Tribune, former Centurion & friend of Priscus & Fronto.

Servius Fabricius **Carbo:** Primus Pilus.

Atenos: Centurion and chief training officer, former Gaulish mercenary.

Eleventh Legion:

Quintus Tullius **Cicero:** Legate and brother of the great orator.

Titus Mittius **'Felix':** Camp Prefect for the 11th & former Primus Pilus.

Quintus **Velanius:** Senior Tribune.

Titus **Silius:** Junior Tribune.

Titus **Pullo:** Primus Pilus.

Lucius **Vorenus:** Senior centurion.

Twelfth Legion:

Titus **Labienus:** Lieutenant of Caesar. Currently Legate of the 12th.

Gaius Volusenus **Quadratus:** Tribune.

Publius Sextius **Baculus:** Primus Pilus. A distinguished veteran.

Lucius Annius **Gritto:** cavalry Decurion.

Thirteenth Legion:

Lucius **Roscius:** Legate and native of Illyricum.

Biorix: Gallic-born legionary & engineer.

Fourteenth Legion (reconstituted):

Nasica: Surviving soldier of the 14th and now aquilifer (eagle-bearer) of the reconstituted legion.

Other characters:

Marcus Falerius **Fronto:** Former Legate of the Tenth.

Masgava: Former gladiator and confederate of Fronto.

Palmatus: Retired Pompeian legionary & confederate of Fronto.

Marcus **Antonius:** Senior officer and close friend & distant relative of Caesar.

Quintus **Balbus:** Former Legate of the Eighth, now retired. Close friend of Fronto.

Faleria the younger: sister of Fronto.

Lucilia: Elder daughter of Balbus & wife of Fronto.

Balbina: Younger daughter of Balbus.

Galronus: Belgic officer, commanding Caesar's auxiliary cavalry.

Marcus Licinius **Crassus:** Caesar's partner in the triumvirate. Currently in Syria.

Gnaeus **Pompey** Magnus: Caesar's partner in the triumvirate. Currently in Rome.

Publius **Clodius** Pulcher: Powerful man in Rome, client of Caesar and conspirator.

Gaius Fusius **Cita:** Former chief Quartermaster of Caesar's Army.

Vercingetorix: Gallic chieftain & rebel, referred to also as 'Esus'.

Ambiorix: Eburone King who recently destroyed the 14th Legion.

Cativolcus: Eburone King.

Indutiomarus: Treveri chieftain.

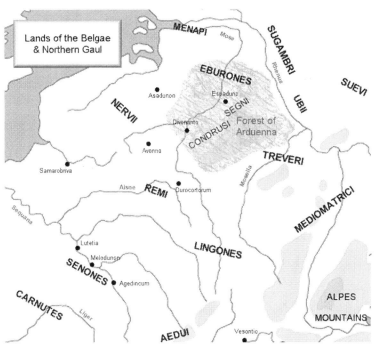

Lands of the Belgae
& Northern Gaul

MENAPI
Mosa
SUGAMBRI
SUEVI
EBURONES
UBII
Asadunon
Espaduno
SEGNI
NERVII
Divonanto
CONDRUSI
Forest of
Arduenna
Avenna
TREVERI
Samarobriva
MoBella
Aisne
REMI
Durocortorum
MEDIOMATRICI
Sequana
LINGONES
Lutetia
Melodunon
SENONES
Agedincum
ALPES
CARNUTES
Liger
MOUNTAINS
AEDUI
Vesontio

**The ruined farm
in the forest**

a

b

c

f

d

e

e

Key to locations

a - Dry stream bed
b - Lookout rock
c - Granary
d - Farmhouse
e - Ruined building
f - Lookout

Prologue

'I will hear nothing more of it, Priscus.'

Caesar drummed his fingers irritably on the table top as his brow twitched, leaden-cold eyes locked challengingly on the man before him. The general, Priscus noted, looked more tired than ever, yet there was something about him that had been lacking in evidence this past year or two: a fire. A purpose. Something had changed in Caesar, and it revolved around the missives he had sent to and received from Rome.

Priscus scratched his chin - bristly and none-too-clean - reflectively, wondering how far he could push the general this morning before he was properly upbraided. The state of his chin brought him back once more to a regular theme in his musings: just how much it seemed he was becoming Fronto. When he'd borne the transverse crest of a centurion the very idea of a morning unshaven would have stunned him. A three-day growth would have been unthinkable - he'd slapped month-long latrine duties on soldiers for less. And here he was, looking like some callow Roman youth emerging from his debauched pit after the Lupercalia festival, eyes red-rimmed with too much wine, wreathed in a smell faintly reminiscent of old dog. He would have to make a short sharp visit to the baths when he left here and get himself in shape.

'With respect, General, you've sent for reinforcements. You will command the biggest army Rome has raised since that Thracian gladiator stomped up and down the countryside freeing slaves. Gaul is unsettled and troublesome - more than ever - and now is not the time to concentrate on small things, but to look to the security of the fledgling province as a whole.'

Caesar glared at him and he took a steadying breath, aware of how close to the edge he was treading. 'I will hear nothing more of it' was a warning sign.

'Again, respectfully, you could stand on the throat of all the Belgae tribes with just eight legions; nine if you really feel the need to flatten them. All I ask is *one* legion. Even a green, untried one as long as the officers are competent. I'll take one legion and unpick this whole damn land until I've revealed every sign of trouble. We do know that Esus...'

He stopped abruptly as Caesar slapped his palm on the table angrily, his face contorting with a snarl.

'Enough with this damned 'Esus', Priscus. I am sick to the back teeth of hearing about mythical Gallic rebels who consort with druids and foment discord behind the scenes. If he exists, how come we have discovered nothing about him in over a year of campaigning?' He pointed at the officer before him, denying Priscus the right to reply. 'Simply because he is a fiction! Or if not a fiction, then the emphasis that you and your pet spies place upon him is vastly overrated. If he *does* exist, most likely this Esus *is* Ambiorix.'

Priscus prepared himself. He had bent the reed just about as far as it would go and it was clear what would happen unless he acquiesced now. Sadly, a dishevelled appearance was not the only thing he seemed to have inherited from Fronto. A pig-headed unwillingness to halt in the face of trouble seemed to have taken hold in his spirit too.

'I do not think that is the case, Caesar. Ambiorix was a *small scale* rebel...'

'*Small scale*?' snapped Caesar. 'That piece of Belgic filth wiped out a legion, lost me two veteran commanders - of Senatorial rank, no less - and endangered the rest of the army, almost finishing off Cicero in the process. And despite our timely arrival in force, still the mangy dog escaped us. Now he runs around free once more, gathering warriors to his banner in defiance of Rome. Get out of my tent, Priscus. Go bathe yourself in wine and forget all about your Gallic demi-God and his machinations. This army has a purpose at this time, other than the simple pacification of tribes: vengeance, Priscus. Simple revenge. Now go see to yourself and your fellow officers.'

Priscus winced at the sharpness in the general's voice. Caesar was controlling his temper by a fine thread at best, and another word could snap it. Not even risking an apology, the officer simply bowed curtly, turned and left the tent.

Gaius Julius Caesar, Proconsul of Cisalpine Gaul and Illyricum, governor of Transalpine Gaul, beloved of the Roman people and descendant of Venus, pinched the bridge of his nose and tried to ignore the blinding headache that was rising in his temple with every crunch of Priscus' footsteps crossing the frosty grass away from the tent.

Gaul was killing him by degrees.

Every morning he felt slightly more worn, as though the very act of waking up in this rebellious world abraded a little of his spirit and body both. He had always reproached Fronto for his drinking

2

habits, and had taken to doing so with Priscus, and yet was forced to admit to himself that his own consumption had risen drastically the past two years. Once upon a time, he had rarely slept, working through the hours of darkness and taking but a few hours of rest before launching into the coming day with renewed vigour. Not so these days. The wine helped him sleep of course, but also the days seemed to press on him so much now that rest was becoming more of a necessity.

Gaul had to be settled.

Straightening, he stalked across the tent to the door, pulling aside one of the hanging leather flaps. Two of Aulus Ingenuus' horse guard stood at attention outside, one to each side. Other than that the nearest activity was a collection of senior officers - including Priscus - chattering away by the water tank near the camp prefect's tent.

'I am not to be disturbed,' he announced to the bodyguards, who saluted without tearing their eyes away from the camp and any potential trouble. Ingenuus was always serious about his task, and that professionalism filtered down through his men.

With a nod of satisfaction, Caesar returned to his tent and allowed the leather flap to drop back behind him. Ignoring the table with its huge map of Gaul and collection of tablets and scrolls, the cupboards and desks that held all his records and correspondence, the chairs and banners, standards and trophies, he turned to the door in the dividing wall.

Caesar's tent was, needless to say, the largest in the camp by a sizeable margin, given the fact that it served as both his private apartments and the army's headquarters. The front room was large enough to comfortably accommodate a briefing of twenty officers, and that was only a third of the whole structure.

The Illyrian slave who stood folding Caesar's tunics ready to place them in the shelves turned at the general's sudden entrance, bowing low and then replacing the linen and scurrying over to his master. Caesar frowned. For some reason he couldn't remember the slave's name. He'd had a series of miscellaneous house and body slaves during the campaign, but they never seemed to be up to the task and in the end they were all sent on to other duties, some not even hanging around long enough to remember their face. The latest seemed to be obsessed with neatness, which was fine, but was never there when Caesar discovered he needed him.

'Leave me.'

3

The slave bowed respectfully, and then scurried towards the other doorway that led into the general's sleeping chamber.

'Not that way. Outside. Go and wash something.'

Nodding nervously, the young Illyrian shuffled through the room and disappeared into the public area and then outside. Caesar sighed and allowed himself to sag a little as solitude enfolded him in its comforting embrace. It was an unfortunate consequence of public life and military command that he rarely ever found himself alone unless he was actually asleep. Privacy was a precious commodity, though he'd had a little more of it these past few months, since Labienus was away east with his legion keeping the Treveri busy and some of the more vocal and time-consuming officers were either back in Rome or gracing the fields of Elysium.

Soon, that respite would vanish. A couple of months of wintering with the troops had brought its own hardships, but at least there had been a certain level of inactivity. No one campaigned in the winter. But the weather was perceptibly changing, and in a matter of weeks the first hints of spring would show, which meant that ships would start to sail and Antonius would arrive in Gaul with a new herd of eager officers. Then the business of command would become fraught once more.

His eyes fell upon the thing to which he must now tend - the reason he had dismissed the slave and sought privacy.

The altar.

Most of the officers had brought small altars on campaign with them, replete with portable divine figures cast in bronze or sculpted from wood or ivory. The Olympian Gods graced shrines in every officer's tent, and even the common soldiery would carry miniature figures of their chosen deities with them to pray before.

The general's, of course, was something a little grander. A full-size altar of carved marble shipped with his personal gear from Rome, decorated with scenes of the Goddess granting favours - and dallying with Mars of course - painted in bright colours with the care and skill of a true artist. Atop the altar - a flat surface surrounded by delicate scroll-work - stood the statue of the Goddess herself. Unusually for her divine portrayals, this particular Venus was clothed for modesty, though her shapeliness showed through the diaphanous gown, and her languid pose suggested less than modest pursuits.

The various offerings he had found cause to place upon the altar top around the lady's figure remained in situ. The slight bowl-shaped depression between her toes was stained a deep dark red from old dried wine libations. Small piles of ash abounded - all that remained of silver frankincense, brought from Arabia via Rome at the cost of a legionary's yearly pay for each shipment. Tiny bronze, orichalcum, silver and gold charms commissioned from Gallic smiths for the honour of the Goddess were scattered here and there. All in favour of Venus Genetrix, the mother of the Julian family line and patron divinity of the general.

This shrine, with its altar, statue and offerings, represented an outlay of money that would make even Crassus wince. And while Caesar only had passing time for Gods as a whole, preferring to trust his own abilities and knowledge, he was careful to keep the family Goddess appeased and on his side.

Yet, despite this, his grand plan seemed to be foundering.

When he had initially secured his command and the Proconsulship - hurriedly, after the end of his Consular term - he had imagined that by now he would be back in Rome, reaping the rewards of his campaign and securing a previously undreamed of level of power for his descendants.

And now here he was in his sixth year of Gaul, on his second extended term of governorship, still struggling to keep the tribes under control, his mother perished in a conflagration, his daughter passed away without issue and taking with her all hopes of peace and reconciliation with Pompey, the senate beginning to speak against him and even his beloved mob of plebs questioning his ability to control Gaul.

It was vexing, to say the least.

With a deep sigh, the general collected his folding campaign chair from the small desk in the corner and placed it before the altar, opening it out. Supplicants may generally kneel or bow or prostrate themselves, but few supplicants could claim to be one of the leading figures in the greatest nation the world had ever known. Besides, he was no longer a young man, and a seated position was sensible for the sake of his joints.

'Beloved Venus, mother and queen, I entreat you...'

He paused. Was it an entreaty? Or simply a vow?

A shrug. It was, of course, both... a deal of sorts.

'*My* line is *your* line, Divine Venus Genetrix. *My* family is *your* family. My *mother* is your *daughter.* Yet our house ails and falters. Julia is gone, and with her any hope of a grandchild. Young Brutus could provide me with one, but to make *that* progeny claim

5

public would tear down much of what I have built and bring shame upon his mother. Barring perhaps Antonius - who has his own demons with whom to wrestle - none of my collection of greedy, self-obsessed and degenerate cousins or nephews would be worth the time and effort of grooming.'

He closed his eyes and rubbed the corners of them wearily.

'Except possibly Atia Caesonia's boy. The lad shows promise, even at only nine summers. Given what he seems to know of the world and its workings, he has the makings of a strong politician, and feasibly a commander of men. But he is still several years from taking the toga virilis, and I would see him grow into manhood and display some sort of sign that he is ready before I entrust the future of all that I strive for to him.'

He sighed and opened his eyes, flexing his fingers.

'And that, great Venus, is the crux of the matter. My family - *your* family - is in flux, and has no clear future. What is the point of my dragging our familia from poverty and obscurity to become the most prominent in the Republic if it all crumbles and falls to dust when I pass on to Elysium because there is no one suitable to follow? I would entreat you to watch over the Julii and to strengthen us, to clear out the chaff that fills the granary of your seed and leave us only the strong grain that forms the pure, healthy bread. If Octavian is to be the future - and my gut tells me he could be that one - give me a sign. If Antonius might be worthy - despite the distance in our lineage - let him leave behind the debauchery that has plagued him since his youth and stand tall on the shoulders of the devils that now ride him. And if Brutus…?'

He straightened.

'Great Venus, I have vowed to the senate and to the Roman people that I will bring to heel the rebel leader Ambiorix, who roused the tribes against us, killed Cotta and Sabinus and all-but obliterated the Fourteenth legion, and who even now remains at large. I have vowed his end to them, and now I vow it to you. In the name of vengeance and good Roman piety I will hunt down and destroy this snake that would ruin all that I have achieved, and with his demise, the senate and the people of Rome will throw their support behind me and our line will rise to heights undreamed of.'

He reached out to the small table beside the altar and collected a pinch of the frankincense, depositing a small pile of it on the stone beside the Goddess' heel. Grasping the taper that smoked on the stand, where the slave kept it permanently smouldering, he placed it among the powder and resin until tendrils of blue-grey smoke began to rise, filling the tent rapidly with the heady exotic scent.

'Give me an heir, Divine Venus, mother of the Julii, and in return, I will give you *Gaul*.'

With a long intake of breath he sat back and watched the smoke writhing about the statue. Collecting his small tablet and stylus from the stand, he quickly scrawled the promise - not an altar or a temple, but a whole province - to the Goddess, sealed the tablet and tied it in the age-old manner to her knee. He would start with a temple - perhaps at Vienna? Or Aquae Sextiae or Arelate perhaps. Somewhere civilised to begin with. Satisfied, he turned back towards the doorway that led into the headquarters.

'Ten legions, you Belgic rat. Ten. With the auxilia, that's almost a hundred thousand men. How long can you hide, Ambiorix of the Eburones? How fast can you run?'

Chapter One

The fast moving liburna leapt like a dolphin as it crested a particularly impressive wave. Fronto stood clinging to the rail with whitened fingers, grateful to the swells of the previous day that had ruined his appetite and left him with nothing inside to bring up. Instead, he retched empty breath out across the sea, his stomach flipping this way and that as the vessel once more descended into the trough and shuddered with the force of Neptune's wrath.

'Dearest, divine Fortuna, who I have loved and graced with my devotions these past decades, if you see fit to just drown me now and put me out of my misery, I will consider it your last blessing.'

The ship bucked once more in answer and Fronto felt his foot slip for a moment.

'I wouldn't beg to drown now, Fronto. The worst of it's over.'

The sea-sick officer turned from the rail to examine the speaker and immediately wished he hadn't. Marcus Antonius was striding up the deck as though out for an afternoon stroll in balmy sunlight. He had no grip on the rail, despite the dangerous rise and fall of the boards, since one hand was wrapped tightly round a greasy chicken leg and the other clutched a goblet that slopped and splashed with rich, unwatered wine.

'How in the name of Bacchus you can drink anything while this ship jumps up and down like a startled horse is beyond me. And how you can...'

His voice tailed off as the very thought of chewing on the wobbly, dripping chicken leg made every organ inside him turn over and pucker. By the time he had finished emptying himself of nothing yet again, Antonius was leaning beside him, watching the waves rise and fall as though it were a comic play. Damn the man.

'Wine inures one to the motion of the ocean' Antonius grinned. 'And anyway, you should be thanking the Gods for our passage. See those lights ahead?'

Fronto blinked against the salt spray.

'Frankly, no.'

'Well I can. That's Ostia, with its welcoming wharves, whorehouses and taverns. In less than an half an hour we make landfall and then we'll be able to make the most of a thriving port town for the night before we move on.'

'If we make it to the dock, just lie me down on the stone and turn me over every now and then so I don't drown when I throw up.'

Antonius laughed aloud and slapped Fronto on the back, bringing on a fresh bout of retching. 'Keep your eyes locked on those lights and watch them grow as we approach. I'm going back inside to finish this rather delectable chicken, empty the last of the amphora and win all that remains of Rufio's sparse coin before we dock and the thieves can try their luck on him.'

He straightened, somehow miraculously staying upright as the ship crested a wave, hovered almost as though floating in the air, and then suddenly crashed back down into the brine with a jolt.

'Want me to send out your wife? She's complaining that she's hardly seen you all voyage.'

'Then she should have agreed to go by horse with me.'

Again, the senior officer laughed and, turning, strode back towards the stern, where the party of travellers sheltered from the chilling, salty winds within the ship's sturdy rear housing. Fronto watched him go with irritation.

Antonius was an engaging and eminently likeable man. He had been good to Fronto and the ladies during the journey, and was a fine wit and a shrewd gambler, despite the fact that he was rarely to be seen without a cup in his hand and Fronto had yet to see him add water to his wine.

Really, they would have been a good bunch to be travelling with, had he not spent the journey either standing at the rail and emptying his stomach contents into Neptune's garden, or in the port taverns where they stayed the night, wishing he was dead and avoiding all temptation of food.

Lucilia and Faleria travelled with them, as well as the sad and silent young Balbina, her father - the ageing former legate Balbus - keeping the girls safe and busy. Palmatus, Galronus and Masgava had largely kept themselves to themselves, not wishing to intrude their selves into the business of the Roman nobility on board. In fact, the three seemed now to be as tight a group of friends as could be found anywhere, and Fronto somewhat resented his sea-sickness keeping him from their circle. Masgava seemed to be recovering from his dreadful stomach wound with disturbing alacrity. Apparently the sea air was helping. It wasn't helping Fronto, that was for sure. It would be months yet before the big former gladiator could comfortably ride a horse or undertake any form of physical exercise, but he had been proclaimed safe and out of danger, and the big man had grinned like a lunatic when he'd learned he would now have a scar twice the size of any other on his much-battered torso.

Most of the others were the usual bunch of Roman nobiles, stiff and formal and not greatly forthcoming. Volcatius, Basilus, Aristius, Sextius, Calenus, Silanus and Reginus had all passed the time of day here and there with Fronto, and Antonius had assured him that every man in the party of new officers was a highly competent military mind, but they had yet to make any sort of impression on Fronto, other than that of bored nobles.

Rufio was a little less ordinary. Apparently the son of a freedman, he was a world apart from the nobs aboard, and yet he seemed to have found his place among them with consummate ease. Still, despite that, he managed to retain something curiously low-born in his manner that put Masgava, Galronus and Palmatus at ease in conversation with him too. Fronto had found him engaging and clever, and had quickly formed the opinion that if the man was as good a commander as Antonius claimed, he would go far in Caesar's army.

Caninius was one of the 'new men' of Rome - a self-made noble in the vein of Crassus or Caesar himself. By all rights, Fronto felt he should dislike the man, but found nothing about him that was wanting. Indeed, Caninius seemed not to miss a trick. He was aware of his surroundings to a level that surprised the others, and Fronto noted to himself that he would have to watch the man. If Fronto said the wrong thing at any time - something he was well aware that he was wont to do - he felt sure Caninius would retain the words.

The other figure aboard had come as something of a surprise to Fronto. Cita, the former senior quartermaster of Caesar's army, who had retired the previous year, had somehow been persuaded by Antonius to return to the general's service. A year in the Campanian sun seemed to have done the man good. He had lost the worry lines, the darting eyes and the numerous twitches that had marked him throughout his former service, and seemed more at ease with himself. It had, however, made Fronto smile how the mere sight of him had brought back one little facial tic to Cita's otherwise carefree face.

Including himself, that made twelve veteran officers making their way back to Caesar's service - more than enough to revitalise the army that Priscus had apparently found flagging. Of course they were still in discussion with Balbus as to his position. The old legate

10

had stated his intention to stay at Massilia with the families and not proceed north to the army. Antonius had been very persuasive, and Fronto had found himself hoping that his old friend would change his mind, but a small part of him was grateful that when he went north a trustworthy friend - his father-in-law in fact - would have a watchful eye on the womenfolk.

What Palmatus and Masgava intended to do was more of a mystery. The former legionary had shrugged and admitted that a return to his fairly impoverished lifestyle in the Subura would be dull to say the least, and had decided to accompany his employer north. The former gladiator still felt honour-bound to serve Fronto, despite having been granted his manumission some time back. Fronto felt sure that both men, solid martial characters that they were, would find a good place in the army. He would do everything he could to make sure that happened.

Of course, given his recent history with Caesar, it remained to be seen whether he would succeed in securing a good place in that army for himself. Antonius had assured him he would take care of it, but with every mile that brought them back towards the general, Fronto felt his doubts grow that little bit.

He returned to the mnemonic that he'd devised in order to remember the new officers:

'*Veteran Roman commanders sense calamity rising back at Samarobriva.*'

Volcatius, Rufio, Caninius, Sextius, Calenus, Reginus, Basilus, Aristius, Silanus. Funny how they spelled such a portentous phrase. Fronto had wondered for a moment whether divine Fortuna had a part in its devising.

For the following quarter of an hour and more, Fronto tried to pick out something memorable about each officer as he ran through his mnemonic, attempting to keep his mind from the motion of the vessel and what remained of his stomach lining on the inside.

Gradually, as he repeated by rote and peered into the spray, he spotted the lights that sharp-eyed Antonius had seen earlier occasionally dipping beneath the waves and then rising into the evening gloom. At least there hadn't been a storm. The ship's captain had been convinced a tempest was on the way and had flatly refused to sail until Antonius talked him around with honeyed words and a fat purse.

The journey had been rain free, but the high, cold winds of late winter had turned the sea's surface into something that resembled a relief map of the Alpes, and the journey had been far from comfortable.

He watched with growing relief as the diffuse orange blooms gradually resolved into distinguishable lights glowing in windows and the shipping beacon on the end of the dock, and slowly the buildings of Ostia began to take shape in the purple blanket of evening. Finally, as the ship bucked ever closer to the city, he began to make out individual figures on the dock and sighed with happiness. Antonius had promised a stop-over of a few nights in Ostia before Caesar's trireme took them north to Gaul. Apparently the man had business to attend to in Rome before they left, and he would have to meet up with Caesar's agents to pick up any new information.

As they rounded the breakwater and made for the river and the dock that sat beside it, the waves fell to blessedly low levels and the ship settled, leaving Fronto feeling surprisingly disorientated with its deceptive calm. He gripped the rail as the ship closed on the dock and forced himself to stand upright and look military, rather than preparing to leap over the side onto land in order to kiss the stonework like a long lost lover.

Ostia slid closer and closer until a thump that made Fronto scrabble to maintain his grip on the rail announced that they had docked. The crew of the liburna ran back and forth securing lines and running out a ramp, and Fronto finally let go of the rail and attempted to walk on unstable, wobbling legs towards the plank. The other passengers emerged smiling and laughing from the rear housing and converged on his position, Balbus and the ladies leading the way.

Lucilia gave him what she probably thought was a smile, but put him more in mind of a predator weighing up whether its prey was worth the effort. Faleria had much the same look, but Fronto knew her well enough to recognise she was well aware of her expression and had cultivated it on purpose.

'Gods,' he thought to himself in a moment of dreadful realisation and with a wicked smile, 'I've married my sister!'

'What are you laughing about, chuckles?' Lucilia asked, raising an eyebrow as they approached the ramp.

'Nothing. Just making sure I got today's good mood out of the way before I had it forcibly ripped from me.'

'Don't be so over-dramatic Marcus. Sea travel always makes you so cranky.'

'It would make you 'cranky' too if you'd turned inside out once an hour and not eaten in three days.'

'Well we're having a stop-over here. Dear Antonius has agreed that we can stay as long as we need to in order to pay our proper respects to mother, on the proviso that Caesar has no urgent demands.'

'Good. Maybe by the time we put back out to sea I'll have had sufficient time on land to recover enough to eat a piece of bread. Extra fuel for sickness on the next leg.'

'Oh do stop complaining and lead us down the ramp.'

Fronto glared at his young wife and turned, stomping angrily down the ramp. She was right, of course. Lucilia was rarely anything but loving and courteous, but sea travel made him tetchy even at the best of times, and the knowledge that her new husband was about to abandon her for months on end and march off to war had done little to raise her spirits.

He forced himself to calm a little. He was being selfish and he knew it. Lucilia was facing her first summer of married life alone - apart from her sister-in-law and father - and even before then they were about to visit the tomb of her recently-deceased mother. He mentally chided himself for not having smiled straight away.

'Marcus Antonius?'

Fronto blinked as he turned his attention from the beautiful young woman behind and to the source of the voice. On the dock, amid the working sailors and dockers, stood a man in the uniform tunic and cloak of a military officer, though lacking weapons and armour. He was a tall man with a pinched, mouse-like face and a twitching nose. His thinning hair was a strange mix of blond and grey.

'No,' Fronto replied. 'Antonius is back up there.'

Stepping off the ramp and holding out his hand for the ladies to alight, he watched until Antonius appeared at the rail. 'That's your man,' he noted to the tall soldier.

'Marcus Antonius?' the man repeated, this time up to the deck.

'That would be me,' Antonius replied. Without waiting for the ramp to clear, the somewhat inebriated commander simply stepped up onto the rail and leapt down onto the dock. Fronto stared as the man made a hard landing which probably jarred every bone and organ in his body. A fall like that could have broken his leg!

13

Antonius grinned, his cheeks flushed. 'Marcus Antonius, lately cavalry commander for the Proconsul of Syria and now aide to the Proconsul of Gaul.' He stopped, frowning as his gaze focused on the tall man. The newly arrived officer stepped back suspiciously, his gait reminding Fronto of a crane fly. 'Hirtius?' Antonius hazarded.

'Ah, yes?' the man replied with a furrowed brow.

'I was told to watch out for you,' Antonius smiled. 'The descriptions I was given are startlingly accurate.'

Hirtius' frown deepened and Antonius let out another deep laugh. 'Nothing bad, my friend.' He turned to Fronto. 'This, Marcus, is Aulus Hirtius. He's Caesar's man, lately of Aquileia.' He turned back to Hirtius. 'What brings you out of hiding in the general's provincial palace, Hirtius?'

The mantis-like man cleared his throat disapprovingly, and took another step back, grimacing. Fronto suspected the wine on Antonius' breath had been the reason for that particular retreat.

'I have been summoned to Samarobriva, along with the rest of you, but I was instructed to meet you here and impart further instructions from the general.'

Fronto's ears pricked at the news.

'Go on?' Antonius encouraged the new arrival.

'You are to dispatch a number of your companions to Cisalpine Gaul. Pompey's former legion - the First - is quartered at Aquileia, courtesy of an agreement ratified by the senate, and you are to send a man to take command of it and lead it north to Samarobriva at the earliest opportunity. That man will have to be accompanied by a second, who will take command of a fledgling legion - the Fifteenth - which has been levied there and supplied with veteran officers from the surrounding cities. I have horses and a suitable military escort ready to leave with them. They can take the Via Flaminia across country for speed.'

Antonius seemed to take in the surprising news of two new legions without blinking, especially one of them being a Pompeian one. He nodded. 'Anything else?'

'Yes. Another man is to head north to the camp at Cremona, disband the camp and collect every soldier, be he veteran or raw recruit, officer or legionary, taking them to Samarobriva to reform the Fourteenth, who were wiped out a few months ago.'

Fronto stepped back as if struck. A legion *wiped out*? Then things were every bit as bad as Priscus had implied. Suddenly, all his attention was on the matter at hand, his sickness entirely forgotten.

14

'Caesar levies new legions? Then he has a new campaign in the works?'

'That, I cannot say,' Hirtius replied. 'I just have the orders to pass on.'

Antonius turned to Fronto. 'I do believe that the campaigning season is to begin a little early this year. At least we'll have no time to pick up cobwebs before we get our teeth into the fight.' He smiled apologetically at the girls. 'I am so sorry ladies, but we will have to cut short our visit. For the sake of family and propriety, we will remain long enough for you to pay your respects, but then, the morning after next, we must be aboard the trireme and making for Massilia.'

He turned his eager smile on Fronto and the veteran legate was suddenly - and worryingly - put in mind of an excited puppy.

'Fabulous,' he grumbled.

* * * * *

Fronto scratched his head as he reached the end of the street and looked this way and that.

'I don't know. Apart from Pompey's new theatre and his house, the last time I set foot in the Campus Martius I was a fresh faced tribune. The whole place is different now. When I was last here there were a few scattered houses and insulae and a lot of greenery. Now it looks like the bloody Subura! When did the senate ratify selling off all the land?'

'You've been away from Rome for a long time,' Palmatus sighed. 'The senate would rip out your kidney and sell it back to you if they thought they could get away with it. Rich men selling land to other rich men to erect shoddy death-traps to rent to the poor.'

Fronto frowned. 'You're an absolute barrel of laughs, you are.'

'I tell it how it is,' the former legionary shrugged. 'By rights I should be sitting in one of these side streets joining the rest of the plebs as they glare at you and mutter curses against the nobles. Strange how the fates lead a man, eh?'

Balbus, his face dark and humourless, gestured to the right hand fork. 'If you two have quite finished bickering, we'll go that way first.'

Fronto nodded, falling quiet. He quite enjoyed his banter with Palmatus. The low-born soldier was unusually outspoken for a

15

pleb among patricians, but that tended to happen when Fronto got to know them, much to his mother's constant irritation. When confronted with loss and sadness, Fronto habitually resorted to either irreverent humour or vengeful anger, as circumstances dictated. Neither, however, was appropriate today, and he was having trouble maintaining the serenity that he felt his friends and family expected.

Balbus led the group on towards the family mausoleum of the Lucilii, Palmatus and Masgava prowling along the sides of the party like wolves, watching for trouble. There was no real reason for them to have come along. The streets of Rome were dangerous these days, but Fronto felt certain that he, Balbus and Galronus would be able to handle any trouble that came their way. The pair had refused to stay behind, though, and had appointed themselves as guards in the mean streets of Rome, Masgava occasionally pausing to rest his still-aching gut.

'Sad, the way all the mausolea that have stood out on these roads for so long are getting lost among housing now,' Fronto sighed. 'Shouldn't be allowed, really.'

'Rome grows,' shrugged the practical Palmatus. 'New residents have to go somewhere, and the insulae are already too tall. Where else are you going to put them, if you don't expand the city?'

'Still seems wrong. A decade ago, Balbus' family would have had a nice little garden plot around their mausoleum. Maybe a few cypresses in a line. Now half a dozen families of dirty scrotes will stand in its shadow, scratching their privates and pissing on the path.'

His sister shot him a warning glance, and Fronto realised too late how insensitive that had sounded. He opened his mouth to apologise and back-track, but decided he needn't bother. Neither Balbus nor Lucilia were paying him any attention, their spirits troubled as they approached the tomb's location, and young Balbina - once a lively spirit - was her usual silent self, unseeing and apparently unfeeling.

The group wandered on in silence a few more moments, taking two more turns until Fronto could no longer guess which way was north, though the further they went, the less housing was in evidence, with more open green spaces between. The rush of water that underlay the everyday sounds of the city confirmed that they had come close to the Tiber, probably at that section where it turned from north to the west and then south. A large, white residence, clearly the property of a wealthy merchant or suchlike - a 'wannabe' noble, judging by the level of ostentation in such a low priced region - stood within an area of untouched scrub land and just beyond it, a small square garden surrounded on three sides by ordered rows of cypresses contained a modest brick-built columbarium, a garland-and-wreath decorative panel running around the structure at head height and a marble panel set into the front bearing an inscription detailing the family who owned it.

Balbus took a key from the chain on his purse-string and approached the building's side, unlocking the iron gate and swinging it open. There was no solid door, but the bars on the gate had been spaced close enough to prevent birds entering the mausoleum and nesting there.

Taking down the small oil lamp from the shelf by the door, Balbus scrabbled around, found the flint and steel and struck a few times until the light-source began to flicker, its guttering flame illuminating the building's interior with a warm orange glow. Palmatus, Masgava and Galronus arrayed themselves outside like a defensive force, the latter handing over to Fronto the bag he had brought with him as the rest entered the structure. Fronto allowed Balbus and the ladies in first, bringing up the rear and withdrawing a small jar from the bag, cracking the seal.

As with all columbaria, the building's walls consisted of row upon row of small arched recesses, reminiscent of a dovecote, each one for a family member's cinerary urn, though only a dozen or so had been filled. The Lucilii were not old nobility, apparently. Given the lack of occupants it did not take long to locate the niche with the new urn, the identifying plaque beneath freshly-made.

Fronto found suddenly, and unexpectedly, that a lump had risen in his throat. Corvinia had been a delight to know. She had been a haven of civility in that first bloody and androcentric year of Caesar's campaign, with her small and neat Roman house incongruously placed among the military camps near Geneva. She had invited him - a complete stranger - into her home as though she had known him for years and had fed and watered him. She would have been his mother in law, he realised with surprising sadness.

And she had died - indirectly, admittedly - because of him. Or rather because of blood feuds *against* him. Though he had done nothing as far as he was concerned to bring it all about, he could not deny more than a sliver of guilt over the matter.

Sorry, he mouthed silently to the shade of his mother in law. By tradition, they should be eating a sacred meal - he'd bought cakes, bread and a few bright flowers in the market especially - but he doubted, given the means of Corvinia's passing, that any of them would have much of an appetite.

Balbus was talking quietly - barely a murmur really - to Corvinia. Fronto deliberately closed his ears to the conversation - it was a private thing and he had no wish to intrude. He was here mostly for them to lean on should they feel the need.

But instead of murmuring, Lucilia was silent and still. If she was talking to her mother, it was in the privacy of her skull, while no hint of emotion showed upon her stony surface. Trying not to interrupt their private thoughts, Fronto shuffled quietly across to the small altar in the corner and made a libation of the expensive wine they had bought at an overpriced stall beneath the columned front of the temple of Portunus, filling the bowl-shaped depression on the altar top and mouthing the words of dedication silently. With a small shrug he retrieved one of the cakes from his bag, broke off a piece, placing it on the altar, and then consumed the rest while he waited.

As the moments crawled by, Fronto started to feel uncomfortable in the almost-silence, pursing his lips curiously as he saw a small smile cross Lucilia's face as though she had shared a private joke with her mother. More worryingly, as soon as she smiled she turned to look directly at him, and then returned her gaze to the urn with a chuckle. Clearly whatever the joke was, it was at his expense. Under most circumstances, that would irritate him intensely, but given the situation he was inclined to let this one pass uncommented.

It seemed an age that he stood there, and he kept glancing at the oil lamp, wondering when it would go out, trying to determine where the spare flask of oil was kept to refill it should the room be suddenly plunged into darkness.

Finally, after a couple of decades of discomfort, Balbus turned and made a questioning face at his daughter. Lucilia nodded, and he took a deep breath. 'Let's move on, then.'

Fronto was the first outside, followed by Lucilia and her little sister. He felt with relief the cold winter air slap him in the face. It felt like emerging from a cave.

'Farewell.' A voice. Small. Broken.

Fronto turned in surprise, looking down at Balbina, the younger of the sisters. Lucilia and Balbus' heads had both snapped round in surprise.

'Balbina?'

But she had returned to her silent, uninterested façade - so swiftly, in fact, that Fronto would have thought he'd imagined her voice had not the others turned too.

'You heard that?' Balbus said quietly.

'Yes.'

The old officer leaned over and reached out, taking his daughter in both hands and gripping her shoulders. 'You *are* in there, my girl. Come back and talk to me.'

Silence. Balbus stood still for some time and waited, but nothing more seemed forthcoming and after a while he straightened and sighed. 'Well that can only be good,' he announced with a shaky smile.

Fronto nodded his agreement but remained silent as the older man blew out the oil lamp and locked the gate to the columbarium before striding back out onto the rutted track that served as a road here. Galronus, Masgava and Palmatus, who seemed to have been having some sort of tactical martial discussion during the visit, fell in once more as guards for the party, their eyes watchful as they scanned the surroundings for any hint of danger.

'I think you're right, you know, Fronto?' Balbus said with a restorative breath. 'I think that when I have the time and the opportunity, I'll have a new columbarium built somewhere further out and move the family there. Maybe somewhere up the Via Flaminia. Seems to be a popular place for good families these days, so it won't be lost among insulae any time soon.'

Fronto nodded his approval, scanning the area. 'Anyone know where we go from here?' he asked with a frown.

'I thought you said you knew where it was?' Balbus replied, rolling his eyes.

'I do. *From the forum.* But I haven't the faintest bloody idea where I am now. I couldn't even *find* the forum now. Another couple of turns and I'd have trouble finding my own arse!'

'Give me a clue, then,' Balbus asked wearily.

'It's across the way from the ovilia, maybe a hundred paces.'

Balbus turned to the others and pointed off across the road towards a stand of pines that surrounded an almost identical columbarium. 'Should be down that way, then?'

Palmatus nodded and pointed off at an angle. 'More that way. Look over to the right of the trees... you can see the top of Pompey's monstrosity. It'll be near there.'

Trusting their directions to the only member of the group who had spent any length of time in the city in recent years, the party crossed the road and took what looked more like a farm track than anything else, heading towards the monumental marble curve of Pompey's new theatre which towered distant over the roofs and trees of the Campus Martius.

They walked on in silence, each with the company of their own thoughts, back through the greenery and into the more populous area of recent constructions which marked the parts of the sacred space that had been parcelled up and sold on to the senate's cronies. It would have irked Fronto had he not all-but given up caring about the city itself anyway. It seemed these days a seething hive of snakes, rats and cockroaches all in human form, and anyone with any value as a human being seemed to have moved away from the capital into more rural retreats.

Let them have their city. He would reside in Massilia or Puteoli from now on, as would his family, only coming to the capital when business required. Slowly they approached the estimated location of their goal. Soon enough the great arc of the theatre was lost to sight behind the various buildings of the greatest city in the world, and Fronto once more had no idea of his location, relying on Palmatus' sense of direction.

Finally, after half an hour more of travel, the group emerged onto a paved road with a drainage channel - a luxury after the tracks they had wandered 'til now. Ahead, amid the new houses rising each year and filling the land, and the monumental structures of the rich, the ovilia stood as a strange sight. The place where the population gathered to vote, the ovilia was an open space some thousand feet long and the same wide, surrounded by a neat, well-maintained fence and subdivided into aisles for individual assemblies to vote within, the whole thing dotted with plaques and signs to direct the people to their appropriate places. Despite everything that happened these days in the city, it was somewhat heartening to note that the thugs, drunks, whores, hooligans and so on seemed to have left the place alone, respecting its function in the governing of their city.

Turning, he was surprised to realise that they had emerged from a side street almost at their intended location. A brick columbarium of some size, graced with a marble façade and a tall statue of Venus stood surrounded by neatly-clipped box hedges and small flower beds, a row of shaped and pruned pines defining the boundaries behind and to the sides. Elegant. A sign of nobility, but with taste and a modicum of modesty.

'There,' he announced, somewhat redundantly, given that the others had already turned with him to look at the tomb. The building housed the remains of the Julii and the component lines of the extended family. Only a decade ago, when Fronto had first visited with Caesar on the death of his first wife, it had been simple brick - like the others they had seen this morning - but the great general and Proconsul who was currently the shining star of the house had embellished the façade and made sure the family's progenitor Goddess was appropriately honoured.

'It will be crippling Caesar not to be able to visit his mother at Parentalia,' Fronto sighed. 'Is it sacrilegious for us to do it for him? I mean, I knew Aurelia, but she's not our mother.'

'I suspect the Gods are more flexible and forgiving than most priests would have us believe,' Balbus smiled sadly. 'It's just a shame we can't get inside, but at least there's a pleasant garden to sit in while we eat and an altar there by the statue for libations.'

Fronto nodded. He'd contemplated going to visit one of Caesar's nieces to ask for a key, but the three Atias were very much not his kind of people - social climbers given to ostentatious displays of new money. Better to steer clear of them for such small favours. Even Caesar had intimated to him more than once how disappointed he was with his sisters' progeny.

He peered into the shadows cast by the pine trees and frowned.

'The door's open, Quintus.'

Balbus followed his gaze and his own brow wrinkled in surprise and suspicion. If the Julii had come to celebrate Parentalia, there would be a dozen armed ex-legionaries surrounding the place to keep trouble away, so whoever was inside was likely up to no good.

Fronto turned to Palmatus and Galronus and used what he hoped were clear and obvious gestured instructions for them to circle the mausoleum, check out the rear and then meet him and Balbus at the door, effectively trapping the intruder within. To Masgava he gestured a need to protect the women. The former gladiator nodded and took up a defensive position next to Lucilia, Balbina and Faleria, his eyes darting around the street, taking in every tiny movement.

Fronto watched the pair of warriors edge around the corner of the columbarium, and once they were out of sight, he and Balbus

21

began to creep quietly towards the doorway and the open iron gate. Fronto found himself smiling with satisfaction despite everything. A year ago he would have been grumbling about his joints and muscles and making more noise than a triumphal parade as he snuck across the garden. Ha. Who was he kidding? A year ago he'd still be two miles further back, sat on a bench, rubbing his knee and almost in tears. He'd never even have *got* here. Masgava had done a damn good job getting him back into shape.

With perfect timing, just as Fronto and Balbus reached the near corner of the building, Galronus and Palmatus emerged at the far corner, signing that they had found nothing. Good. Whoever it was would still be inside, then.

While none of them bore weapons, even though they were now outside the city boundary, all four would be able to make good account of themselves if trouble arose. Fronto flexed his muscles and nodded.

The four men closed on the door. The padlock hung open, suggesting that the intruder either had access to a key or was skilled at opening locks. A faint orange flicker danced on the darkened portal's stonework and Fronto squinted, narrowing his eyes against the daylight as he approached, so as not to find himself all-but blind when he peered into the gloomy entrance.

Stepping into the doorway, he opened his eyes wide again - fast, in case anyone was lurking close to the exit - his hands coming up ready to defend or attack as required. Even as he took in the scene before him, he was automatically stepping inside and sideways so that the other three could enter.

The occupant appeared to be alone.

Fronto blinked.

The orange glow illuminated a single figure - a young man of perhaps ten or eleven summers, standing by the altar with a silver cup in his hand. The light glinted off the surface of a fresh wine libation in the bowl atop the stone, and the crumbs and pieces of several cakes sat beside it.

While the other three moved in beside him and shuffled around the edge as the figure turned to face them, Fronto stepped forward so that the small oil lamp on the shelf would light his face. The young man seemed entirely unafraid.

His hair was clearly blond, though the shade was hard to tell in the dancing orange glow. He wore a well-tailored and expensive tunic of some pale colour and light calf-skin shoes. He was slightly built - one might even say spindly - and short for his age, which was apparent from his face, but something about him carried a power that defied his physical presence.

'If you are here to cause damage or thieve goods, I would remind you who owns this columbarium. There is nowhere you could hide from the Julii after such dishonour, as I'm sure you will realise. So if you are here on ill business, I recommend you move on immediately.'

He tipped the last of his cup's contents into his mouth, swallowed, and placed the vessel on the altar top. 'But you're no intruders, are you?'

Fronto felt, rather than saw, Balbus relax and take a step forward.

'We could be.' the older man said quietly. 'Dangerous for a boy of breeding to be abroad in the city alone. Where are your escort?'

'At home,' the young man replied nonchalantly. 'Probably searching the house for me at the behest of my tutor. But I know this city, old man, and how to traverse it safely. I am in no danger.'

'Not even from us?'

'Hardly!' the boy gave a humourless laugh. 'Four men - three of them wearing studded military boots - all reeking of fresh sea salt, one of them a Gallic nobleman and another wearing a Gaulish torc?'

Fronto blinked. How had the lad picked all that out so quickly, especially in near darkness?

'How is my uncle?' the lad asked genially. 'Send him my regards when next you see him.'

'We could have been Pompey's men' Fronto suggested with just a hint of irritation.

'I think not. He has no active legions now that he's signed over the First to my uncle, and in any case, he would hardly countenance an army in whose ranks a Gaul served with authority. That's my uncle's kind of decision. Wine?'

Fronto was still shaking his head in surprise as Balbus stepped forward. 'Octavian? Atia's boy?'

'That I am. Are you men returned from Gaul, or bound for there?'

'On our way north,' Fronto said quietly. 'We thought to stop by and honour your great grandmother, since it is Parentalia and your

23

great uncle is trapped so far away with the army. The same occurred to you, perchance?'

'After a fashion,' Octavian smiled. 'Suffice it to say that I was unimpressed with the devotions I had witnessed thus far, and felt the balance had to be redressed.' He straightened and flexed his shoulders. 'However, it is time now for me to return and allay the fears of my womanish tutor. Do avail yourself of the rest of the wine in this jug. I shall leave it here, and it is a Caecuban of the Opimian vintage, worth more than a centurion's yearly pay. It would be a crime to waste the rest.'

Fronto realised that he was still shaking his head and stopped, scratching his chin instead.

'Would you like an escort back to your house?'

'That will not be necessary. Pay your respects, soldier, and good luck to you all. Help my uncle as best you can, and you could urge him to finalise matters with his new province as soon as possible? Whatever his plans for the governorship, he cannot afford to leave Rome to its own devices much longer. The city becomes more of a festering pit of lunacy with every passing month. Soon it will be safer in northern Gaul with nothing but a spoon and a tunic than in the forum surrounded by guards.'

He gave a pleasant, slightly lop-sided smile and with a nod of acknowledgement stepped out past Fronto and Balbus and into the light, where they heard him exchange pleasantries with the ladies.

The four occupants of the tomb shared glances.

'I don't know about you three, but that lad seems to resemble his great uncle disturbingly closely.'

Balbus nodded. 'Of Caesar's nieces, Octavian's mother was always the clever one - the best of the brood. She's a distant cousin of mine, of course.'

Palmatus shook his head with a curled lip. 'In my experience nearly every noble in Rome is a little *too* closely related, if you know what I mean? Pale, with bulging eyes, a throat-apple the size of a cabbage and all the mental flexibility of a donkey with the shits.'

He turned and noticed in the low flickering light the glowering looks Fronto and Balbus were casting at him.

'Present company excepted, of course.' He grinned a wicked grin. 'Anyone else itching to try the lad's special wine?'

Fronto maintained his scowl for a moment longer before cracking and chuckling at the irreverent humour that he'd come to expect from the plebeian ex-legionary.

'Why not. Let's make libations to Aurelia Cotta and young Julia and drink a toast to the general and his great nephew's generosity.'

As he crossed to collect the jar of rare and extraordinary wine the young Octavian had left them, he mused on family. Curiously, now that he'd tied himself by marriage to Balbus, and Balbus was Atia Caesonia's cousin, that meant - he supposed - that there was a very distant familial connection between him and the general. He almost laughed at the realisation.

The morning would carry them north again towards war. But for today, the group would relax and enjoy what they could of Rome.

'Galronus, you'd better go outside and bring Masgava and the girls in. Lucilia seems to have gone off wine these days, but Faleria will relish this vintage.'

* * * * *

Bucephalus whickered with irritation, apparently feeling the urge to run and stretch despite Fronto's stern words and careful grip on the reins. He'd not ridden much in the past year or so, and his beloved horse - which Longinus had bequeathed to him a lifetime ago and a world away - had spent much of that time stabled and limited, run out only briefly by the equisio at Puteoli. Indeed, the journey below deck on first the liburna and then Caesar's trireme from Ostia to Massilia seemed to have made the beast twitchier than ever.

'Steady, you big black bastard,' Fronto grunted through clenched teeth as he used both reins and knees to try and steer Bucephalus to the right. The carriage, lent eagerly by one of the more helpful of the city's assembly, rumbled along behind bearing the three women, while Balbus rode ahead and the other three brought up the rear.

Fronto shaded his eyes from the late afternoon sun and peered off across the hill at the line of horses and men disappearing at a tangent towards the north and the Rhodanus valley. Marcus Antonius had taken the bulk of the new officer corps straight for Samarobriva at his earliest opportunity, departing in the evening, hoping to make the mansio at Aquae Sextiae for the night. He had expected Fronto to go with them, as any extra delay would make the placation of Caesar all the more difficult, but Fronto had been adamant that he must see the family safely to their homes before he could consider riding north. Besides, Lucilia deserved at least one last night in a real bed with her new husband. He'd not announced that to Antonius, of course, but it was true nonetheless. And so he would follow on with Galronus, Masgava and Palmatus the next day. He would miss out on the escort of a hundred cavalry that Antonius had had waiting for them at Massilia, but he'd ridden the route to Samarobriva enough times now to know he was safe. Besides, he wore a Gallic torc and travelled with a prince of the Remi. Who would challenge him?

He tried not to list the answers to that, and failed until Bucephalus' next attempt to take him for a long, leg-stretching run dragged all his attention back to the business at hand.

As they approached the road that led to Balbus' beautiful rural villa with its cultivated vineyards and orchards, its sheds and stables and the view over the sea, breath-taking even in the changeable weather of late winter, Fronto first laid eyes on the new villa the old man had spent a year constructing in secret for his daughter and new son-in-law.

Almost a mirror of Balbus' villa, and close enough to loose a scorpion bolt from the one to the other, the only visible differences between the two houses were the newness and cleanliness of the stonework and the lack of plant life and gardens about it. And the huge tracts of farmland, of course, but Balbus knew just how little Fronto saw himself as a farmer. The old man had apparently taken that into account.

'By Fortuna and her golden tits that's something,' he muttered, drawing the big black stallion to a halt so that he could take it all in. Balbus paused slightly ahead and turned with a smile.

'My villa *is* perfect, so I thought 'why change a good thing?' and had the new one built to the same design. The only difference is that yours might be a little more exposed to the sea winds, being closer to the slopes, so I've had hypocaust flooring put in all the downstairs rooms to keep the place warm, and the flues take the hot air up past all the upper rooms. The courtyard's just overgrown grass at the moment, mind. I didn't bother with any gardening, as I felt sure you'd want to personalise that - blooms and the like.'

Fronto pictured himself choosing flowers and positioning them just right. The image made him laugh. 'Lucilia, perhaps.'

Balbus grinned in reply and the two men kicked their steeds into motion once more as the carriage rattled closer behind.

'It's just occurred to me that there'll be no staff,' Fronto said, slapping his forehead.

'True. I can build the thing for you, but staffing it's a different matter. You and Lucilia will have to do that.'

Fronto shrugged. 'Actually, since I'll be gone in the morning, it'll have to be *you* and Lucilia. Is there a good slave market in Massilia?'

'Where do you think all the poor buggers Caesar's captured over the last five years end up?' Balbus asked with a grim smile.

'Hmm. Perhaps we'll be selective and choose Greeks and Spaniards and so on. I can't see the family of one of Caesar's legates being a popular master for enslaved Gauls or Belgae. We don't really want another Spartacus rising in southern Gaul, do we? Or another Berengarus!' For a fleeting moment he wondered how the crippled giant was faring in his cave prison at Puteoli, fed scraps by the villa slaves. Hopefully he was suffering an eternity of torment for what he'd done. More likely by now he had given in to despair and starved himself to death. He became aware suddenly that Balbus was talking again, and refocused his ears.

'… and I'm certain my daughter will be fairly sure of what she wants. In the meantime, I'll send over a couple of the better slaves from my villa to see to your needs - get the furnaces stoked and all that - and I'll have Agathocles double up on whatever he prepares for the evening meal and bring half of it round to you.'

'Thank you, Quintus. It's going to take some getting used to, though I spent a little time a few years back in the seaside villa of Longinus' widow near Tarraco. It's quite similar, really, apart from the precipitous slope, and that just reminds me of home. It's the remoteness of the place from civilisation that worries me.'

'You'll be surprised when you explore Massilia a bit more just how urban it all is. It's got a nice agora full of cheap taverns, a theatre - don't pull that face, I know you don't like plays - and a stadium that they use for foot races, but occasionally for the horses too. There's good wine from Italia, Carthage and Greece - a lot of the latter - as well as olives and garum from Hispania and a lot more. And you'll find a lot of it at only half the price you'd pay in Rome.'

Fronto grinned. 'Alright, you're starting to sell it to me now.'

His friend laughed as they reached the entrance arch to the unkempt courtyard garden with its deep lawns.

'I'll leave you here,' Balbus smiled, 'and head off to get my own house in order and warmed up. I'll pop back round and see you in the morning before you leave.'

Fronto nodded. It would have been nice to invite his old friend in for the evening, especially in a new, unfamiliar house still cold from the winter and lacking the comforts of a home. Lucilia would see to all that over the next week or two, of course, but at this time they would only have the few sparse blankets and cushions Balbus had seen fit to have brought round in preparation. Among the various goods back in the baggage cart behind the carriage, escorted by the other three warriors, sat a chest of the family's denarii from Rome that would easily see the house furnished and staffed in short order. He smiled as he imagined the glee on Lucilia's face as she set to in the agora of the city choosing drapes and furnishings.

'You'd best take Masgava and Palmatus with you, Quintus. You'll have the spare comforts for them, unlike us.'

'I'll do better than that, Marcus... I'm taking Galronus and your sister, too. You and Lucilia should have the first night on your own. You've had precious few opportunities, and even those few are about to dry up.' His knowing wink brought a childish flush to Fronto's cheeks and he nodded and clambered down from Bucephalus to hide his embarrassment.

The carriage pulled up behind and the door opened, allowing Lucilia to alight with a wide smile.

'Oh father, it's perfect.'

'Of course it is, child. Would I do anything less? Now go on. I've arranged everything with Marcus and food and comforts will be brought across shortly.'

Without pause for farewells - knowing he would be spending the next few weeks in his daughter's constant company - Balbus nodded at Fronto and then kicked his horse forward towards the homely villa a little further along the road.

As the carriage rattled on once more, the cart full of goods following, Galronus, Masgava and Palmatus nodded and smiled at him as they passed. Though none of them said anything, Fronto had the distinct impression that they were silently laughing at him for some reason. He felt an irrational rush of irritation and, still gripping Bucephalus' reins, strode into the courtyard in the wake of his young wife.

'I don't even know what to do with this big softie. No idea where the stable is and whether there's food and water there.'

'Father will send his equisio round to deal with it shortly, beloved, be sure of that. In the meantime the grass in this garden is horribly overgrown. Close the gate and let the poor beast wander and stretch his legs and eat for a while. If he's half as sick of being cramped up on board ships as I am, he'll need it.'

Fronto nodded and closed the gate, turning to the big black head with the glistening, intelligent eyes. He pointed his finger at the stallion's forehead as he let go of the reins.

'No jumping the wall and running away, and try not to eat the gate, you big numb bugger.'

Bucephalus neighed and turned, stomping off across the gravel and onto the deep grass. Fronto thought the noise sounded suspiciously argumentative, and glared at the animal as it set about demolishing the overgrowth.

'Come on,' Lucilia called from over by the door.

'Wait there.' Fronto jogged across and ducked between her and the portal, bending and putting his arms around her.'

'What are you doing?'

'Picking you up to carry you across the threshold.'

'I think not.'

'But it's *tradition*. What about the bad luck? Or the Sabine tradition?'

Lucilia huffed and folded her arms. 'That's for the *newly* married. We've been married best part of a year. Besides, I would rather not be carried right now.'

Fronto, deflated, stepped inside, noting with relief and a little gratitude the jars of wine and water standing on the table in the atrium and the two beautiful glasses that rested beside it. Quintus had apparently anticipated his initial needs.

'Come on.' he strode across to the table and picked up a glass. The house may be sparsely furnished, but there would be enough to keep them going for the night. Lucilia, smiling with happiness at her new home, shut the door behind her, lowering the level of light in the atrium to the glow of late sun that penetrated the open roof at the centre.

'We should move through to the triclinium and see if there are lamps to be lit. It won't be light for much longer and the dark just adds to the chill.'

'In a moment,' Fronto sighed. 'It's our new home, we're finally here after a long trip, and I'll have to move on in the morning.

Right now I rather feel I need this glass of wine, and we should toast the house and welcome the lares and penates to the new home.'

'Pour yourself a glass and bring it through with you.'

Fronto looked crestfallen once more. 'Will you not raise a glass with me?'

'Wine makes me feel nauseous at the moment.'

'What is wrong with you?' Fronto snapped grumpily, waving the empty glass in his hand at her.

'Can you not guess, you great oaf?' she replied with equal vehemence.

'Stop talking in riddles, woman.'

'I am with *child*, Marcus!'

Fronto stopped in the process of opening his mouth to argue further and let it hang wide in surprise. His glass slid from suddenly numb fingers and smashed on the floor next to the atrium's small impluvium pool, sending glittering shards across the marble.

'Wh…?'

'I don't know, Marcus, but I must be two months gone now. So do as I ask: use the other glass, pour yourself a wine - don't bother with the water, I think you'll need the full strength of it - and come through to sit with me in the triclinium.'

'The…?'

'Father's slaves will clear up the mess when they come round. Just step carefully until then. Now come on. I feel the need for a sit down and I would rather like to talk to you properly. I had envisaged telling you the news in more luxuriant circumstances than standing in the cold empty atrium in our travelling clothes, but as usual you forced my hand until I was left with no choice.'

'Bu…'

'And when you have recovered sufficiently to recall more than a syllable at a time, we can discuss the speed with which you will carry out this year's campaign so that you can rush home to my side in time to welcome your son or daughter into the world.'

Fronto stood gawping until Lucilia reached down and poured him an unwatered glass of wine, grasping his wrist with her free hand and guiding him between the shards of glass towards the triclinium beyond.

The Gauls had better behave themselves, Fronto found himself thinking. *I want to be home before the autumn rains set in.*

Before my child arrives!

30

Bibracte, in the lands of the Aedui of central Gaul

The druid stood within the nemeton - the sacred grove - and looked around with an expression of distaste and dismay. The palisaded site had been a thriving religious centre for the mysteries when last he had visited. Four years now there had been no druid here, in this city of a tribe that had welcomed the invader's crushing heel to their throat and revelled in their servitude. Four years the shepherds of the people had lived in exile from their own tribes while fomenting resistance against the Roman dogs. Four years the once marvellous nemeton of Bibracte had been left to rack and ruin, overgrown with gorse, its stones green with moss and lichen, its shaped and tended trees grown into misshapen things.

Four years.

And even now, with many of the more powerful nobles of the Aedui actively inviting the Gods and their mysteries back into their lives, even now he had been escorted to the grove in secret in case that section of society that still lived in hope of scraps from the Romans' table took offence at his presence.

All that would change, of course. All would change, and soon. Plans were building rapidly, with everything falling into place, barring a few mishaps and mistakes, the matter of which had brought about this meeting.

'This is a disgrace.' he snapped. 'Do the Aedui not honour their spirits anymore? Could they not at least tend the sacred places even when they are not used?'

The small party of Gallic warriors, clad in mail and with bronze helms displaying wings or animals or ritualistic horns simply paid him no attention and talked among themselves. It infuriated him. Their chosen leader had been given everything he needed: support, power, goods - even the approval of the Gods and the secret ways of the druids - in order to free the land of the invader, and yet he and his men still went about their business as if the whole thing were *his* achievement - *his* doing - rather than theirs. He treated the shepherds of the people as an inconvenience. As though they were tantruming children!

'What do you intend to do about Indutiomarus and his tribe?'

Vercingetorix circled his head, stretching his neck so that the bones clicked, and sighed.

'Nothing.'

31

'*Nothing?*'

'Nothing.'

The druid clenched his free fist, the knuckles of the hand that gripped his staff whitening. '*Something* has to be done. Ambiorix lost us tribes we might sorely need in the next year, and now the dog-faced, idiot Treveri threaten to get themselves wiped out too.'

The big Arvernian noble shrugged as he nudged a fallen carving with his foot, watching beetles and woodlice escape from beneath. 'The Treveri are no loss. We let them tangle with the Roman commander and watch with interest.'

'We need every tribe in the land to support you. Those across the fast cold sea, as well. And even those across the mountains and across the great river if we can. You know that Rome's army is coldly efficient. No matter how brave your warriors, unless you can convincingly outnumber them you will never have a chance. Even with our help!' he added bitterly.

'You fail to see the tactical advantage. Ambiorix kicked the Roman wasp nest and now the bulk of Rome's soldiery in our land is concentrated in the territory of the Belgae trying to put out the repeated fires of rebellion. But Ambiorix's power is waning and his time is almost past. He has been useful in keeping Caesar occupied, but while he wanes and loses his value to us, the Treveri are on the rise to take his place. We need many months yet to tie our plans and people together; to arm them and train them and organise. And we cannot do that in total secrecy with Roman officers breathing down our necks. It is useful to have places like Bibracte, from which even their supply garrison has been recalled, leaving the route in Aedui hands, because Rome thinks these places settled and safe. A man does not look beneath his own roof for his enemy. And while we make use of these advantages, and put our plans into place, it is vital that Rome keep its hooked nose out of our business. The Treveri are doing us a great favour by sacrificing themselves on the altar of resistance.'

'The shepherds among the Treveri speak out against action.'

'Then your shepherds speak against their own purpose. Stop them.'

The druid narrowed his eyes and clenched his teeth for a moment before speaking again. 'I will ask them to support the revolt, though we are brothers in faith rather than ordered ranks, and they may not agree and decide against it. You had better be right about this, as we wager the future of our people on you.'

'I am rarely wrong, druid.'

'And what of Ambiorix? Now, with the Eburones shattered and worn, he scrabbles around, trying to pull together tribes to support him and resist Rome. Is he still a useful distraction for you, or is he becoming a danger to us. Unlike the Treveri lunatics, Ambiorix knows all about us - about *you*! If he falls into Roman hands all our plans could be for naught.'

The big Gaul gave a nonchalant shrug once more - an irritating habit in the eyes of the druid - and scratched his neck idly.

'For now, he is of more use than danger. And the man is resourceful. Let him keep the Romans hopping from foot to foot in Belgae lands while we grow and strengthen, and when the time comes that he is too dangerous to us, I will have him dealt with. Even now I have men in their lands ready to act, should such action become necessary, as well as a contingency in place with his brother King, Cativolcus of the Eburones.'

'Cativolcus is a doddering old fool.'

'But he is loyal, and he has no love of Ambiorix. We are safe yet. Stop your shepherds making waves among our Belgae cousins and you will see the great Julius Caesar devoting all his attention to a nagging rat at his heel, while the great bear that truly endangers him wakes far off among the Arverni.'

The druid could not help but smile. Whatever he thought of Vercingetorix and the big man's ways, he was a natural leader and a silver-tongued speaker, and when the time came, all the peoples would follow him against Rome.

They had made a good choice, after all.

The sacrifice of Ambiorix and the Treveri, then, buying them, with their lives, the time they needed.

Chapter Two

Titus Atius Labienus, commander of the Twelfth Legion, lieutenant of Caesar and pro-tem representative of Rome in the eastern Gallic and Belgic lands, struggled into his cuirass while the body slave laced up his boots, and then held it in position while the young Samnite laced up the armour.

'It is beyond me why I need be armoured in order to receive one of my own spies.'

The legion's senior centurion, Baculus, officially confined to the sick hut but proving somewhat difficult to contain, leaned heavily on his stick, his grey features shining unhealthily.

'Firstly because as senior officer in the region, legate, it is a matter of principle. Secondly, because your scouts and spies are natives and, given what's happened this past winter, I would not advise any Roman to get too close to one of them without armour on, especially someone of value.'

'My spies and scouts are Mediomatrici, centurion. They are our allies, not the enemy.'

'They have spent months wintering among the Treveri, legate, and the Treveri would like nothing more than to tear out your heart through your arse. Better safe than regretful, sir. Buckle up and look good.'

Labienus sighed as the slave handed him his baldric with the fine sheathed blade attached. Settling it over his shoulder, he narrowed his eyes.

'You need to be back in the sick hut, centurion. The medicus has told me that he's considering putting a guard on the door to stop you straying.'

'There's nothing wrong with me a bit of fresh air and exercise won't cure.'

'On the contrary, the medicus tells me that even a minor wound can kill if the infection takes hold too strongly, and that the infection which eats away at *your* wound is brutal and life-threatening. He puts the fact that you are still alive thus far down to the fact that you are - and I quote - 'a pig-headed angry bastard'. I do not like to countenance a future for the Twelfth Legion in which you are not there to bully them around, so kindly go back to the sick hut, lie down and stop interfering with the running of things until the physician pronounces you 'healthy'.'

Baculus managed to sneak in an unhappy grumble before saluting quickly, so that he could grab back hold of his stick for support, and turning to leave.

'Get better, and do it quickly. Things are too unsettled around here for me to be missing such an important officer.'

Labienus watched the centurion leave and shook his head with a slight smile. The medicus had actually told him that Baculus was generally out of danger and would stay that way as long as he didn't overdo things and set himself back. The chances of the veteran sitting back and not overdoing things were, he had decided, miniscule.

'Am I ready?'

The slave nodded. 'Yes, Domine.'

Labienus shrugged his shoulders so that the red cloak hung slightly better and then strode from his quarters - one of only five wooden buildings in the camp, the rest of the men making do with their tents. The mud, despite the periodic fall of near-freezing rain, was being kept well under control in the camp by the judicious use of timbers sunk into the main thoroughfares for stability, and scattered gravel and chippings brought by the men from a local rock outcropping.

Nodding a greeting to some of his tribunes and centurions who were going about their business around the headquarters and the larger officers' tents, he strode off down the gentle incline towards the north gate.

Two of the veteran legionaries assigned to guard their commander fell into step behind him and escorted him towards the small knot of men gathered inside the gate. A Belgic warrior in his colourful tunic and wool trousers stood rubbing his hands as legionaries held his steed by the bridle, kept his spear and sword out of reach and blocked off any possible route for the native to escape into the camp. Labienus sighed. What the Twelfth had experienced earlier in the winter had put the men on guard enough, but the news of what had happened to Sabinus, Cotta and Cicero had brought about an atmosphere where no Gaul would be given a sliver of respect, let alone outright trust. Sad, really. Labienus was still sure that Gaul could be tamed peaceably if only the army and its more rabid officers could be persuaded to a more tactful approach. Of course Caesar's own actions did little to promote such a diplomatic solution.

35

'Have you confirmed his identity?' he asked the duty centurion as he approached the knot of men.

'Aye sir,' the centurion - a surprisingly young man for such a role - nodded, passing over a wax tablet with a list of names and details. 'Litomaros. Birth mark shaped like a fat amphora on the left shoulder and 'L' shaped scar on lower left of belly. Unless they've been very creative, it's him.'

Labienus nodded, satisfied. He'd sent a dozen men out among the Treveri and their sub-tribes in the area to gain intelligence and provide forewarning of any trouble, and on Baculus' recommendation had had each one's distinguishing features noted to provide proof of identity should they return. Labienus had shaken his head at the time and replied that such a means of security stopped a man masquerading as one of the spies, but did not mean they could not be turned. Baculus had grunted and said that half a measure of safety was still better than nothing. Despite his misgivings, Labienus had to admit that he felt that little bit more sure when the centurion had confirmed it.

'Litomaros?' he said, gesturing for the other soldiers to step aside and moving forward to face the spy.

'Legate.' The man bowed his head respectfully.

'What news from the Treveri?'

'Trouble, sir,' the Gaul replied, his face dark.

'Indutiomarus stirring up his tribe for another try on us?'

The native warrior cleared his throat, rubbing his cold hands together. Labienus noticed his frosting breath and realised the man must have ridden twenty miles or more in the freezing morning air. With a gesture to wait, he turned to the legionaries beside him. 'Someone get this man some heated wine. Can you not see he's chilled to the bone?'

As one of the men ran off, Labienus filed away the looks on the other men's faces for later attention. Not one of them cared that a native might freeze to death.

'Right. Now tell me the news.'

'Treveri are unhappy at Roman warband camp in their lands.'

'This is nothing new. Are they unhappy enough to make war on us?'

'Treveri know they are too small to beat Roman warband. Indutiomarus try to talk other tribes to attack Rome, but they not fight.'

'Good. There is still *some* sense in this land, then.'

'So Indutiomarus send men across river to German tribes.'

The legionaries shared a worried look and Labienus tried to keep his composure without reacting obviously to such unsettling news. If the tribes across the Rhenus decided to join the Treveri in force, then the Twelfth Legion would likely be a mere stain on the memory of the campaign in a few weeks, just like Sabinus and Cotta's command a few months back.

'How many?'

The Gaul shook his head. 'Suevi and Ubii and Chatti refuse to help.'

Labienus felt his spirits lift at such news. It seemed unlike those tribes not to take the opportunity for a little havoc and plunder among the lands of their Gallic cousins and against the might of Rome, but Labienus could be grateful for their recalcitrance without seeking the reasons.

'So the Treveri do *not* come? Why then did you feel the need to leave them and seek me out?'

The Gaul took a steadying breath. 'Indutiomarus not needing Germans now. Chief gather to his boar standard all thieves, murderers, bandits, killers and rebels in Gaul and Belgae lands. His army grow with men who hate Rome.'

'How large can an army be if it's formed of countryside brigands?'

The Gaul frowned as if the question made no sense.

'Is it really a force that presents a threat to us?' Labienus rephrased.

'Yes,' the Gaul replied. 'You surprise how many Gauls hate Rome and run to Indutiomarus because their druid say not fight.'

Labienus sighed. He would not be at all surprised, if he were to admit it. It *was* a surprise, however, to hear that the druids were counselling non-confrontation. While Labienus was of firm belief that the Gallic tribes and their leaders could be persuaded to a diplomatic solution, the druids had always seemed immovable objects in the path of peace. What was their game?

He pursed his lips. 'There are enough to do to us what the Eburones did to Cotta and Sabinus?'

Again the Gaul nodded.

'Then we are faced with three choices. We abandon camp, give the Treveri the run of the countryside, and join up with Caesar's army back west. Upside: no one dies unnecessarily. Downside: the

37

Treveri are given a victory and the freedom to cause further trouble. Or, we sit and hold tight and work on our defences in the belief we can hold against a siege until Caesar arrives and breaks them, like he did with Cicero. Upside: we have time to strengthen our position. Downside: we are trapped and if Caesar does not come, the Twelfth become a memory. Or... we strengthen ourselves while weakening them.'

The duty centurion frowned as he leaned closer. 'Sir?'

'The man said the druids are counselling peace. The Treveri still have druids among them, and still listen to them. There will be warriors of honour within the tribe who are in two minds about any attack. If they recognise that the druids are against it and that half their army is made up of criminals or men from tribes they don't even know, a lot of their warriors might find cause to desert any attack.'

He wagged his finger at the Gaul. 'It is asking a great deal, but do you think you can get back among the Treveri without suspicion?'

'I think,' the Gaul nodded.

'Good. Go back to them. Take up your former role but now, instead of gathering information for me, I would like you to sound out their druids and, if they are truly opposed to an attack, help spread their dissent among the warriors of the Treveri. Try not to get yourself caught though, and steer clear of these thugs they have recruited.'

The Gaul nodded and Labienus smiled sadly. 'You know I want naught but peace for us all, and I know you will be returning to terrible danger, but I'm trying to bring matters to a close without strewing the countryside with the bodies of all our people. Go with your Gods and ours.'

As the Gaul held out weary hands to the man holding his spear and sword, Labienus turned to the duty centurion.

'We have a full legion, barring a few wounded, but we are lacking in cavalry.'

The centurion's face showed his low opinion of horse soldiers - an opinion shared by many of the legion's officers and men.

'Cavalry have their place, centurion. I have commanded mounted forces and while there are things that the legion can do that they cannot, there are activities that require the speed and flexibility of riders. We have less than three hundred horse - probably only half that if I look at the figures. I want that upped to more than a thousand, split into four alae, each with the few regulars we have mixed among the native levies.'

The centurion shook his head. 'Sir, Caesar has already levied every cavalryman he has the right to. If we try and call for more levies, we are exceeding our agreements with the tribes.'

'It seems curiously out of character for you to care, centurion?' Labienus asked with an arched brow.

The centurion looked a little taken aback, but made a quick recovery and shrugged slightly. 'I'm not over-bothered whether they get irritated about having more of their unwashed hordes recruited, true. But I'm not a lover of the idea, when faced with a sizable enemy, of stirring up the other tribes around us. I don't want to suddenly find we're also facing the Mediomatrici, the Leuci and all their little friends.'

Labienus smiled.

'Not a thought I relish either, centurion, but also not something I intend to bring about. I want your most eloquent men, accompanied by a few of our native auxilia, to head to all the larger oppida within a day's hard ride. They will petition the tribal councils for volunteers to help us against the Treveri.'

The centurion's eyes widened. 'That's mad, sir.'

'Remember to whom you speak, centurion.'

'Apologies, sir, but these people don't give two wet shits about us already - even the ones who are supposedly our allies. I really can't see anyone volunteering to save us from the Treveri.'

'That's because you have haven't thought of it from their point of view, centurion. You need to brief the men you send on the necessary angle of attack and bring up all the following salient points: the local tribes are peaceful now and have good trade relations with us. We are demanding nothing of them other than a small tithe agreed years ago with Caesar to help us against the rebels. The Treveri may be distant cousins to our locals, but you need to emphasise the fact that their leader has tried to petition the Germanics across the river to join him. *None* of the local tribes will like that. The Germanic peoples have only ever been aggressors and invaders. I think you'll find that many of the Gauls hate the tribes across the river more even than they hate us. Moreover no settled, law-abiding and honourable Gaul will like the idea of an army of bandits, murderers and other scum moving into their lands. Appeal to their honour and their sense of self-preservation. Remind them that we are here trying to build links between our people, and remind them of the last few times the tribes across the river came into their territory. I think you'll be surprised just how many volunteers you get.'

The centurion grinned. 'No one likes a thief in their garden, that's for sure, sir.'

'Precisely. Succinctly put. Now get your best rhetoricians saddled and ready to go. We don't know how long we have before the Treveri decide to come and stand on us, and I want a cavalry force to be reckoned with assembled by then.'

'I still don't see what good that will do us, sir,' the centurion replied.

'That, my good man, is because you have never ridden a horse into battle.'

As the centurion saluted and disappeared off to find the men he would need, Labienus watched the Gallic spy riding out through the gate towards the Treveri once again.

It was a gamble. But it was always worth gambling a little if the stakes were the prevention of a full scale war. Now to make the camp impregnable, or as near as damn it. It was always worth preparing for the worst.

* * * * *

Sextius Baculus, Primus Pilus of the Twelfth Legion, veteran of dozens of engagements and eighth highest-ranking man in the camp - including several pointless boyish junior tribunes - struggled upright at the end of his cot.

'Lie down, centurion,' said the orderly from across the room, where he was engrossed in some arcane medicinal duty involving bottles and dangerous looking liquids.

'I will forget that you just tried to impose an order on your senior centurion, *soldier.*'

'With respect, Primus Pilus, the medicus' authority exceeds your own in this place, and I speak with his authority, given by the man himself.'

'Unless you want that authority bottled and stuffed up your arse, go about your business and forget that you saw me,' Baculus growled. He was being unusually bad tempered, he knew, but his temper had seemed to decline with his general state of health. He looked to one side, to where a legionary he didn't know was

40

grinning. The man's smile disappeared as Baculus' glare passed across him. 'Laugh it up, lad. It's your diseased bowels polluting the air in here that's half the reason I'm vacating for a bit. If you keep farting like that you're going to turn inside out. Every morning I expect to see your liver hanging out of your arse.'

The soldier, embarrassed, turned his gaze down to the bed.

'That's better.'

He struggled to his feet, tottered a little, and then reached out for the stick at the foot of the bed. Grasping it, he staggered towards the door. While most of the men were still in their military tunics, soaked with sick-sweat, Baculus had also retained his belt and baldric'd sword. He wouldn't be parted from them until he was dead, and probably not even then. With a deep breath - one that he wished he hadn't taken in this nauseating miasma - he took a few unsteady steps across the room until he managed to strengthen his stride, and pulled open the door.

The valetudinarium of this more or less permanent *temporary* camp consisted of the sick-hut in which he was currently confined, a tent that performed a similar role for the less fortunate, a surgical tent and the medicus' own quarters. As was often the case, the hospital complex was kept as far apart from the headquarters and the barrack lines as possible. In the case of this particular camp, that put it out near the east gate, close to the stables and the workshop tent, away from the bulk of the population, in case of infection.

The upshot was that when Baculus pulled open the door, he was confronted with the area given over to the small cavalry detachment that had accompanied the Twelfth to its winter quarters.

Small no longer. Two days ago, new allied auxiliaries had started riding in, in groups of a dozen or more - sometimes nearing a hundred - and now the entire cavalry section had been expanded to cater for them. The workshops had been taken down and stored, their space donated for more stabling. He'd heard men grumbling that their amenities had been removed - three large communal social/mess tents that were only ever erected in winter quarters - in order to provide space for the new horsemen to make camp.

He'd peeked out of the door a few times over the past two days, keeping an eye on things and watching the cavalry contingent grow. He'd wished Labienus would drop by so he could get some answers over this whole thing, but the legate had not appeared and, despite his resilience and refusal to obey the outspoken physician,

Baculus would have to admit if pressed that he was weak as a kitten and really could not bring himself to go find his commander.

But this morning things were different. He'd heard the warning blasts from the legion's musicians, summoning the men to stand to, indicating an enemy force in view. This had been followed only a short while ago by sudden frenzied activity among the cavalry outside. Baculus could hardly contain himself any more.

'You!' he snapped at one of the few regular cavalrymen he could see.

'Sir?' replied the soldier, startled, turning with the reins of his horse in his hand.

Taking a deep breath, Baculus hobbled out of the building and onto the lightly-gravelled road. 'I'm feeling a little weak. I need your horse.'

The trooper opened his mouth to argue, noted the look on the centurion's face, and saluted, holding forth the reins. Baculus hobbled over and without the need for a request, the soldier helped him into the saddle, grunting with the effort.

'You'll have it back before you need it,' said Baculus, noting the slightly panicked look on the soldier's face as he shuffled into the saddle. Grasping the horns, he turned the beast and trotted it back to the headquarters section at the camp's centre and then north towards the gate where there was a great deal of commotion. He could see from here a seething mass of Gauls assembled on the low rise opposite, with more still arriving from the northeast.

Wincing with effort, he held tight to the reins until he bore down on the party at the gate, and then slowed. Never a natural horseman, his current condition made his control of the skittish beast less than impressive. The tribunes had gathered at the gate with Labienus and a number of standard bearers and musicians, and their horses were being led out by the camp equisio from the intervallum road that wound around inside the wall. Labienus and his lesser officers looked up at the sound of the approaching horse and the commander's eyes rolled.

'I thought you were confined to your cot, centurion.'

Baculus made to slide from the horse, but Labienus waved him to stop. 'Stay in the saddle man. At least you won't fall over up there. Besides, we're mounting up, ourselves. I presume you're aware of what's happening?'

'The Treveri have arrived. I thought my presence might be useful, sir? I should be in full armour I know, but there was not enough time to find it after two weeks of convalescence.'

'Never mind that. Just try not to look as though the ferryman's standing in your shadow and make sure you don't pass out and fall off the horse. It would not convey the right impression.'

Baculus gave a weak salute and waited patiently as the officers mounted and the gate swung ponderously open. The number of warriors arriving across the open grassland to the north had fallen off, and it seemed almost the entire enemy force was here. As the small party of officers rode out of the gate, an honour guard of regular cavalry - along with a few carefully selected local volunteer noblemen - at their back, the centurion peered at the enemy ranks.

He had fought in almost every engagement of any worth in the five years since they'd first stepped into Gaul and felt he knew enough about Gallic warbands to form easy and fast opinions concerning their strength, morale and capabilities, but this was unlike any force he had laid eyes upon in that time.

Since every army they had faced had been formed by one or more major tribe, along with their lesser neighbours, the armies tended to have more than one knot of 'royalty' where a chieftain would direct the battle, surrounded by his close kin and personal bodyguard. The main force would be infantry, gathered around and in front of the leaders, usually with the more bloodthirsty or desperate for recognition at the front, jostling for position and itching to get into the fight. Behind them would be the lesser warriors: the older men who had nothing to prove, the farmers who had more to gain by staying alive than by winning prestige, and so on. The equipment would vary according to the wealth of the individual, and there was no rule to say the best armed and armoured would be at the front. In basic terms, it was barely-controlled chaos. The only disciplined force would be on one or other of the wings - the cavalry, mostly manned by noblemen, though again rarely armoured.

Such was the general makeup of Gallic forces.

Not so here.

Only one knot of leadership was in evidence, and that was at the rear, where Indutiomarus and his cronies 'commanded' the force. There was precious little evidence of cavalry and what there was seemed to be kept at the rear, in reserve. The bulk of the army, as usual, was formed by the infantry, but they were clearly organised in an unusual fashion, with the typical force - likely the Treveri

43

themselves - at the rear, and the front ranks filled with slavering mercenary killers. These men were heavily armed, for Gauls, many bearing captured Roman equipment. These then would be the criminals and rebels that had flocked to the chieftain's banner. The Treveri seemed not to be putting themselves forth for the chance of prestige, leaving the front with its dangerous initial clashes to the volunteers who had joined up either through pure hatred of Rome or more likely for the chance of loot that would follow the battle, a distinct gap separating the two groups.

'Slow down,' Labienus commanded the party. 'Let's give the man time to come out the front and talk to us. I've no intention of riding through or past his army to open negotiations.'

'Seems little point in talking to them at all, as far as I can see, sir,' one of the tribunes chimed in.

'I agree that little is likely to come from it other than a little name calling,' Labienus smiled, 'but I have some of our most important local nobles with us and I want them to get a good look at this force of vagabonds and murderers so they remember just why they're here when the fighting starts.'

Baculus nodded his agreement and the party slowed. 'It looks to me very much like the goat-buggerer has no intention of moving.'

The tribunes, frowning at the language, turned to look disapprovingly at Baculus, though Labienus simply nodded, used to the senior centurion's outspoken tongue. 'I suspect you're right, centurion. It looks like there will be no parlay today.'

'Then why are we still riding towards them, sir?' the inquisitive junior tribune hazarded.

'Tell him, Baculus.'

The centurion rubbed his grey, sweating forehead. 'Because it's how things are done in a civilised war, and we want the local royalty to see us as the righteous ones. We do things by the rules and then when the Treveri and their hired bandits fail to meet our standards, the locals will see what they're facing and steel themselves a little.'

'Precisely. Now we're close enough that our allied volunteers can see the quality of the shaved apes at the front of Indutiomarus' force. Our friends can see that these men are killers, bandits, rapists, thieves and the like, and the sight will confirm what we initially informed them, sealing them to our cause.'

Baculus shook his head slightly as they approached. 'Something bothers me though, sir. Their army's more than twice the size of ours and the way it's formed it should be even less organised and disciplined than usual. And yet look: there's a gap between the front rank of mercenaries and the rear where the Treveri wait. Why? It's not like they use our tactics? They're not going to rotate the ranks during battle, so why the gap?'

The officers and their escort rode slowly towards the line of waiting Gauls, close enough now to pick out the armour and the torcs and arm rings of the warriors, to see their spiked hair and drooping moustaches. Close enough that if Baculus had a rock in his hand, he...

'Retreat!' he shouted at the party. The tribunes and the commander turned to face him, frowns creasing their foreheads. Baculus was already turning his beast.

'Back to the camp!' he yelled. Labienus turned his frown on the enemy in time to see the front ranks crouch or bow, the gap between the two infantry forces suddenly filling as the archers and slingers that had hidden there rose to their feet, weapons in hand.

'Mars protect us!' barked the legate in consternation as enemy weapons were discharged with the hiss and hum of airborne arrows and the zip and whine of sling stones.

Three of the escort cavalrymen, used to manoeuvring their horses in battle, charged forward to protect Labienus, arriving just in time to take half a dozen strikes to their shields that were meant for the Roman commander. Labienus looked in grateful surprise at the three men as he turned his horse to retreat. Two of the men bore the professional straight faces of career cavalrymen. The third tried to smile, but a torrent of crimson erupted from his mouth and he slumped forward over his saddle, his shield falling to the grass below. Two arrows jutted from his back between the shoulder blades where they had ripped straight through the mail with the force of a short-distance blow, and a third stood proud from the back of his neck, driven in so far it had almost emerged from his windpipe.

Labienus rode for the camp, watching the talkative young tribune suddenly stiffen in his saddle as he wheeled his horse and then tumble to the ground, an arrow jutting from his lower back.

Two of the volunteer noble cavalrymen were already down, thrashing about on the ground in agony, their horses bolting for safety, and a third was trying to control his mount, which had taken an arrow in the flank and was dancing in a panic.

45

A second volley from the hidden archers and slingers began, this time at a sporadic release rate, but now the party was on the move, harder to hit and at a greater range. Another of the regular cavalrymen went down, a sling bullet smashing a dent in his helmet so deep it shattered his skull beneath, and another tribune's horse was struck, though he managed to keep the pained beast enough under control to head for the fort.

By the time they were out of range of the missiles another half dozen arrows and bullets had struck, but the reduced force at such a distance caused only bruising and stinging pains. Leaving seven men dead or dying on the grass, the Roman ambassadorial party reached the north gate of the camp and rode inside, their horses dancing excitedly.

'Well, it would appear that the negotiations are over before they began,' Labienus sighed, shaking his head and climbing down from his horse. 'It's my belief that the majority of the Gauls consider missile volleys and traps to be lacking in honour, so I think that tells us all we need to know about Indutiomarus' intentions and abilities. He clearly plans to conduct this attack in a most atypical fashion.'

He handed the reins of his horse to the nearest soldier and rubbed his hands together in a business-like fashion. 'Moreover, it tells us that either Indutiomarus is unwilling to field the Treveri unless he has to or, more likely, the Treveri themselves are less willing to bring the fight to us than the mercenaries. Either way, the main force we face now is the mercenary army he has attracted and they will have no discipline. They will falter at our defences unless he can commit the Treveri as well. I am decided as to our course of action, gentlemen, but it is all a matter of timing. We need the time to be just right before I put my plan into action and until then we need to hold them off and keep our defences and morale strong.'

'I will see to the disposition of the men, sir,' Baculus announced, swaying slightly in his saddle with weariness.

'You will do nothing of the sort, centurion. You will report to the medicus and return to your bed and stay there until either your infection passes and you take on a healthy complexion or until we are desperate enough that I am forced to send for you.'

Baculus began to shake his head, but Labienus held up a warning finger. 'The medicus tells me that every time you come out and about and push yourself to the limit, not only do you endanger your life, but you also set back your healing progress by several weeks. Simply: if you do not lie down and rest, you will never heal and I will be forced to have you put down like a horse with a broken leg. Now go!'

The Primus Pilus stared helplessly at Labienus and finally sagged a little, saluted and turned his horse to ride back through the camp. Labienus, he knew, had been nicknamed 'soft touch' by the soldiers. The commander knew nothing of it of course, and Baculus had already disciplined every man he heard use the phrase. And it was, to some extent, a fair appraisal. Of all of Caesar's officers, only Titus Labienus had repeatedly - even constantly - attempted peaceful relations and diplomatic solutions with the Gauls. One man had even called him 'Gaul-lover' and had been scourged until his back ran red for his wit. But while they were right about his desire to avoid conflict where possible, there was still a steel in Labienus that Baculus could see and respect. The man might favour the diplomatic option, but he would never put his army in the situation in which Sabinus and Cotta's force had found itself a few months back. And he would brook no argument, even from Baculus.

The legate had a plan, and the centurion knew his commander well enough to know that a shrewd, tactical military mind churned away within that peaceable exterior. Despite being outnumbered and cut off from the rest of the army by a force whose capabilities and actions they could not predict, Baculus felt certain that Indutiomarus would rue the day he brought a force against the Twelfth.

* * * * *

Labienus cinched the belt around his cuirass and stood still while the slave brushed out the long red plume on his helm.

'You don't have to do this, sir,' said one of the junior tribunes, quietly.

'Yes I do, Lentulus. I know you've studied your Herodotus and the like but no amount of tutoring can match the experience of long-term command, and you're very new to this. A good commander knows when to sit back and when to throw in his lot with the soldiery. That is where half of Caesar's genius lies, and it is he who taught me the value of 'getting involved'. The value of the boost in morale and strength it gives the men to find their commander amongst them in the thick of it far outweighs the danger I will face. And that is why I must look as 'noble Roman' as possible. Caesar wears his crimson cloak and rides a white horse so

47

that the men can see him and take heart that he's with them. A horse is of little value when under siege, but I can do my part, and I shall do so.'

'But legate, why go to such lengths to levy local cavalry and then allow ourselves to be besieged? It makes no sense! We should have met them in direct conflict on the hillside before they reached the camp. Now our cavalry cannot be deployed and we sit and wait while they continually harry our defences.'

Labienus sighed patiently.

'Lentulus, the cavalry are part of my long-term plan, so please stop concerning yourself too much. I realise that I am keeping my strategy somewhat obfuscated but we must learn the lesson from ourselves. I have spies among the Treveri and their allies and bearing that in mind we cannot rule out the possibility that there are enemy spies among our own native levies. It has not even been unheard of for a *legionary* to turn informant for promises of rich reward, though I would prefer not to suspect my own men of such low dealings. I will continue to keep my strategy contained until the time arises to open the carceres and let the horses run. Now... you stay here, go over my latest engineers' reports and make sure I've missed nothing. If you can think of anything to add, be my guest and do so.'

Leaving the exasperated young tribune, Labienus strode out into the cold, slightly damp late winter air in his most resplendent gear. Lentulus was almost laughably young and naïve, but Labienus could remember being just like him as a junior tribune in Vatia's army against the Cilician pirates. Still, in this current situation, better the boy kept himself busy with the records than getting in the way on the defences.

The camp was quiet, but it was a quiet that Labienus knew well. It was that specific, eerie, leaden quiet that presaged another attack. The thugs and bandits that made up roughly half of Indutiomarus' force had committed themselves to the assault almost immediately, but had not come with the force and skill of a tribal war band or a professional army, and had broken on the defences like a small wave on the beach.

They were doing damage, for sure, and two rows of tents had been taken from their occupants and given over to the medicus for extra hospital space. Men were being brought in at a steady stream, wounded by blades and missiles, and the area left largely clear - due to being the site of the most recently backfilled latrine pits - was now stacked with bodies awaiting the pyre when timber supplies and time allowed.

But it was all remarkably easily fought off and contained. While Labienus had lost maybe two dozen men to the 'dead pile' and more than a century's worth to the hospital, it was a smaller figure than most sieges would have brought on. And the number of Gallic dead in the ditches around the camp was substantially larger by comparison. A satisfactory situation.

Two things had occurred to Labienus as he ran his reports this morning:

Firstly: while the situation was perfectly acceptable to Labienus, the failure to make a dent would be driving Indutiomarus mad and soon he would snap and commit the Treveri to the attack as well. When he did that, one of two things would happen. Either the Treveri would turn on the man and refuse, which was Labienus' main hope and great suspicion, or they would throw their full weight into the attack, and in that case the camp would be overrun before the next sun set.

A gamble.

Secondly, that the troops were well provisioned, well armed, and not being particularly tested in the current attacks. They were handling the siege with all the professionalism he could have hoped for, but there was every likelihood of them becoming over-confident and lax, believing their position unassailable. By going among them as he was, he could help fight off the ennui that would be infecting the defenders, as well as gauging the enemy's situation. All he needed was a sign that Indutiomarus' control was faltering.

The quiet was reaching that tense point and would snap at any moment. Another attack was about to launch - he could feel it crackling in the air. With a smile of self-assuredness, he slowed his step as he approached the east gate. This side had not seen a concerted attack yet, and he felt certain it was due, but he didn't want to arrive too early and stand uselessly in the chilly air, passing the time of day with the men.

Almost as if he had given the signal himself, a roar arose beyond the walls as he reached the earth bank and the wooden steps built into it which led up to the gate top walkway. Climbing the steps with practiced ease, he emerged atop the wall just as the first shower of arrows and stones whipped, whined and thudded into the defences. The centurion in command of the section saluted, holding his shield - circular and smaller than the legionaries' - up behind his

49

head to deflect the missiles as he stood proud. His men cowered behind the parapet and their large shields waiting for the barrage to end and the infantry assault to begin.

'How goes it, centurion?'

'Very good, sir. The 'braid-monkeys' seem to have little heart for it.'

'Pray it stays that way, soldier.'

'Oh I do sir, but I'd be happier down on the grass out there, facing them in a shield wall.'

'I'm sure, but my purpose is other than the complete destruction of the Treveri and the corresponding losses to the Twelfth.'

The centurion looked a little unsure, but the cacophonic honking and booing of the Gauls' carnyxes ordering the infantry forward drew their attention. Labienus stepped across to the wall and peered over the top. The mob of unsightly, disorganised killers was coming again, swarming across the grass, passing the archers and slingers who were stepping back away from the fight, and thundering towards what remained of the ditches.

Had it been Romans on the outside, or some of the more civilised and advanced Gaulish tribes, men would have come forward first, covered with shields and carrying bundles of sticks and earth to fill in the ditch and make crossing easier. Not so with this rabble of criminals. They had simply charged and filled the ditch with corpses in the first two attacks. It was grimly effective, if very costly to the attackers.

'Best get back down, sir. Here they come.'

Labienus rubbed his neck and drew the blade from his sheath. 'I think it's time to get my sword dirty, don't you?'

The centurion grinned. 'I'll try and leave you one, sir.'

'That's the spirit. Share the fun.'

They both turned their gaze back to the exterior, where the enemy were pounding across the triple ditch, the bodies of their former compatriots forming an effective causeway.

'Ready, men!' the centurion bellowed. 'To the wall!'

The soldiers, who had been sheltering behind shields and parapet leapt up and forward, taking their places at the timber palisade and preparing to meet the attack.

Labienus found a gap where a slick of blood rapidly drying on the timbers marked the absence of a man - wounded or dead - and fell in between two legionaries who instinctively moved slightly apart to allow him plenty of room. He had no shield - had decided against one to allow for a more impressive profile among the men - and so drew his pugio dagger from its sheath and held it in his free hand. The men were not leaning into the wall to get a good view of the attackers - that was a good way to receive a spear point in the eye.

A moment later there was a barked Gallic curse in front and below Labienus - hidden by the wall - and grubby fingers came over the parapet, gripping the timber and whitening as they took a man's weight. The wavering tip of a sword appeared, glinting, as the man tried to get high enough to take a swing at the defender he couldn't yet quite see.

With a grim smile, Labienus reversed his grip on the dagger and slammed the blade down onto the clutching fingers, easily severing all but the thumb and digging into the wood beneath. Blood sprayed from the stubs of the fingers before the hand disappeared outside once more, withdrawn with a howl of agony.

The sword point also vanished and, despite the danger in doing so, Labienus leaned forward to take a quick look. A long blade sliced out and cut through the air a few finger widths from his face as he pulled back. Startled, he forced himself to grin at his neighbour as though it had been intentional and even amusing.

Off to the right, a loop of rope appeared from the far side and settled on a protruding tip of one of the wall's constituent stakes. The legionary closest lowered his shield and leaned in, using his gladius to saw at the rope even as it tightened. Such an enemy tactic could be effective if not dealt with quickly, as it would only take one stake pulled out of the palisade with ropes and brute force to begin the complete collapse of a section of wall.

The legionary sawed madly at the thick cable and was so intent on his work that he did not see the next attacker reach the top of the parapet and stab out with his sword. Labienus shouted a warning, but he was too late - the long Celtic blade jabbed deep into the legionary's shoulder and he cried out, dropping his own sword. With a howl of triumph, the Gaul began to climb over the palisade. Recovering himself from the painful and debilitating - yet clearly non-mortal - wound, the legionary leaned forward and head-butted the attacker, the bronze brow of his helm smashing and pulping the man's face. As his victim fell away down to the ditches below, the soldier hissed in pain and, collecting his sword, shuffled back towards the steps down to the camp's interior.

'Reserves!' bellowed the centurion, but half a dozen legionaries standing at the bottom of the grass bank were already moving, climbing up to take the place of the wounded and dead, orderlies among them coming to help the injured back to the capsarii who tended them a little further from the wall.

Labienus heard the next Gaul before he saw him, and ducked aside as a spear shaft appeared, lunging for his head. Contemptuously, he knocked the spear aside against the timbers and brought his sword down in an arc, cutting the leaf-shaped blade from its tip. The man withdrew the broken shaft, but there was no time for Labienus to revel in his latest success, as a Gaul with a scarred face and a tarnished torc appeared atop the wall, propelled up by his fellows, heavy sword already swinging.

Labienus ducked the scything blade and lunged out with his gladius, jabbing it deep into the man's chest, twisting it and wrenching it from side to side for good measure before withdrawing it. The man gurgled and disappeared over the wall again, dead before he hit the ground.

A noise resembling the anguished cries of a family of wounded oxen echoed out across the field and the attack broke off once more, men rushing back across the ditches towards the Treveri force on the far rise.

'That was bloody brief!' the centurion announced, peering out over the parapet at the retreating Gauls.

'Shorter than usual, sir,' an optio agreed a little further along.

Labienus peered into the mass of Gauls. What the others had failed to notice was that the call of the dreadful carnyxes was different from the ones that had sounded the recall in the previous dozen assaults. This was a *new* call.

'Watch them, centurion. Most importantly, watch the commanders and the Treveri themselves, and forget this rabble in front. If you see any concerted movement before I do, shout out.'

Tensely, he watched the mercenary Gauls return to the fold of the enemy. Though he could not say what the call precisely meant, he was convinced that this was the crucial moment - the tipping point for the battle. His breathing slow and deliberately calm, he squinted into the air, shivering in sudden recognition of the chill now that the brutal activity had stopped and his blood was cooling.

'There! Did you see that?' He pointed at the enemy with his dagger.

The centurion shook his head. 'No, sir. What?'

'The Treveri. They're splitting up.'

A moment's silence, and then the centurion cleared his throat. 'I see it, sir. Three groups separating off from the main force. A new tactic you think, sir?'

Labienus gripped his blade tight. 'I hope not. If it is, we could be in trouble. Either they're moving off to get into position around the other sides or…'

He paused and a grin spread across his face.

'No. No new tactics or attack. They're leaving.'

'The Treveri, sir?'

'Not yet; not as a *tribe* at least. But *some* of them are. Look. They're following noblemen and a druid. They're leaving the field.' He laughed out loud as he managed to locate the figure of Indutiomarus on a horse near the back of the army. The rebel leader was yelling and gesticulating angrily at the departing sections of his force.

'Excellent. Everything is falling into place. Prepare for another assault, centurion. This will be a brutal one, too. That lunatic is going to throw everything he can at us now, because he knows as well as I do that unless he makes significant in-roads in the next hour, that will not be the last time he watches whole chunks of his army depart. Pass the word round the walls. Hold the defences, but don't do anything stupid. No heroics. I just want the camp secure, not a bloodbath.'

'Sir?'

'I have something else in mind.' Labienus grinned as he moved to the stairs down into the camp. Spotting one of the legionaries on courier duty awaiting orders, he gestured the man over.

'Go find Quadratus at the stables and tell him to have every trooper equipped and in the saddle in the next half hour and every native levy on horseback and armed. Their time is about to come.'

With any luck he would be able to end this entire uprising with minimal carnage, remove the ongoing threat and bring the Treveri back onto Rome's side. There were days when Mars clearly looked down favourably upon him, and today seemed to be one of those days. Indutiomarus had better hope *his* Gods were watching over *him* too.

Chapter Three

Gaius Volusenus Quadratus waited impatiently for the gates, watching the twin leaves open under the straining arms of the legionaries. Gathered behind him at the southern entrance to the fort, a force of cavalry - some two hundred local auxilia and thirty two regulars - champed at the bit ready to move. Still, even with the open gate before them, he held his hand high, waiting to give the signal.

His arm ached.

Labienus had waited until the last moment to reveal his plans, as was his command style, Quadratus knew. Really, with the many and varied local tribal auxiliaries, it was a safe and sensible thing to do, but really he could have at least dropped an advance warning to a fellow senior Roman officer.

The waiting seemed interminable, but finally he heard the low honk of a horn - three short and relatively subdued blasts designed to be heard across the camp, but not to carry to the enemy force.

The Treveri army had been breaking up now for more than an hour, separate groups of nobles taking away their people, sick of the siege and disenchanted with Indutiomarus' failure to provide them with victory and loot. The Gallic chieftain had been ranting and railing from the back of his horse, waving his sword at the departing groups and threatening them, but still they had gone.

Now more than half the Treveri themselves had left the scene, and between desertions and death, perhaps half of the mercenary force had gone too. The odds were more or less in parity with the defenders and a pitched battle would have almost guaranteed victory, but still Labienus had held back his forces.

Quadratus could understand why, of course. In a full scale battle, the rebel chief could launch his army at the Romans and sit safely protected behind them. Hundreds or thousands of Romans would die, as would even more thousands of Treveri, in a bloodbath on a monumental scale. Labienus had avowed time and again his desire to see this corner of the world settled without heavy Roman losses, but also without Gallic genocide, given that the Treveri were not as committed to the attack as their leader would have them. To attain victory without such a death toll would mean finding a way to take down Indutiomarus without having to engage his army in bulk.

And that was where the cavalry came in.

At the east gate, the rest of the mounted contingent had gathered under the command - despite Quadratus' misgivings - of a native, a prince of the Mediomatrici who had been utterly incensed by the actions of the Treveri leader and had been urging Labienus to let him and his men off the leash ever since the attack had begun. It was not that Quadratus thought the man a coward or a traitor. There was no question of him refusing to attack, but the problem was something rather opposite. Given his spiteful invectives against the Treveri and their bandit allies there was every possibility that the angry noble would forget his orders in the thirst for blood and simply launch into the nearest enemy he found. And that would put Quadratus' considerably smaller force in great danger.

But it was all moot now. The anvil was in position and the hammer was falling.

Those three short blasts had indicated to Quadratus that prince Messirios of the Mediomatrici and his force had fully committed and the east gate was now closed. If the blood-crazed lunatic Gaul was still clinging to both sanity and his orders, he would now be racing in a wide arc, circumventing the bulk of the enemy force and threatening their flank enough to draw out the reserve that sat behind - the Treveri noble cavalry, the most dangerous and effective fighting group on the field. With any luck, even now Indutiomarus was spotting the danger and sending the cavalry - one of his few remaining loyal units - off to the east to meet the Roman auxiliary force. And with luck Messirios had not simply charged his cavalry at the murderers and thieves in the front lines. If he had, Quadratus was in for a short and brutal trip, as he came across the entire Treveri mounted contingent.

He shook his head irritably. No point in brooding on the possibilities. The attack had to go ahead regardless. He would just have to pray to Mars and Minerva that the prince stuck to the plan.

His hand dropped and the cavalry began to move out through the south gate at his signal.

The enemy had long-since abandoned the siege of the southern and western sides of the camp, partially because of the diminishing numbers of their force they could rely upon, but also because they knew that the swift, dangerous Mosella river - which formed a wide horseshoe at this point - curved around those sides and effectively prevented the Romans from fleeing that way in force. Indeed, their force was small and unimpressive even to the east, theoretically allowing the rest of the cavalry to burst through them

55

and complete their task, depending upon the reliability of that Gaulish prince.

This concentration of enemy forces around the north and east left an area to the south devoid of enemy warriors, giving Quadratus the golden opportunity to leave the camp unnoticed while all Treveri attention would be on Messirios' attack.

In line with the series of orders Quadratus had issued before the gates opened, the small but effective force of veteran cavalrymen raced across the causeway that spanned the camp's double defensive ditch, and down the gentle slope which led to the Mosella river, the thunder of hooves lost to enemy ears amid the tumult of the attack by Messirios, and sight of them hidden by the slope.

Quadratus reined in close to the rushing torrent of ice cold water brought several hundred miles from the Vosego mountains to the south. To be caught against that river by a superior force would be the end - the main reason for the lack of enemies in this arc. Nobody would be able to escape across it without the aid of a bridge or a ford, and the only local ford was the one behind the Treveri, across which they had come when they first arrived.

Swiftly the rest of his force assembled around him, and Quadratus paused as they arranged themselves into their tribal sub-units, his veteran regulars forming up on him, bearing their banner to relay his orders to the rest, no signal horn in evidence in case its blasts led to their discovery.

As soon as the various sections were ready he nodded to the signifer, who waved the red *vexillum* flag in the approved signals. In moments the entire force was moving along the bank of the river, following it downstream in a northerly direction towards the ford at the rear of the Treveri army. It was a measure of the skill and competence of the cavalry, both regular and native levy, that they managed to maintain their unit cohesion and move at speed given the narrow confines afforded by the raging torrent to their left and the slope that hid them from the enemy to their right.

The horsemen raced on blindly, able to see only the gentle curve of the river valley, the location of the Roman camp and the Treveri army pin-pointable by the sounds that echoed across the landscape. The first gamble had been whether the other cavalry force would commit as intended. They would soon know the answer to that. The second gamble was that Quadratus' own unit could leave the river and move up onto the enemy-controlled plain in just the right position to reach the commanders from the rear without engaging the entire force.

Evicaos, one of the more senior native mounted scouts, had assured him that if they followed the river as far as the ford and then turned back directly south, they would fall upon the unprepared and lightly defended Indutiomarus with ease. Quadratus hoped the man was right. There was still every possibility - even if they made the right position to leave the river - that his small cavalry unit would arrive at their turning point, rush up the hill and find themselves confronted by the entire Treveri cavalry force defending their leader.

* * * * *

Lucius Annius Gritto clung to his spear and shield tightly as he steered his nervous steed with his knees in the fashion taught by Roman cavalry trainers. His mail shirt felt as though it weighed more than he did, dragging him down to the ground, but he clenched his teeth and held on.

How he had drawn the duty of second in command of the native cavalry attack, he was still unsure. He was certainly not the most senior decurion in the camp, and far from the most experienced. He *was* lucky with dice and had fleeced a number of his peers recently, including the commander Quadratus, and it was tempting to blame that as a reason, though he hoped he owed this dubious honour to something more substantial than his affinity with lady Fortuna, bless her shapely breasts. He wished he had a free hand to grasp the pendant of his favourite Goddess hanging around his neck, but settled for a mental prayer - short and to the point.

The briefing had taken mere moments and was simple:

Make sure the native prince and chieftains kept to the plan and didn't either race off into the open ground and freedom or launch against the first warrior they saw. It *sounded* simple, anyway.

In reality, given the lack of regular cavalrymen in the force and the absence of Roman officers or Roman training, what he actually found himself part of was a headlong, disorganised charge in true Gallic style, with a lot of shouting and screaming, threats and promises, some crazed laughter, more than a little jostling between the riders, occasional falls and mishaps and so much noise that it felt as though his ears might turn inside out. It had occurred to him within only moments of leaving the camp that his presence was about as pointless as tits on a bull, since even if any of them could hear his orders and calls over the general din, none of them seemed to be paying the slightest attention to him anyway.

His initial fears were first realised when he shot out of the gate like some sort of projectile, squeezed through among the Gauls, only to see the remaining western force of Treveri running towards the open gate. There were not many of them, given the size of the Gauls' army - perhaps three hundred, which was minimal given that until the desertions had begun there were more like two thousand outside this gate. They were rabid and wild, just like the horsemen he was riding amongst, and they sought blood, but they could easily be avoided, given their numbers.

Indeed, the prince in charge, one Messirios - identified by the dragon standard that rode alongside him - immediately took the lead units out and swept around the Treveri group, as the plan had dictated.

Two of the other chieftains leading their auxiliary volunteer regiments seemed to have different ideas and turned their forces directly on the small besieging mob, rushing to meet them and crashing into them like two opposing waves.

Gritto had shaken his head in exasperation, realising there was virtually nothing he could do about it, and rode on with the bulk of the force, hoping that the loss of a hundred or more cavalry to this unintentional engagement would not alter their chances of the main objective.

Then they had found themselves in the clear, riding hard to circumvent the main enemy force. It had been exhilarating, momentarily. They were on-task. The discordant honking and lowing of the carnyx horns and some frantic waving from the Treveri command group confirmed that they had been seen and were being taken seriously, just as intended, and even the enemy cavalry began to move as if to intercept them.

And then things had gone wrong.

Another bunch of the chieftains among the cavalry had apparently decided that they liked the look of the nearest bunch of Treveri scum and had peeled off with their units, heading directly towards the main force. As Gritto had shouted himself hoarse, his voice totally lost in the noise of the attack, he'd felt his heart sink as he watched two more of the native units peel off to support them.

A very quick rough estimate in his head now suggested that almost half the attacking force had separated to wage their own private wars, and not only was it therefore not a given that the enemy would consider the attack enough of a threat to engage their own horse, but it was also now a worrying possibility that the Treveri might come after them and win…

Ahead, what was left of the main cavalry attack was still skirting the main force, heading for the Treveri horse and their commanders at the rear, and Gritto scanned the crowd of his own men as he rode until he spotted the standard that betrayed the position of Messirios.

It was dipping to the left!

Though he had absolutely no idea of the signalling systems the natives used, if indeed they used any kind of signalling at all, given their propensity to chaos, an intentional dip of the standard to the left could only signal a move that way, as it would with a Roman unit.

And that meant straight into the bulk of the infantry.

Gritto felt his spirits sink even further - if that were at all possible, since they were already bounding along at ground level and cutting a furrow in the grass. If the prince turned against the main force, so would all his men and his allied chiefs. Then they would be engaged with the wrong group. Very likely the enemy cavalry would not even bother to commit and would just watch the fun, given that the infantry that would be dying would be the mercenary bandits anyway, and not their own tribesmen.

How could that Mediomatrici moron be so short-sighted? He would cost them the battle.

In the most futile of gestures, Gritto tried desperately to shout for them to hold their course, waving his spear and almost gutting one of the nearest Gauls in the process. He might as well have been throwing mouldy cabbages at the walls of Rome for all the difference his attempts were making.

His heart raced. The legate Labienus and commander Quadratus were relying on this attack. If it failed, what should be a short, surgical cut would turn into a chaotic slaughter on both sides. And, far more important than that, Gritto would be decommissioned, chastised, punished and then sent home in disgrace, where Aurelia would never speak to him again, her father would call off their betrothal, and his own parents would push him into some awful administrative role.

The thought of spending the rest of his life shuffling and shelving scrolls with records of public works brought on a worse fear by far than that of simple death.

He had to do something to make this work.

The Gallic horses were larger than his Roman one - Roman cavalry preferred the easier trained and more even-temperamented smaller beasts - so he could hardly make his presence felt and was barely visible among the crowd. But his horse was a noble beast, trained in the Roman military and therefore so obedient that he barely had to twitch his knees to make his intentions felt. And he knew that the Gallic steeds were more angry, more nervous and considerably more awkward.

He would have to *make* his presence felt.

Raising himself as best he could, he locked on to the position of the prince's standard and noted its location and then, taking a deep breath, leaned forward over his steed's neck and held his oval shield out in front at an oblique angle. Keeping his spear point up, so as to avoid accidental wounds, he kicked his faithful steed onwards, driving it as hard as he could.

He felt the shield smack into the Gauls slightly ahead of him, who were moving as fast as they could in the chaos, but not with the speed and purpose of Gritto and his smaller beast. The shield bounced off a man's leg and the angered Gaul, either not realising whose shield it was, or more likely not caring, smashed his sword down on it as Gritto pushed and heaved past.

Then he was out between the two horses ahead, his shield battered but in place. The angry shout of the Gaul whose knee he had hurt rang out behind him but he ignored it, aiming for the position he remembered the standard to be and driving on the horse as hard as he could. He felt the shield bounce off the haunch of a larger horse and sensed the beast veering off, away from this discomfort. That rider of the animal roared at his steed and tried to turn back, only to find Gritto there, pushing past, shield up and yelling imprecations in Latin.

The push went on. Another three times, four, five, and he had actually received a punch and a kick in the process, but had forged ahead through the mass of horsemen by sheer control of his horse and force of will.

Slowing for a moment, he risked rising above the shield and was both surprised and relieved to see the standard of Messirios bobbing about almost in front of him. The horses had already turned slightly off-course, heading for the infantry. Any moment now, the prince would give the command to go from a messy gallop to an unrestrained charge, and then it would be too late to stop them.

Even if the prince would consider listening to him, it was exceedingly unlikely that he would hear him in the din. A moment of undecided panic, and Gritto settled upon a course of action, somewhat regretfully dropping his shield and spear among the running horses where they were immediately trampled and smashed to pieces.

Driving his horse on for that standard, he elbowed aside a Gallic nobleman, who in return delivered him a sturdy kick to the thigh in anger. A push, a lunge, and suddenly he was next to the standard bearer. The Gaul, his drooping moustaches bouncing comically with his gait and the breeze, his head topped with a bronze helm that looked as though a metal seagull had impaled itself on the tip, had not even noticed he was there, too intent on watching the prince a few paces ahead, waiting for the nod.

Aware that he might just die for his presumption but seeing no other choice, Gritto reached out and delivered the hardest punch he could muster to the upper arm of the standard bearer. The Gaul let out a yelp, the blow - as intended - deadening his arm for a moment and causing him to lose his grip on the shaft. As the Gaul's head swung round in a mix of shock and anger, Gritto grasped the shaft of the falling standard and raised it high, tipping it to the right once, twice, three times.

The course of the attack changed instantly, and after a matter of mere heartbeats Gritto found himself on the periphery of the force, along with the Mediomatrici prince, his standard bearer, and his personal cadre of noble warriors.

The standard bearer raised the sword he had held in his other hand ready to bring down on this sudden attacker, but faltered as he recognised the uniform of a Roman officer, the sword quivering in his shaking hand high above them.

Prince Messirios seemed to have realised that something was amiss, and had turned to look at the scene behind him, his eyes wide as he realised his army were veering off to the east, skirting around the enemy. His eyes, blazing, fell upon the Roman officer holding his royal standard and he barked something furiously in his own tongue.

Gritto felt his heart skip a beat, knowing that the heavy Gallic sword was poised to fall on the prince's command and that when it did so, it would smash open his head like a ripe melon. He realised that he was probably ashen faced and gawping like an idiot and forced his open mouth shut, lowering his brows into an expression of arrogant defiance such as the one his father seemed to have permanently affixed to his face.

'Indutiomarus!' he snapped and, to try and make his point all the more obvious, used his free hand to mime a cantering horse (though in all fairness it probably more resembled a drunken spider) and then pointed over the enemy to the cavalry at the rear.

For a long moment, the prince of the Mediomatrici glared at him in anger and finally, showing no sign of letting up his fury for even a moment, nodded and turned his horse away, racing off to catch up with his men as they skirted the Treveri army.

The Gaulish standard bearer lowered his sword with a glance after his departing lord and punched the Roman heavily in the arm, retrieving his standard before riding off to join his compatriots.

Gritto sat for a moment rubbing his arm and watched the fruit of his labour as the attack moved back on track. After a few more heartbeats, though, a rising noise attracted his attention and he realised that the nearest group of mercenary killers among the enemy force were moving out to try and attack this now-lone Roman on his small horse. It occurred to him in the blink of an eye that his shield and spear were somewhere back across the hoof-churned grass, smashed and splintered, and that defending himself against this bunch with just a sword was plain suicide.

Drawing his blade anyway, he wheeled his horse and raced off to join the cavalry attack - preferably somewhere safe and near the back.

Now it was time for a short and brutal attack and the rest was down to the commander and his small mounted force at the ford.

* * * * *

Quadratus gestured to the slope leading up from the river. According to what might laughably be called 'the sun' which shone as little more than a pale reflection of the moon in the marble grey sky, they were roughly at the position where the river curved around north of the fort. The scout's initial suggestion that they turn at the ford had proved less than helpful in the commander's opinion given that, despite the season, the rainfall had tailed off in the last couple of days and the river's level had dropped sufficiently to reveal two more of the seven known fords in this area as opposed to the only one visible the past few days.

Still, the scout had been insistent as to which shallow strand was the ford he'd meant, and the sun never lied about directions, so Quadratus had little choice but to accept his appraisal.

The scout nodded at his commander's gesture and cupped a hand to his ear meaningfully.

Quadratus tried to steady his thumping heart and listened carefully. The general mob noise of battle was all he could hear, and it sounded exactly the same to him as it had the past three times they had paused to listen since nearing their objective.

No. Different, now that he concentrated. The main clash of battle had become more distant, muted by the tense bulk of the army gathered between. The other cavalry force had drawn the Gallic riders away to the far side of the field as they had intended. It was the only explanation.

With a nod, Quadratus had his signifer wave the standard and ready for the advance. The unit would move up the slope as quietly as possible to maintain the element of surprise until the very last moment, and would then break into a charge as soon as they could see the command party and target the Treveri leader.

With quiet speed, the horsemen urged their mounts up the rise, which at this point seemed to be so much higher than when they had descended to the river, perhaps twice as high in fact. Logic dictated that the same plateau could only be the same height above the same river, but clearly something about the landscape had thrown out that particular bit of logic and the rise was difficult on horseback. Quadratus was immensely grateful, though, that he was climbing it rather than trying to coax a horse safely *down* it.

He was impressed with the Gauls in his small force on two counts: firstly their surprising level of control over their mounts. The ease with which the auxiliary volunteers mounted the slope took him quite by surprise, and a number of them could have taught his regulars a thing or two - though in fairness, when it came to the act of joining battle, the reverse would certainly be true.

The second was that the units were not vying with each other for prime position in the coming fight, which was the normal Gallic way, each man desperate for the most glorious and prestigious kill. Instead they were holding to their given formations almost as tightly as his own regular ala, each unit staying in position behind his lead.

If he were to be uncharitable, he might suspect that to be a matter of letting him and his men fall into the shit first...

63

Quadratus was the first to crest the slope, with his regulars arrayed behind him and his signifer by his side, standard lowered so as not to give any more advance warning than necessary

'Oh, shit.'

It had been the signifer that had spoken, but he had voiced Quadratus' own thoughts.

Certainly most of the enemy cavalry had been committed to the far side of the plateau to deal with the more major cavalry feint. Only a few hundred at most had stayed with the command group and that would not have been a great issue. The problem was that the Gallic commanders were fleeing the field, with that remaining cavalry about them. And that meant riding for the ford.

The result was that Quadratus crested the ridge at a steady pace only to see several hundred Gallic cavalry, along with their chieftains, musicians and signifers, bearing down on him at breakneck pace. A little more worrying than that was the fact that behind them, he could see the bulk of the Treveri force turning and taking to their heel in his direction too.

The other cavalry attack had been *extremely* effective. *Over-*effective, in fact. It had totally broken the already-flagging spirit of the Treveri army, and the entire force was now turning to leave the field, only to find Quadratus - and his roughly two hundred and fifty men - directly between them and the ford.

Desperation gripped the commander. Suddenly things looked rather worrying, and they had perhaps a count of thirty at best before the Gallic cavalry reached them. Would the Treveri slow to engage, or...?

A slow smile spread across his face as he realised the approaching riders, rather than slowing down, had increased their pace! They were moving to charge the Romans. Idiots.

He was suddenly filled with a smug sense of relief that over the past day he had given the auxiliary cavalry extensive tuition in the various calls, orders and standard relays for different manoeuvres, not knowing what Labienus had planned. The result was that he could be relatively confident that he had a good Roman command over the native force behind him.

'Sound the 'halt' and the 'form line'.'

The signifer had the effrontery to look puzzled, but his professionalism prevented any real insubordination, and he waved the standard madly. For a moment, Quadratus worried whether the Gauls under his command would manage to form up as intended, but their control over their beasts was truly excellent, and in a matter of heartbeats the bulk of his force was forming a line only two riders deep at the crest of the ridge, others still arriving up the slope behind them and falling in to make a third line where the terrain allowed.

He remembered with a smile that the native scout was still close by, and explained his plan in a few short words, which was then relayed with shouted orders in both directions along the line.

'Shields forward, spears out!' he bellowed.

The signifer and the native scout relayed the command. A count of ten...

'Ready!'

Eight...

'Signifer!'

Six...

The man nodded, fingers ready on the standard.

Four...

'Now.'

Simultaneous with his call, the scout relayed it in the local dialect and the signifer waved the flag, giving the command to form squares by ala. It was an infantry-style manoeuvre usually carried out with precision in drills or with the leisure of awaiting the call to attack an enemy.

But not usually with only two heartbeats before a rabid charging enemy crashed into you.

All along the line, the formation disintegrated as men moved into their new positions. With thirty two men in each ala - the Gauls had been befuddled at being organised into Roman unit sizes - the square was perhaps six men wide and near the same deep. Of course, the native levies could not be expected to form with the same sort of precision as his regulars, who created a good solid forward edge and powerful wings, but left the centre and rear less compact, yet their efforts were laudable and more controlled than he would have expected.

Quadratus would have laughed out loud, had he not been suddenly thrown into deep combat as the fleeing Treveri cavalry charged him. The sudden forming of a line had led the enemy to believe that they had an easy - and stupid - kill awaiting them. But as the line reformed into blocks the enemy suddenly discovered that the majority of their number were racing at unstoppable speed over the crest of a slope that disappeared at a steep gradient towards the fast, icy torrent of the Mosella below.

More than half the Treveri cavalry charge swept helplessly through the empty space where the Roman forces had been only moments before. While the odd one managed to regain some sort of control and slow themselves or direct their descent and a few found themselves engaged with Quadratus' men who had not quite got out of the way, most of those charging Gauls instead found themselves hurtling unstoppably down the hill, faster and steeper than their mounts could cope with.

The result was carnage.

Quadratus knew what it would look like, though he could hardly turn to see the slope covered in fallen riders and downed, injured horses. Of the perhaps one hundred and fifty horses that had passed between the Roman squares, they would be lucky if two dozen made it to the river bank alive. The slope would be an appalling sight.

The cavalry charge of the Treveri had failed dismally, and those who had still found themselves facing an enemy had crashed into a solid block of riders rather than a wavering double line, only to grind to a halt in a brutal horseback melee.

Quadratus hacked and chopped with his blade, his shield held forward and moving up and down with the enemy's strokes in an attempt to protect his torso or legs and steed as required. The cold, damp air was supplemented with a faint drizzle of pink as the numerous blows from both sides sent arterial spray up into the morning atmosphere. Half a Gaul's hand whirled past lazily in the air - victim of some stroke Quadratus never even saw.

It could have been bloody and vicious. It could have been - *should* have been, really - a hard fight with a high casualty rate on both sides. But with the siege lifted, the army departing, and half their number scattered broken on the slope below, there was simply no heart left in the Treveri cavalry. Almost as soon as battle was joined at the crest, the horsemen were pulling away from the fight and trying to flee through the gaps between Roman units and down the slope to the river, their momentum now slow enough to afford them a reasonably safe descent.

But as many of them swept past, the sides of the defensive squares - a formation rarely utilised by cavalry - raked them mercilessly, bringing down two of every three riders that passed by.

As the hell of personal combat relented, the enemy either dying or fled, Quadratus paused to take in the situation. The Treveri infantry were moving his way, fleeing the field, despite the cavalry in the way. After all, sheer weight of numbers was with them, and they had to make it across the river to even begin to believe they were safe. Behind Quadratus and his men, down the slope, maybe seventy or eighty enemy riders had managed any kind of safe descent.

Quadratus let slip a loud string of curses and imprecations as he noted the standards that identified Indutiomarus' party at the bottom of the slope, near the river, racing desperately for safety.

'Bollocks! Damn, damn, damn and bollocks!'

With a sigh, he turned to the signifer. 'Sound the pursuit. Full pace. I want that standard and the king's head.'

Aware that many of the Gaulish volunteers around him were listening in, and that his scout was still relaying a translation, he raised his arm. 'Whoever brings me Indutiomarus' head, I will repay with the same weight of gold!'

Barely had the scout relayed the words than the auxiliaries let out wild whoops of delight and turned, directing their mounts over the crest and down the slope with as crazed and dangerous speed as the enemy had attempted, driven by their greed for the royal prize Quadratus had set.

The commander turned with the rest of his force, leaving the small parties of native auxiliaries still locked in a fight with their counterparts to finish it off before following, and began to pick his way back down the slope as fast as he dared, which was less than half the speed of the blood-and-gold crazed Gauls.

By the time he was halfway down the slope, he realised just how quickly word of his offered reward had spread, shouted between the Gauls, and many of the ones who had been farthest down the slope to begin with were even now racing out into the water in an attempt to head off the foremost fleeing enemy and capture the command group.

Quadratus slowed his descent, his gaze flicking alternately between the dangerous incline down which he walked his horse and the events unfolding at the ford in a vast tableau. As he realised what was happening, he paused and reined in to watch.

Seeing the Roman's Gallic auxiliaries closing in on both sides and pulling ahead to seal off the ford, the Treveri cavalry had collapsed into a disorganised, panicked shambles. In the centre of the remaining enemy force, the small knot of nobles and the standard bearer were trying to push their way out ahead.

Indutiomarus - or at least, Quadratus assumed it had to be the Treveri king, given his ostentatious armour and garb, raised himself as high as possible on his steed and started throwing around commands like a man in a state of extreme desperation. Quadratus nodded to himself happily. His own riders had got ahead now and were sealing off the ford. The enemy king was doomed. He hoped momentarily that Labienus might stand the reward, rather than leaving him to pay it, but if need be, he was willing to cough up the gold. It would be worth it.

He almost bellowed out with laughter as the Treveri king yelled at one of his nobles, shaking his arm and pointing to the far side of the ford, and then failed to hold in the mirth as that same noble simply raised his sword and slid it deep into Indutiomarus' chest.

The Treveri king - would-be architect of their destruction and aspiring hero of Gaul - gave a cry of agony that was audible even halfway back up the slope and tumbled from his horse. The mass of auxiliary cavalry swarmed in like locusts, each ignoring their own peril and leaping from their horses, rushing the disorganised and panicked Treveri in the desire to be the one to retrieve the head of the dead king. Quadratus wondered, still chuckling, whether he could get out of the reward on the technicality that the king had already been killed by his own, but shook his head at the thought. Honesty in all dealings.

The Treveri at the ford had thrown down their weapons and were begging for clemency, but the auxiliary cavalry were having none of it. The body of Indutiomarus was still in among them somewhere, and the idea of a head's worth of gold was overcoming any of the riders' notions of nobility in battle. Quadratus considered giving the order to accept their surrender, but he knew it would do no good. His local levies had blood and gold in their sights now, and no mere Roman order would stop them from collecting. Besides, they would have finished it before the order ever reached them and, truth be told, he wasn't entirely sure he *wanted* to stop them.

He would take Indutiomarus' head, and that would help put the final end to this irritating and dangerous rebellion in the east. His memory furnished him with an image of the entire Treveri force running on foot for the ford, and his heart lurched suddenly.

Somewhere down at the ford there was a whoop of delight and a Gaul was running for his horse, a heavy weight swinging from his hand by the hair, half a dozen of his compatriots chasing him angrily while the rest finished off every last Treveri soul in the river in their disappointment at failing to take the prize. It was over down there.

So, given the approaching Treveri infantry, should his small force leave, heading back the way they'd come, upriver and along the bank, or try to bring the army to a halt? He knew the answer, of course. He had the suspicion that Labienus would let the survivors go free anyway, but *he* would not be the one to allow the entire Treveri force to flee the field without explicit orders from a superior.

'Signaller! We form up on the fords. Their army's coming this way and I intend to deny them the crossing.

The soldier with the standard stared for a moment in disbelief, and then began waving the flag in an attempt to attract the attention of the rest of the cavalry. A quick pause and with a little concentration, Quadratus could hear the fleeing Treveri nearing the crest of the slope. This was going to be extremely bloody unless he could persuade them to surrender.

With a quick uttered prayer to Mars, he made his way on down the slope to the river bank, where his men were forming in the shallow water.

* * * * *

Barely had the small cavalry force assembled in the ford than the first of the fleeing tribesmen appeared over the crest of the hill, beginning their descent to the river. Some of the discipline seemed to have evaporated among the native levies with their easy victory at the ridge and the ensuing bloodthirsty executions of the Treveri commanders in the river, which even now ran with a pink tint from the numerous bodies snagged on the stones of the ford and the rocks and branches at the river's bank.

Still, despite the elation and blood-drunk enthusiasm of the Gauls under his command, they had managed to form a rough block that defended the river crossing, some ten men deep. It was a formidable obstacle. They would be hopelessly outnumbered by the fleeing Treveri, but the width of the ford would negate much of that disadvantage, since no man in his right mind would try to cross the Mosella anywhere but at a ford. And the height advantage of a horseman meant that as long as a rider could keep his beast from harm, he was relatively free to manoeuvre, stabbing with his spear into the attack, while the enemy infantry would be hampered by the waist-deep flow and the numbing cold.

On a straight field, Quadratus would never contemplate attempting to stand with around two hundred riders against many thousands of infantry. But this was no straight field, and there *was* a chance. A *good* chance.

Still his heart lurched as he watched the endless ranks of the Treveri and their hired killer allies swarm over the crest and down towards the waiting horsemen. They were coming fast. Far too fast for comfort. Any sensible enemy, even fleeing, would take that slope with just a little more trepidation, unless he savoured the thought of tumbling and plummeting, breaking bones and then being trampled by his compatriots.

They looked like they were planning on charging!

No one - absolutely no one - charged an enemy in a river. It was utterly pointless. The current would drag any speed from the attack within five paces of leaving the bank. Charging in waist-deep water was impossible. So why rush headlong down the hill and risk death or injury only to be slowed by the waiting torrent? Surely not because of the other cavalry attack? There had been a lot more of them, for certain, but not enough to send such panic into a vastly superior force.

The rhythmic crunch was faint, but unmistakable, and it brought a smile to Quadratus' tired face.

After a few more heartbeats, he could hear the Gauls around him chattering away in their own tongue and from the light-hearted tone and the knowing smiles, he could tell that they knew that 'crunch, crunch, crunch' for what it was.

The waiting cavalry watched the stragglers of the fleeing Treveri begin their dangerous descent. All across the slope men were tumbling and sliding, bringing down knots of their fellows in a painful and damaging fall. Panic had gripped them all and drove them on to the ford and the promise of freedom.

And then at the top, the gleaming line of Roman helmets appeared in perfect ranks, close on their enemy's heels. Pilum points glinted in the pale sunlight as the ranks halted on the command of a buccina at the very lip of the slope. The long line was broken into two separate sections with a gap in the centre, the entire force stretching from the curve of the river left to the distant knot of trees at the right. Two cohorts at least. An immense force, and certainly one to drive panic into the hearts of an already anxious enemy.

The nearest of the fleeing Treveri suddenly realised what they were coming up against in the river and drew themselves up on the bank, unwilling to be the first to charge into that waist-deep icy water and face the waiting horsemen. The quicker thinking of them began to run up- or downstream along the bank, but already a third cohort could be heard moving off to the south to seal off that path, and the rumble of the victorious Roman cavalry assault could be heard the other way. The Treveri were boxed in and it was quickly becoming apparent to them.

Even as many of their compatriots were still descending the slope beneath the steady, flinty eyes of the legion, Treveri and bandit alike began to throw down their arms in surrender.

Quadratus grinned. The legate was a crafty old sod.

* * * * *

Titus Labienus walked his horse forward between the ranks of the First and Second cohorts, his command party close behind. A musician and his standard bearers accompanied him, along with his camp prefect and the tribunes.

And Baculus.

That man turned up like a bad smell any time anything happened, despite having received direct commands to stay in his convalescent cot from both medicus and legate. But despite the man's borderline defiance and his bad temper, his tendency to become outspoken when in discomfort, and his pale grey, wheezing and disconcerting illness, it was always comforting to have the veteran centurion close by, and Labienus could hardly deny it. That was why he let Baculus get away with as much as he did.

The small mounted party reached the crest of the hill and spread out as much as possible, the musician and standard bearers - and the tribunes, surprisingly - hanging back slightly to allow Baculus to take prime position at the front. One of the native scouts in his party rode forward to join them at the legate's gesture.

Labienus peered down at the field before him and felt a wave of relief wash over him. The Treveri standards were in the hands of Quadratus' men. Though he could not see Indutiomarus, it seemed almost certain the man was captive or dead. Either suited just fine.

'People of the Treveri!' he announced, just to make sure he had their full attention, though the majority of the enemy were now looking back and forth despondently between the cohorts atop the

71

slope and the cavalry in the ford and were dropping their weapons to the turf. The native scout relayed a translation in a deep, booming voice.

'People of the Treveri, you have brought unlawful and unsought war upon the forces of Rome, who are here in this place with the blessing of your own Gaulish assembly to defend your lands from the aggressive Germanic tribes beyond the Rhenus and from the treacherous Eburones.'

He paused to let the scout translate.

'You have besieged our garrison in contravention of your prior agreements with Rome. The penalty for such transgressions is clearly written as death!'

A number of the frightened Treveri picked up their weapons again, fearing the worst as the translation was relayed.

'But that penalty has been paid by your leaders,' Labienus continued 'whose standards even now rest in the hands of my cavalry. Your king has paid your price, which is fitting, since it was he who led you into this fool's crusade in the first place. I have no wish to persecute an entire tribe of loyal, peaceful and noble Belgae for the whims of a dangerous fool.'

The crash of more and more weapons falling to the floor spoke eloquent volumes as to the opinions of the surrendering tribesmen.

'Moreover, I make no distinction in my magnanimity between the great Treveri and the mercenaries and vagabonds who have flocked to their banner. I have conditions for your surrender, and I know that you will not be so foolish as to refuse them, particularly since they are so light.'

Another pause for translation, and Baculus leaned closer. 'I know this is not going to be a popular suggestion, legate, but you have one of the more powerful tribes in the east in your grasp here, and they've already risen against us twice. You have the singular opportunity right now to remove them from the board of the great game entirely.'

'I will not execute an entire tribe, centurion, who were already wavering in their loyalty to their king in light of their oaths to us.'

'They wavered for *fear* of us, sir, not for any oath. And anyway, those who wavered had already left. Those who remain here are the ones who stayed loyal to that royal menace Indutiomarus.

And what of the thugs, murderers and thieves among them? You'll free them too?'

Labienus turned an angry glare on the centurion.

'I know all the arguments. I heard them all when I consulted the tribunes, including - I note - the value of the prisoners in terms of the slave trade. But I am not Caesar. Caesar may have the habit of executing and enslaving entire peoples, but if we are ever to have Gaul settled like Hispania or Illyricum or Greece, we have to start building bridges more often than we burn them. Caesar's tactics have led us to five years of stamping out the fires of rebellion on half a dozen occasions each season, and it is time to try and create some sort of lasting peace.'

Turning his attention back to those at the bottom of the slope, Labienus cleared his throat.

'You will turn over to us one hundred hostages of noble birth to ensure your continued goodwill' he paused and whispered sidelong 'Good enough?' at which Baculus simply shook his head in exasperation, and then continued. 'You will take a renewed oath to Rome that you will not raise arms against her in future times, and that you will make no alliances with other tribes without the consent of both the Gaulish assembly and the Proconsul or his appointed representative. If you agree to this oath and to the giving of hostages, you will be permitted to return to your lands as free men to continue your lives, though your weapons will stay with us.'

He waited for the relayed translation again, and for the enemy to deliberate before replying. Whatever minor nobles and/or druids remained among them would accept the terms, of course. They were more than merely generous. And they were also the only feasible option. The rest of this meeting was a formality. The threat of the Treveri had been neutralised with the death of Indutiomarus, as he'd planned from the beginning.

'This is going to come back and bite you on the behind, legate.' Baculus grumbled quietly enough not to carry to the others nearby. Labienus narrowed his eyes in irritation.

'What will be, will be, centurion, as the Gods will it. But for now, I will take the renewed oath of the Treveri, their hostages and their weapons, while you will return to the camp forthwith and clamber into that sick cot of yours and not emerge again unless your own backside is on fire. Do you understand me?'

Baculus saluted, grumbling, and turned to ride away.

Leniency was a mistake, and the centurion knew it.

73

Chapter Four

Palmatus raised himself from the horse's back to rub his sore rear end once again and Fronto rolled his eyes. Yes, the former legionary was a trained infantryman and had never ridden a horse for more than a few moments in his life before signing on with Fronto, but the man had now ridden over three hundred miles and even if he was never destined to make a horseman he should at least by now be numb enough to resist the pain.

Masgava gave a low chuckle. *That* man, on the other hand, seemed to have an almost preternatural affinity with horses despite not having ridden one since leaving his native land in a wheeled wooden cage. He put it down to his people's native abilities with riding beasts, be they horse or camel.

Fronto himself was a little sore, given the lack of time he had spent in the saddle recently, but he was damned if he was going to show it in front of the others. Galronus, of course, was unaffected. It was like sitting on a comfortable couch for a man so born to the beast.

'This place is so green.' Palmatus frowned. 'And damp.'

'Like the lands of Cisalpine Gaul,' Fronto nodded. 'I spent plenty of time around Cremona and it's much the same there.'

'This is the first time I've ever been north of Rome,' Palmatus said in a flat voice. 'It's different to Armenia and Pontus, I'll give you that. Less barren rock. More squelching.'

Masgava gave a deep belly laugh and slapped Palmatus on the shoulder. 'You should try the ergs and dunes of Numidia, my friend.'

'Anyway...' Fronto interrupted before he was treated to yet another diatribe on the glories of Masgava's homeland. 'That town is Bibracte. It covers the whole hill. Big place with a couple of nice taverns. There's the place where the Gaulish chieftains' assembly usually meets, and an old druidic site that's gone out of use. Should be a Roman supply station in a compound outside the walls too, but I can't make it out and, since Cita left and Priscus was in charge, who knows how the supply lines have been organised. You can just see a couple of hills over to the north from here, looks suspiciously like a pair of boobs from this angle. That's where we finished off the Helvetii five years ago.'

'So a lot happened here is what you're saying?' Palmatus mumbled irritably.

'Moan if you like, but after all those small Roman way stations and local hovels since Massilia, it'll be nice to be somewhere civilised for a change.'

'Civilised?' Palmatus cocked an eyebrow sarcastically and received a cold look from Galronus of the Remi for his efforts.

'May not look it,' Fronto replied blithely, 'but this place is almost a home from home after five years of passing backwards and forwards through it. Even the first year we were here the place was welcoming, and you can get proper wine here. Not just that frothy brown latrine water that Galronus' people make.' He flashed a cheeky grin at the Belgic prince, who simply shrugged. Galronus had moved to Roman wine as his chosen tipple more than a year since.

'Bloody hell!' Fronto said in astonishment and reined in his horse suddenly. The others hauled to sharply, looking about for whatever had caused their friend such consternation.

'Trouble?'

'Not now. A few years ago, yes. Come over here.' Kicking his horse into life, Fronto trotted over to a low, curved ridge. The others joined him curiously.

'It's a ditch!' Palmatus said with a snort. He saw the look on Fronto's face - dreamy and distant - and smiled sympathetically. 'Don't get me wrong... it's a very pretty ditch. Nice and wide. Almost like a bowl. Pretty. You shag someone here?'

It was a mark of how distant Fronto had suddenly become that he failed to reply with a sharp or witty line, instead just nodding as he scanned the depression.

'Not a ditch. Too uniform.' he replied eventually.

'What?'

'Man made.' Fronto said with a sigh. 'By the Tenth. Under the careful supervision of a man called Pomponius who still commands the legion's major engineering works - or he did a year or two back anyway.'

'So what is it?' Palmatus frowned.

'What does it look like?' growled Masgava, his face dark. 'It's an arena. A gladiatorial ring. Seen enough of them in my time.' He turned his spiteful look on Fronto. 'Native sport? Entertainment for your men?'

Fronto saw the rising ire in his friend and shook his head. 'No, Masgava. Not that. In actual fact only one combat was ever fought there. One of the combatants was a Gaul, yes. A native cavalry officer named Domiticus of the Aedui - from Bibracte as it happens. The other, though, was a Roman. Me, in fact.'

The other three riders stared at him, all anger draining from Masgava's face to be replaced by a strange and complex mixture of curiosity, shock and sympathy. Fronto paused for a moment and smiled.

'Well don't get all morbid on me. After all, I won. Otherwise I'd not be here to show you it.'

He waited for another moment, but the silence weighed, so he shrugged. 'Needed a show to boost the men's spirits as they were heading for starvation. And that bastard Domiticus had assassinated a good friend of mine - a tribune by the name of Cominius. I wanted revenge. The whole Tenth did, so there was nothing unfair or wrong about it. Domiticus met his Gods that day, and Cominius smiled at us from across the last river. And then I got so drunk that night that I couldn't stand.'

'You,' Palmatus shook his head, 'are a constant surprise. You know that, Fronto?'

'I like to keep people guessing,' the legate smiled. 'Come on.'

The small party rode on, the former legionary, the Belgic officer and the ex-gladiator gazing up at the main oppidum of the Aedui as they approached, taking in its strong defensive walls and surprisingly urban style as far as possible from the outside. The town marched away up the slope and must occupy an area much larger than a lot of supposedly settled Roman towns.

Fronto rode slightly ahead, his gaze scouring everything he passed, his mind floating on a cloud of memory and seeing the place through five years of history. He could almost hear the buzzing of the summer bees, smell the flowers and the warm sun and feel the place pulsing in his blood. He'd not realised it, but not only had he missed life in the army, but he'd apparently, and curiously, missed Gaul, despite the fact that he'd seen much of it from a position knee deep in body parts.

His gaze strayed as they climbed the lower slopes and approached the outer edge of the town and its walls, and he felt uneasy suddenly.

The low rectangular earthwork off to his right had been the Roman supply station the last time he was here. Clearly it had been gone for a year or more now, the timber palisade and wooden huts pulled down and the Roman presence removed. He made a mental note to ask Priscus about the new system. Were they now wholly reliant on local produce, tribute from the tribes and foraging? Seemed unlikely, given the number of men Caesar had, so the supply line must have moved.

Causing him more consternation, though, was the fact that the last time he had been here, the town had clearly outgrown its walls and new homes and other small structures had been built on the slopes below.

No longer.

The walls reared up impressively, and no external constructions obscured the line of sight for any man atop them. The spread of the city had been halted and those offending buildings had been torn down, the wounds they had left on the land remaining to mark their passing.

His gaze took in the figures of Aedui warriors on the wall, watching with spears in hand.

Fronto felt a shiver run up his spine. Bibracte looked for all the world like a city on a war footing.

'Is something wrong?' Galronus asked, sensing Fronto's discomfort.

'Maybe. Not sure. I don't like the way the walls have been cleared for line of sight and lookouts stand guard. It's not the relaxed and peaceful Bibracte I remember.'

'Maybe your memory's at fault?' Galronus shrugged. 'People often look back on their past with a biased view. The Remi are Caesar's men to the hilt, and yet our towns are still defended and ready. Regardless of treaties with Rome, there will always be other hungry tribes in Gaul and Germania who eye our cities with greed.'

'I hope you're right and this is just something internecine and simple,' Fronto said quietly. 'All the same, I was planning to stay here a few nights before we leave but I think, in the event, we'll move on first thing in the morning.'

Palmatus and Masgava nodded at the sense of the decision, and the four men rode towards the gate, which stood open under the protective gaze of half a dozen solid, well-armoured Aedui warriors.

'Want me to do the honours?' Galronus asked as they approached.

Fronto shook his head. Despite the fact that the cavalry officer spoke his Belgic tongue naturally, it would sound almost foreign to the Aedui, the accent so different that he might as well be a German. Besides, Fronto was interested to see the reaction of the guards to a Roman in their midst. The legate was relatively incognito, unarmoured and just in his riding gear with an officer's tunic beneath his heavy wool cloak, even wearing his Gallic torc - a gift from Galronus - around his neck. Palmatus wore old leathers and tunic, Masgava hardly appeared to be Roman, and Galronus was clearly a native. But as soon as Fronto opened his mouth, his origins would be clear. What would the Aedui say?

As they approached, the riders slowed. Palmatus and Galronus staying back a little and Masgava at the rear, holding the rope to the pack horses that carried all their main gear, including their armour.

He took a deep breath.

'In the name of Rome and the Proconsul Gaius Julius Caesar, greetings,' the legate intoned in an official manner. 'I am Marcus Falerius Fronto, of the Proconsul's staff, and these three are my colleagues. In the absence of the Roman supply depot here, we seek shelter for the night in your oppidum.'

There was a long, strange pause and Fronto began to wonder whether he had been incomprehensible. When the army had been here regularly, the city's leaders had made sure that the men who stood by the gates spoke enough Latin to communicate with the soldiers and officers, and Fronto had assumed that, with the presence of the supply depot, the same had held true ever since. Perhaps since the demise of the supply post, Latin was no longer a concern among the guards.

He was about to gesture Galronus forward when one of the Aedui stepped to the parapet and held up his arm in salute. 'Greetings, Fronto of Rome, legate of the Tenth Legion. You and your companions are welcome within our walls.'

Fronto heaved a sigh of relief but even as the man clambered down the steps out of sight and then emerged through the open gate, his oppressive feeling of unease refused to lift.

'I am Danotalos of the Aedui. You are welcome to Bibracte and are known here.' The Gaul looked him up and down. 'I remember you myself. You have grown strong.'

'Thanks,' Fronto said drily. 'This place seems... quiet? Nervous?'

Danotalos shrugged. 'Our neighbours to the north - the Carnutes - stir up trouble. Your Seventh legion has been placed among them to quell the trouble, and the Carnutes' arrogance and stupidity brought Roman uncertainty even upon us. We had your

79

Thirteenth legion quartered in the north of our lands until the snows lifted. In such times it is wise for a city to look to its security.'

Fronto nodded his agreement, and could see out of the corner of his eye Galronus' satisfaction at hearing the reasonable explanation of the city's readiness, but somehow his spine was still tingling and he reached up and touched the little figure of Fortuna hanging on the thong around his neck before forcing a smile to his face.

'There was a small tavern not far from this gate run by a man called Lugos, I think? A nice place on a steep street, with a shady garden covered in trees and vines?'

'Lugulcos' the man smiled. 'The tavern is still open and its owner as miserable and cheap as ever. He may even still have some of your wine. The supply of new Roman wine dried up when the garrison outside left, but few here have the taste for it.'

Fronto nodded, noting something that unnerved him about that last phrase, or rather about the way it was said.

'Will he have rooms in his place for four men for the night? We'll be moving on in the morning.'

'I am sure Lugulcos will make room for such men.' the Gaul grinned. 'Though you might regret it when he offers up his bill!'

Fronto fell silent once more as the four men followed Danotalos up the street from the gate and made their way towards the small tavern that had played host to some of Fronto's favourite moments of the entire campaign in Gaul.

Each and every person they passed, be they man, woman or child, nodded their respect to Fronto and quite a few of them smiled, even warmly. And yet there was an atmosphere over the whole place that refused to let up. Even as the shady, tree-covered garden of the tavern appeared around a corner, Fronto was already looking forward to being gone from this place.

* * * * *

Fronto pushed his plate across the table and slid his wine cup into position before him. With care he poured a small quantity of the strong rich red liquid - imported from Cisalpine Gaul across the mountains - into the cup and watered it thoroughly. It had not kept over-well and had a sharpness to it that tingled the tongue but beggars, as they said, could not be choosers, and it was still better than the frothy ditch water being consumed by the locals in the tavern.

The discarded plate still contained some of the thick, rich gravy and morsels of meat with some soggy uneaten bread. The portion had been more than adequate and he felt his waistline stretched to the limit - almost to the width at which it had normally sat a year ago, he thought wryly.

Masgava was giving him a meaningful look and he simply nodded. At the signal, the big Numidian reached over and swiped his plate, stuffing the leftovers into his face like a man possessed. How he could eat like he did and not gain even the slightest fat was beyond Fronto. If *he* wanted to maintain his new lithe figure he had to be extremely careful. He only had to look at honey cakes and he felt his weight increase. But then he was older than Masgava by quite a margin.

Palmatus had finished his plate completely and was now supping down the wine with aplomb. Galronus had left half his meal and was toying with a piece of bread, dipping it in his wine cup and letting it soak up the red, then nibbling at it. The rest of his dinner had already made its way across the table to Masgava and had vanished into the empty pit that was his stomach.

'I notice they still refer to you here as legate of the Tenth,' Palmatus said quietly. 'You must have made an impression.'

Fronto smiled wearily and took a sip of his wine. 'I know Pompey shifts his legates round as the situation demands - in the old way - but Caesar's tried to keep the same legate with the same legion for as long as possible, unless the need for change arises. Thinks it increases their efficiency. I think he's right, too. I was legate of the Tenth for a number of years. Thought I always would be.'

He fell silent with a slightly morose expression.

'You think you'll be made legate of the Tenth again then?'

Fronto looked across at Palmatus. 'The way the general is likely to receive me I'll be lucky to command anything other than a latrine pit. I understand he took my departure sort of personally.'

Galronus shook his head with a smile. 'You basically called him an amoral power-monger and told him you'd have nothing to do with him. It *was* personal.' He leaned back with his soggy bread. 'But the general is ever the player of the game. He will forgive if you are of value, and Antonius seems to think that is the case.'

Fronto nodded slowly. He would have to play his arrival somewhat carefully. Too familiar or arrogant and Caesar would simply take offence. Too humble and quiet and he might not make enough of an impression to gain the general's trust again. The answer, of course, was to be himself, as he always had. The general would come around eventually, and he would be given some sort of command.

'I'm hoping to get a legion, I have to admit. It would be nice if it were the Tenth, but there are good men in the others, too. So long as I don't get to take over from Plancus. He'll have ruined his men at best. Or one of the new bunch... can't see a former Pompeian legion taking to me all that well, and the others will be so green you'd mistake them for a cabbage.'

'I'm a former Pompeian legionary, and I only find you mildly irritating,' grinned Palmatus.

'Funny.'

'But seriously, Fronto. Any legion is better than nothing. You're a man of the army and you know it. You'll not be happy anywhere else.'

Fronto nodded slowly. 'It will happen. And when it does we're going to have to sort you two out. Galronus will go back to his Remi cavalry, but you two would make good centurions. Masgava: you should be a chief training officer. Any legion you train will be a nightmare to face.'

'Piss on that idea,' smirked Palmatus.

'What?'

'I'm no centurion, Fronto. I have no interest in bending over and letting the young tribunes have their way with me. Never yet met a centurion I like, so I'm damn well not going to *be* one.'

Masgava was nodding. 'Too restrictive. Too rigid. Not for me either.'

'Then can I ask,' Fronto sighed, 'what you were hoping for when you came north with me?'

'We signed on to serve you, Fronto. Not the general.'

'Well don't look for anything higher than a centurion,' Fronto said, sipping his wine again. 'I can't make tribunes or prefects of you. When I'm given a command again, I'll be able to push transfers through for centurions, but Caesar will veto any attempt to put you two in higher office.'

'Don't worry about us. Arrange a tent for us and meals and leave us to it.'

Fronto shook his head. There was no arguing with them. Theoretically they both worked for him and, although he'd not paid them a wage since Puteoli, he'd sprung for all the food and drink, transport and accommodation on the journey. They were living free.

'Well just don't get yourselves into trouble. Or me.'

'No,' Palmatus grinned. 'We'll leave that up to you.'

The former legionary picked up the eating knife from the table and placed the point down onto the much-scarred wooden surface, twiddling it this way and that with the fingers of his left hand while he drank wine from his right. As he drained the final dregs, he lowered the cup and grinned.

'Thing is, Fronto, I've been thinking.'

'You should watch that,' the legate replied acidly. 'You could strain yourself.'

'I've been thinking,' Palmatus repeated 'about what we'll do when we get there. I'm assuming Caesar has a Praetorian guard?'

Fronto nodded. 'A horse regiment led by a professional young soldier called Ingenuus. Why? Surely with your saddle trouble you're not planning to turn horse-humper?'

Palmatus shook his head, smiling. 'Back in Pontus I served for a while under Quintus Metellus Celer. He was a legate of Pompey's and he formed his own guard - his singulares - like a Praetorian guard. Apparently it's not unknown for a legate to do so?'

Fronto shrugged. 'I've heard of it being done, but usually only by those legates who have reason to fear, or those who like their pomp and show. I remember a few years ago young Crassus did it for a few months, and Plancus was going to until Caesar gave him the hard word.'

'Well I see no reason why you shouldn't have your own 'singulares'? As a legate you'd have the right, and certainly you seem to have a habit of getting yourself into trouble. Maybe it wouldn't be a bad idea to have a few broad-shouldered lads close by when you decide to go off into the fight?'

Fronto shook his head flatly. 'Not a hope. I have no intention of swanning around with a bodyguard unit in shiny steel and crimson plumes, looking like some ponce from a triumph. Forget it.'

But Palmatus simply turned and looked across at Masgava, whose brow furrowed in thought before he nodded his agreement and then started into the last morsels on his plate.

'You can plan all you like,' Fronto shrugged, 'but I will not sanction a 'singulares' unit for myself, and neither will the rest of the officers. Caesar doesn't like his legates to build themselves up like that. He allowed Crassus, but only because of his father. Start thinking differently. Make other plans. Maybe you could set up an independent training school for legionaries with too much pay who want an extra edge?'

But the two men were sharing a look that Fronto knew well. It was the look his sister and his wife shared when they had plans for him and no intention of letting him interfere with them.

Refilling his wine cup, he tried not to allow his thoughts to wander down the avenue of home, though his mind furnished him with a speculative image of his wife stumbling around the villa in Massilia with a large, pregnant bump.

He drew a deep breath and took a swig of the wine. Time to think more on the present rather than the future or the past. He glanced around the bar surreptitiously. He'd have liked to have sat outside in the tree-shaded yard he remembered so well, but the season was against it. They'd sat at the outside bench for half an hour but as the sun began to disappear behind the hill of Bibracte the temperature plummeted and they soon moved inside.

There were eight other inhabitants of the bar and most of them had been there since the start of the evening, eating or drinking and talking in small groups, playing some sort of dice game that was unknown to him. With only a couple of people leaving or arriving during that time there had been polite acknowledgements of his presence, but mostly locals minding their own business.

Now, as he scanned the place, the other occupants were all busy with their own social lives. He was struck once more how, despite the war and the cultural differences between Gaul and Roman, there was so much they had in common when you got down to the bottom line.

Leaning forward, he kept his voice low enough to not carry to other tables yet clear enough to be heard by the other three. 'I want to be gone as soon as it's light in the morning - possibly before that. And I know you'll probably think it ridiculous, but I want one of us awake and on watch in the room tonight at all times. We can take shifts of two hours once the bar closes. I'll take the last shift, though, 'cause I want to be ready to get everyone up and gone sharpish. Alright?'

The other three nodded their agreement.

'Good.'

Palmatus leaned forward to speak in a similar low voice, but paused, his eyes flicking off to his left. 'Hello, what's this?'

Fronto turned to look in the same direction, along with the others at the table.

The door to the tavern had stood open all evening, despite the breeze it caused, allowing some of the dinginess of the interior to clear, and now figures were coming in from the cold and dark outside. That locals might enter the tavern in the evening was no surprise, but Fronto couldn't help but note the fact that, despite the lack of armour and swords, these dozen men were all warriors, well-built and with quality clothes and torcs and arm rings, speaking of their valour and success at military endeavours. All of them had a large hunting knife at their waist.

If he had required any more evidence that something was amiss, it was supplied by the sudden apparent shift-change in the tavern. As the twelve men moved into the bar, spreading out, all but two of the current occupants drained their drinks, pushed their plates aside, gathered up their dice and left the room hurriedly, not casting a glance in the Romans' direction, and throwing a nervous one at the new arrivals.

'Told you something was wrong,' Fronto muttered.

'Trouble,' agreed Galronus, his hand going to the large knife at his belt, similar to those the Gauls wore. Fronto was already regretting the fact that his swords were in the kit stored in the room upstairs. From their faces, so were Palmatus and Masgava.

Two of the new arrivals sauntered across to the bar and purchased a tray full of mugs filled with frothy beer. Another pair moved to the stairs leading to the rooms above, and a third stayed by the door - almost in position as guards. The rest moved across and sat at tables near Fronto and his party.

'I'm not well-equipped for a fight,' Palmatus sighed, looking down at the small eating knife on the table before him.

'They're not here for a fight' Fronto replied quietly. 'Whatever they *are* here for, it's not that. This is their town, so they could have brought swords. They could just have done for us outside, or even during the night.'

Despite his certainty that the new arrivals were not intending violence - or at least not immediately - Fronto found himself pushing his chair back slightly to allow for freedom of movement, and noticed the other three doing the same. Palmatus' hand came down over his eating knife and when he leaned back and folded his arms casually, the knife had vanished.

85

'I do not think that these men are Aedui,' Galronus hissed quietly.

'Why?'

'Look at their arms.'

'What?'

'The arm rings.'

Fronto peered. 'Some sort of snake?'

Galronus nodded. 'A winged snake. It's a symbol of Arvernus. You'd call him Mercury, I think. While he'll be as revered here as most places, he's the chosen father of the Arverni. And every warrior here has that arm ring.'

Fronto scanned the room. Galronus was right. Each of them wore individual clothes and torcs and jewellery, but all of them bore the same arm ring on their left bicep.

'Arverni?' he asked, turning to Galronus. 'They're from the south, yes? Almost in Narbonensis. We've never had any trouble with them. Not for the best part of a hundred years.'

Galronus simply shrugged.

Fronto watched the new arrivals with suspicious interest. The presence of a group of warriors from another tribe could feasibly explain the taut, tense quiet that overlaid the town of Bibracte, but it raised as many questions as it answered.

'Aye, aye,' Palmatus said, gesturing at the entrance. Fronto turned once more. A man stood in the doorway, almost blocking it. From his high quality leather boots up through his leg-bindings, his checked blue trousers, his pale grey linen tunic and the gold torc around his neck, he was every bit the Gallic noble. Bearing no weapons, his muscular arms hung easily by his side and his long brown hair hung low, swept back from his face and tied in a braid at either side. His heavy brow was expressive and powerful and thick, drooping moustaches hid his mouth.

There was about this man the sort of power that instantly filled the room. Druids probably wished they had it. Senators would kill for it. Caesar already *did* have it, for all his faults. A natural power, born of leadership and charisma. A man to whom other men would look for sanction.

'If I remember rightly, the Arverni stopped being ruled by a King when Ahenobarbus and his legions flattened them.' Fronto said quietly. 'Part of the peace settlement with Rome required they no longer rally under royalty.'

The others shrugged, but Fronto nodded to himself. He remembered the tale from his studies of the Gallic tribes when they'd first come north of the Alps. The Arverni had no royals now, but this man could easily have been a King.

The big Gaul strode into the room in a relaxed manner, nodding to his men and to the tavern keeper, before turning and making directly for their table. Without being bidden, one of the warriors nearby pushed a chair across the floor with a jarring scrape until it sat at the end of Fronto's table.

The big man wandered over to the chair and indicated it with a large, powerful hand, an unspoken question in his expression. Fronto nodded and gestured back to the chair in answer. Whatever was happening, he found himself curious as to the powerful Arverni warrior's intentions.

'Do you speak Latin?' he asked conversationally, taking a sip of his wine.

There was a pause and the big man toyed with his moustaches for a moment, and then nodded.

'I learned your tongue young. My people trade with your merchants across the border, and Latin is widely spoken in my tribe.'

'Good, 'cause frankly I'll never be able to get my tongue round your language.'

The big man gave a humourless smile and sank into the chair. A low murmur of ordinary conversation arose across the room. Fronto was not fooled by this apparent ordinariness. As far as he could see the general drone would nicely mask any of their own words and prevent the two remaining local patrons and the tavern keeper from hearing whatever they all had to say.

'You are a Roman officer, I understand,' the Gaul smiled, 'despite the good Belgic torc around your neck.'

'A complex question right now, given my lack of command, but I'll settle for a simple yes. I ride for Samarobriva to rejoin the army.'

'And your companions?'

'Friends of mine. Two from Roman lands - an ex-soldier and a warrior from the southern deserts, and Galronus here is a nobleman of the Remi.'

'The Belgae are here too?' the big man mused. 'Fascinating, though it perhaps explains your decorations. I must apologise for interrupting your evening, and I will not keep you long, but I find myself in Bibracte at the most fortuitous moment when Roman officers pass through, and I would be wasting a great opportunity were I not to come and speak to you.'

Fronto gave the warmest smile he was capable of right now and took another sip of wine. 'I have to admit to wondering what the Arverni are doing so far north and in the guise of warriors?' he asked pleasantly.

The Gaul gave a low, throaty chuckle. 'We are simply passing through, much like you, on our own business. But enough of this duel in which we slowly circle our opponents, Roman. I see from your tunic that you are a nobleman yourself?'

'My wife might argue, but I suppose that's a fair assessment.'

'You are acquainted with Caesar?'

Fronto scratched his chin. It was a humorous tendency among non-Romans to assume that any nobleman would know any other nobleman. Ridiculous assumption, really, given the population of the city and the size of Rome's noble houses. And yet, it so happened that the man had selected someone who was closely acquainted with the general. What was he up to? What was the man trying to learn?

'I have been, yes. I've not seen him for over a year, but I have served with him.'

'Tell me of him. I wish to know of this Roman '*Brennus*' who would conquer all the lands of my peoples. What is he like?'

Fronto shrugged. 'His reputation is well known and well-founded. If you are as bright and as well-informed as you appear to be, then I doubt I can tell you anything that you do not already know.'

'Humour me.'

Fronto shrugged. 'He is brilliant. A tactical mind like no other, charismatic and loved by his men, capable of the most astoundingly rash decisions - and brutal ones, too - but tempered by the knowledge of his abilities and the certainty that he is capable of succeeding in everything that he attempts. He is not a man to cross, for he has a short temper and a long memory, but those who deal fairly with him he holds in high esteem.'

He laughed. 'Gods, that sounds like a eulogy! But it's true, nonetheless.'

The Gaul nodded. 'I hear he is also a shrewd negotiator and a clever speaker.'

'I'd say so.'

The Gaul leaned forward and steepled his fingers. 'Many fleas are biting the back of his army in these troubled times. Might the great Proconsul be persuaded to an advantageous peace which will bring him glory and gold to take back to Rome, if the price is just that: that he takes you all back to Rome?'

Fronto felt a sudden easing of his pulse. This was the nub of the matter. A potential negotiation? No, surely not for such a man. And if he had no interest in a negotiation, why ask?

'You would offer Caesar money and glory to get him out of Gaul?'

'It has been suggested before,' the big Arverni shrugged.

'I am not sure whether the general would ever accept such an offer, though this war does drag on, while Rome seethes in his absence. Two years ago I would have laughed in your face. Now, I am not so sure. But two things occur to me.' Fronto took another drink and placed his empty cup on the table. 'Firstly, you are Arverni, who are allied with us and under no threat, and yet who have no royalty who could legitimately make such an offer. That is why we don't see you at the annual assembly of the Gaulish chiefs. And I have to point out that no tribe - no matter how big - could manage to gather enough gold and slaves to buy the general off. Even the Arverni and the Aedui together. It would take a meeting of the chiefs at the assembly to do something that big.'

'But you think it would be possible?'

Fronto tapped his lip in thought. 'Perhaps. But the more your 'fleas' bite the Roman back, the less the general will be inclined to negotiate. I understand from reports that the Eburones under a man called Ambiorix destroyed a whole legion this winter. Not a good first step in negotiation.'

The Gaul laughed again.

'It seems to me very reminiscent of *Roman* negotiations. The Arverni have languished half a century in the shadow of tribes that were once our lessers because of what your General Ahenobarbus did to us.' As Fronto narrowed his eyes and leaned forward, the Gaul held out a placating hand. 'But I concede your point. Ambiorix is a troublesome pest for your general, but he is something of a difficulty for those who would see our lands free of your iron-nailed boots also. He has too much avarice and need for acclaim and recognition. His failings pushed him into launching his own petty war and he damages both Rome and his own allies, but most of all he damages himself.'

89

'How so?' Fronto asked, genuinely intrigued.

'His tribe are now fragmented and scattered and he is sought by the Romans and all their allies for what he has done. His time is past. Worry not over Ambiorix for he is naught but a fly and will soon be swatted. Indeed, if you took his head, you would do all the peoples of the land a great favour.'

He laughed again.

'Look, Roman, how my simple questions have led to my being interrogated by you instead. Such is often the way when my people talk to yours, I find.'

Fronto nodded slowly. 'I presume you will not tell me who you are?'

'It is of little matter. I am a warrior of the Arverni, friend of druids, and a wanderer of the ways with my small band. You would not know my name, nor that of my father.'

'I suspected as much,' Fronto replied, noting the reference to the druids and connecting it with the potential for peace negotiations. It sounded unlike them, too. 'Then is there anything else I can help you with, or are we done here?'

Slowly, the warrior stood, stretching.

'Thank you for your time and your honesty, Roman,' the big Gaul smiled. 'I trust we will meet again under happier circumstances.'

'Somehow I cannot see that being likely,' Fronto replied quietly, 'but only the Gods know the future.'

'Perhaps with *your* people,' the man laughed. And, turning to the nearest warrior: 'Come Vercassivos. We have much to do.'

With a final nod at the four men, the big Gaul strode from the room and the man he had last addressed - a wiry warrior with flame-red hair and moustaches - nodded in turn and followed him out. Slowly the bar emptied until only the four of them remained, along with the tavern's owner.

'Now what do you make of that?' Palmatus asked quietly in the suddenly empty bar.

'There was so much being conveyed there without words that it'd practically fill a book,' Fronto sighed. 'I would say that man is a man to watch carefully if we had the opportunity. I'd give good money to know who he was, but you saw the reaction of everyone when his men entered. No one in Bibracte's going to tell us. An Arverni nobleman seeking information on the army and its general.'

'But you said the Arverni were allies of Rome.'

'Yes, but you'll note how he said he was a friend of druids, and a 'wanderer of ways'. I've heard that last expression before, more than once, and usually in relation to an exile. Whoever that man is he's noble-blooded and in with the druids. And he's here among the Aedui who have stepped up their defences.'

Masgava leaned forward. 'He spoke of peace? Of negotiation?'

'Those were his *words*, yes. But not his intent. He and his men are warriors and 'free' Gauls to the hilt. And the way he talked of his people and Ahenobarbus, it sounds as though a grudge is still held. I think he needed to ask the question on behalf of his druid friends or someone else. But that man had no intention of settling peacefully.'

He shivered. 'Suddenly I am extremely uneasy among the Aedui. I can hardly wait to get going in the morning. Caesar is going to be interested to hear all of this.'

'Would it not be worth the detour to follow these Arverni and see where they go?' Masgava asked.

'No. We'd not find anything out, and we need to head north as quickly as possible and make up time. I have been slow and dawdling, but it seems there is more urgency required in our arrival than I had previously anticipated. We're only half way to Samarobriva yet, with a long journey still ahead. Let's have one more drink and then head up for some shut-eye.'

As Galronus strode across to the bar for another jar of wine, Fronto's eyes slipped once more to the door. Trouble was brewing, and it was far larger even than a revolt that had wiped out a legion.

He shivered again.

91

Chapter Five

Priscus drummed his fingers irritably on his chair arm as he listened. The more he argued, the less the general listened to him, it seemed.

'There are reports coming in from a number of my scouts concerning minor unrest and isolated incidents across a number of Gaulish tribes. I have considered calling the assembly of Gaul earlier this year, but I fear that once we make our fears and intentions known we will lose any edge upon which we can currently rely. It is still winter and all Gaul knows that Romans do not campaign in winter.'

'Respectfully, General,' Plancus gestured, 'there are good reasons for that. Rotten feet in icy swamp water. Mildewed and stinking tents. Snowdrifts. Floods. The list goes on…'

Priscus' fingers stopped drumming. What could possibly be happening to the world when Plancus of all people became a font of common sense?

'Sometimes hardships must be endured and risks taken to achieve grander goals.'

'And,' Priscus added 'we're still waiting on your new officers and replacement troops.'

'Regardless,' Caesar replied, casting a cold glance at Priscus, 'I am planning on campaigning before the spring thaw, while the Gauls think themselves secure. Tell the officers what you know,' he said, gesturing to three native scouts standing by the map at the room's rear.'

'Ambiorix has all-but vanished,' the taller of the three said in good Latin but with an accent everyone was beginning to recognise as Remi. 'After the battle in the winter, he went to ground with his personal band of warriors. There have been reports of his being seen at the court of his brother King, Cativolcus, though it is common knowledge that there is no love between the two rulers, and none of the reports can be substantiated. Equally uncertain reports have placed him in Nervii lands and in Menapii territory.'

'Cativolcus,' the second scout cut in, 'has made it known that he is not willing to join any rising against Rome in the wake of what happened in the winter. He sits on his throne in the near-empty Eburones lands and trembles.'

Caesar nodded. 'Then *he* is no current threat.'

92

'There have been rumblings among the Nervii and the Menapii recently,' the tall scout said, pointing to those lands on the map. 'There is no overt sign of a rising, but there is the very real possibility that Ambiorix's anti-Roman venom has spread wide through their lands, and that might give us a hint as to his current location.'

'And what of the Treveri?' Caesar asked.

'The Treveri are involved in their own private war against your legate Labienus, General,' the third scout, a short and wiry man in a Roman-style tunic and native trousers replied in a matter-of-fact voice. 'There is a rumour that they have suffered a sound defeat at the hands of the legion in their territory, but I am waiting for confirmation from my own people of that. As yet there is no record of Ambiorix treating with the Treveri, but given the latter's current activity, if he has not yet been in contact with them, rest assured that he will be.'

Caesar nodded.

'You see, gentlemen? Unrest in the Belgic tribes and open warfare from the Treveri. And all linked by rumour to Ambiorix, despite there being no solid evidence as to his location or current activity. This supports my ongoing suspicion that Ambiorix is the man behind all the trouble we have faced these past few years. His tendrils snake among the Belgic peoples, inciting them against us while he flits around in the shadows like a ghost, hidden and untouchable.'

Priscus' fingers began to tap again.

'Ambiorix is an agent of chaos,' the general went on, 'stirring up rebellion wherever his oily hide slithers. He has destroyed one of my legions and killed two of my most trusted and most senior officers, and he almost did the same for another legion and for Cicero, leaving me short many men and officers. He has clearly spent the last month rebuilding his web of power and influence since we stopped his advance. I *will not*, under any circumstances, allow him to repeat his treacherous successes into the spring.'

'And what of these rumours of which you speak, of minor unrest coming in from other parts of Gaul?' Priscus asked pointedly.

'The rest of Gaul can wait. Minor unrest is trouble, of course, but when weighed against the danger posed by that madman Ambiorix? I think it is clear where our primary concern should lie. If small fires break out here and there, we will contain them as

93

required. Our two new legions that should be here soon will give us ample manpower to deal with small unrest here and there while still concentrating a major force on Ambiorix.'

'But what of this Esus?'

'Your mythical rebel, Priscus?' Caesar asked quietly. '*If* he exists, what makes you think that he is not Ambiorix himself?'

'Gut feeling, General.'

'I will not risk our entire presence in Gaul on your gut, Priscus. Ambiorix is my concern now. I have vowed his death to Rome - the senate and the people - and to Venus herself, and that vow I will not break. Ambiorix must...'

The general's voice trailed off as his eyes rose from Priscus to the rear of the room. The gathered officers turned and followed his gaze to see Fronto standing in the doorway. Priscus could swear Caesar was actually growling as he stepped back to his campaign table and folded his arms.

'Marcus Falerius Fronto reporting, Caesar.'

Priscus squinted. Fronto was silhouetted by the pale watery light from outside the door, and the gentle drizzle pattered down around and behind him. Something about the man was odd. As his eyes adjusted, Priscus sucked his teeth in surprise. Fronto had apparently been on a fitness regime. The trim, muscular figure standing in the doorway looked like the Fronto who had served under the searing sun of Hispania all those years ago, not the older, overweight officer he had been recently. The difference was quite startling.

Caesar narrowed his eyes dangerously and Priscus realised that the general was fighting for control of his anger. When he *did* say something it would likely be highly acidic and might drive an ever-greater wedge between them. In a moment of fuddlement, he tried to think of something to say that would defuse the situation and calm the atmosphere without rubbing either man up the wrong way. The words would not come.

'Fronto!' announced a pleasant, warbling voice. 'You took your time. Did you manage to get lost even with a Gaulish guide by your side?'

Marcus Antonius stood and beckoned to Fronto, gesturing to a chair beside him. Caesar looked for a moment as though he might explode when the newly arrived officer, still in his travelling clothes, strode across to the proffered chair and bowed momentarily before sinking into it.

'You smell like a dead bear,' Antonius laughed. Noticing the silent form of Caesar, Antonius fixed his commander and old friend with a look that conveyed far more steel than Priscus had realised he was capable of, and then smiled easily. 'Do go on, General.'

Caesar stood silent for a long moment - trying to recall what he was saying, Priscus suspected.

'If I might venture some new information for your consideration, General?' Fronto said quietly and with a surprisingly calm and controlled voice. 'I overheard the tail-end of your conversation. Seven days ago, my companions and I stopped off at Bibracte - I'm assuming everyone here is familiar with the place - and there are signs there of unrest or uncertainty. I wouldn't necessarily put it down to the Aedui themselves, but it seems they were playing host to a bunch of warriors from the Arverni, with a nobleman of that tribe in command.'

Curiosity seemed to slowly wash the initial anger from the general's face, and he tapped his chin in thought. 'The Arverni are virtually part of Narbonensis. They have no nobles and no power without Rome's authority. Are you sure they were Arverni, Fronto?'

'Galronus was, and he knows the tribes better than any Roman. I think we can safely say that's who they were. I suspect they were a mercenary band serving under an exile of the tribe, but they elicited fear and respect in equal measures from the Aedui, and their leader engaged us in conversation. It seems he is in cahoots with the druid class and knows a lot about the troubles we've had.'

'Esus?' Interjected Priscus.

'No idea what his name was. He's far too shrewd for that. But he did tell me straight out that Ambiorix was essentially an upstart who had played his move ahead of the great game and threw out the plans of his allies. He intimated that most of Gaul would be happy if Ambiorix were dead.'

Priscus nodded. 'I think that Fronto's encounter supports the theory that Ambiorix is not the central power in all this, Caesar.'

'Perhaps,' the general conceded. 'But with no further information, all this does is give us a fresh set of rumours to worry over. I will not turn from the hunt for Ambiorix without something more solid to persuade me, especially given the vow I have undertaken.'

Fronto nodded. 'Respectfully, Caesar, I don't think this man who spoke to us was so simple to have told us the plain truth over Ambiorix anyway. I've been thinking about some of the things he

95

said all week, and I still cannot decide whether he was trying to persuade us to leave the man alone, or whether he was trying to get us to hunt him. Either way, I think I would like to hear what Ambiorix has to say under the threat of Roman interrogation.'

Caesar raised an eyebrow at this, unused to support from Fronto even before the division had been drawn between them more than a year ago.

'Still,' the general went on to the room as a whole, 'this information does not alter the fact that all the rumours suggest that Ambiorix is somewhere among the north-eastern Belgae, hemmed in and trapped. If he can only rely on the Treveri, the Nervii and the Menapii, then he has the great Rhenus river at his back, Labienus to the south, the Britannic sea to the north and our main force to the west. It seems to me that we have him surrounded and we could utilise what is left of the winter to squeeze those lands until he shows himself. We can chip away at the edges and shrink his region of influence.'

A figure gestured with a raised arm and Priscus noted the younger Crassus brother - current legate of the Tenth - rising from his chair.

'My father had great success hunting one of his clients who had betrayed him.'

Caesar gestured for him to go on.

'The criminal hid from father's men in a maze of insulae on the Celian hill. Problem was that father *owned* those insulae. He had the outer ones pulled down to create a fire-break, set his men to guard that perimeter, and then began firing the wooden insulae one at a time until the man surrendered, choking on fumes and half burned.'

Priscus shook his head. The somewhat brutal and inhuman tactics of Crassus' family were well known and he'd had a lot of hope that this young officer might turn out to be the white sheep among the black, but occasionally the fellow dropped something into conversation that chilled the blood.

Caesar, on the other hand, seemed to be nodding his appreciation.

'It is a costly method both in terms of resources and of reputation, but effective, no less. I must - I *will* - have Ambiorix, and if I have to burn every house, every tree and every human being I come across until he turns up, I will do it. I still need to hear the reports of a number of scouts who have yet to return, and for now I have much to ponder before I settle on our precise course of action, but be aware that the army will be moving within the week, so I want every legion and auxiliary force ready for the off at short notice. Look to your units, gentlemen, and be prepared for another meeting in the next two days.'

The various officers stood, bowing or saluting the general and filing out of the headquarters. Priscus paused at the door, peering with distaste at the saturating drizzle outside and waiting for Fronto, who was clasping forearms in camaraderie with a number of officers he knew of old. As the travel worn former legate approached, Priscus folded his arms, his lip curling into a smile.

'I can only imagine that you scraped too hard with a strigil and that in some bath house somewhere there is a pile of blubber you scoured off yourself?'

'Good to see you too, Gnaeus.'

'Seriously, what did you do? Wherever that pile is it must be almost *half* of you.'

'A friend helped me get into shape.'

'You were already in shape. Admittedly that shape was 'circular'!'

Priscus snorted with laughter at the look that passed across Fronto's face, and behind them Marcus Antonius let out a bark of laughter. 'Come on you two young lovers, get out of the door and stop blocking everyone's way.'

As Antonius herded the pair out into the drizzle with his broad hands, Priscus slapped Fronto on the shoulder. 'In truth, you have no idea how glad I am to see you.'

'Trouble?'

'Isn't there always? But at least Cita's back now, and he's taken over the quartermaster chief's job, so I can concentrate on my own duties. Caesar's got me back doing the camp prefect role again.'

'A job you are well suited for Gnaeus, or will be when you put on a little more weight and stop exercising.'

Another snort.

'I was meaning to ask, by the way:' Fronto said quietly as they stepped outside, 'when we passed through Bibracte, the supply depot had gone. Is this a new system?'

Priscus shrugged. 'We've been somewhat short on manpower and our forces have been concentrated in the north-east. We've a second supply line now coming over the mountains through Helvetii lands and on to Vesontio, but this one's still operational occasionally. We've left several legs of it in the hands of Aedui merchants. It gives them an opportunity to make a little on the deal, and saves us manpower and endless organisation. I suspect that now Cita's in charge again, things will change, but it's worked quite well in the meantime.'

Antonius put an arm around each of their shoulders. 'This is heart-warming and fascinating, but I am slowly becoming wetter than a fish's private parts, and I'd rather like to be inside, near a brazier and with a jug of wine in my hands. Any offers?'

Priscus sighed. Antonius had only been in camp for four days, but already his prodigious drinking habits had become a talking point among the officers - only quietly and well out of his earshot, but there nonetheless. Priscus had already had to requisition more wine at an inordinate expense due to the new officer's evening visits.

'My quarters, then. It so happens I have a new jar of Rhaetican untried.'

Two figures emerged from a knot of soldiers to one side of the path and stepped in front of the three officers.

'And who, might I ask,' Priscus said with quiet force, 'are you?'

'These are friends of mine,' Fronto grinned. 'Priscus? Meet Palmatus and Masgava. Don't get into a fistfight with the latter or a war of puns with the former. In fact, you and Palmatus should get on like an insula on fire. Just don't tell him you used to be a centurion.'

'This place stinks of sweat and piss and no one can tell me where to get a cold drink, a hot meal, and a warm woman,' Palmatus grumbled sourly.

'See?' said Fronto with a grin. 'You two are going to get on just fine.'

* * * * *

Fronto lounged in his chair, slumped like a sack of grain. His head felt as though someone had pushed a ferret in through his ear and left it there to nest. He'd intended to be slumbering in his cot not long after dark, but Antonius had had other ideas.

He looked around the tent.

Priscus leaned heavily against the trunk that contained most of Fronto's gear, still packed from the journey. His eyelids were dark and heavy and hung like saddlebags. Even as Fronto's gaze played across him, he heard the prefect snore and realised with a start that

Priscus was actually asleep but with his eyes open. How long had he been gone?

He would have chuckled if he'd had the energy.

Brutus was still awake and arguing with Antonius, though his speech had sunk into a weary drawl and his wine cup had gone untouched for more than an hour.

Varus was toying with his bootlace, trying to tie it in an effort to escape the sucking whirlpool of the tent's atmosphere.

Atmosphere! That in itself was a laugh. Having spent over a year in townhouses and villas and then in a variety of Gallic inns and taverns, he'd forgotten the discomfort of living in a military tent. The smell of slightly wet leather combined with the cloying smoke of the brazier that provided warmth and light, sweat from the occupants and... feet. Most overriding of all odours, that of feet.

He shuffled in his chair.

'I know I'm sounding repetitive,' he said, trying to cut through the debate raging in his tent, 'but before very long the birds will be singing and the camp will be up and about, and I really think it's time we got our heads down.'

Antonius held up a hand as if to say 'just bear with me for a moment' and gestured at Brutus with his cup - a cup that had just been refilled once more, Fronto noted, and with unwatered wine, no less.

'Decimus, you have to accept that it takes a strong hand to guide any group,' the new officer said brightly. Alert and shrewd and with a clear voice, which was absolutely unfathomable to Fronto, given the quantity of wine the man had consumed. Even on his best days, had Fronto drunk that much unwatered wine, he would now be lying face down in a puddle somewhere muttering about boobs. And yet the only effect it seemed to have had on Antonius was to bring forth a hard loquaciousness. The man had launched into arguments and debates with relish, like a horse with the bit between its teeth.

'In the military, I agree, though with reservations,' Brutus replied wearily and with a slight slur. 'Discipline is important and without it we're just a well-armoured rabble. And you and I both know that the grand strategy requires a single mind, though we also both know how misguided that single mind could be without a staff of solid officers to advise. And although the legatus can direct a legion into a battle, his tribunes might as well be garlands hanging round his neck for all the use they are. And moreover,' he slurred, pointing at Antonius and only missing by a few feet, 'we all know that when sword hits shield, it's the centurions that run the show.'

'Pah!' Antonius swept the argument aside with his hand. 'Look back to armies commanded by more than one man. Back to the days of the wars with Carthage or of the last slave revolt. Flaminius and Servilius with half the army each and look what happened to them! Or Gellius and Lentulus against that Thracian gladiator and his thugs! Divisions in command, you see? And in both cases it took a single strong hand at the reins to put things right. Crassus for the latter and Scipio for the former. Quod erat demonstrandum.'

Varus, having given up attempting to lace his boot and leaving the leather thong flapping, waved his arm. 'In fairness, that was down to Pompey as much as Crassus, and *two* Scipios - younger and elder.'

Antonius waved the words aside irritably and Varus sensibly fell quiet. Fronto and the others had seen Antonius' ire beginning to rise several times throughout the evening, and had moved to defuse it as quickly as they could. Though he'd not seen Antonius angry, there was something about him which suggested to Fronto that he might not want to do so.

'Anyway,' Brutus cut in, 'the same cannot be said for the Republic. The last time we had a 'strong hand on the reins' as you put it was in the age of kings, and look at what that was like. We are a Republic and proud to be so. All the freedoms and advantages of a government by a concerned group of citizens without the randomness and failings of the Greek model.'

'Sulla!' snorted Antonius in reply, as he threw the entire cup of wine down his throat apparently without the need to swallow. Fronto sighed and gave up on the idea of disbanding the gathering for much needed sleep.

'Sulla was a bump in the road - a tyrant trying to wrestle power from the legitimate government. He was a butcher and a villain. The lesson there has been learned, though, and Rome will not allow something like that to happen again.'

'You are short-sighted, Decimus, if you think Sulla was the last tyrant Rome will see. And whatever you think of the man, he halted and reversed the chaos gripping the Republic. A strong hand. The damned place could do with another Sulla, if you ask me.'

'I dearly hope you're wrong, Antonius.'

'Will somebody please fasten my bootlace?' drawled Varus wearily.

'Pila!' yelled Priscus, causing everyone's head to snap round in shock, only to realise that the prefect was still fast asleep, his eyes open and his dreaming fingers twitching around the haft of an imaginary javelin.

Fronto snorted with laughter and, as the debate on the nature of command burst into renewed vigour, interrupted periodically by Varus' complaints concerning his boot, he hauled himself wearily out of his seat and staggered across to the bed. Taking his lesson from Varus, he didn't even bother trying to fiddle with the laces and leaving them on, simply collapsed, face down on the cold blankets and buried his head in the pillow allowing the argument to drone on around him.

For perhaps half an hour he lay there, breathing in the linen cover of the pillow and attempting to shut out the conversation that raged over the rebellion of Sertorius and the dangers of breakaway states, trying to picture nothing but blackness in an attempt to let sleep overcome him.

Unfortunately, every time his mind emptied enough to permit sleepiness, his aching gut acted up and his head thumped in a sickening way, between them pushing the welcoming arms of Somnus far beyond reach.

After a time, he gave up, sitting upright in an attempt to fight off the fiery indigestion that coursed through his system. His body was simply not used to this sort of activity these days. A couple of years ago it had been the norm, and he could easily imagine slipping into his old ways, but he was not willing to relinquish his newfound strength and health to the vine.

'Are you lot settled in for the night?'

Antonius waved at him in answer and Fronto sighed, aware that he'd basically lost his tent and along with it any hope of sleep.

'Try not to throw up on my cot and don't let the tent burn down. I'm going out for a walk.'

Leaving them to it, Fronto stepped across the tent, his foot brushing Priscus' leg and eliciting a muttered 'testudo' order given to the dream army that he commanded.

'If you'll fasten this pigging bootlace, I'll join you,' Varus grumbled.

Pausing near the entrance, Fronto leaned down to Varus. Being charitable, he assumed that Varus' trouble stemmed from the wounded arm that still gave him trouble in wet weather, and went to help him fasten his lace, only to discover that one end of the lace turned out in fact to be threaded wrong through the eyelets in the boot. With an almost paternal sigh, he spent a few moments re-lacing the boot and then tied it off.

'Come on, you daft sod.'

With a grunt, he helped lift the cavalry commander from the floor and the two men ambled unsteadily out of the tent door, leaving the sleeping Priscus as silent witness to the heated debate going on within.

The damp pre-dawn air settled onto them, almost immediately chilling them to the bone and leaving a fine layer of dew on their tunics.

'Why are we not wearing cloaks?' Varus asked, shivering in the cold.

'Because you didn't bring one with you, while mine is underneath Priscus, and if I try to retrieve it, he'll probably punch me in his sleep.'

'Fair enough. Bracing, isn't it?'

'That's one word for it.'

The huge encampment spread northwards before them, rolling down the gentle slope to the wide river, with the Gallic oppidum over to the west side. Camp fires and braziers burned here and there providing light and heat for the few men still on duty. A faint glow off to their right, over the crest of the hill, suggested that dawn was not a long way off, and Fronto blinked wearily. There were no stars and the moon was obscured by a thick grey layer, warning of a high likelihood of rain.

'Going to be a shitty day' Fronto noted.

'Not unusual up here at this time of the year. Seems odd that we've been in Gaul for so long that we're used to its climate and changes.'

'Come on. Let's stroll.'

The two men pottered past the tent that had been requisitioned for Palmatus and Masgava, where snoring and farting confirmed that the two men were in residence and asleep. On past the gathered tents of the tribunes and prefects the pair strolled, their feet squelching in the grass until they made it onto the sunken-timber walkways that criss-crossed the semi-permanent camp and prevented the main roads turning to a quagmire in the wet.

The decumanus led down to the east gate from here and, for want of anything better to do, the two men strolled on towards the defences, thinking to climb the ramparts and gain a good view of the low hills and wide plains of the Ambiani tribe stretching off towards the rising sun.

'You heard the news as well, then?'

Fronto jumped at the sudden voice at his shoulder and turned to see Rufio and young Crassus falling into step behind them, the former rubbing his eyes sleepily and the latter still fastening the expensive belt around his middle and hoisting his knee-length tunic up, cinching it in place.

'News?'

'Just a night owl then,' smiled Rufio. 'Messenger at the gate.'

'At this time of night?' Fronto shook his head. 'What is he: half-man, half-owl?'

'Curious, eh? But then the Gauls all seem to work on a different schedule to the rest of the world.'

The four men strode down the road at a faster pace, converging on the gate, where a knot of officers stood, surrounded by legionaries and lit by the braziers of the watch. As they closed, Fronto noted a small group of natives at the centre, dismounted, their horses snorting and huffing in the cold air. There was something about the colours of their clothes - more russets and browns than the colourful blues and greens of the Gauls that suggested they were Belgae, from the east. It struck Fronto as interesting that he had spent long enough out here that could actually pick up on such details, even after a year away.

'Sir!' barked the duty centurion, snapping to attention and saluting the four approaching officers, though clearly uncertain as to whom to defer as the most senior. Fronto allowed the others to step ahead of him. Whatever position he might hold in the army right now, he was fairly sure that he could claim less seniority than any of these men, even the young relatively-untried Crassus.

Rufio, seeming to sense the need for a spokesman, stepped ahead and saluted the centurion in return. 'Your runner said we had a messenger?'

'Yessir. A scout party that's been out in the forest of Arduenna. One of them's wounded, so I sent for the capsarius from the Tenth. Should be here any moment.'

'Wounded?' Fronto queried, stepping in.

'Yessir. Arrow in the back.'

Gazing past the cordon of guards, he could see that there were four riders, but one of them was being held upright by two legionaries, clearly in agony and pale as a moonlight ghost.

'What happened to you?' Rufio asked of the native scouts. One of the three unwounded men stepped forward and nodded his head in deference.

'Nervii patrol in Viromandui land. Chase us for many mile. Ategnio lose much blood. Need get to healer.'

'The healer is on his way,' Rufio said as comfortingly as he could and then turned to Fronto. 'Nervii and Viromandui?'

'The Nervii are one of the biggest Belgic tribes in the north. Caused us a lot of bother in their time. And the Viromandui are smaller, on their border. Sort of under the Nervii. Their land's maybe forty or fifty miles from here, as the bird flies.'

'Looks like they might be causing us more trouble, then, unless this was an unrelated and accidental incident.'

'No attack by the Belgae is accidental,' Fronto sighed. He turned to the scout. 'What news do you carry?'

'Caesar's enemy,' the man said slowly. 'Nobles meet at Aduatuca one week go. Ambiorix with them.'

'And who else?' Varus asked quietly. 'I'm guessing the Nervii?'

The scout nodded. 'Nervii. And Menapii. And Treveri.'

Fronto whistled, mentally picturing the map of the Belgae lands in the general's tent. Between those three tribes - and the Eburones of whom Ambiorix was still a King, at least in theory - they constituted most of the northeast, from the great cold sea in the north to the foothills of the Alpes in the south and along the entire western bank of the Rhenus.

'That's a big coalition. Caesar might have been right in planning to move before spring. Clearly Ambiorix has.' He turned to the others. 'Best get the word to the legion commanders, as the general's going to want to move as soon as he's held his briefing.'

'Is it not a little previous to pass word to the men before it is given to us?' Rufio asked, his brow furrowing.

'When you've known Caesar for a while, you'll realise it's worth getting a couple of steps ahead, 'cause he hates being made to wait when he's itching to move. Warn the officers. Trust me.'

Crassus nodded his understanding and cleared his throat. 'Where will we move, do you think?'

All three men seemed to be looking to Fronto for answers, despite his current uncertainty of rank or position. He shrugged. 'The Treveri are bogged down with Labienus and won't move anywhere with him on their flank. The Menapii are way up north in the swamps of the delta. And Caesar already avowed his intention to chisel away at the edge of Ambiorix's power. So I would wager my money on a march into Nervii lands.'

Varus nodded. 'And they're closest. We can be in their lands inside two days at a forced march. Caesar can take the poor bastards by surprise.'

'Then let's get back up the hill. Antonius will want to know about this before he gets dragged in front of Caesar with the rest of us.'

* * * * *

The sudden order to march came as no surprise to Fronto, or to any of those used to Caesar's decisiveness when it came to campaigning. Barely had the capsarius reached the wounded Gaul before the rest of the scouts were escorted to Caesar's headquarters and debriefed. An hour later, when the first chirps of the dawn chorus issued from the trees and faint tendrils of orange crept through the clouds to the east, Caesar had called his staff meeting and given the entirely predictable order to break camp and march for the lands of the Nervii. Four legions had departed - the Tenth under Crassus, the Ninth under Trebonius, the Eighth under Fabius and the Eleventh under Cicero, and many of the staff had come along too, leaving only a small garrison at Samarobriva. By the time any man in his right mind would be having his 'morning movement' and contemplating breaking his fast, the legions were already a mile from the camp and marching east-by-northeast along the shallow river valley.

Fronto had felt appropriately ill all day, half-dead on his feet with fatigue, regretting his timing of the previous night's activity - or rather that of the ever-vigorous Antonius. He had ridden Bucephalus as though every hoof-step that touched the ground might make him hurl, and had not been able to look at food whenever it was offered throughout the journey. The only consolation was that Varus and Brutus appeared to be feeling similarly unwell. Priscus seemed his usual dour and irascible self, though he was reasonably rested but for a kink in his neck from the way he had slept.

The irritating thing, of course, was the fact that with no sleep at all - and having consumed more wine than even an elephant should be able to comfortably stand - Marcus Antonius rode gaily along beside the general discussing this and that as though he had gone for an early night with a glass of warm mulsum. Damn the man.

If he wasn't so bloody likeable!

Fronto had ridden in silence all day, alone with his discomfort and at the rear of the staff, away from anyone he really knew who might try to engage him in conversation, and it had been with an immense sense of relief that Fronto had watched Caesar hold up his hand to halt the column at the position the advanced scouts and engineers had selected as the site for the night's encampment.

While the legions, under the watchful eyes of their centurions and optios, had broken up into work parties, digging ditches and raising ramparts, excavating numerous deep latrine trenches at the edge that was currently downwind, gathering water from the river nearby, raising tents and lighting cooking fires, setting the watch, assigning pickets, and the myriad other tasks required and allocated by Priscus as camp prefect, the staff and the four legates had gathered on a low hill nearby to discuss the next stage of the march and to await their accommodation's raising and furnishing - one of the first tasks of the workers.

The scouts had confirmed that the next day would bring them through Viromandui lands and into the territory of the Nervii. The former, smaller, tribe had no links to the latter's treachery as far as the native levy were aware and had been nothing but obsequious and accommodating as the army had passed through. Things might change in Nervii lands, though.

'From the morning, we slow the march a little, with cavalry scouting in a wide arc ahead and beside us,' Caesar announced. 'I want no chance of us blundering into a trap and we have no idea how long the Nervii have been plotting with our enemies. With the blessing of Fortuna we will have taken them by surprise and they will be totally unaware of our approach and thoroughly unprepared, but I will not rely upon the fact. When we move, the Eighth will play rear-guard, behind the baggage train. The Ninth will take the lead, and the Tenth and Eleventh will march side by side in two wide columns, with the officers, artillery, baggage and auxiliary infantry in the centre. If we *are* taken by surprise I want my veteran heavy infantry on all the edges to form shield walls.'

106

This was greeted by nods all around and Fronto looked out across the landscape. Much like the lands they had just left, the Viromandui's territory was mostly flat and covered with a patchwork of fields, with occasional ripples of low hill to break up the monotony. A wide marching formation was no trouble in this land, and it would be exceedingly difficult to launch a sneak attack upon the legions until they reached a hillier, more forested area.

As Fronto pondered, wishing he could collapse into his bed and sleep instead of sitting on his horse in the chilling cold and the fading light, Caesar continued to give out commands and answer the questions of his officers, and Fronto was almost asleep in the saddle when the general clapped his hands in a business-like manner and dismissed them all.

'You look like a drunk on a four-day session,' Antonius grinned as he pulled his dappled grey alongside Fronto. 'And you smell like my aunt Hybrida, which cannot be good as she suffered from a permanent and debilitating bowel complaint and had to have her own separate latrine.'

'Thank you. Thank you very much. Particularly given that this is largely your fault.'

'My mistake, Fronto. You see I had you pegged as a soldier, not as a flagging woman.' He grinned, waiting for an outburst, but Fronto was too tired to play the offended victim.

'Let's just go find our tents so that I can fall over and not move again until the sun has gone and come back again.'

Antonius laughed and the pair rode on down the slope in the wake of the other officers, towards the already-half-constructed camp. The officers' quarters were already in position, the tents raised and legionaries unloading the furnishings from the wagons at the camp's edge, carrying cots, tables, chairs and more into the confines.

Fronto looked for his tent. It used to be easy, as it would be located with the Tenth, but these days his was one of the miscellaneous ones in the staff area near the general's own accommodation. After scanning the area, he picked out an officer's tent no different from the rest, but with a smaller legionary tent pitched close by. Masgava and Palmatus. That was the best way to identify his.

'Care for a drink?'

Fronto turned a withering gaze on Antonius. 'Do you never stop?'

'One of the advantages of a strong constitution and a position in command is that I never really have to. Similar tales are told of you, you know?'

'I can hold my own, but I do like to have a day off occasionally to rest. Anyway, the answer's no. I want nothing more than to fall face down on my bunk and drool into my pillow. Find Priscus. He'll want a drink after watching the men ruin his carefully laid camp plans, mark my words.'

Antonius gave a low chuckle as they passed the first groups of workmen, crossing the causeway that overlaid the already-excavated ditch.

'Why do you hate Crassus?' the man said suddenly. Fronto blinked.

'What?'

'Crassus. I've seen the way you look at him, as though you'd trodden in something distasteful.'

Fronto shrugged, too tired to maintain a civil fiction. 'I don't, really. I sort of resent him, is all. He's young and pleasant and not half as vicious or grasping as the rest of his family, and there's nothing about him to dislike. But he commands my legion.'

'*Your* legion?'

'The Tenth. I know, I know,' he said quickly. 'It's the Proconsul's prerogative to select his legates, but I commanded the Tenth long enough that they're like my family. It's like watching your children with another father.' He frowned, wondering where *that* analogy had sprung from, given that he *had* no children. Well, not yet, at least. He fought down the rising image of a pregnant Lucilia with difficulty. 'I keep waiting for Caesar to call me in so that we can talk but he seems to have no interest in speaking to me at all. And as long as I'm on the periphery, I'm just along for the ride. I'm no use to him without a legion. You know that.'

'I know. Give it time. I keep speaking to him, but Gaius is stubborn; you know that. I will get you your command in time. Maybe even the Tenth, but be patient. Let me work on him.'

'Thanks.'

He reined in Bucephalus as he rounded the tent of another officer and beheld his own small empire. The big black steed huffed in irritation and stepped high in place, itching to exercise more, having been restricted to a plod on the march. As well as Fronto's tent and the smaller one that belonged to Masgava and Palmatus, another tent was busy rising in the lee of his own - a traditional legionary soldiers' tent.

'It appears your entourage grows,' mused Antonius. Fronto frowned at the men hauling the leather sections into position and tying them into place. Though they all wore military-style tunics, they were plain off-white wool rather than the russet colour favoured by Caesar's command. Some of the men were of Roman origins, as was obvious from their swarthy appearance and neatly-trimmed military haircuts, but three of them appeared to be Gauls stuffed into Roman uniform. Not drawn from the Gallic-blooded legions, though, since *they* had now all adopted the Roman model at their officers' urging. So these three must be from the native auxiliary cavalry units.

'Eight men. A contubernium of the most mixed variety,' Antonius said with more than a hint of curiosity in his tone.

As they watched, Palmatus appeared from his tent, dressed in a similar colourless tunic, with a well-used but well-maintained mail shirt over the top. Fronto couldn't help but wonder how the ex-legionary had managed to come by a good mail shirt here. He didn't have that much money and now that Cita was back in charge of the quartermasters there was more hope of the outspoken Roman growing a second bumhole than persuading the supply officers to give out a freebie.

'Erm, Palmatus?' Fronto said quietly. The unshaven former soldier turned and, noticing Antonius, gave a half-hearted salute. The smiling senior officer waved the formality aside, given the fact that the man in the mail shirt was officially a civilian and a Roman citizen.

'Sir?' the man replied with more deference than Fronto had heard him use all year.

'What is this?' Fronto took in the rising tent and its workmen with a sweep of his hand.

'Singulares unit,' Palmatus replied airily. 'Told you we were working on it.

'And I told you to stick it up your arse, didn't I?'

'Legate with your record of danger and combat should have a bodyguard,' Palmatus said dismissively, nodding to Masgava as the latter emerged from the tent, similarly dressed in pale tunic and mail shirt - though his enormous bulk strained the shirt and made it look like a winesack stretched over a ballista.

'Palmatus, I am not a legate. In fact I'm little more than an observer at the moment. The chance of me actually getting close enough to any action to experience any danger is tiny, so I hardly need a bodyguard. What I'm more in need of is an entertainer to keep me busy. Or a mallet to knock me out and send me to sleep.'

'Don't tempt them,' grinned Antonius. 'I can see these two complying with your request.'

'And who are they, anyway?' Fronto grumbled. 'Weirdest looking bunch.'

'Chosen men. Pick of Galronus' best, along with four veterans of the Tenth who opted for this rather than their honesta missio and a friend of Carbo's who has been deemed a little over-excitable by his optio. Good men, every one. I'm working on getting the Gauls to cut their hair and shave off their 'taches, but it's an uphill job.'

'Send them back to their units. Even if I wanted a babysitter - which I don't - Caesar will have nothing of it, even if I'm made legate again. Certainly not before that.'

'No, wait,' Antonius grinned. 'It's a splendid idea. It'll give you something to do until your command comes through, putting your little house in order. And until you're made legate, at least you'll have your own command.'

Fronto threw an appropriately venomous look at the other officer and cleared his throat. 'Caesar will not authorise it.'

'Caesar will do as I advise, and *I* authorise it. Go ahead, you two, and get your singulares set up. In fact, get another contubernium together too. Eight men is too small for comfort. Just run any transfers by me. And tell Cita to give you what you need. Those Gauls will need kitting out properly.'

Fronto sighed deeply and looked back and forth between the implacable faces of his new bodyguard officers and the second most important man in the army. Shaking his head, he glowered at Palmatus. 'Get at least a couple of archers from Decius' auxiliaries attached to the Eighth. And a good engineer, too. Ask around and see if a Gallic legionary called Biorix is here. He was serving with the Thirteenth three years ago, and he could be dead or transferred, but if he's in one of these legions, get him.'

Antonius grinned. 'That's the spirit,' he laughed. 'To it, Fronto! Your men need you.'

'My *bed* needs me,' Fronto grumbled.

Palmatus gestured towards the larger of the three tents. 'It's in there waiting for you. Leave the rest to us.'

Fronto gave his new command a last disparaging look and with his deepest sigh yet entered his tent, seeking the oblivion of sleep.

Chapter Six

'We're certain that we are in their lands?' Marcus Antonius asked carefully. 'We could cause ourselves more than a spot of bother if we move in and they turn out to be an allied tribe.'

Caesar watched the scene before him and replied to his friend and subordinate without moving his gaze. 'They are Nervii. The scouts are natives, so they know these things. And in my gut *I* know they are. I can almost feel it in my blood. These animals ambushed us four years ago not a great distance from here and we fought hard for our lives. I stood in the line with the dying men that day, covered in the enemy's blood, sweat and stink. I know the Nervii of old and accord them appropriate loathing.'

Antonius simply nodded, his own gaze playing across the oddly tranquil scene.

Not so for much longer.

The first settlement they had come across in Nervii territory was no city or oppidum. No fortress or druidic site. It was a simple village of poor, dirty and apparently frail farmers and their families. To Antonius - and to Fronto, standing on the periphery of the staff - they did not look capable of ambushing a sheep, let alone a sizeable force of Roman legionaries.

But Fronto knew otherwise.

They may *look* peaceful and frail, yet they were anything *but*. These very people may well have been among that force that almost halted the Roman campaign in Belgae lands four years ago. They may be the very men who besieged Cicero a matter of months ago. Yes, they held hoes and rakes, fed pigs and kneaded bread. But give them a rousing anti-Roman speech and in moments they would be wielding any blade they could lay hands upon and charging the hated Roman enemy. The Belgae were, as Caesar had once said, the bravest and the fiercest of all these peoples. Even their farmers were dangerous. Even the women.

The officers watched in silence as the two cohorts began to move in. As soon as the village - a shabby collection of huts that played home to some fifty souls - had been located, Caesar had ordered two cohorts of the Ninth ahead, sweeping to both sides in a wide arc and then moving in like pincers to surround the settlement and pin them against the approaching army.

Panic gripped the natives as the first signs of the two cohorts were seen between the trees and scrub, closing in on the village. A wall of steel and bronze and red wool, rattling, clanking and thumping, with the rhythmic crunch of booted feet in an ever-tightening circle of death, leaving only a single gap which even now was filling with the rest of the approaching army, moving around both sides of the small hillock that played host to the staff officers, like a river around an island.

Native women grabbed their dusty, half-naked children and ran into their huts as though a few handfuls of dried mud and wattle would stop the advance of a determined legion. The men variously grasped whatever offensive items upon which they could lay their hands and gathered in a group, or helped the women and children to 'safety', one man actually wasting time releasing a large horse from a corral gate and leading it by the reins to his hut!

Horses were expensive, after all.

'Come!' Caesar commanded and applied heels to horse, urging his steed down the gentle incline towards the village, where the panicked and desperate males had now formed up into a small warband of twenty or so, armed with scythes and sickles, shovels, and even the odd real sword here and there.

The Ninth legion's ranks parted at calls from their centurions, clearing a path for the staff officers to traverse and reach the centre of activity. Caesar and his cadre of officers entered the small settlement, passing between a barn and a small pig pen where the beasts wallowed, grunting and carefree, unaware of the drama unfolding around them.

'Galronus?' the general asked, to which the Remi noble, commander of a large auxiliary cavalry wing, stepped his horse forward, falling in near Caesar's side.

'Sir?'

'I will need my words translated to these people, since I doubt they have a word of Latin.'

Galronus nodded respectfully, and the general cleared his throat. With a wave of his hand, he gave a signal and small groups of legionaries detached from their units and began to move towards the various structures.

'My soldiers will search each of your huts,' he announced, pausing for Galronus to echo his words in the local drawl.

'If you wish to see another dawn, you will drop your weapons and gather peacefully in the corral there, offering no resistance. Your women and children will leave their buildings and join you. If they do not leave the huts voluntarily, my men will drag them out, and if they offer continued resistance, they will simply be killed inside the huts. Do I make myself clear?'

There was the obligatory pause in translation, and then a long silence as the menfolk looked at one another in panicked indecision.

'You number perhaps a score of men, while I command some thirty thousand in your lands alone. There is no doubt about your fate if you disobey, and you know who I am and what I will do. Now drop those weapons and move.'

By the time the translated words had become echoes among the huts, the men had begun to drop their spades and rakes and scythes, and a number of small groups of women and children and the elderly had started to appear, blinking, from the darkness of their hovels.

Caesar waited patiently as the villagers traipsed despondently into the horse corral. Two centuries of legionaries moved off at a command from Trebonius and surrounded the enclosure, leaving only the open gate for the remaining natives to move through.

When the last of the visible Nervii had entered the makeshift holding pen, the small parties of soldiers began to move into the buildings, most of them coming out a few moments later with a signal for 'all clear', others shoving panicked, screaming women out into the cold light, crying children clamped around their mothers' legs, inhibiting their movement.

In one hut there was the sound of raised voices, the words indistinct, shouting in the Belgae tongue and then a blood-curdling scream, after which four legionaries emerged, grim faced and dragging two young boys, their mother's blood still running from one soldier's sword.

Moments was all it took, and so far with miraculously only one death.

Fronto had watched it all in hard silence and noticed that Galronus had not flinched or looked away either. It was a hard fact that with these people there was no distinction in war between warriors and the rest. He remembered with a sudden ache the Germanic woman that autumn so long ago who had sunk her teeth into his ankle and very nearly done for him. The Nervii had plotted twice before to defeat the legions, and their underhanded sneak attacks had been brutal and costly. They could not be allowed to do the same again under the command of Ambiorix.

114

He hardened his heart against the violent demise of the poor unseen woman. She would not be the last. The legionaries moved to close the gate, but the centurion in charge halted them, selecting one middle-aged farmer with a tap of his vine stick.

As the man was dragged out by the legionaries, the gate closed behind him, other work parties moved around the farm. Some were igniting hastily-made torches and then moving to the huts of the village, holding the flames to the thatch or wattle until the fire caught and raced across the walls and roofs of the buildings, quickly turning them into an inferno. Others rounded up all the animals of the village, that fine horse retrieved and led to the cavalry detachments, much to the sullen chagrin of its owner. The pigs, sheep, cows and chickens were butchered quickly and efficiently, loaded into the empty supply carts that were being brought forward, where they would provide good fresh meat for the army. Other units began to move off into the vegetable plots and the granary, gathering the food, uprooting or harvesting everything of any value and storing it for the legion's consumption. The village would be utterly devastated within half an hour of their arrival.

But the scene at the centre was the important part, and they all knew it, Roman and Nervian alike.

The farmer was manhandled to the central space, where the temperature was now becoming uncomfortably warm from the burning huts all around. The damp earth had been churned to mud by so many feet. One of the auxiliary cavalry drawn from the Remi stepped forward to join the centurion who stood near the captive. The pair waited quietly while the two legionaries hauled the farmer into position and then kicked him hard in the back of the legs, dropping him painfully to his knees with a squawk.

One soldier grasped his hands and yanked them up behind him, eliciting another yelp of pain, while the other drew his pugio dagger and tested the edge with his thumb, nodding his satisfaction.

Everything fell to an eerie silence, broken only by the cries of the animals being slaughtered and the tears and wails from the women and children in the corral - and from some of the menfolk.

'Where is King Ambiorix of the Eburones?' Caesar said, with deliberate slowness and clarity, enunciating each word carefully, so that there could be no mistaking what it was that he asked. The Remi cavalryman next to the centurion repeated the translation equally slowly and carefully. The farmer simply stared at his captors in panicked misery, shaking his head with what appeared to be genuine incomprehension.

The centurion looked around at Caesar with an unspoken question. The general nodded and, at a gesture - reminiscent of that of the editor of a gladiatorial combat - the legionary put his pugio beneath the farmer's chin and opened his throat from one ear to the other.

Blood spurted, fountaining out onto the wet dirt. The cut was so wide, deep and professional that the watching Romans saw the man's face change colour rapidly, going from a ruddy and healthy pink, through purple to a rubbery grey. His eyes bulged and his mouth worked silently but he remained in position, held in place by the iron grip of the legionary behind him. At another nod from the centurion, the soldier let go and the dead farmer, still twitching, fell to his face in the mud.

By the time two more soldiers had arrived and grabbed the farmer's arms to drag him away, he had stopped kicking. The legionaries hauled him over to one of the burning huts and, taking his arms and legs, cast him into the flames to be consumed by the conflagration. By the time they had finished their grisly disposal and returned to the central space a second farmer - this time a young man, fresh faced and defiant - had been hauled out of the pen and to the centre. The performance was repeated and the man sank to his knees in the churned mud and blood, his defiant, cold blue eyes fixed on Caesar. Back in the pen his woman screamed her love and fear for him.

'Where is Ambiorix of the Eburones?' asked Caesar slowly. The Remi horseman repeated the translation. The farmer simply heaped more scorn and arrogance into his cold gaze and at Caesar's nod, the centurion gave the order.

The young farmer's blood arced and sprayed, adding to the russet coloured mud before them.

As the body was hauled away, leaving dark red streaks through the dirt, the young Crassus appeared between Fronto and Antonius, his face bleak and unsettled. If ever there was a sign that he was not a facsimile of his father and brother it was the difficulty that he was clearly experiencing in watching such efficient brutality. The older Crassus brother would - Fronto knew - have performed the task with gusto, and his father would have positively revelled in it.

'What happens if they don't know? Any of them, I mean? Will they *all* die?' Crassus' voice was little more than a whisper, but

116

Galronus and Caesar both apparently heard and turned their heads while the next victim was being brought out.

'We decided to set the limit at ten,' Antonius replied quietly so that the natives would not hear, in case any might speak Latin. 'After that it's slavery for the rest.'

Crassus seemed slightly relieved to discover that there would be an end to it at some point. 'And if none of them know the answer?' the young legate persisted. 'It seems farfetched that such low peasants would know of the doings of kings.'

Galronus shook his head. 'They know. That last man knew. You could see it in his eyes - in the defiance and arrogance. He knew, and he took the knowledge with him to his Gods. And if *he* knew then others do too. Do not be fooled by their rustic appearance. I am Belgae and I know these things - no man in these lands is less than a warrior, no matter how much he kneads the bread.'

Caesar nodded his agreement and the two men turned back to the scene as the third victim, this time a woman, was dropped to the bloody, wet earth on her knees.

'Where is Ambiorix, king of the Eburones?'

A repeat in translation.

The woman spat a string of words at Caesar and received a slap to the cheek from the knife-wielding legionary. The slap was hard enough to break cheek or jaw, as the loud crack announced, and the woman slumped slightly. Caesar threw a questioning look at the Remi translator, but he shook his head and replied that the woman had simply cursed Caesar for a devil.

'And now she is useless anyway since she cannot answer through her ruined jaw,' the general added irritably. At a gesture, the centurion gave the order and her throat was opened.

Fronto watched impassively along with the other officers, including the slightly pale Crassus, while the next few farmers and their wives were brought out, questioned, and executed quickly and efficiently. Crassus muttered his gratitude that the Ninth had been vanguard and therefore given this grisly task, and not his Tenth. Fronto fought the irritation at that last part, but could only echo the young legate's gratitude that the Tenth had not been set to executing farmers.

Seven dead now, their bodies blazing in the inferno of one of their homes.

Crassus gave a sharp intake of breath as he watched a boy of perhaps seven summers being dragged from the pen. The lad's

117

parents were shouting desperately and clawing at the hard legionaries holding them back.

'Where is Ambiorix of the Eburones?'

'Surely he cannot know?' Crassus whispered in a hollow voice.

'Unlikely,' Antonius nodded, 'but his parents might, and it could shock some sense into them all.'

Crassus watched in horror as the boy shook, making his throat-cutting a difficult chore, but the legionary was a professional, and held the boy's head while he was dispatched. The rising wails and shrieks from the corral confirmed the effect this brutal display had had upon the locals.

Caesar gestured, and the centurion gave the commands, but the Remi translator waved his hand and shouted something to Galronus. The cavalry officer turned to Caesar and raised his own arm to pause the string of deaths.

'Three of the Nervii are shouting Avenna,' he said quietly.

'And what is Avenna?' Caesar asked.

'The Nervii are quite advanced for a Belgic tribe,' Galronus said, with what appeared to be grudging respect. 'Almost as advanced as the Remi,' he added pointedly. 'They have a council, like the Roman senate and a capital city like Rome, which is the heart of their tribe. Avenna is less than a day's march north of here.'

'Avenna sounds as likely a place to find Ambiorix as anywhere else, then,' Antonius noted.

'More likely than most,' agreed Caesar. 'Very well.' He returned his attention to the centurion and raised his voice. 'End it. We are done here and ready to move on.'

The centurion nodded and began shouting his orders to the men. As the last of the livestock and grain was being loaded, the huts burning down now to orange embers billowing with black smoke, the rest of the villagers were roped together at neck and wrist and sent off with three centuries of men to lead them back to Samarobriva and a future of slavery, the profits of which would supplement the income of the army by a minute sum.

'It seems almost too good to be true,' Fronto noted to Antonius. 'To pin the bugger down so quickly, I mean.'

'Agreed,' the other officer replied. 'With any luck we'll deal with him in short order and the army can be moved out into garrisons to deal with these various other threats we keep hearing about.

Fronto nodded, though he couldn't help but fear that this was far from over yet. Something was still nagging him about that Arverni noble back in Bibracte and the way the man had spoken of Ambiorix. There was mystery wrapped up in all of this and he couldn't believe it would all be this easy.

* * * * *

Avenna was, Fronto had to admit, impressive. As far as Gallic or Belgic defended settlements went, it ranked up there with the best. It was not large, being perhaps a third of a mile across at the widest point, and claimed no benefit from the topography, lying fairly low in an area of even lower, featureless ground.

But its defences were solid.

A low earth rampart had been topped with a wall of the type they now knew was typical of the Gallic peoples: constructed from a framework of wooden beams, the outer of which was faced with heavy stones between the supporting timber, the inner backed by a solid, earthen bank, and the framework itself packed throughout with a core of rubble and dirt.

It was a solid system and a good one, very hard to bring down with siege engines.

The oppidum seemed to have been constructed in three sections, with a separate enclosure to the west, consisting of perhaps a quarter of the whole, with its own west-facing gate, while the main enclosure with its southern entrance contained a further individual and double-walled hill at its easternmost edge.

'Why the three sections?' Antonius mused.

Fronto, however, had spent years traipsing around similar fortifications all over Gaul. He shrugged. 'There's very little uniformity in the Gauls' settlements, even within the same tribe, so unless you get in and have a look, there's no knowing for sure, but I'd wager that the separate western enclosure is a sacred druid grove. You can see even from here that there's no smoke from household fires rising over the top, and there seem to be a lot of treetops there. If not religious, then it's perhaps some sort of animal and farming compound? The main section is the city itself - you can see the chimney smoke rising. The heavily fortified hill is interesting. I'd expect that's where their council meets, and their leaders live.'

Antonius nodded. 'Seems a fair assessment. And here's mine: this place is too bloody strong by far. It'll take a week to

119

demolish enough of those defences to get inside in sufficient numbers. The cavalry are no use, and any infantry assault is going to be extremely costly. Have you seen that gate?'

Fronto grunted an affirmative as he squinted into the slightly misty cold air. The huge, heavy walls - easily the height of two men - turned sharply inwards, forming a wide approach to the gatehouse, which was set back some way, providing a killing zone perhaps twenty paces wide and as deep before any attacker could reach the huge double gated entrance with its tower above. An attack there would invite death from a hundred arrows, bullets and rocks. Not that the rest of the defences would be any easier, of course. Antonius was right about the cost in manpower.

'Then let's hope we don't need to breach it then, eh?'

Ahead, Caesar gave the signal and the knot of mounted officers, along with Caesar's bodyguard under the command of young Ingenuus, trotted out ahead of the slowly assembling army, making for the gate. Fronto glanced to the side to see his own bodyguard drawn up behind Masgava and Palmatus. They looked somewhat unhappy at remaining with the legions, but Fronto had put his foot down and refused to let them join the staff officers. The general kept giving him funny looks and he was sure it was something to do with his new singulares unit. What he really *didn't* need at the moment was something else to irritate Caesar. The man still barely acknowledged Fronto's existence, despite Antonius' frequent attempts to bring him around. If this went on for much longer, it would hardly be worth remaining in Gaul.

Grumbling under his breath, Fronto rode on with the other officers, sticking close to Priscus and Antonius as they approached the solid, defiant ramparts of the Avenna oppidum. Already the walls were thronged with Nervii, standing with spears or bows and watching the assembling might of the Republic on the plain before them. It had to be a daunting sight, and yet there appeared to be no trace of fear or panic emanating from the city.

As the party approached the gatehouse, more and more figures appeared on the ramparts above and around them, and Fronto began to spy that killing zone before the gates with some trepidation. For a moment he wondered whether Caesar intended to ride straight into that deadly space, but then the general held up his hand and the column halted, Ingenuus and three of his men riding to the front to flank their commander.

There was a long, pregnant pause, and then a groan and a series of thumps as the gate was unbarred and swung open ponderously. A small party of Nervii strode out through the portal on foot, armoured in mail and Gallic helmets, with russet coloured or grey or brown woollen trousers and a variety of equally dour tunics and cloaks. They wore little in the way of jewellery or accoutrements, barring a few torcs or arm rings that indicated their noble rank or their worth as warriors. Three men behind them carried standards bearing stylised wolves and boars, and another group held the huge carnyx horns aloft, preparing themselves. Fronto clenched his teeth against what he knew was coming, and just in time, as the horns started blarting out their 'dying bovine' song of discord.

Antonius, next to him, paled.

'If that is their idea of a fanfare, then the whole world should thank us for trying to silence them for good!'

Fronto shook his head. 'That's *tuneful*. You should hear the songs of the Armorican tribes. It's like a swan trying to swallow a tuba! Or a dog having one inserted from the rear, perhaps.' He grinned, his teeth grinding slightly.

The party of Nervian nobles stopped some twenty paces from the Romans, safely within the reach of their own archers and right in the centre of the killing zone, Fronto noticed. Whatever you could accuse the Nervii of, they apparently were not daft.

'Say your piece, Caesar of the Romans, and begone!' barked out one of the Nervii in surprisingly good Latin. Studying the crowd, Fronto picked out the ubiquitous druid, safely lodged amid the nobles, wearing a dirty grey robe and clutching a staff like some sort of badge of office.

'Arrogant sods, aren't they?' muttered Antonius. 'Do they not see the thirty thousand men lining up behind us?'

'Ridiculously, they're not afraid,' Fronto replied. 'Even if there were only ten of them, they'd show no fear. The Belgic tribes are all mad, and the Nervii are the worst of them. You've met Galronus, yes?'

Caesar raised himself slightly in the saddle, though he already towered over the horseless Nervian nobles.

'You afford us neither fear, nor respect,' he said loudly, 'not that I expected any such thing. But if you think to turn us away so easily, you are not simply brave, but deluded.'

He waited for the words to sink in. The general always knew how to treat with his opposing numbers, and a meaningful pause was only one weapon in his verbal arsenal.

'The Nervii have proved themselves to be repetitive enemies of Rome, rising against our armies time and again, despite the fact that we are here legitimately and at the behest of the Gallic assembly. It is the considered advice of many of my better officers and some of the senators of our Republic that it is time for the Nervii to be removed from the world of men altogether, and left as nothing but a hollow memory of a people.'

Another pause to let that sink in, and Fronto noted a few heads turning at the implication of these words.

'I took a significant step towards agreeing with them when news reached me that our great enemy, the traitor *king,*' - the word spat almost as an insult - 'Ambiorix of the Eburones, has entered into negotiations with the Nervii, among other tribes. Since I know that you are aware of the damage dealt to our legions by the traitor only short months ago - you yourself being involved to a great extent - you will know just how much we owe Ambiorix. This army will not stop killing and burning until he is found and made to suffer the consequences of his actions, and anyone who stands in the way of that retribution is begging to become a part of it.'

An uncomfortable silence.

Perhaps, despite their legendary bravery, the Nervii were realising now just how much they were putting their own necks on the line by maintaining an alliance with the fallen Eburones' king.

'Despite everything, in the hope that the lands of the Belgae can once more be settled into peace and harmony, I am willing to overlook the treacherous decision of your leaders to ally with this snake. If you deliver him to us - or give us the details of his whereabouts if he is not here - I will personally guarantee the life of each and every occupant of Avenna. If you do not comply, I will not leave this place until the charred remains of the houses are indistinguishable from the charred remains of your tribe. You know me as a man of my word, so consider this your final ultimatum. You have the count of one hundred to oblige or I give the order to cut down, burn, kill, rape and crucify every living thing my legions find in Avenna.'

Fronto found himself nodding at the sense of this. While the ultimatum was brutal and impossibly harsh, with the Nervii little other than the threat of utter annihilation would even make them

122

blink. But Caesar had judged his words carefully before he gave them, and the deliberate, slow delivery had produced the desired effect: the small party of nobles were muttering among themselves. While displaying no obvious fear, they were clearly considering the clear threat to their very existence that the gathering legions posed.

The general turned to his standard bearer, holding aloft the 'Taurus' bull emblem of Caesar's command party. 'Give them the count out loud. Let's keep their nerves frayed.'

As the signifer began to count down from one hundred in a loud, clear voice, the activity among the Nervian nobles became a little more frenetic and Antonius grinned. 'He was always this good at playing people, you know? Even when I was a boy, he had my family at his beck and call.'

'I know.' Fronto sighed. 'Look at the poor bastards. They know they're done for. They're just trying to decide whether they have any room to negotiate.'

The signifer had reached 'thirty six' when the Nervians turned back to the Roman party and the apparent 'spokesman' stepped out front. The druid, Fronto noted, had pushed his way angrily out of the rear of the party and was even now making for the gate.

'At least we won't have to make the assault,' Antonius sighed with relief.

'I wouldn't be too sure about that,' Priscus muttered from behind them, and Fronto could only nod his agreement. Somehow he couldn't see Caesar simply walking away from this.

The Nervian leader cleared his throat. 'Since, though you are a low, murderous Roman beast, you are also noted as a man of your word, and you have vouchsafed the lives of our people, the council authorises me to inform you that your enemy Ambiorix is not at Avenna. He has not visited this place at all, but his small party of ambassadors approached our lands and treated with us at the town of Asadunon, which is two days north of here, close to the border of our lands. Whether or not he was among them, we are not certain, but it is very likely the ambassadors remain there still. This is all the knowledge of them we have for you, and it is given freely in return for your clemency.'

Caesar smiled then and Fronto, catching the corner of it from one side, recognised that smile. He took a deep breath.

'Prepare yourselves. Here it comes.'

123

Antonius turned a frown on him just as Caesar opened his mouth with his reply to the Nervii.

'Do not mistake my offer for childish clemency, Nervian. I did not guarantee your *freedom*... just your lives.'

Turning away from the falling faces of the Belgic nobles, who were just now realising what they had done, Caesar gave his clear orders to the entire staff and all the senior officers assembled on the plain loudly enough to be heard even over the walls and inside the oppidum.

'Take Avenna. Do not kill any man, woman or child unless they offer you resistance. When you have the town, chain every last occupant for the slave markets of Narbonensis, commandeer everything of value, butcher the animals, impound the grain and have everything shipped back to Samarobriva.'

The Nervii were blustering now, shouting imprecations and accusing Caesar of breaking his word. The general turned to them with an arched eyebrow.

'I do *not* break my vows. *Ever*! I vouchsafed your lives and you have them, under the conditions I have set. If you resist, however, I am absolved, as you are committing suicide. Now you have my conditions, do not test me further.'

Without further exchange, Caesar turned his horse.

The first few arrows began to come, loosed by archers on the gate tower or the nearby walls, sent without the need of orders from a noble. Ingenuus and his cavalry threw up their shields to protect the general, but he was already almost out of range, having carefully stopped for the parlay at a distance that would render arrows largely harmless.

As the group moved back towards the army, the Praetorian horsemen sheltering their rear ranks, the Nervii rushed back into their gate and the huge timber portal began to close. Caesar turned to Antonius.

'They will resist, of course. You have a solid reputation, Antonius - built upon your years in the east - for ending engagements quickly and decisively. Take Avenna for me. Do it quickly and with as few losses as possible.'

Marcus Antonius nodded to his friend and commander, and turned to the rest of the staff as the general rode off to where other members of his guard were overseeing the erection of his headquarters tent.

124

'Alright. You heard the general. We need to take Avenna quick and easy. I need ideas.'

* * * * *

'This wasn't what I had in mind when I said he needed a small force.' Fronto eyed the soldiers around him.

'We *are* a small force' Palmatus replied with a shrug.

'I was thinking more like three centuries to a cohort. Not less than twenty men who barely know each other.'

'How did you get volunteered for this?'

'Sort of by accident. Antonius asked for ideas. I gave him one, but he thought it was mad and unfeasible. I tried to convince him it could be done and next thing I know, I'm being told to make it happen. In the old days Caesar would either have listened to me and given me a full unit to command or given me a flat no. Antonius is an odd one. Unpredictable, I'd say.'

'Priscus reckons he's dangerous,' Palmatus added quietly.

'He might be right. But there's no denying that he's also good at what he does.'

'Sounds like someone else we all know.'

'Shut up.'

Fronto looked around at the men once again.

He had just shy of two contubernia of soldiers, with his friends commanding one each.

Palmatus' squad of eight men consisted of hand-picked and dangerous legionaries from the Tenth - and one from the Eighth who had been recommended as a homicidal lunatic, which had sparked Palmatus' interest enough to give him a try out. The former legionary had settled on a unit of traditional soldiers, for all their oddities, since he knew the drill and the commands well.

Masgava's squad consisted of three Gauls drawn from the auxiliary cavalry, two Cretan archers from Decius' auxiliary cohort, a slinger from a Balearic cohort and an engineer from the Ninth who had been with the army since the action at Geneva five years ago and had been involved in nearly every project since. There was still one space left in the contubernium, but he and Fronto had decided to leave it empty until he could locate Biorix, who would likely still be serving with the Thirteenth.

So in all: eighteen men, himself included. Against the most important and best fortified city of the most dangerous tribe among the clearly battle-mad Belgae. The more he thought about it, the more deranged it sounded.

Still, he had insisted himself into this situation, and now there was a certain amount of professional pride involved. He knew it *could* be done, and so now he had to prove it, not just to Antonius the disbeliever, or even to himself. But to Caesar. The old man might be made to reconsider his position if Fronto gave him Avenna.

The small knot of men - a motley collection to be sure - stood in a low, tree-lined dell, where a trickle of spring water flowed into a stream, a weathered, unrecognisable shapeless lump of an ancient Gaulish deity overseeing the flow. A sacred spring. For luck, Fronto pulled the small figurine of Fortuna from his neckline, kissed it, splashed sacred water over it and then dropped it back onto the thong beneath his tunic.

He was unarmoured. In fact, he wore no helm and carried no shield, clad in only a drab tunic and with his sword on the baldric - just like the rest of his unconventional singulares. This action was about being fast and quiet, not slow and well-defended. His gaze played across the other fourteen figures in the dell. He had tried to remember names, but he'd only been introduced to them twice, and simply could not hold them. He knew there was a man called Quietus, because the irony of taking him on a crazed hectic night-time raid was not lost on him, but he couldn't remember which one he was. He had the suspicion, with ever increasing irony, that he was the big fellow who kept snorting his runny nose and appeared to have a permanent twitch.

The missing three men were even now on their way back. He could hear them moving through the undergrowth, light as cats, recognisable only because he was expecting them and because they were making the strange '*kua kua*' noise of the little crakes that inhabited the lower swampy areas of the region.

The trio of native riders had been the obvious men to send out as scouts and had disappeared on their mission half an hour ago, and it was with a great sense of relief that Fronto watched them appear through the brush and slide down into the hollow, pausing only to make a brief devotion at the spring and take a sip of water before reporting to Fronto.

'How is it?'

'Poorly defended.' One of the scouts scratched a map in the dirt with a stick, drawing the three circles of the settlement's walls, two linked like a figure 8 and a third within the eastern, larger, loop.

He pointed to the one at the west. 'You were correct in your thoughts, sir. It is a nemeton - a sanctuary of the shepherds. There are three buildings only, and a grove that is still used. The ramparts are guarded by men from the main city, but widely-spaced. They do not apparently consider it important to defend. They know it is separated from the city itself by a wall.'

'And that is true,' Fronto smiled. 'But it is a mental weak spot. They will not expect an attack to come through there. Two things bother me, and two things only. How do you three feel about mounting an attack through this 'nemeton'?'

The three Remi horsemen shrugged. To the Remi, the Nervii would be more of an enemy than Rome could ever be. Until Caesar had brought the army here, the tribes of the Belgae had spent hundreds of years at war with each other. And the Remi may still respect the druid class, but these were *Nervii* druids.

'Good. And you two?' He looked across at the archers. 'How fast can you get a fire arrow off?'

'With a ready-prepared arrow, a count of twenty at most.'

'Impressive. Try to be faster. Time will likely be an issue.'

He looked around at everyone again. 'Alright. Is everyone happy with their tasks?'

There were a variety of nods and mumbled affirmatives and he took a deep breath. 'Let's do it then.'

With no further words - there would be no more speech until stealth was no longer an issue - the group scurried out of the dell and through the scrub land. The shadows were now becoming intermixed and almost indistinguishable in the fading light. The timing had been very carefully selected. Dusk would help mask their movements, given the sparse cover that nature had afforded them, and the men on the walls would be weary, their eyes tired, and less alert than usual. Plus Roman forces attacked during the light - usually working from dawn, so no one would expect this.

But it had to be done quickly. The scouts had had the reasonable light to work by. Now the attack would go ahead in the dim hazy indigo of evening. But they had to achieve their goal while there was still enough light for Antonius to bring the army to bear.

Moving from tree to tree and ducking behind scrub, trying to stick to the hollows afforded by streams or natural ditches, the motley assault moved across the flatland towards the western end of the oppidum. Squinting as he went, Fronto finally started to see the walls more clearly and could pick out the men on watch there. He smiled in gratitude. The druidic grove was indeed sparsely guarded, with only three men visible from this southern approach. Three men. Perfect. Thank you, Fortuna.

On and on they crept, as fast as they dared - the natives faster than Fronto would have recommended, but still they closed on the ramparts without an alarm going up, and Fronto found himself gripping the figurine on the thong through his tunic, mouthing prayers and offers as they moved.

Masgava gave a silent hand signal and the attack separated into three groups, one peeling off to the left and the other right, six men in each group, including one missile weapon and one native. Fronto followed the one to the right, the man in front of him a stocky legionary with a rope coiled over his shoulder - again one of three. The engineer from the Ninth, Fronto noted. Iuvenalis, he seemed to remember suddenly.

His world had then shrunk from an attack of eighteen men to an assault by six. He realised that the archers had gone off the other ways and his unit was relying on the slinger. Some might say slingers were less effective, but Fronto had nearly had his brains knocked out of his head with a slingshot twice now, and he would disagree. The Remi scout led the group, the slinger behind, then two lithe and dangerous looking legionaries that he vaguely recognised, followed by the engineer, and then him.

It took what appeared to be only a couple of dozen heartbeats to reach position behind an ailing yew tree and its surrounding undergrowth, and the Remi gave another little crake call. It was answered in only a few heartbeats by a 'kua kua' from somewhere nearby, out of sight. A heart-stoppingly long pause was finally followed by a third call.

No sooner had that final noise risen than the Spaniard who had been crouched near the tree, bullet already in his sling, rose and whipped it round just once, his arm coming up and over as he released the cord at the top of the arc. It amazed Fronto to watch a skilled slinger at work, and there were no better than those drawn from the Balearic Islands. Youths and the unskilled would whirl the damn thing round for hours, making a 'whup-whup' noise. Even the damned treacherous tribune Hortius a couple of years ago had whirled it three times before striking Fronto, but a truly skilled professional would be able to rotate it just once, the only sound being the faint flap of the loosened thong after and the hum of the bullet through the air.

The figure on the rampart disappeared instantly, thrown backwards by the blow to the face, most certainly dead before his feet left the ground. As Fronto strained to look left, the next man had also gone and even as he squinted he saw the third vanish silently, a shaft - invisible at this distance - through his throat.

The wall was clear.

Without the need for commands, the engineer with the rope ran forward and uncoiled it, holding the end near the iron grapple - a naval design, but put to good use here too. With a few test swings, the soldier heaved the rope up over the rampart. Fronto couldn't see the other groups, but the engineer with his party was clearly an expert, and the grapple caught and held, even when he tested his considerable bulk on it. Pulling it taut, he nodded to the Remi scout, who grasped hold and began to climb fast, hand over hand and legs dangling.

Fronto hated climbing ropes. Always had. It was one of the few exercises Masgava had had him doing last year that he truly loathed. But now, at least, he was grateful for the practice.

By the time the Remi had reached the top - Fronto mentally noted that he must learn these men's names - the engineer was already on his way up and the slinger was spitting on his hands and rubbing them ready for the climb.

Fronto, determined not to be that officer who was 'just along for the ride', made sure he was next, before the other two legionaries, and as the slinger, light, lithe and energetic, neared the top of the rope, Fronto grasped and began to haul.

Once more he marvelled over the difference last year's fitness regime with Masgava had made. As he struggled up the rope, using his feet and his hands both to pull and push, he considered how two years ago he would never have stood a chance of making it to the top, let alone quickly and without exhausting himself.

As he reached the parapet, one of the men reached out and helped him over onto the rampart top, where he stayed in a crouch and scanned the area. The same was happening at the other two assault points. Because there was a good chance that other guards across the compound were watching the walls occasionally, the Remi scouts were standing, taking the position of the dead defenders, while the others crouched out of sight.

The area enclosed by this rampart was heavily green and wooded, with a small cluster of huts near a clearing at the centre, where rituals were presumably carried out. It was empty, apparently, or at least the priestly inhabitants were safely ensconced in their residences. The far rampart had men spaced wide-apart along it, around to the western and northern sides, but no alarm had been given. There was only one single guard on the wall between the nemeton area and the main town, and he appeared to be slumped, possibly asleep, but certainly inattentive in any case.

Where the two walled areas' ramparts joined, Fronto had expected some sort of barrier, given the lack of a gate between the two enclosures, but it seemed he was in luck. The wall carried on uninterrupted from where he crouched all the way to the main gate, though the concentration of men increased there.

Even as he was turning to give a signal, he realised it was unnecessary. The parties that had scaled the walls further along were already in motion, led by the irrepressible Masgava and Palmatus. The Remi scouts remained in position to allay any suspicion while the other ten men scuttled along the wall to join him, keeping low and in the shadows.

In a matter of twenty heartbeats, fourteen men were gathered around Fronto and moving off, drawing their weapons with a quiet rasp and leaving the three Remi standing silent and still in position.

A thrill throbbed in Fronto's blood and he realised only as he caught the worried expression of the legionary next to him that he was probably grinning like a jackal, or possibly a wolf. He was right where he should be at last, after almost two years of faffing about, and even more than that of meddling in political chicanery. He was in the midst of combat. He had trouble stifling the laugh that almost burst from him. The legionary next to him afforded him a couple of feet of extra space, in the manner that sane men avoid the mad.

He didn't care.

The party of fifteen soldiers burst onto the main town's defences like a wave breaking over rocks, overrunning the two guards standing closest, who hardly had the chance to see their death approach in the failing, dim light. Fronto felt his blade meet the resistance of only tunic and cloak before sliding between ribs and tearing the life from the Nervian guard, while his other hand went around the head and clamped over his mouth to prevent the cry. The next guard along the wall opened his mouth to yell a warning and toppled backwards, a dark arrow shaft jutting from his eye socket.

Other Nervii were trying to bring weapons to bear and shout out a warning, but Masgava was faster than any of them, dispatching one with a backhanded strike across the neck as he ran and then ploughing the other down to the wall top, knocking all the breath from him and killing him with one masterful blow. Behind him, legionaries moved to take care of others. Palmatus was pointing out targets before he himself slammed open the door to the tower above the gate and rushed inside.

They were here! It had sounded like an impossible task, as far as Antonius was concerned.

A cry went up from the wall at the far side, but they'd reached the tower above the gate. The game was up and they were discovered, but it no longer mattered. Two legionaries were busy putting down another guard.

'Now!' he yelled.

With the professionalism and discipline of the Roman military, his force split off and splintered. The archers and the slinger disappeared into the tower, along with another legionary, fast on the heels of Palmatus. Two brief squawks within announced the success of the Roman officer, and then two of the missile troops appeared at the openings, loosing arrows and bullets down at any defender they could see. The third was not visible for a long moment, but then finally appeared, his arrow blazing with golden fire as he drew his bow string back and released. The fiery shaft shot up into the air, trailing smoke like a comet.

Fronto and the engineer took up positions on the wall, to either side of the tower, preparing to hold the gate top from any more Nervii coming along the wall, which they would be doing in force as soon as the alarm had spread throughout Avenna and they had mobilised a stronger defence. The three Remi were now on their way to lend a hand, and the remaining legionaries split into two groups of four and descended the rear slope of the rampart, Masgava leading them as they rushed the men on duty at the gate below. The four Nervii on the ground had no chance, and were butchered with little resistance. Fronto peered over the edge and realised that he had lost two of those men in the assault, but Palmatus and three others were standing in an arc, preparing to meet the Nervii from the city, who were approaching with a roar, somewhere back among the houses, while the other two heaved open the gates.

A pained cry drew his attention and he looked along the wall to see that the three Remi scouts had run into a little trouble, one of them on the floor, yelping and clutching his stomach. The other two finished off their attacker and then granted their companion a mercy blow, finishing him off before running on to join Fronto at the gate,

The sound of the approaching legions began to rise above the action at the walls, and the rhythmic beat was a balm to him. Antonius, true to his word, had had the Ninth and Tenth poised ready to move at the signal, and even before the fire arrow had touched the ground the first cohorts were approaching the gate.

The Nervii were coming from inside. The legions were coming from outside.

It might appear to be a race, but Fronto knew better. The Nervii were unprepared and would be coming in dribs and drabs as they armed. The gatehouse and its killing zones were designed for easy defence and it would be just as easy for them to defend as for the Nervii. They would hold until the army were through. And then it would be easy. And bloody.

Fronto laughed like a man possessed.

Chapter Seven

It took less than half an hour for the elation of swift victory to wear off.

Fronto stood in the main public forum-like area at the centre of Avenna, before a large stone-and-timber construction that seemed to have served as some sort of crude curia for the Nervian 'senate', with a temple to one of their hairy, hammer-wielding Gods off to one side and a number of shops around the periphery, a well - where they had gathered - in the centre.

Carefully, he examined the beautiful blade in his hand, lifting it so that the pale watery sunlight gleamed on the perfect Noric steel. There was no trace of the gore that had encrusted it half an hour ago - Fronto had always been careful to clean his blade after a battle, but since acquiring the murderous tribune Menenius' astounding gladius, he had become almost obsessive over the matter. The great Gods of Rome smiled approvingly from faces of perfect glittering orichalcum. With a sigh, he slid it into the sheath and tried to block out the activity all around him.

'Not pretty, is it?' Palmatus muttered, and Fronto looked around in surprise at the statement only to realise that the former legionary - now officer of singulares - was actually speaking to his counterpart, Masgava.

Palmatus had dealt with the removal of the tower's occupants with the casual brutality of a veteran legionary with experience of more than one war, and had then returned to help hold the wall top until the army broke through the defences and began the systematic destruction of Avenna. The result was that he now stood here in his drab, dun-coloured tunic, the same as the rest of theirs, so liberally splashed and spattered with mud and blood that it was difficult to tell where material ended and skin began.

Masgava, conversely, had stood in a line of soldiers - a fighting style totally unfamiliar for an arena trained combatant - and defended the gate from all comers until Antonius' men had swept past them and relieved the small attacking force, and yet the only marks on him were three small lines and splashes of red. His gut wound had held up and stayed closed throughout his first real action, though he complained of discomfort. He did, however, look somewhat hollow-eyed and angry. Not at the battle - death was an old friend and constant companion to the big Numidian gladiator. No… what happened afterwards was the cause of *his* concern.

'Why is this being allowed?' the big man replied with his own question.

'Because the general wills it.' Fronto replied in a weary voice. 'It is in the nature of the career soldier to take every opportunity to make the most of a situation for financial gain. And beyond simple loot, some are simply too blood-drunk to stop. Their centurions will eventually take control of them and instil order, but without the general specifically forbidding it, a little looting and destruction is almost expected. In fairness, Caesar is generally quite humane in this respect. He doesn't often approve of wanton post-battle chaos, but in light of Ambiorix and Caesar's need for revenge, the standing orders now have changed. At least he's forbidden random rape and murder.'

'Some of the things I've seen in the last quarter hour might challenge that.'

Fronto shrugged. '*Random*, I said. The orders to hold back only applied to those who surrendered willingly. Those who choose to resist have no defence, and Caesar won't blink twice at their fate.'

Masgava still seemed unimpressed.

Fronto turned and took in the havoc he had been blocking out. Already, sizeable portions of Avenna were aflame. While legionaries had herded the captive survivors into the smaller squares here and there and roped them together for transport to Samarobriva and then the slave markets, others had begun the systematic looting and impounding of anything of use or value. Once an entire neighbourhood had been emptied, it was fired.

Here and there warriors, women, or even children fought back. Most of them were killed on the spot by the legionaries, who had little interest in struggling with a difficult native when loot was there to be had. Many of the struggling children had escaped where the legionaries had simply let them go rather than wrestle and then murder a minor, but the women had been treated worst, as was always the case in the aftermath of a siege.

Black, oily smoke poured into the air from three neighbourhoods and the crackle and roar of flames was periodically punctuated by the crash as a building fell in. Screams and shouts and occasionally the ring of steel on iron echoed across the city.

'What was the final number?'

'Five,' Palmatus said with a satisfied tone. Fronto nodded. Five losses was more than just acceptable, given what they had achieved and under what conditions. Of course, five of eighteen was more than a quarter, but still, for their success…

'One of the Remi, three of the good old boys from your Tenth and an archer, who just managed to get his fire arrow off before he collapsed.'

'Somehow,' Fronto replied quietly, 'I can't see replacements being a problem with Antonius backing us.'

'I take it you've warmed to the idea of a singulares guard then?' Palmatus smiled.

'They have their uses, yes.'

'Oi, oi,' Masgava nudged Palmatus and the three turned to look in the same direction. Fronto's remaining ten men were gathered in a knot nearby, rubbing their arms and feet and sloshing water down the nape of their neck, while at the corner of the square legionaries were dragging a reluctant future-slave from his ravaged house. Between the two groups, though, Galronus was trotting over on horseback with half a dozen Gauls behind him.

'Not much for cavalry to do here,' Fronto said as the Remi officer approached and reined in. It was sometimes hard to remember that Galronus was of the Belgae. Though his hair and moustaches were long and braided, and he wore a torc around his neck and the long 'trousers' of the Gallic peoples, his clothing was exquisite, sewn in Rome by a craftsman at an extortionate price in fabrics acquired from as far afield as Arabia and Hispania, and dyed the madder red of the legions. Indeed, his tunic was of a Roman cut anyway, cinched with a Roman belt buckled with a silver Medusa head. He even sat atop a four-horned Roman saddle. Fronto found himself wondering whether his ever-more-Romanised friend was a talking point among the men under his command.

'Not a good place for my people to be at all,' Galronus grunted as he swung down from the horse and gestured to another of the riders. 'But I thought I would let you hear this yourself.'

Fronto waited patiently, Palmatus and Masgava edging closer to listen in.

After a moment of silence, the man Galronus had invited stepped around his horse and approached with a nod of recognition. Short and wiry for a Gaul, he was instantly familiar.

'I know him. A scout?'

Galronus nodded. 'Searix of the Condrusi. One of the senior scouts in the army. His tribe are as loyal as the Remi, but their lands are trapped between the Nervii, the Eburones and the Treveri. Danger lurks there for a supporter of Caesar.'

'Then he's to be commended for sticking to his oath,' Fronto said quietly. 'Many tribes in less difficult circumstances seem to be having trouble doing so.'

'That's sort of the problem, Marcus.'

'Go on.' Fronto had a sinking feeling as he saw the darkness in the eyes of the scout. Galronus nodded to Searix, who moistened his lips.

'The officers say that you are a man who listens without judging.'

'The officers,' Fronto replied carefully, 'apparently do not know me that well.'

Galronus gave a meaningful frown and Fronto sighed. 'Alright. Let me guess: you have a problem with something but will not take it to Caesar either because you think he won't listen to you, or you think he will and then won't like what he hears?'

Searix had the decency to look slightly uncomfortable.

'Go on,' Fronto prompted wearily.

'This is bad for the allegiances to Rome.' Searix indicated the burning city with a sweep of his hand. 'For those who took oaths.'

'It's considerably worse for the Nervii, who didn't. Bear in mind, Searix, that the Nervii have never even claimed to ally with us and we are under no obligation to them. Whereas the Remi and your own Carusi -'

'Condrusi.'

'Them too - have a standing alliance with Rome and this treatment will never be visited upon Rome's allies.'

Again, Searix looked uncomfortable.

'That promise is not enough?'

'For some,' Searix replied in a defeated voice. 'The Remi are in no danger and enjoy Roman favour. Other tribes, though, for all their oaths and loyalties, lie in direct danger from Rome's most bitter enemies. My people sit as an island of your Pax Romana amid a sea of rabid Rome-haters. It will not surprise you to hear that there is always a small portion of our tribe that maintains we would be better discarding our oath.'

'Of course. In their position, I might think twice myself,' Fronto replied. 'But two things remain fact. Firstly: Rome will win any war she sets her mind to. The world knows this. A hundred beaten enemy peoples know this. And siding with Rome is the fast track to a glorious golden age, while facing off against her is a sure path to destruction. Secondly: breaking an oath is the act of a coward and a traitor, and just as Rome hates an oathbreaker, the Belgae are also a people founded on the nobility of spirit and the reliability of a man's word.'

It was truth. These two facts had become instrumental in Rome's rapid expansion over the past two centuries, and every new campaign made them more central and certain.

'Honour,' Searix nodded 'is paramount to a warrior. And our tribe honours their oath. But the more we watch your army act *without* honour, the more voices join that minority in our tribe that condemns Rome for a butcher. This new policy of Caesar's is destroying his reputation among his allies.'

Fronto sighed and sagged back onto the well's lip.

'If you think this is the be-all and end-all of Roman savagery, you really have seen nothing yet. Ask a Carthaginian about Rome's vengeance - if you can find one! And Caesar is far from the most forgiving and peaceable of Romans. But the fact remains that these are our avowed enemies, and they are suffering for their actions. No such cruelty would be visited upon an ally.'

'The Condrusi are still your allies,' Searix replied somewhat stiffly. 'We will remain so as long as those of us who respect our word outnumber those who fear your betrayal. But as I say this, remember that there are other tribes out there sending you grain, supplying you with horses and warriors, guarding your backs, who will be experiencing the same difficulty as us. And some of them may have less of a grip on their oath than us. If Rome is to maintain her alliance with the tribes and continue to enjoy their support, someone is going to have to turn Caesar from this most dangerous path down which he has us walking.'

Fronto rubbed his scalp and was surprised when his hand came away stained pink. Other people's blood, of course, but still...

'Thank you for confiding in us, Searix. See what you can do to reassure your people. They may be trapped, but the Eburones are a shadow of what they were and the Treveri are having too much trouble with Labienus to turn on them. And of course, the Nervii are now suffering.' He saw the darkening of the scout's expression and held up his hands defensively. 'Frankly, Caesar is considerably less likely to listen to me than he is to you, but I will see what I can do. To some extent, I agree with what you say.'

137

Searix nodded and turned, striding back to his horse.

Galronus waved away his men, and they escorted the scout back through the city, in case he be mistaken for a Nervian and enslaved or butchered. At a gesture from the Remi officer, they took his horse with them. Galronus rolled his shoulders and produced a skin of wine from somewhere about his person.

'Today I feel the need,' Fronto grumbled and reached out as Galronus passed it over.

'It is more serious than it sounds,' Galronus said quietly.

'What?'

'Searix down-played the trouble for your benefit. But I have heard unhappy rumblings even among the Remi.'

'That'll be the fault of your turd-flavoured beer,' Palmatus snorted, earning a gimlet stare from the Remi.

'Still, Marcus, feelings are starting to turn against Rome at the sight of burning houses, enslaved grey-beards and dead children. Some feel that Caesar went back on his word here, whatever the general says about his actual terms. If he keeps to this course, he may soon find that he is facing all of Gaul rather than a few rebellious tribes.'

'It's all about bloody Ambiorix,' Fronto snapped. 'That one man is costing us dear. Far more than the legion and a half and some senior officers he's credited with. Even with his tribe smashed, he manages to stir up trouble against us. But worse still, he's earned Caesar's wrath, and we all know that Caesar is not a man to turn from a path laid down in anger. The general is set to harrow all of the north in order to flush out that little Eburone rat, and nothing we say will likely turn him away from it.'

He threw an arm out to what he thought might be the north-east.

'Somewhere out there is a town called Asadunon. Ambiorix or his runt advisors might be there - and pray he is, as that'd end this whole mess - so be prepared. In the morning we march to Asadunon and they will be lucky if they get half as good treatment as the people of Avenna. And it will continue to get worse until Caesar has his hands around Ambiorix's neck and squeezes.'

'Then something needs to be done.'

The four men fell silent for a long moment and finally Fronto grunted and stood, passing the wine skin back to Galronus. 'I am going to find Antonius and try and pass this news on as nicely as possible. Thank you, Galronus. And you two? Best get everyone back to camp and rested and fed. We'll be on to Asadunon first thing tomorrow. And start asking around for five replacements for our losses. Looking at the situation after the last fight, we could do with someone who knows their way around a poultice. Find a capsarius – preferably one who ignores orders from his patients. They're the good ones.'

Masgava and Palmatus nodded and Fronto turned and left, seeking the army's second most senior officer. Galronus shook his head sadly. 'This gets worse year upon year. Four summers ago, when my tribe were first tied to Rome, we saw a future of mutual benefit, with greatness for us all. We made our mark in Caesar's ledger, as did others, but we thought that by now there would be a lucrative peace. Instead we exist in a state of interminable war. I have seen enough of Rome now to know that there is no point in turning away from you. You will win in the end, and we are better to accept the *tunica* and the *wine* now and benefit than to disappear from the histories in a swathe of blood. But how long can this land stand continual war before it becomes a waste ground habitable only by scavengers and ghosts?'

Palmatus and Masgava seemed to be having an unspoken conversation, their brows and eyes doing most of the work. Galronus narrowed his own. 'What are you two up to?'

'You're right, Galronus. Something must be done. And I think we know what it is.'

'Care to elucidate?'

Palmatus shook his head. 'Not at this point. But could you do me a favour? We need to replenish our men and - though Fronto wants a capsarius - I'd like to take on four of the five from Gallic stock. I'll look into the Thirteenth and Fourteenth when we get back to them, since I hear there's a lot of staunch Gauls among them. But I'd like another of your Remi, and one of the Con... the men from Searix's tribe... if you can arrange that for me. Preferably one of the cleverest and quietest.'

Galronus' already narrowed eyes almost closed with suspicion.

'I will see what I can do.'

Masgava grinned. 'I like the way you think, Palmatus, my friend.'

* * * * *

'That is an *oppidum*?' Antonius snorted.

'After Avenna, it lacks a certain something, does it not?' the scout said quietly. Galronus, sitting next to Searix, peered off into the mist, nodding at the other horseman's words. The weather had warmed somewhat this morning for the march, but a thick, fleecy mist had overlaid the entire land and seemed unwilling to dissipate, or even to thin a great deal.

The party of a dozen senior officers, plus scouts and bodyguards, sat on a low rise with the best view afforded of the oppidum of Asadunon in the obfuscating mists.

It was, as Searix had noted, lacking.

Defence-wise it had a low rampart of the more basic form: a tall timber palisade, revetted with an earth bank that produced a walkway atop. The single gate - this place hardly needed more than one - was a simple matter of two wooden leaves that closed and barred. No walkway over. No tower.

There did not appear to be anyone on the walls, though the mist made everything uncomfortably indistinct.

Of the apparent size and complexity of the oppidum the scouts had reported less than a hundred inhabitants at an estimate, and perhaps forty houses. No public buildings or the like. No towers on the palisade for the entire circuit. Fronto estimated that a single century could overrun the place faster than they could put up their tents.

'Tell me of the other compound,' Caesar commanded quietly, his voice slightly muffled in the fog.

'There is a sanctuary to Epona, the Lady of Horses, to the north. It is perhaps half a mile distant and the two compounds will probably be hidden from one another in the mist. The sanctuary has a similar defence system to this, a temple and a nemeton, both cared for by perhaps a dozen men.'

'Do we take Asadunon first and risk our prey fleeing if they are in the druidic centre, or move on and attempt to take the religious compound and the village simultaneously?' Antonius asked quietly.

'Speed is now of the essence.' Caesar sighed. 'The more we tarry, the more chance there is of the Nervii becoming aware of our presence and our quarry escaping.'

'If they're here,' Fronto noted sourly. Caesar gave him a sharp glance, but said nothing in reply. It was a possibility that had been discussed under people's breath all day.

140

'Take the cavalry out in an arc and secure the druids.' Caesar gestured to Galronus. 'One wing should be sufficient and your men will be comfortable in the terrain.' He shifted his glance to the former legate of the Tenth. 'Take Fronto with you - he seems to have acquired a talent for opening up tight-sealed clamshells.'

It was, Fronto noted, the first time since his arrival at Samarobriva that the general had actually indicated that Fronto was both present and of value. Despite the dark, unfriendly voice in which the general had addressed him, it was progress.

With a quick nod to Masgava and Galronus, who sat astride horses some twenty paces away, Fronto turned Bucephalus and walked the big black beast back towards the waiting army. The small knot of Fronto's singulares who had been exchanging looks of mutual distrust with Caesar's own Praetorian guard, turned their mounts with varying degrees of skill and bumbled after him like some sort of comedy troupe that would entertain arena-goers before the main events. Masgava had insisted that if Fronto was to be mounted it made sense for his singulares to acquire horses too, else how could they be expected to protect him. The decision had been warmly accepted by the Gauls, who were all-but born in the saddle, and by a few of the others, who either had experience on horseback in earlier life, or who simply relished the idea of not marching from A to B to C. Others were less impressed. Most particularly Palmatus, who clung to the fact that he would rather walk a thousand miles than ride a hundred. In the end, Masgava's logic had overridden his defiance, and even Fronto could not find a reasonable argument against. The singulares were now a mounted troop, courtesy of Galronus' gifts.

As the group closed on Galronus' wing, Fronto pulled alongside the Remi officer, Palmatus and Masgava behind him.

'It's exceedingly unlikely that Ambiorix is here. Even if he is in the area, he won't be around the druids.'

'Oh?'

'Remember that nobleman back at Bibracte? He was a friend of the druids but no friend of Ambiorix, apparently. If that's the case, Ambiorix will not be here.'

The Remi noble nodded thoughtfully. 'You realise that druids are not going to meekly surrender?'

'A dozen men? I have more than that number of singulares, without your thousand cavalry, Galronus.'

141

'But you must take at least one of them alive, for Caesar to interrogate.'

Fronto nodded. 'I'll do you a favour. None of your lads are going to be stunningly happy at ravaging a sacred grove. You lot surround the place and prevent escapes and we'll go in and deal with it.'

Galronus nodded. It would sit better with his men not to be arresting and executing druids.

Moments later, they were moving off along the route the native scouts had taken, down into the shallow dip that led in a gentle curve around to the west of Asadunon, and then out onto a gentle incline that rose to the north beyond.

The terrain here looked like a ruffled blanket, with gentle humps and dips. The analogy brought back a flash of memory, and Fronto had a mental image as clear as day of the gentle and soft-spoken Crispus sitting opposite, surrounded by their friends, some three years ago and a lifetime away.

'This land is somewhat like a lumpy sleeping pallet,' the young legate had said. 'You cannot sleep comfortably, so you have to flatten out the lump, but then a lump forms somewhere else. No matter what you do, there will always be a new lump forming somewhere. And the more you play with it, trying to make it comfortable, the more lumps you have until, in the end, there is nothing else for it but to discard the pallet and begin again with a new one.'

Asadunon and the Epona shrine were yet another bump in this seemingly-interminable lumpy pallet. And Crispus. Poor, young, promising Crispus, had been brutally murdered by Gallic traitors. *A lump to be flattened.* Caesar's current policy may be dangerous, but there were times when Fronto could hardly deny the pull of it. Crispus would never rest well until revenge had been taken.

'You stay safely outside. I'd send my Belgic singulares out with you, but they have to be reliable, and I have to know that they will do what must be done.'

Again, Galronus nodded.

As they neared the top of the slope they slowed, remembering the words of the scouts. Asadunon was now lost in the mist almost half a mile to the south. The white blanket that covered the rumpled pallet of the land deadened noise so effectively that he could hear no sign of the thousands of men less than a mile away, moving to take Asadunon.

At the crest of the low hill, they were afforded their first view of the shrine compound of Epona.

A low rampart with a palisade surrounded a circular area perhaps fifty paces across. Despite what the scouts had said, the rampart here was, to the experienced eye of a Roman officer, nothing like the one that enclosed the village. This was lower and simpler. More a social divide than a defence. Inside, the trees had been trained into two concentric circles, surrounding what appeared to be a paved, central oval, bounded by low steps and squat standing stones. At the northern end stood a small hovel - a shrine apparently, built in the stone-and-timber style of almost all northern Gallic structures. There appeared to be tall wooden posts standing to either side of that temple building, and half a dozen other structures evenly-spaced around the outer edge.

Only two figures were visible from here, both at the near edge of the central oval, one seated on a stone, while the other appeared to be raking or hoeing the ground. It looked so sickeningly peaceful and pleasant that Fronto had momentary cause to doubt his plan. *Only* momentary, though. Images flashed through his mind of druids cursing him, defiant as they drove the Gauls to rebellion, of the maiming and burning of horses and riders by Germanic priests back in their first year in Gaul, of that bastard druid with the sword and the iron crown in Britannia who had tried to carve him into a new shape.

Don't be fooled by their apparent pacifism! He grunted to himself.

'How do you want to do this?' Galronus muttered.

'Quickly and simply. Send your men out in both directions and surround the place, then close in until you're just outside the rampart. In this fog there's little chance of us getting a signal and Asadunon could already be under attack. We'll go straight in.'

Galronus nodded and, with a couple of simple gestures, sent his riders off to the east and west to surround the sacred enclosure.

Fronto looked back at his small force. They were still short three men, until they returned to the rest of the army - Palmatus and Masgava had been adamant about saving space for someone, but with sixteen in total, and all fighting men, they could hardly expect trouble from a dozen priest-folk.

With the assurance of a force superior in every way, Fronto and his singulares rode down the gentle slope and towards the gate which still stood wide open. As they approached the defences,

Fronto felt the hair rise on the back of his neck. For a moment, he chided himself on his over-superstitious nature, but then Bucephalus wrenched his black head this way and that, his muscles bunching unnecessarily, breath coming in short heavy snorts, steaming in the air, betraying his state of heightened nerves.

The shiver began and Fronto noted that several of his companions were looking apprehensively back and forth. The place was exuding an almost tangible aura of something unpleasant, and everyone felt it, especially the horses.

'There's no wildlife,' Masgava whispered on his left side. Fronto cocked his head. There was certainly no birdsong and no rustle in the grass or undergrowth, but that was not necessarily a surprise, given the conditions.

'Could be entirely natural.'

'Why are the horses nervous?' Palmatus added, struggling to control the steed over whom he had minimal mastery at the best of times.

'Same reason as us, I guess.'

'But isn't this a shrine to a horse Goddess?'

Fronto's shiver came back and brought some friends.

'Swords out, lads. Something's amiss.'

The men around him unfastened the carrying straps and lifted their shields from their backs, each still encased in its leather cover for travelling, shouldering the shields and drawing their swords.

Knowing that despite his nerves it was his duty to enter first, he pushed Bucephalus out front, Masgava and Palmatus hurrying to join him, the rest following on closely.

The gate remained open. There was no sound of movement from within. No shouts of alarm or running feet. All there was, floating almost ethereal on the top edge of the air, was a haunting melody of strings and a hollow, childlike voice, raised in sad song.

The family of shivers formed into a thorough, spine-tingling shudder as Fronto passed across the threshold of the sacred site and between the carefully manicured trees towards the central oval. It reminded him - somewhat unpleasantly - of walking down a darkened corridor to enter the oval floor of an arena, something he'd done once or twice in his life.

'Can we just leave and say there was nothing here?' muttered Palmatus, his horse struggling for dominance over the rider.

Even Masgava, a master horseman, and a man Fronto had never yet seen fazed by anything, looked distinctly uncomfortable.

'Just be prepared. Things could turn horribly ugly at very short notice.'

The Roman force, walking their beasts, moved into the centre of the sacred enclosure and Fronto reined in close to where they had observed the two men. A long rake stood leaning against one of the taller stones, the gravelled ground surrounding the oval 'arena' perfectly weeded and raked flat and neat. The taller figure had disappeared. The shorter one was still seated on the stone and Fronto now realised, as they closed on the youth with the delicate lyre, picking out a sad tune and warbling along to it, that it was a girl. With surprise, he found himself suddenly re-evaluating his plans. The death of pre-pubescent girls was not high on his list of priorities, whatever her religion or people.

While his eyes took in every part of the *nemeton*, a part of him wondered what the tune was, though a quick glance at the Remi and the Condrusi among his party suggested that he'd be better off not knowing. The colour had drained from their faces.

Despite the eerie stillness and the neatness of the place, there was a faint aroma of horse dung that they had not brought with them. Remembering the nature of this shrine, Fronto wondered if Epona had sacred horses in her groves and - if so - were they in one of the huts rather than roaming free among the trees?

Shudder.

'This compound,' he announced, his voice cracking irritably, 'is now under the control of Rome, as is the oppidum of Asadunon across the hill.'

The girl seemed to ignore him completely, continuing her song. The reaction unnerved him more than ever. Quietly, he turned to the nearest of the Remi riders, who looked close to panic.

'Your druids have girls with them?'

'*Uidluia.*' The man announced, his voice shaky.

'And for those of us with less command of Gaulish?'

'A seer-poet, sir. Revered. Blessed. Sacred.'

Well, Fronto thought to himself, he had wanted to test the loyalty and obedience of his new unit, and this looked like it would probably be the strongest test he could ever throw at them.

'You,' he gestured. 'Girl? Where are the others?'

Expertly edging the lyre into the crook of her elbow so that she could continue the tune one-handed, the girl used her other to point to the small temple of Epona on the far side of the oval. He gestured to the capsarius in his group.

'Damionis, come out front and watch her. Don't hurt her.' His words seemed to resonate well with his Belgic men, and they settled their skittish horses as best they could, as the reedy, pale figure of the capsarius rode out to the girl.

Fronto gestured for Masgava and Palmatus to follow him and, dismounting, he led Bucephalus to one of the larger standing stones which had iron rings driven into it, almost as if designed for a hitching post.

The three men continued on foot, crossing the oval and approaching the shrine. The structure was the same as most of the better class of Gallic buildings - of stone courses half way up the door frame, and then of timber and thatch. A step up from the wattle and daub of peasant dwellings, but still poor compared to the great temples of the Roman world. There were no windows in evidence, and the door was shut.

Fronto quickly pictured every possibility, from hidden archers in the darkness to traps devised to behead in the doorway, and approached the door nervously, reaching up with his free hand, the other wrapped whitened around the hilt of his glorious sword.

He swung the door open...

...and had to swallow down the bile that rose to his mouth. The smell of an abattoir hit him in the face, filling his nostrils with the stench of meat and blood and faeces and flies. He took a step forward, coughing up bile, and his foot skidded on the mess that had leaked as far as the door on its way outside. After all, the small temple was at least a finger-breadth deep in liquid.

But the *source* of that liquid...

Both Palmatus and Masgava gasped behind him.

The two horses, which had apparently been fine beasts, had been killed quickly, with a slice across the throat, but someone - actually at least three someones from the animals' size - had taken the time and effort to prop them in a pose, slumped to either side of the old woman, their big, sad, dead heads on her lap. The woman had removed her own tongue and then cut her own throat, as was evident from the open mouth, the sheets of blood, and the knife still gripped in her hand.

It was a grotesque parody of the frieze that stood behind her, spattered with their blood, which showed the Goddess Epona with her twin sacred horses by her side, nuzzling her.

146

Around the floor were the rest of the druids and helpers from the shrine, all suicides, apparently - no warriors like that British nightmare with the crown, just old men in robes.

Getting as much of a grip on himself as possible, Fronto leaned down and prised open the mouth of an ancient, grey-bearded man, confirming his fears. The druid had also removed his tongue before slitting his own throat.

'What in the name of seven hills of shit happened here?' Palmatus breathed as he stepped back into the light with Masgava.

'Defiance.' Fronto sighed as he stepped out and joined them. 'Defiance and certainty. They're informing us they will never be taken alive, and the tongues are to be certain that they will never talk to us, whatever world they find themselves in. Stupidity.'

'Why the girl alive, then?'

Fronto shrugged. 'Don't know, but let's get her back to the army before...'

He heard a shout and turned to look across the oval arena, his heart sinking as he realised all too late that the song had ended just as they stepped back outside. He had only moved two steps before the dead girl fell from the stone, the lyre clattering across the ground beside her. The capsarius had leapt from his horse and run across, not quite in time to catch her.

'Why didn't you stop her?' he yelled at the rest of his singulares. But he knew the answer. Well he knew it for *two* answers: None of them had expected it. And even Damionis, close by, had failed to react in time, so entranced was he by her song. And even if they'd had a *week* to react, the Remi who were nearest would not have stopped her. While he could easily throw his weight around and bring them up on charges, in all fairness, Fronto was not at all sure that *he'd* have stopped her in the same circumstances. There was something almost otherworldly about the whole event.

'Saddle up. Ambiorix's men are long gone and Asadunon is dead to us. We'll find out nothing here, so let's get back and hand the good news to Caesar.' He looked down at Damionis. 'You can't help her; or any of the others.'

Reaching out to untie Bucephalus, he breathed deep of the fresh, misty air, trying to clear his nostrils of the stench of death and his throat of the taste of bile. He tried not to look down at the girl's twisted, leaking corpse as he passed. The sooner this land was under Roman control the better, if only to get rid of the damned, sickening, idiotic and dangerously-unbalanced druids!

* * * * *

'So what now?' Antonius sighed, leaning against the gatepost of Asadunon and watching the last of the slaves being led away. The legionaries were occupied removing anything of value from the village, torching the buildings and tearing down the ramparts. In an hour's time all that would remain to show that Asadunon had existed would be an encircling mound and a pile of carbonised timbers.

The general, his face lined with fatigue - and bubbling, barely subdued anger - looked around at his senior officers.

'Since there is no sign of Ambiorix or any other Eburones here, we need to turn our attention beyond the Nervii. Their power centre is gone, the place of their treaty is empty and burned. Our trail has run cold and left us at their most distant border empty-handed.'

'So which tribe is next?' Rufio asked quietly. Despite having looked over the maps whenever he'd had the chance, the new officer still had only a tenuous grasp of tribal geography.

'The Menapii,' Priscus sighed where he leaned beside Antonius.

'Is that a problem?' Rufio asked, seeing the weary look on the camp prefect's face.

'We've gone at them before, but they just melt away into the delta and the forest and swamps like fog on a hot day - which I wish *this* was, incidentally. Then it's a matter of hunting down and taking out endless small settlements on reedy islands or hidden in wet woods. Awful.'

'And for which we need more men,' Fronto noted. Even Caesar nodded at that.

'The army will return to Samarobriva and wait for the arrival of the new legions,' the general said finally and decisively. 'Then we will have adequate forces to root out the Menapii and find the miserable little Eburone king. But I want the Nervii thoroughly downtrodden first. We have broken them, yes, but we broke them once before, and they simply rose whole again. This time I want them to be flattened and cowed and never able to rise beyond the ground. The army will divide: each legion - along with a quarter of the cavalry and adequate scouts - will take a different route back to Samarobriva, through Nervii land. Every Nervian settlement you find - regardless of size or importance - is to be enslaved, looted and

148

burned. When we meet once more at our base of operations, I want to know that nine of every ten Nervians is face to face either with his Gods or with our slave traders.'

Fronto threw a meaningful glance at Antonius. After Avenna, he had spoken to Caesar's friend about the concerns of the allied Gauls, and Antonius had wholeheartedly agreed with the problem, promising to speak to the general as soon as the opportunity arose.

Antonius took a moment to notice his look and then frowned in confusion. Fronto mouthed three words at him. 'GAULS'... 'BURNING'... 'TROUBLE'.

Antonius shook his head dismissively, and Fronto ground his teeth for a moment and then took a deep breath.

'General, if you continue to do unto the Belgae what Rome did to Carthage, you're going to lose the support of the allied tribes. They grow restless.'

Caesar turned a cold look on him and Fronto rose to the bait, suddenly overwhelmed with the idiocy of his being here if he wasn't to even be consulted or listened to, let alone given a command.

'I *know*! You're not happy with me. We *all* know it. It's not a surprise to any man here, General, but the fact remains that whether you think you need me or not, you *do* need the allied tribes.'

'Our forces still outnumber our enemies now, even without the allied tribes,' Cicero said airily.

'Not if you add those allied tribes to the enemy!' Fronto snapped in reply. 'Then it starts to look a little ropey, I think you'll find. I only advocate a more restrained approach. As the medicus would say: 'surgical'. You'd stand more chance of removing a gut worm with a knife than a mallet, if you get my drift.'

Antonius was glaring at Fronto, but Caesar simply narrowed his eyes.

'I'd forgotten how outspoken and contrary you can be, Fronto, but you do have a point. Very well. You have proved yourself as resourceful as ever so far, so you find me a way to excise Ambiorix with a knife, and I will consider withdrawing the mallet. But if you cannot do so, I will continue with this course until either Ambiorix kneels before me or the entire northeast of this land is a smoking ruin.'

Fronto felt a small hard gem of hope somewhere deep inside. For the first time, Caesar had actually listened to him. Now he had to come up with some sort of plan, and a damn good one, if he was to halt this swathe of destruction sweeping across the Belgae.

'Now attend your legions, gentlemen.' The general straightened. 'We march as soon as the slaves and booty are on the move. All proceeds when we return to Samarobriva will be divided as spoils among the men. Your legions will appreciate this, so bear it in mind as you pass like a cleansing fire through the Nervii. Every sestertius you tear from those benighted settlements will improve the mood and loyalty of your men. Now: off, gentlemen.'

As Caesar and the other officers dispersed, returning to the staff group or their individual forces, Antonius strode across to Fronto.

'You have Gods' awful timing, Marcus.'

'You said you would speak to him!' Fronto snapped in retort.

'And I did. But the more I thought about it, the more I realised that the best way to help the Condrusi of your scout friend is to remove the threat from their border. If we keep going as we are, whatever their dissenters think, we'll have removed the Nervii from the map, and that will give the Condrusi some breathing room - a cowed Nervii to the north and a preoccupied Treveri to the south, courtesy of Labienus. And if Caesar moves on to the Menapii and then the remains of the Eburones, we'll have freed the Condrusi from danger entirely. Then we could even smash the Treveri.'

'You're talking about genocide here, Antonius, and of more than one tribe.' The smell of wine on the senior officer's breath was strong, and possibly even the stench of Gallic beer? When had he found the time? They'd been marching all day and then fighting! Fronto was impressed in a slightly worried way, Even at the times when he was deepest in the arms of Bacchus, he couldn't have found the opportunities Antonius did. Probably wouldn't have been able to stand, either!

'The genocide of more than one *enemy* tribe,' corrected Antonius, showing no sign of inebriation, 'freeing up room for our allies.'

'And there's no guarantee that Caesar burning every house in the north will get him Ambiorix. In fact it's more likely to push him into hiding or across the river to the dubious, white, flabby bosom of the Germanic peoples.'

'*Caesar* is the one who cares about Ambiorix, Fronto - not me. *My* job is to make this campaign a success for him, and crushing these rebellious Belgae is part of that. If you want to go rooting out his obsession like an 'attack ferret' that's up to you, Fronto, but I'm going to keep this war on course.'

With a last defiant look, Antonius turned and stormed away after Caesar.

Fronto spotted Masgava and Palmatus with the rest of his men standing not far away, looking tense. Quickly, once more grateful that his knee was strong again and his marching speed better than he could remember, he strode across to them.

'Alright you two. Start thinking of any way we can get to Ambiorix. I want to come up with a near-to-fool-proof plan before we reach Samarobriva so that I can present it to Caesar. If we want to stop Gaul burning, we need to think hard and fast.'

'Already way ahead of you there, Fronto!' Palmatus said, winking at Masgava.

'Do tell.'

'We've been thinking on something along those lines,' Masgava admitted. 'Sometimes a large force can be a handicap. After all, you wouldn't send a bull down a hole to catch a rabbit, would you?'

'I just got called an 'attack ferret' by Antonius. Be careful how you proceed with this conversation!' Fronto warned with a dark look.

'And when we get back to Samarobriva,' Palmatus added, 'you might note a Gallic theme to your singulares.'

Fronto frowned. He had an inkling what they were suggesting, and it was a thought that had been rattling round his subconscious too. 'Let's go see Galronus. If you're suggesting what I think you're suggesting, he could be of great help.'

Chapter Eight

'What are you two looking at?' Fronto asked wearily. He'd only been back in Samarobriva along with the rest of the army for a matter of hours, and everything seemed to be utter chaos. In Caesar's absence, the three legions levied in Cisalpine Gaul had arrived - Pompey's First, the reformed Fourteenth, and the new Fifteenth - and their commanders had already put their stamp on the quarters in the commander's absence.

'Shocking,' Priscus shook his head. 'No organisation. Look at the way they've pitched.'

Fronto shook his head. He could see nothing wrong, but Priscus' term as camp prefect had given him an extra level of grumpy perfectionism that Fronto could hardly believe found room in the man's head, given how it already overflowed with ire, irritability and gloomy pessimism.

'Looks textbook legion procedure to me.'

'For some situations, but we've learned over long years in Gaul to tailor the camp to current need. Regardless of tradition, we pitch the centurions' tents uphill from the rest and the troublesome bastards at the bottom because it rains in Gaul every quarter of an hour and the rain should respect rank. And they've taken the tent space of the auxiliary cavalry, which might seem fine to good upstanding no-lip, fat-necked, dung-brained patricians, but might piss off the commanders of the only real cavalry we have. And they've dug their latrine by that copse of trees with the big *'menhir'* stone in the middle. It doesn't take more than a rudimentary thought process to recognise that as a native shrine. Gods, they have them in the south, in Roman land. When the princes and chieftains in the cavalry see that they're going to drown a few gleaming, bronzed patricians in that trench!'

Fronto nodded in wonder. He'd missed all three issues and Priscus was absolutely right that they would cause trouble. 'The new fellas can't be expected to know these things, Gnaeus.'

'There was a caretaker garrison here who should have made it clear. Do you see what happens to things when I'm not around to nail a few arses to walls?'

Galronus, next to the prefect, nodded wearily. 'I'll talk to the auxilia and try and keep tempers calm until you can sort it out with the general.'

'Thank you. Fronto? You coming too?'

152

'Actually, yes. I'm afraid it looks like I'll be leaving things in your hands again, Gnaeus. Masgava and Palmatus have planted the seed of an idea in my head and I can't help but see it growing big and producing a bountiful crop. I need to ask Caesar for a little independence.'

Priscus narrowed his eyes as they turned and made off towards the general's tent. He was intrigued almost to bursting point, but he knew his old friend well and remained silent as they walked.

Fronto's gaze played across the newly arrived legions and he frowned.

'Why are they in white?'

Priscus shrugged. 'That's Pompey's First. I asked Furius and Fabius about it. They said Pompey only paid to have the officers' gear dyed red. That way he could spend the spare money on more useful things like armour.'

'He may be a rabid shit-weasel, but he might be onto something there,' Fronto acceded. 'Eminently sensible idea. We ought to put it to Caesar.'

Priscus sighed and shook his head. 'Tried that. Cita and I both spoke to him, but Caesar is adamant that he would rather pay the extra for madder to dye the whole army. He thinks red and silver is a statement that shouts 'ROME' at the enemy.'

'Another good point. He might be right. Seems to me that that's a pretty good assessment of the two men: Caesar believes that half the battle is image, and he thinks too deeply about everything. Pompey seems to be relaxed and even slightly slovenly, but underneath he has a Spartan warrior's mind. They're never going to agree on anything, Gnaeus. You know that? This war is a bloody Gods-send for Rome, 'cause when it ends those two bastards are going to end up in Rome together, tearing each other to pieces.'

Priscus smiled at the thought. 'Then we'll just have to pray to Minerva that Crassus makes a swift job of the east and returns in triumph to keep the pair of them apart.'

'Yes,' Fronto agreed with ironic bile, 'That's just what the world needs: a bit more Crassus!'

The pair wandered on, heading for the command tent where Caesar would be busy... doing whatever it was the general did when he wasn't shouting at officers. Aulus Ingenuus himself - commander of the general's Praetorian guard - stood beside the tent's entrance, berating an unfortunate soldier for a poorly-polished belt. The young officer's three-fingered hand waved angrily at the soldier as he unloaded aggression upon him, and then turned as he watched the soldier's expression shift, to see Fronto and Priscus.

'Morning.' The young man gestured to the tent doorway. 'I wouldn't if I were you. He's in a worse mood than me.'

Fronto shrugged. 'Nothing new there with me. And Priscus could out-spite a cat with an itchy arse. Think we'll cope. How's things?'

'Dreadful. Since you seem to have acquired your own bodyguard, we're getting scrutinised by every officer with a self-importance complex - which seems to be all of them. The general insists on us not only being good at our jobs but looking better than your lot - not that that takes a lot of work, with such a motley collection of homicidal lunatics!'

'I love you too, Aulus. Can we go in?'

'Go on. But don't say I didn't warn you.'

Fronto and Priscus stepped up and rapped on the wooden frame of the general's tent door. There was a pregnant, heavy pause.

'Get in here, Priscus!' a voice barked from within. 'I can hear you grumbling under your breath even through the tent.'

Fronto raised his eyebrows at Priscus. He had apparently been out of the general's close council long enough that Priscus seemed to have acquired his former relationship. The prefect gestured for Fronto to go first, but the legate grinned and sketched an elaborate bow, gesturing for Priscus to lead.

The interior was dim, lit by the same guttering braziers that kept the room warm. Seats were folded against the outer edge, soaking up the wetness from the leather skin of the tent, awaiting the next staff meeting. In the meantime, Caesar had the centre clear - in front of his desk and chair and reams of maps and documents. Fronto smiled. The general always needed room to pace.

'Oh Good,' Caesar snapped, 'you brought the prodigal too.'

Priscus sighed and saluted, standing at attention in the room's centre. Fronto echoed the gesture half-heartedly. If Caesar was hardly bothering to register his presence, he felt unwilling to offer too much respect in return.

'We need to do something about the new legions, General.'

Caesar pursed his lips angrily.

'I intend to release them on the Menapii shortly. Is that enough for you, prefect?'

Priscus practically bristled, and Fronto was impressed at the level of equality that seemed to exist between the two men - a thing he had once had himself.

'Not really, General, with respect. The new boys don't know how things work here and the garrison we left didn't explain things to them. They've annoyed all the native cavalry commanders. I've not had a chance to speak to the three legates in charge yet, but I can guess with some conviction that the garrison tried to direct them to our tried and tested systems and were entirely ignored. We get this with every officer new to Gaul. I need to invoke your authority in order to shift the pillocks and their badly-set camps and put everything right, before there are fistfights and even latrine murders between them all.'

Caesar narrowed his eyes for a moment as though weighing up Priscus' words and finally nodded. 'You have it.' He scribbled something on a scrap of vellum and dripped wax, stamping it with his Taurus seal. 'Get them organised and keep everyone happy. Are we done now?'

He had not looked at Fronto since they first entered the tent.

Priscus shrugged, with a sidelong glance at his friend, and stepped forward to collect the authorisation. 'Happy with that, General. I'll leave you with chief bronze-balls here. If he's suggesting what I think he is, then he's got testes of orichalcum.'

With a last raised eyebrow at Fronto, Priscus saluted, turned, and strode from the tent.

'This had better be good, Fronto. I'm in no mood for your insolence,' Caesar said, coldly.

'Were you ever, General? I need to ask for something and to offer something, but before I do, we need to clear the air, you and I.'

The general's gaze hardened yet further, if such were possible. 'You and I are colleagues, Fronto. You need the army, and I need your command experience. Do not expect anything more than that relationship!'

Fronto stepped three paces forward and placed his hands on the desk face down. 'Bullshit. If that were the case you'd be putting me in charge of men right now, where I could be of use to you. Or asking my advice. Instead, you're excluding me and ignoring me out of spite, because I turned my back on you. Get over it, Caesar.'

The general's expression faltered between anger, surprise and pride. 'I will not be spoken...'

155

'I will speak to you as I see fit until you acknowledge that I am here as one of your officers and put me in charge of a legion.' He bridled. 'Preferably the Tenth!'

Caesar actually gave a low chuckle, though there was little humour in it. 'The Tenth *has* a legate. *All* the legions do.' He stood from his chair, hammering his fist on the table to punctuate his words. 'You turned your back on me, Marcus! But not only that! I could have worked *around* that. I am not infallible, but I know it. I would have taken you back into the fold even that very day. But you walked off into the arms of that overweight, overemotional, warmonger and despot Pompey! And you did it willingly, because you saw him as an *improvement* on me!'

Fronto blinked. He'd never considered it from that angle.

'How do you think that sits with me, Fronto? You've clearly come to a sensible conclusion in the end, though, since you're back. So now you know. You know that Pompey is a rabid dog, ready to savage the Republic, barely contained in a smiling human shell. Shall I tell you about Crassus? Shall I tell you just how much I have to do just to keep a level of balance that maintains safety for the whole of Rome? You think I fight here for glory?'

He stepped out from behind the desk and marched on Fronto with such force that the former legate actually took a couple of steps backwards, the general's finger wagging at his chest.

'You do - I know that. You and Cicero and the others. The dissenters and pacifists. You think I do this for vainglory. Whole portions of the senate are of the same opinion. But you and they have no idea, Marcus. You have not the slightest clue about the pressure under which I find myself every waking moment. Pompey is a raging, bloodthirsty lunatic wearing a thin veil of civility. And Crassus is a plutomaniac. He would *sell* Rome if he was offered the right price. And me? You think I wade through the swamps of Gaul and hunt criminals for fun? Tell me!'

'Sir?'

'Tell me why I am here. Knowing now what you do about my peers in the city.'

Fronto's mind was racing. Caught horribly on the back foot in a situation where he'd expected to have the upper hand, he was struggling, but new thoughts were battering his subconscious. New opinions were beginning to form in his mind. He cleared his throat.

'You fight to stay ahead of them.'

156

'Yes. Yes I do. Pompey is the hero of the pirates and the slave wars. He is a three-time triumphant general of Rome. All the people see - the senate as well as the plebs - is a hero. They might very well hand him a damned crown if he won another victory for the Republic. But you know what Rome would be like if Pompey ruled the roost?'

'Hades. It would be like Hades. Constant war at the expense of the people.'

'Yes it would.' Caesar stepped back and made use of his carefully cleared pacing space. 'And what of Crassus?'

'Rome would be a commodity. Everything in it would be a commodity. The only reason he hasn't risen to the top is because he hasn't...' The truth came crashing in on Fronto and silenced him.

'Precisely!' Caesar snapped. 'Pompey has the military record but has to keep his true face hidden. He builds the people theatres and woos them in his bid for supremacy so that they do not see him for what he is. Crassus has the money but needs a triumph to go with his purchase of senators. Both seek the power that Rome cannot bestow - never has since Tarquinius the Proud was exiled and the city abolished the monarchy. And both could conceivably actually *achieve* the unthinkable. And here am I. I am the third player in this Greek tragedy - The Aeneas to their Paris and Hector. I have to do whatever I can to stay ahead of them both. I have less money than Crassus, but more support among the people, and a better record. Pompey is a threat, but with every victory we achieve, I win the plebs over and remove a strut from beneath him. Gaul is my stepping stone to climb above the pair.'

'And then take the crown.' Even as Fronto's lips closed, he started, aware that he'd said out loud something he would barely even contemplate thinking to himself.

'No, Fronto,' Caesar said quietly. 'The Republic has provision for putting a man in charge when necessary: Dictator. It has its uses. But no Roman will wear a crown while I am alive.'

Despite himself, Fronto was impressed. How far he felt this to be the truth was immaterial. The general was born to lead and to persuade, and he had Fronto in his purse now. Both men knew it.

'I apologise, General.'

'It was a stupid, short-sighted comment, made in a heated moment.'

'Not for the comment about the crown. For doubting you against Pompey. The man is an animal.'

157

'Better!' Caesar stopped pacing and leaned back against the table. 'The fact remains, Fronto, that I have no space for a legate right now. You should stay on staff and advise. Roles will develop in due course.'

'Ah, well.' Fronto said and stepped forward, his excitement giving him an edge. 'The thing is: you asked me to find you a way to excise your Gallic infection and I intend to do so. Give me free rein with my singulares. Give them whatever equipment and supplies they need, and give me the room to work. I will take my small unit and I will bring you Ambiorix.'

'An offer I can't refuse?'

'An offer you *shouldn't* refuse. For the loss of one officer and a score of men, I will bring you the enemy. But that's only my side of the deal.'

'I wasn't aware this was a deal?'

'Well it is. In return I ask you to halt your obliteration of the Belgae. Hold off the destruction in order to keep your Gallic allies and start the healing process this country needs. And...' he grinned, 'when this is over, you give me the Tenth.'

Caesar frowned. 'You ask a lot, Marcus. I have vowed to bring Ambiorix down. Not only to the senate and the people, but to Venus herself! Would you ask me to defy a God?'

'You're not defying her. I will be your proxy.'

Caesar took a deep breath, his eyes flicking to the map, to the altar through the open doorway into the rear of the tent, and then back to Fronto. 'I will meet you part way. I will give you weeks. A month, maybe... a head start in your hunt. I need to raise more cavalry, and I need to assure myself of the tribes' loyalty, so I am calling the Gaulish assembly to meet here. It will allow time for the three new legions to acclimatise and will grant me the opportunity to increase our mounted contingent. Until that is done, I will hold off. But then I move on the Menapii unless you bring me Ambiorix's head.' He smiled cruelly. 'And if you grant me the death of Ambiorix, I will move Hades itself to give you back your legion. How does that sound?'

'Better than a poke in the eye with a shit-sponge, General.'

'Then get moving, Fronto, and Fortuna be with you - as it seems she always is.'

'We'll move out in the morning, as soon as I've raped Cita's supplies for everything we need. But before I go, I thought I should tell you about Rome.'

'A hive of villainy. I know the place. Has Clodius got himself killed yet?'

Fronto smiled. 'Not yet, Caesar. But we were there for Parentalia as we travelled north.'

'Your father was a sad loss to the Republic, Marcus.'

Fronto felt a sudden pang of guilt. He had not even thought to visit his father's tomb before they'd left, though it had not been Parentalia then. His mother would have been there for the festival.

'Perhaps, General, but father was interred in Puteoli. Quintus and I thought it would be fitting to pay a visit and a libation to your mother and your daughter while we were there. After all, with you being a thousand miles away...'

He saw a sudden flair of pain in the general's face. Almost as quickly as it arrived, it was gone.

'Thank you, Marcus. All is well? Did you see Atia?'

Fronto shook his head. 'We had our little meal and made our offerings. Atia had apparently visited earlier. But we had the fortune to cross paths with your great nephew.'

'Octavian was there?' the general frowned. 'Why?'

'It seemed he felt that the ladies and your ancestors required a little more devotion than had already been given them. He gave them Caecuban wine. A vintage. *The* vintage!'

Caesar nodded and a slow, knowing smile began to reach his face for the first time. 'He is a good boy, that one. Had Julia had children, they would have been like that, I think.'

'He's far too damn worldly-wise for his age in my opinion,' Fronto said with a sly smile. 'He reminds me dreadfully of you.'

And Caesar laughed. Just once - and for a moment, Fronto was newly arrived in Gaul once more, with his ambitious general, sharing a joke. The feeling passed in the blink of an eye, but it had astounding cathartic effect. Somehow, it felt as though an obstacle had been overcome.

'Are we...' Fronto couldn't decide what word it was that he sought. Friends? They *had* been friends. And confidantes. Compatriots. Sword-brothers even, at times. But he couldn't quite put his finger on the word he needed.

Caesar simply nodded. 'I won't renege on a vow to the Goddess, Marcus. I give you time to bring me Ambiorix, but once the Gallic assembly is done with, I will move. Find me the villain.'

Fronto stepped back to the doorway and gave a salute. Suddenly he felt like a soldier again, for the first time since he had returned. It felt good. 'I will, General. Good luck.'

'And to you. Fortuna seems to coddle you, Marcus. Let us hope she continues to do so. I think I will call a meeting of the officers and make the plans known.'

* * * * *

Fronto approached the tent cautiously. He had no real reason to see Antonius, given that he would be leaving before the council was convened, and certainly not attending the meeting of the general's staff that was about to be called. In fact, he had plenty to do. But for some reason, the way he'd left things with Antonius after Asadunon was preying on his mind. The two officers had not spoken on the return journey, since they had travelled with different forces.

But, before he and his singulares went off on their insane quest to hunt Ambiorix, he felt it might be important to settle matters with the officer.

Antonius' own singulares guard stood to either side of the door, their dark skin sheened with sweat in their heavy armour. The men wore a scarlet, eye-piercing red, their cuirasses burnished to mirror brightness. Their helms were of a strange, eastern design, and both men eyed him with hard, unflinching stares. Syrians. Apparently, Antonius had brought them back from their own land. They'd been with him for years.

He'd heard the other officers talking about Antonius' guards. They were not popular.

'I need to see Marcus Antonius.'

'What yo business.'

'That is between he and I.'

'No business. No go.'

Fronto ground his teeth. 'Listen, you weird, tunic-lifting, inbred easterner: I am a staff officer of the army, as is Antonius. He is also a friend. I will speak to him and I see no reason to pass my business though your greasy, dubious hands. Your job is to stop assassins or the unwanted bothering Antonius. Nothing more. Feel free to go in and announce me, but that's as far as your remit extends, soldier.'

The Syrian who'd spoken stepped forward, his friend coming to join him. Their air of menace was palpable.

160

'Get... out... of... my... way!' Fronto growled at him slowly.

'What... yo... business?' Equally forcefully. The second Syrian, he noted, had his hand on the hilt of a slightly curved sword.

'Is there a problem?' Fronto jumped as the sudden voice behind his right ear almost made him soil himself. Recovering as best he could, shaking like a leaf, he saw Palmatus and Masgava step past him to confront the Syrians.

'I jus' ask he business.'

Palmatus grinned unpleasantly. 'Perhaps 'he business' is 'he own'? Get out of the way, you sickening catamite.'

Next to him, Masgava flexed something that made every muscle across the upper half of his body dance, even through a mail shirt, and Fronto almost laughed at the expression that passed across the Syrians' faces. The second guard stepped back into place, and the first lingered only a moment - long enough to realise he was without support - and then saluted and stepped back.

Fronto turned a smile on his friends.

'Thank you. I was just on my way to see you two. Have you got everything ready?'

'Getting there. We still need a lot of supplies and equipment and some spare horses. You've cleared it with the general, sir?'

'Yes. We go as soon as we're ready. Go back and get everyone assembled in my tent.'

'And these catamites?'

Fronto gave the second - less sure - Syrian a nasty look.

'I once tore out a Gaul's eyeball with my hand while he was trying to cut me to shreds. I'm not frightened of this knob.'

Paying no further heed to the Syrians or his own men, he knocked on the wooden tent frame.

'Antonius?'

Silence.

'Antonius?'

Still silence. Fronto took a deep breath. If the man wasn't here, his Syrians would not have been so vehement, would they? Reaching out, he pushed aside the door and stepped into the tent.

As the leather flap fell back into place, returning the tent to its Stygian gloom, his eyes began to adjust slowly. His nose adjusted considerably faster.

The smell of vomit filled the front room of the subdivided structure, having apparently been trapped within for some time.

161

Fronto could feel his own gorge rising, but was determined not to make a big thing of it. If he walked out now, he would lose face to the Syrians outside.

A bed. The room was a complete state, with clothing and armour scattered among the overturned tables and chairs, cushions and blankets. It looked as though the tent had been trashed by burglars, but for the shape under the blanket on the bed - which was clearly a human figure - and the rhythmic snoring.

'Antonius!' he yelled. Nothing moved. For a strange moment, Fronto worried the man might have been murdered. After all, stranger things had happened in the legions' camps in Gaul. But in his experience the dead rarely snored, so he soon put away that thought.

Carefully, he took a couple of steps into the room, avoiding a puddle of something yellow and viscous, which may or may not have been the source of the smell. He lifted his leg high over an upturned chair and consequently almost tripped over a fallen table obscured by a rumpled blanket. He had a momentary flashback of his room back in Rome when he'd been young - just old enough to take the toga virilis and just old enough to have acquired a drinking habit. He had always thought his mother had been over-critical of his untidiness. Now, looking at Antonius' tent, he could perhaps finally see it through her eyes.

'Antonius, you daft bugger. Get up.'

With increasing care, slipping on occasional 'things', he approached the bed and peered down. A pale bare foot poked out from the bottom of the blanket. A surge of childish delight vanished as quickly as it came and instead of tickling the sole of the foot, he reached down and grasped the corner of the blanket, yanking it back and whipping it from the bed.

He grinned like a sadist.

His grin vanished.

The two naked girls in the bed untwined slowly, like a flower opening for the sun. The pair, apparently exhausted, looked up at their torturer. There was no shame or panic about them. Just a sense of mild surprise. As Fronto stared, wondering whether it would be politic to look away, the two girls embraced, kissed briefly, and returned to their entwined sleep.

Fronto felt the uncomfortable panic of a man confronted with a situation so unexpected he is completely wrong-footed.

'Nice, aren't they, Fronto?'

162

He looked up in surprise to see Antonius pushing his way through a curtain that closed off part of the tent. The senior officer wore only a linen subligaculum, his hair wet as he rubbed his face with a rough white towel.

Fronto searched for something intelligent to say, but came up short.

'Your vomit or theirs?'

'Bit of both, I expect. We were rather energetic, after black olives, Gallic fruit and a skinful of mulsum. Lucky you're not knee deep in it, I think.'

Fronto stared.

'You can have one, if you like,' Antonius went on conversationally as he dropped his linen loin cloth and began to rub himself dry. 'They're best together, but they're quite good apart too. The one with the redder hair is Bissula, The other is Elica. Sisters by different fathers.' He paused and frowned. 'Might be the other way around,' he admitted with a dismissive wave of the hand.'

Fronto realised he was staring wide-eyed at the two girls and, reminding himself that he had a lovely wife carrying a child to term, turned to lock eyes with Antonius.

'I worried that we had not spoken, but had left things with a rift. It would be a shame, seeing as how we seem to be so… oft matched in our views?'

Antonius frowned for a moment as though dredging his memory, and then shrugged. 'We argued? I don't remember. Whatever it was, consider it forgotten.'

Fronto's turn to frown.

'We had a conversation…'

'I have a lot of them. Few are memorable. Come on.'

Fronto blinked as the man strode past him and hastily threw on a tunic. 'Where?'

'I have somewhere to visit in town. You should come.'

'Is it a bar, or a whorehouse?'

'Neither, interestingly, although I may be tempted to sample both on my return journey.' The officer bent to fasten his sandals, threw a hasty belt around his middle, cinching up his tunic, and stretched before walking to the door.

'You forgot your underwear.'

'No. I make it a rule only to bother every other day. Gets healthy air to the warmest parts and means I'm always ready.'

Fronto shook his head. In his experience, not wearing underwear in Gaul was a sure way to acquire 'blue balls syndrome' but he was rapidly learning that Antonius was not like most men.'

'So where are we going?'

'Temple.'

Fronto blinked again. 'To whom?' But Antonius was already out of the tent and moving.

* * * * *

'Tell me again why I'm traipsing through ankle-deep grot on a chilly day to visit a temple to some random hairy, hammer-wielding Gaulish God?'

Fronto stumbled on a protruding stone. Samarobriva proper - rather than the enormous Roman camp that had become synonymous with the native settlement, sat on the opposite bank of the river, on what might pass for a hillock in this endless flat country. It was a disorganised place that had grown from an organised centre into a sprawling mess of Gallic houses and hovels, interspersed with what the locals probably considered civic amenities.

Antonius strode purposeful and bright - certainly brighter than he had any right to, given the previous night's activity.

'Not a hammer, Marcus. A club.'

'Semantics. Why are we here?'

'I like to consult the auspices every now and then, especially when we're about to do something that might have far-reaching effects. Before Caesar summons the Gaulish assembly I'd like to know what the Gods have in mind. And before you disappear on your little errand, it might serve you well to know more, too.'

Fronto frowned irritably. How Antonius had found out already that Caesar was summoning the assembly before word went out was concerning enough, but how he knew about Fronto's plans was baffling. The man was a constant bag of mysteries. *Amphora* of mysteries, he corrected with a quiet smile.

'The temple in question is apparently to some local God named Ogmios,' Antonius shrugged, 'but this Ogmios seems to be their name for Hercules, and Hercules is my family's patron deity right back to the earliest times. It seems as though he's almost demanding to be consulted, really.'

'I don't like temples,' Fronto grumbled. 'Temples and me have a bad history. And priests annoy me. And all the auspices ever

164

tell you is that the goat died in surprise and that the priest's going to eat well that night.'

'Come on.'

Antonius led him to the door of a large hut. A standing stone with a flattened surface stood to either side of the door. One was carved with curious designs and the other held a relief of someone who bore a passing resemblance to Hercules, or would have done if Hercules had had some sort of strange hat, one hairy leg and one bald one and a pronounced paunch that leaned to one side.

'This is pointless.'

But Antonius had already stepped inside. Fronto followed in hesitantly, shuddering as he passed across the threshold.

'Will Caesar approve of you consorting with druids?' he grunted.

'They say he is not a druid, but a seer or something. The druids all left the area when the legions settled the first winter. A *'Uidluia'* they call him, apparently.'

Fronto paused for a moment as his eyes became accustomed to the gloom. Images of a young girl with a harp singing her last, suicidal song swam through his mind and he shuddered yet again. Temples: always bad news.

The room was surprisingly bare, resembling more an ordinary house than anything religious. The seer-poet sat on a chair formed from a single piece of carved stone facing the doorway and behind a brazier of dull bronze with handles shaped like twisting vines. A low orange glow emanated from the bowl, and tendrils of smoke rose towards the small hole in the room's roof. A table near the man's hand held a collection of oddments, including - Fronto noticed - animal parts and a set of sharp knives.

'Good day, priest,' Antonius said jovially as he strode across towards the man. Fronto shuffled slightly to the side, trying to stay comfortably distant. The Uidluia was dressed much the same as any ordinary Gaul, rather than the almost uniform robes of the druids. He was of indeterminate age and with a hook nose and sharp eyes that glittered in the firelight.

'Ogmios does not speak for Romans.'

'But you speak for Ogmios, and you speak surprisingly good Latin,' Antonius smiled. 'Your Ogmios, as you call him, is the patron of my family. I will make plentiful offerings for your help.'

The man made a noncommittal, throaty noise.

'We seek augury. I on the Gaulish assembly being called, my friend on a journey he is about to undertake. Will you read for us?'

'Silver,' the man said. Antonius smiled and reached to the purse at his belt, removing three denarii and placing them on the table next to a wicked-looking jagged knife. The man lifted the coins, examined them, seemed to find them satisfactory and nodded.

Gesturing Antonius to the side, the bearded seer lifted a charm of some sort of pale stone - so thin as to be almost like smoky glass - enclosed in a ring of bronze. With his other hand he grasped a handful of something powdery and grey from a bowl on the table and cast it into the brazier. The fire leapt into life, burning first green and then fading through yellow to orange once more. The smoke rising from it increased and the seer held up his charm, putting it to one eye while squeezing the other shut.

Fronto rolled his own eyes. It would be virtually impossible to see through the stone, and with the smoke as well, he might as well stare into a brick. Yet the man seemed to angle things so that he peered through his charm and the smoke at the white rectangle of the doorway.

'Two wolves fail to eat with the pack. The bull will spoil the pickings for all.'

'Typical rubbish.' Fronto snapped, earning a hard look from Antonius.

'And who are the wolves and the bull?' the officer said quietly.

The seer appeared not to have heard him, for his eyes narrowed. 'But the bull will not find the snake, for the snake slithers into burrows.'

'Someone has been listening to too many animal stories,' muttered Fronto.

'Will you kindly shut up and listen?' Antonius snapped.

'Well, when he tells you that the horse gets humped by the hedgepig, what are you going to divine from that?'

'Quiet!'

Fronto lapsed into silence, glowering at them.

'While the bull does not find the snake, the eagle will bring death to the serpent.'

Fronto grunted as the seer turned at this last to stare pointedly at him. 'Don't look at me, you old fruit. I'm no snake, and I only *serve* the eagle.'

'Fronto, do be quiet.' Antonius sighed.

166

'It's all guesswork and deceptive vagaries.'

'I will argue the authenticity of omens with you another time, Marcus, but right now I want to try and pick apart those phrases, in case they are of use.'

'The final thread snaps!' the Gaul suddenly barked.

'See?' Fronto laughed. 'He's getting unhinged.'

'In the baked sand, the Parthian shot takes the last.'

Antonius frowned and leaned down to the man. 'What in the name of Olympus do you know of the Parthians?'

Fronto was staring at the two men. Antonius, of course, had served out in the east recently, and would likely have come into contact with the Parthians. This Gaul, though, should never even have heard of that eastern empire, let alone the 'Parthian shot'. His blood suddenly chilled.

'Socrates' root.'

Antonius' head jerked round to Fronto. 'What?'

'Socrates' root. Vulcan's Fury. The arrival of the Son. The Parthian shot.'

'Marcus, what are you babbling about?'

Fronto took a couple of steps back and leaned against the wall.

'Marcus, you've gone white as an aedile's toga. What is it?'

Fronto pulled himself together with some difficulty. The hairs were standing proud on the nape of his neck. 'Nothing. I'll tell you later. Let's get out of here.'

'But there could be more.'

'You've got what you want. Two wolves won't be attending the feast. Doesn't take a druid to translate that. Come on.'

Leaving Antonius to finish up with the priest, Fronto strode outside, where he stopped in the slightly damp, chilly air and took a number of deep breaths. The last part of Catullus' prophecy! It had been so long since Julia's death that he'd almost forgotten about it. Catullus, then Aurelia Cotta, and then Julia. Now the Parthian shot for the fourth. It was hard not to take a guess at that one.

Antonius appeared from the doorway, a frown of curiosity creasing his brow.

'Talk to me.'

'Not right now. Now I need to get back to the camp and get ready to go hunt Ambiorix. I think great and terrible things are hovering on the horizon, Antonius, and we need to put our current problems to rest. They'll pale into insignificance against what's coming, I fear.'

Antonius' frown deepened as he watched the rattled soldier turn and almost jog back towards the camp.

* * * * *

Marcus Licinius Crassus, the richest man in Rome, commander of the eastern armies and invader of Parthia stood on the dais, his arms stretched tight and lashed to the wooden frame that kept him in position, head tilted back so that the sun seared his face. Only his legs had any real freedom of movement, and even that minimal. The only relief he felt was that this restrictive position meant he could no longer see the head of his eldest son Publius dancing around atop a Parthian lance among their officers, a prize taken in the mid-phase of the dreadful, appalling, decisive battle.

All he'd wanted was the military glory due to him. Pompey had stolen his credit for the Spartacus campaign, and Caesar was busy racking up the victories in Gaul. Wealth was important, but no man could control Rome without the respect of its people. Was he so disfavoured by the Gods that he must die out here, in the unforgiving sands, never seeing Rome again?

Perhaps the enemy general Surena would ransom him back to Rome? He was, after all, famed for his extraordinary wealth. And though he would never recover from the sight of Publius' severed head, at least he could be there for his younger son, currently out in Gaul with Caesar. He had to be worth the ransom. He could afford to buy the Parthian King of Kings a second empire!

Something metal clamped around his head, digging painfully into his temples, holding his cranium in precise position with no fraction of movement. As he opened his mouth to shout in alarm, something else metal slipped in from either side and then opened like a vice, driving his jaws painfully apart.

What had the cruel monster in mind?

Crassus watched, immobile and totally helpless, as a large iron bowl at the end of a long staff appeared to one side, lifted above him. Thick steam poured from the top and the contents made unpleasant noises.

Blop. Gurgle. Pop.

His eyes widened in terror and his voice came out in a high-pitched, feminine shriek as he saw the pot of molten gold hover

168

above his open mouth and begin to tip. The scream continued for a moment, before it drowned in the liquid metal that burned its way through him in scant moments.

The corpse of the third master of Rome sagged in the frame.

Chapter Nine

Fronto performed a quick headcount and, noting eighteen occupants, nodded to Masgava to close the tent flap and tie it shut. The men of his singulares unit sat around on the various small stools and seats or on the thick rug on the floor, interest showing in their faces.

'Masgava and Palmatus you all know. Some of you might have believed when you were plucked from the drab everyday of your legion or cavalry life that you'd just been handed an easy ride. Now that you're getting used to your two officers, you'll probably have abandoned that notion. I am not a sit-back-and-watch staff officer. I like to put palm to hilt and bloody myself up to the elbows in battle, so your job as a bodyguard unit is likely to be somewhat perilous.'

He grinned. 'Think on that for a few heartbeats, because this is your last chance to back out and request a transfer. I'll grant it, because I only want committed soldiers here.'

He paused for only a moment before gesturing to a pale, willowy figure, seemingly odd-fitting in a military tunic and boots. 'Damionis there is a capsarius that comes highly recommended by my former training centurion, Atenos, and therefore has my utmost confidence and support. If he tells you to do something, you do it. Capsarii are paid well for a reason.'

'At the back over there is Biorix. He will remember me, won't you?'

The big blond engineer from the Thirteenth, still noticeably Gallic in appearance despite having Romanised as much as one could expect, nodded his recognition.

'Biorix was instrumental in the success of the battle of the Aisne river up in Belgae lands a few years back. He's an intuitive engineer and a man of Gaul, to boot.'

He leaned back. 'So that's four of you I know of old, and who know me. The rest of you will probably know of me by reputation anyway if you've been with us for more than a year, and, of course, some of you were with me when we took Asadunon. I don't have an excellent memory for names, and it'll be weeks before I stop calling you 'you there' or 'big nose' or 'lop-eye' or some such. Don't take offence. I've been called worse, and it just means I'm trying to remember who you are. See, there's only nineteen of us altogether, and we lost too many at Asadunon. I want each of these

170

faces still looking up at me from a briefing by the time the army settles into winter quarters later in the year. Alright?'

There was a murmur of agreement, and Fronto poured himself a watered wine, three parts to one in favour of inebriety. 'Very well. The rest of you introduce yourselves. You all need to know who you are and what you do. We'll start with the native levy.

One of the recent recruits - a dark-haired and bearded man with arm rings, a neck-torc and various pendants and sigils attached to his clothing - cleared his throat. 'I am Brannogenos of the Remi, warrior and noble of Acoduro on the Aisne river.'

'And I am Galatos of the Remi, noble of Avacon on the Aisne,' added an old grey-beard seated next to him. His age might be against him, pondered Fronto, but noting the number of battle-won arm rings - including a couple of unusually rich and decorative mixed copper-and-gold ones - and the clearly well-used sword at his side, Galatos was no doddering ancient.

'Magurix,' announced another from nearby. Young and handsome and with muscles that would produce envy in a trained wrestler, Magurix brushed a blond braid aside and smiled a white smile. 'Remi, of no settled home.'

Curious, noted Fronto, filing the nugget away for future investigation.

'Samognatos of the Condrusi,' chimed a strange looking fellow near the door, 'and I did not request this. I am not sure why I am here?' The man had been recommended through Galronus and, while an irregular scout with no paid position in the army, he was perhaps the most important man here. It worried Fronto that the man seemed to wear a permanent half-crazed smile, and his appearance was no easier. With flaming red locks and moustaches, Samognatos had left half his hair long, ragged and knotted, while the other half of his head had been shaved clean. Badly, too, judging by the criss-crossed network of fine white scars. Still, he had been recommended as the best.

'I'll come to you last, my friend,' Fronto smiled. 'We have two archers from Crete, drawn from Decius' auxiliary force, and a Balearic slinger who I've met. Care to introduce yourselves?'

'Myron,' grunted a dark-haired and olive-skinned man with no further explanation. His skin tone marked him as a Greek as much as the accent that tinged his Latin.

'And I am Arcadios,' smiled a man with similar looks, though taller and broader and sitting hugging his knees on the floor.

171

'Myron and I are natives of Hersonissos. My aim is unerringly true, and yet Myron over here could knock my arrow out of the sky with his own. He can bring down a hawk by piercing its wing.'

'Excellent!' grinned Fronto. 'Good eating on a hawk.'

Myron barely acknowledged the conversation, a faint nod his only contribution.

'And you'd be the slinger,' Fronto gestured to a man in a pale grey tunic. 'I remember you from Asadunon. One swing of the leather and you brought the man down. Economy of action. I like that.'

The slinger bowed his head in acknowledgement. 'Luxinio,' he confirmed in a thick Hispanic accent through a bushy, curly black beard.

The remaining eight men sat together, in an almost laughably disciplined double row. If Fronto hadn't already known they'd been drawn from the legions it would have been obvious from the neatness of their positioning and the uniformity of their dress.

'You all from the Thirteenth? I can see a lot of Gallic blood there.'

'I'm from the Ninth, sir.'

'I recognise you. Saw you with a rope and grapple at Asadunon. Engineer, yes?'

'Artillerist mainly. Iuvenalis, sir, of Tibur.'

Fronto nodded. 'Anyone else?'

'Quietus, also of the Ninth,' announced a veritable giant of a legionary with a shock of unruly straw-blond hair. His wrist was probably about the size of Fronto's thigh.

'I remember you from Asadunon too, I think. Good man.'

'We's both from the Tenth, sir' piped up a short man, gesturing to his comrade with a back-turned thumb. 'Served under Centurion Atenos. He were a bit reluctant to let us go, truth be tole, sir, but your two officers is quite persuasive, we think.'

The man next to him grinned and Fronto saw Palmatus frown at them, but Masgava simply chuckled at the apparent compliment.

'Valgus and Celer, sir' the second man explained, fidgeting with the silver Medusa ring on his finger. 'He's Celer. Thinks he's quick, sir.'

A light laughter rippled across the room, including from Celer, Fronto noted. Good. At least he had a sense of humour.

'So the rest of you are from the Thirteenth?'

172

'Sir,' nodded the four remaining men.

'Names?'

The legionaries called out their names in roll-call fashion and Fronto nodded. 'Numisius, Drusus, Aurelius and Pontius - Good Latin names, but I'm guessing from your looks that you're all men of Cisalpine Gaul up around Cremona and Aquileia? N - D - A - P. Never Dice Against Priscus.' He smiled.

'Sir?'

'Mnemonic. Helps me remember names. My wife taught me the way, Aurelius.' He took the last swig of wine from his cup and placed it on the small table, leaning forward in his chair.

'Right. We all know one another a little now and I'm sure we're going to get to know each other quite well in time. Your officers, Palmatus and Masgava, are a little unconventional, as you've probably noticed. They're not centurions, so don't refer to them as such. In fact, I suppose they ought to rank as prefects, given their position, but I think we'll just stick with the word 'officer' for now. They've put you together into a unit because with such a variety of talents and backgrounds, you should be able to handle just about anything thrown at you. But at the same time, you have all agreed - yes Samognatos I know you didn't, so put your arm down - to be part of this singulares unit for a Roman commander. That means I want everyone to treat the unit as though it were a legion. Discipline and order. So...' he took a deep breath. 'Bearing in mind what I've said about peril and unconventionality, now is the last time I will accept any request for a transfer. Speak now.'

The Condrusi 'volunteer' cleared his throat but Fronto waved him down. Other than that there was no sound, just an expectant silence.

'Good. In that case, pass around the cups from that table. You'll find two jugs of good wine in that cupboard and there are several jars of water. Drink a toast to each other and to Fortuna and Nemesis who I'm sure will guide our path well, since they've looked after me for years.'

He waited while the drinks were distributed, and then sat back again.

'Very well. I have been in discussions with Caesar and with your two officers and we have taken on the task of hunting a treacherous Belgic rebel: Ambiorix. I am going to leap to the assumption that you are all familiar with the name?'

173

Nods and positive murmurs accompanied the expressions of surprise and concern.

'Ambiorix has gone to ground somewhere in Belgae lands. Those of you of native blood will no doubt have been a little disheartened by the general's 'loot, enslave and burn' policy regarding the Belgae at the moment. You probably realise that this is all in an effort to bring to justice that Eburone king who massacred a legion a few months back? Suffice it to say that we believe that two contubernia of good men could succeed where nine legions might fail. If we bring back Ambiorix, we can save the Belgae from very probable obliteration.'

He grinned.

'And that, friend Samognatos, is where you come in. Searix and Galronus have both recommended you as a smart and subtle man who knows the entire region well. I hope that is true. While I have no intention of granting *you* a transfer, I hope you realise, given the location and predicament of your tribe, that what we are about to embark upon could be the balm to ease your people?'

The scout pursed his lips and nodded.

'Good. First thing's first. Your officers have arranged requisition of everything we might need, and it is all neatly stockpiled in one of the stores. One of the stables holds a native horse for each of you, fitted with tack and saddle. They are all larger beasts than we're used to in Rome - much like my Bucephalus - but they're all battle trained. There are also six pack horses for us and four spare mounts in case of trouble. Once we're done here I want everyone to return to their tents and pack their kit - we are leaving before the sun rises. While our mission is hardly a secret, news of our absence will soon get round and I would prefer to have a head start on any Gallic spies that might be hiding in the camp. I've cleared our departure with command and with the duty centurion of the east gate. When the call for the eighth watch goes out, I want every man to make his way to the storage sheds near the east gate. You'll know which one, as we'll already be there and the lamps will be lit.'

Again, murmurs and nods around the tent.

'We move out and travel east as speedily as we dare, saving the horses rather than riding them into the dirt. This is where you come in, Samognatos.'

The scout nodded his strange, half-shaved head and his smile remained fixed.

'We need some sort of lead on Ambiorix's probable location. I doubt he'll be with the Treveri, as they're embroiled with Labienus to the south. He's been in contact with the Nervii, though possibly only through intermediaries. He's got ties with the Menapii, and what remains of the Eburones tribe, though I gather his fellow king, Cativolcus, is no friend to our quarry. Whatever the case, what we've known so far will be very much old news by the time we are in his lands, so we need the latest intelligence. Our best, most central, and most loyal friends there are the Condrusi, and so Samognatos here will lead us to his people so we can make enquiries and hopefully know better where to start.'

He gestured at the scout as he poured another wine. 'Where will we be best to go for information, and how far?'

Samognatos shrugged. 'Divonanto.' He announced. 'The sacred valley lies upon the river Mosa, nestled beneath a mountain. There the nobles and druids alike will tell us everything that can be heard among the Condrusi.'

'Are you sure the druids can be trusted?'

'I would stake your life on it.'

'That's comforting' Fronto grumbled in the face of that strange smile. 'And we reckon how many days?'

'I would say four if we rode fast and brooked no delays. With no change of horses available and a string of pack animals behind, I would comfortably estimate six days. Eight if you want to be unobtrusive and avoid encounters, which is what I am thinking?'

'The faster the better,' Fronto said quietly. 'Instead of making camp for the night, we'll have three stops each day for a few hours and we can sleep in rotation. That way the horses will get more rest and we can move at a better pace.'

'Dangerous, sir,' Palmatus muttered. 'Low sleep levels make soldiers less effective. Missile aim can be off, sword and shield reaction times drop.'

'It's a risk,' Fronto agreed. 'But I'm counting on avoiding running into trouble at least until after we've spoken to the Condrusi. We can have a proper rest once we've got there. But I want to get close to Ambiorix before we let up. Caesar is calling the Gaulish assembly and it won't take long. It happens this time every year and the chiefs will be waiting for the call. And once that's over, the army will turn back east and start to slash and burn again. We want to get as much of a head start as we can.'

175

''Scuse me, sir.' Fronto glanced around to see Celer holding up his arm.

'Yes?'

'If we's to be fair subtle and unobtrusive... well in all fairness, sir, we ain't hardly unobtrusive, is we?' He inclined his head meaningfully towards Masgava.

A chorus of nods greeted him and the Numidian reluctantly joined them.

'True.' Fronto smiled. 'But that's not the end of it. We've requisitioned from a local merchant a whole array of Gaulish trousers and long-sleeved tunics, as well as native wool cloaks, belts and boots and the like. I know some of you will baulk at the idea, but we're going to dress native. If you have a mail shirt you can wear it, but remove any double layering at the shoulders and any accoutrements that label it as Roman. Likewise no plated belts. Leather only. I have shields for everyone in the stores, all painted up with nice Belgic motifs, and I've managed to lay my hands on half a dozen Gaulish helmets. Those of you with older, less decorative Roman helms can get pliers from the stores and rip off your crest holders and any decoration if you want and they'll just about pass for Gallic at a glance. You can keep your weapons, though. Subtlety notwithstanding, I want everyone able to defend themselves at a moment's notice. Masgava, you'll have to keep your hood up most of the time.'

There were a number of groans at the thought of dressing in the itchy, all-encompassing Gaulish wool garments, but no open complaints. *Good*, thought Fronto. *Now we're almost ready.*

'Alright gentlemen. That's it. Palmatus and Masgava have already formed you into tent groups, I understand. You will need to get to know each other well - to rely upon one another. But not right now. Right now, you need to go get some shut-eye. You've got nine hours to alter your kit and get some sleep before I want you all standing in the stores, raring to go and nail Ambiorix to a post.'

* * * * *

Over the four days since they had left Samarobriva, Fronto had noted a gradual change in the landscape. Slowly, they had left the wide, flat floodplain of north-western Gaul and moved into the foothills of the undulating Belgae lands. It would continue to change,

176

he knew, becoming steadily more vertical, cut through by deep, cold rivers and covered with impenetrable forest.

The forest of Arduenna.

Priscus had warned him to steer clear of it.

'From what I hear,' Fronto had countered, 'you sent Furius and Fabius out into the forest on their own to hunt men. At least I'm taking a small force with me.'

'I think you missed the relevant fact there, Fronto.' Priscus had smirked. 'I *sent* men. I did not go myself and bring them along for the ride.'

Fronto had been disparaging at the time, but conversations with the men of the singulares had done little to allay his growing unease. It seemed that even the Remi were a little wary of the great forest, which was said to be home to a powerful, vengeful Belgic Goddess and protected by wicked spirits. Only the Treveri and the Eburones, who worshipped Arduenna above all, felt comfortable there. Even the Condrusi, whose land was hidden beneath the edge of Arduenna's green veil, were wary of her, for all they prayed to her.

Still, that was a couple of days away, yet. They would not pass into the territory of the Goddess for another day or more. Here, they were in the hilly territory of the Nervii, not far from Remi lands. Here, they were inclined to be less wary, given the lack of life signs to be found. Upon returning from Caesar's devastating campaign against the tribe only a week or more back, the Ninth had come this way and the evidence of their passing blotted the landscape every few miles. Burned, blackened villages. Empty, ruined farms. Piles of charred wood, surrounded by dismantled ramparts. And in two days of Nervian landscape not more than a handful of people to be seen, with even those weeping as they buried their loved ones or investigated carbonised houses in the desperate search for their possessions.

Fronto had agreed to an extent with Caesar's campaign, and the Nervii had been habitual rebels, but the after-effects, now he had seen them with his own eyes, supported what Searix and Galronus had advised him. Any Gaul or Belgian who witnessed this would question the ways of Rome.

'Stop!' came a hiss.

Fronto almost rode into the back of Samognatos as the scout reined in sharply, close to the grey, smoke-stained bulk of a ruined farm house.

'What?' he demanded quietly. The Condrusi rider pointed off into the distance and Fronto followed his gesture.

'Damn. Riders? Out here? How many?'

Samognatos shrugged. 'More than us. And they are well armed, from the gleam of bronze and iron.'

'They won't be Roman out here,' Fronto replied.

'No. Hide your men. The riders are coming this way.'

Fronto turned in the saddle to see Palmatus and Masgava closing on him. 'Get the men to that copse back there and hide them. Try and keep the horses quiet.

Masgava gave him a disapproving look.

'I won't endanger myself. I'm just taking a look. Do I have to *order* you?'

Still glaring at him, Masgava turned with Palmatus and trotted back along the track to the rest of the unit, who waited patiently. As the men made for the small knot of beech trees - tall and slender with a budding bright green starting to show amid the tops - Fronto followed Samognatos in dismounting and leading their horses into the shell of the ruined building.

Bucephalus seemed happy enough, and Fronto trusted him not to start making undue noise as he tied off the reins to a carbon-stained hinge. The scout seemed equally content to tie his horse up, and moments later the pair were edging along the sooty interior wall towards an aperture that still had one charred shutter hanging at an angle. The wide track that passed the farm and onto which they would be moving shortly was less than half a dozen paces from the window, raised on a slight causeway and unsurfaced, lacking the camber of a Roman road. Already the sound of cantering hooves was growing closer.

Fronto hunched down so that he could see through the cracks in the ruined shutter while remaining almost entirely obscured from the road. The scout found himself an equally hidden position, and the pair waited with bated breath.

Drumming hooves, and now the huff and snort of the horses. The shushing of mail and the jingle of fastenings rattling against armour and sheaths.

Fronto watched.

He had been in Gaul long enough now to tell the difference between some tribes, or at least *groups* of tribes. The Belgae tended to wear different shades to the Gauls of the west. They all had different skin and different colouring to the tribes of the south, beyond the Aedui. Some tended to strange animal shapes atop their helms, while others were more plain. Of course, he would not go so far as to say he could identify a tribe easily, but as the first rider passed, he noted their colouring instantly, which betrayed their southern origin. They were not Belgae, nor a tribe of north-west Gaul.

He glanced briefly at Samognatos without turning his head, and noted the scout narrowing his eyes in surprise at the riders.

More than twenty. He lost count as some of them were three abreast. *Certainly* more than twenty. Possibly thirty. Too small to be a war band of any kind, and they were too well armed and kitted out to be simple bandits. Their very presence here raised huge questions for Fronto and he found himself wishing he had persuaded Galronus to come along on this hunt.

And then he saw it.

A winged snake arm ring.

The symbol of Arvernus.

The last rider passed and the Gauls were gone, the sounds of thundering hooves receding into the east as the Arverni rode on.

Fronto waited for a count of fifty and then gestured to Samognatos with his hand and jerked his thumb back towards the copse where the singulares waited. The scout nodded and the two men untied their horses and retrieved them, walking them gingerly out of the ruins and scanning the horizon until they were sure that the Gauls were out of sight and earshot.

Sharing a quick glance, the two men mounted and began to ride.

'I'm starting to think we should have taken them on,' Fronto said breathlessly as they closed on the copse.

'Dangerous thought,' Samognatos replied with a raised eyebrow.

'They were Arverni from the south. Whatever they're doing in Nervian lands, even if it's not connected with Ambiorix - though I am almost certain it is - it will be something underhanded that we could do with knowing. I would have liked to interrogate one.'

'We'll not catch up with them unless you cut loose the pack horses and we ride fast. And now you'll have no further opportunity to set an ambush.'

'I know,' grumbled Fronto. 'Shame. Confirms that we're headed the right way, though, I'd say?'

179

The figures of Palmatus and Masgava appeared from the undergrowth at the edge of the small knot of trees, leading their horses.

'Trouble?'

'Arverni!'

Masgava frowned. 'Same ones we met in Bibracte?'

'No way I could tell. I wouldn't like to discount the idea, though. Whatever the case, they're up to no good this far north.'

'I'm starting to think we might have been better just going with Caesar and burning the whole damn lot of them,' Palmatus grunted, glancing quickly at Samognatos. 'No offence to you.'

'Arverni in the north and Ambiorix sending out ambassadors,' Fronto sighed. 'It's all very dubious. I'd like to have a nice long chat with some of these people before Caesar brings the torch to bear.'

He turned to look back at the main road.

'Let's get to this Divonanto place as fast as we can. Even this smoking wasteland is starting to feel rather dangerous.'

* * * * *

The narrow wooded valley had descended for the last half mile or so, gradually steepening in its drop towards their destination. The muddy trail had wandered left and right between the thick trees and afforded no view of their goal until the last moment.

Samognatos the scout sat at the bend, waiting for Fronto to catch up, having spent much of the last day or two ranging a mile or so ahead in order to avoid any difficult encounters. There had been no further sign of the Arverni riders, for which Fronto was both thankful and troubled in equal measures. Now, the scout waved for his commander to join him, and Fronto trotted out along the path until he reached the bend where, as he passed the latest clump of trees, he was treated to his first view of Divonanto.

The Mosa river, wide and fast, cut a deep valley through the forested terrain, flowing from out of sight to the right, across before them and around another curve to the left. And across that torrent, nestled on the far bank in the glowing late afternoon sun that promised a good morrow, lay the sacred valley of the Condrusi.

This was no oppidum with walls of stone, earth and timber, nor was it a farmstead, undefended and poor. This was a thriving town with all the hallmarks of peaceful civilisation. Dozens of double-storey houses fronted onto narrow streets, intermittently held apart by wide, paved spaces. A wharf sat on the river's edge, swarming with fishing boats and small trading vessels. Fronto was not sure what he had expected from a sacred place of one of the region's lesser tribes, but this most certainly wasn't it.

The feature that really drew the eyes, though, was the rock.

The far bank with its neat collection of streets and houses sat beneath a veritable mountain that towered up into the darkening sky. At the centre of the settlement, almost opposite the defile along which Fronto had approached, the jagged cliffs jutted out, creating a promontory with an apex two - perhaps even three - hundred feet above the settlement.

Fronto squinted in wonder up at the place. If *he* had ruled Divonanto, there would be a fortress above. Assuming a long slope away at the far side, it was perfect for defence. And given the value of this place to the Condrusi, combined with the pressing proximity of so many unfriendly tribes, such a construction would be eminently sensible.

His eyes told him a different story, though. Wattle fences were just about visible at the top, behind which jutted the regularly spaced shapes of tapering, well-tended trees. A temple, then. A 'nemeton' of the druids. It seemed as appropriate as a fortress, really. For all its defensive value, such a location was also a natural site to honour Gods. Romans were equally predisposed to building temples on the highest ground, after all.

'Impressive,' he muttered, scanning the town.

'Tonight we rest in the town and speak to the council of elders. They will have had men in the forests, watching, and will know we are here. In the morning we climb to the nemeton and commune with the druids.'

Fronto turned, prepared to argue the necessity for speed, but there was a quiet reverence in the scout's face, even straightening his permanently-smiling mouth a little, and the Roman found his words dried in his throat. If it were true that there were druids here who would actually help, it would be a good idea not to irritate them. He still felt uncomfortable with the very idea, though. He'd never yet met a druid who hadn't either spat bile at him or tried to kill him.

Behind him, the others rounded the bend and there were a few whistles of appreciation at the sight of the sacred settlement.

'We're bound for an inn first.' Fronto straightened in his saddle. 'Once there, I will take six men with me, as well as

Samognatos here, to talk to the leaders. The rest of you get the horses fed and stabled, store the kit and secure the rooms. Send out a few men to replenish the supplies we've used so far and then wait for our return. In the morning we're to visit druids and I want to be sure we're ready for anything.'

As he turned and began to walk Bucephalus down towards the river, with the column moving along behind, he leaned across to Samognatos.

'How do we get across?'

'Ferrymen,' the scout replied. 'Pay them well.'

Fronto looked at the fast, wide and deep river and nodded. 'Believe me, I will.'

By the time the party had assembled on the near bank, horses snorting gratefully and taking the opportunity to rip at the lush green grass of the valley, the ferrymen were already on their way. Clearly they were used to dealing with vehicles and beasts of burden. The ferries were wide and flat with high sides, large enough to accommodate a cart with oxen, and there were two such vessels ploughing through the rippling water towards them. As the first approached with surprising accuracy, making for the bank directly before Fronto, the commander noted the iron rings driven into the timbers of the boat and the ropes stacked in a corner for tethering skittish animals during the crossing. As he watched the men work, he realised they were using a line submerged beneath the water, running through a ring on the vessel, to pull themselves across with such accuracy. As one of the ferry's two occupants leapt ashore and began to haul the boat up onto the gravel, the other entered into a brief exchange with Samognatos.

'He says three men at a time. No more. One silver coin a trip. A sestertius would do.'

Fronto nodded his agreement as he made a quick mental calculation and fished seven coins from his purse. 'Sensible. Ask him if he's transported any other groups of riders this big in the last couple of days.'

The scout relayed the question as the ferryman gestured for the first three to board. Fronto dismounted and motioned to Palmatus to join him, leading Bucephalus onto the wooden deck.

'He says no group of this size,' Samognatos relayed, dropping from his own steed. 'A party of foreigners came through here yesterday, but there were only five, and they were not stopping in the town.'

'Were they the ones we saw?'

'They were southerners, he says.'

'So, yes, then.'

Palmatus led his horse aboard, rubbing his sore posterior in relief, and Samognatos joined them as the second ferry approached and Masgava selected three men to cross first.

'I don't like the fact that Arverni have passed through here. I don't trust the druids at the best of times, and that Arverni warrior had close links with them, he said. Everyone stays in the inn except for collecting supplies, and I want them out in pairs for that, too, and armed.' Palmatus nodded his understanding. 'Do you think they know we're out and about?'

Fronto shook his head. 'I don't think so. I think they're on their own business, but I'd sooner they didn't learn about us, just in case.'

The three men fell silent and leaned on the side of the ferry, watching the slate-dark water slide past as the ferrymen hauled on the rope, dragging them back across to the town. The imposing bulk of the tall cliff became ever more impressive as the ferry drifted towards it and the shape, which already loomed, took on an extra level of ominousness with the knowledge that druids who may or may not be in league with the Arverni sat atop it waiting for them.

Fronto was busy trying to make sense of it all when the ferry crunched to a halt on the town-ward side, and he had to grip the timber strake to keep his footing. Moments later, the three men had led their horses from the vessel and the ferrymen had slid their watery steed out into the river once more, making for the waiting horsemen. The next three were already halfway across.

'There will be no inn that can provide proper accommodation for nineteen men,' noted Samognatos. 'Either we split between two or three inns, or many men will have to sleep in a bunk house together.'

Fronto pursed his lips.

'That's an inn, right?' He pointed to a large building at the very end of the wharf, with a ground floor of stone and a timber upper, lights shining in the shuttered windows already and a painting of a mug on the wall by the door.

'It is. Not a large one, though. I was going to suggest the one in the town's centre, which will accommodate the most men appropriately.'

183

'They're soldiers. They'll just be glad they're not in a tent. I like the place. Right on the edge. Come on - let's go and introduce ourselves.'

* * * * *

Fronto straightened as he approached the large, well-constructed 'council building' of Divonanto. For a moment he wondered what the hell he was doing, but the image of the burned-out, desecrated landscape of the Nervii insisted itself into his mind's eye once again, and he steeled himself. Caesar would not stop until Ambiorix was dead, for he had vowed it to Venus. And he would burn Gaul to cinders to do it, if Fronto couldn't bring him his quarry first.

It came to him as he took in the surprisingly sophisticated town around him that, whatever his ostensible reasons for trying to prevent the searing of this land, as much of it was down to his growing respect for Gaul's potential as for the security of the army's auxiliary forces. Just as Galronus' closeness over the past few years had Romanised the Remi nobleman beyond any expectations, Fronto realised that he had come to respect the Gallic aspects of his friend, too: his inordinate strength and self-belief. His honour and his truthfulness, which far exceeded any to be found in the Republic's seething capital. His love of - and protectiveness of - his family and tribe. There were things about the Gauls that should make Rome look to its own morals. And soon, if things proceeded apace, Galronus would be his brother. There would be a great deal of trouble for the family with the die-hard patricians who still believed that no one born outside Latium ranked above cattle, but the Falerii were nothing if not adaptable and hard-skinned.

His reverie was interrupted as Samognatos reappeared in the doorway and beckoned. Fronto glanced round at Masgava and his men. He had wondered whether bringing the dark-skinned Numidian would put the locals on their guard - a reminder of just how foreign their visitors were - but had settled on the ex-gladiator for two reasons. Firstly he was softer spoken and more accommodating than his fellow officer, and secondly, Palmatus had a legionary's grasp of defence, pickets and passwords, and was therefore plainly the man to leave in charge of the inn, with its stores, horses and men.

'Come on.'

184

Putting as much confidence in his stride as he could muster, Fronto strode into the building after Samognatos, blinking as his eyes adjusted to the gloom, the interior lit by a central fire-pit, whose smoke drifted up through a hole in the roof, and by three braziers spaced out around the edge.

The upper floor took the form of a mezzanine around the central smoke-hole area, reachable by ladders. Shuffling in the darkness above announced the presence of people on that floor, though they were invisible from below.

The ordo - the council - of Divonanto sat on a set of stepped benches at the far end of the room, for all the world like a Gallic version of the senate, though undoubtedly with more conviction, morals and sense than the Roman ruling body. Eight old men, each with a torc and silver and gold jewellery in evidence. None were armed or armoured, which gave Fronto cause for relief, since he'd left his own weapon outside with Quietus, along with that of each of the four men he'd brought inside with him.

'Well met, ambassador of Caesar,' intoned one old man, holding up a hand in greeting.

'And to you, elders of Divonanto,' he replied, pleased at the level of introduction. It seemed no one was going to stand on too much ceremony here - at least the cacophonic carnyxes were auspiciously absent. 'We seek your counsel' he added.

'So we are led to understand. You seek news of your enemies?'

'Of one enemy in particular,' Fronto scanned the faces of the council. Impassive, but curious. Not the faces of deceivers or enemies. He felt his posture relax a little more.

'You seek Ambiorix of the Eburones,' the old man said in a matter-of-fact voice.

'We do. We understand that he has made contact with the Nervii, the Menapii and the Treveri. Though we have not heard as much, we also suspect him to be initiating contact with the tribes beyond the great river Rhenus, as well as possibly wresting what remains of his own tribe from the control of his brother king, Cativolcus.'

'First tell me,' the old man asked, leaning forward with an interested frown, 'why a small unit of Romans hunt their great enemy, shunning the trappings and symbols of your Republic?'

Fronto nodded. It was a very fair question and one whose answer he was sure could only strengthen their position.

185

'The general - Caesar, that is - has pledged to one of our greatest Gods to bring down Ambiorix. He will burn the world if he has to in order to complete that vow. I am sure you, living in such a sacred place, will appreciate the importance of a vow to the Gods?'

Nods all round.

'The Nervii have already suffered his wrath for treating with Ambiorix, and he will do the same to other tribes until the rebel king is his. While the Nervii deserved what befell them to some extent, I seek to close the matter early and save the rest of the Belgae from further destruction. Some Romans see the only solution for the troublesome tribes to be their removal. Others - myself included - see that the level of cooperation that exists between *our* two peoples could be extended to all, and as such, we would prefer to avoid potentially opening a crevasse between our peoples with such destruction.'

More nods. Mutters quietly among the nobles in their own tongue. Fronto stood silent, patient, waiting.

'Ambiorix moved among the Treveri little more than a week ago,' the old man announced finally. 'It seems that he stirs up trouble among them. Your general in the south put the Treveri to flight and killed Indutiomarus, but that unfortunate King has living relatives who would see him avenged. Ambiorix fans the flames of their desire.'

'The Treveri,' Fronto noted with a sidelong look at Samognatos. The scout looked unhappy. Not surprising, really, considering the possibility of moving into the lands of one of his tribe's most rabid enemies.

'Hold,' the old man said, raising his hand again. 'There is some indication that Ambiorix and his men passed into the lands of the Segni mere days ago.'

Fronto shook his head. 'Not heard of the Segni. Who are they?'

'The Segni are a small people who lie to our east,' the old man replied.

'They supply a cavalry force to Caesar,' added Samognatos. 'They are a loyal tribe.'

'Perhaps no longer, if they now harbour Ambiorix.' He looked up at the council. 'Is this your latest information?'

The old man nodded. 'Conjecturally, if he has moved from Treveri lands into the Segni's territory, he may be making for Eburone lands again, home into his deep woods under the protection of Arduenna. Pray to your Gods that he has not done so, Roman. If Ambiorix disappears into Arduenna's reach, you will never touch him.'

'Don't underestimate the tenacity and reach of Rome, my friend,' Fronto said darkly. 'Thank you for your aid. It is greatly appreciated, and I will make sure that Caesar knows of it. Before we leave, I would ask if you have had any contact with the southern tribes? The Arverni in particular?'

The old man frowned. The council began to chatter to one another again and Fronto squinted into the dim light to scan their faces. Years of facing off against men across a council chamber or a battlefield or even a game of dice had given Fronto a reasonable ability to read a man's expression, and he was satisfied from what he saw that the council had no knowledge of the men who had apparently passed through here. Certainly if anyone *was* involved with them, he was an excellent liar and a master of maintaining a straight expression.

'We know nothing of the Arverni, Roman. In fact, in these troubled days we see no one but our neighbouring tribes or your own people. Are we to be wary of the Arverni? I was under the impression that they were a quiet and uninvolved people.'

Fronto nodded quietly. 'We were under that impression too, but that might be about to change, if I am correct. Beware any southerner entering your land, and Caesar and I would both appreciate knowing if they make contact at any time?'

'I will make sure to do so,' the old man bowed. 'Will you be staying with us for the day? We were unaware of your approach until the last moment, but would be pleased to lavish a feast in your honour tomorrow?'

'Tempting as that is,' Fronto smiled, 'I must decline. If Ambiorix is headed into the great forest's depths, we must move on him with all haste. I am truly grateful, but we must leave as soon as we have consulted your druids in the morning.'

The old man nodded. 'We will pray to Arduenna for your safety and success beneath her boughs. She is, after all, a huntress!'

Fronto smiled. 'Then with the aid of my own ladies of Luck and Vengeance, how can we fail?'

* * * * *

187

Legionary Aurelius sighed with relief. Despite their position, far from the army and deep in Gallic lands, life had improved for him no end. For all Fronto's warnings of what a place in this unit would mean, for Aurelius it meant no more digging latrines, raising earth ramparts or 'soft duty' - removing and cleaning the tribunes' piss pots from their rooms. Even though he'd drawn one of the black stones and had to make do with finding a sleeping space in the hay loft of the stables, it was still a dozen steps above life in the old cohort.

Carefully, so as not to wake the rest of the slumbering soldiers, Aurelius descended the ladder from the loft, alighting in his bare feet. After all, he'd only be a few moments, and the ground was drier than it had been for months.

Taking a deep breath, he trotted out of the stable's river-side door. The familiar shape of Drusus sat hunched against the wall, cloak wrapped around him for warmth in the chill of the night and fastened with the 'naked girl clasp' which had cost him a bundle a few years back. The heavier-set legionary nodded to him in recognition and Aurelius nodded back before wandering across to the river. Standing at the cobbled dock and grumbling about the ache of the lumpy uneven surface on his bare feet, Aurelius hoisted up his tunic and pulled aside his subligaculum, straining for a moment before a long arc of steaming urine jetted out into the wide, glass-dark river with a loud spatter.

Relief.

He watched the far bank, where only scrub bushes and occasional knots of trees punctuated the monotony of green slopes beneath the black-purple sky. From what they said about the great forest of Arduenna, on whose periphery they now waited, the chances of seeing such open spaces and such an expanse of sky again for some time were rather small. Some people said that the protector Goddess sealed off the sky with the boughs of her trees so that even birds could not enter or flee without her leave.

Turning, he smiled at Drusus, who was shuffling to achieve a more comfortable position under his cloak. Arduenna could go screw herself. No native witch was going to worry him. He took a step forward and something smacked into his forehead, obscuring his vision, scratching... fighting... blinding.

Aurelius felt a moment of true, earth-shaking panic as his vision was occluded by something black and flapping, pincer points digging into his scalp. He shrieked and threw his arms up in panic, simultaneously soiling his woollen undergarment.

The bat that had become tangled in his overlong locks managed to free itself and flit away into the night. Aurelius realised that he was shaking like a leaf and a steady, warm, unpleasant smell was rising from his nethers. Despite the explosion of raucous laughter that issued from Drusus where he sat on guard, Aurelius felt neither embarrassment nor anger.

He was too busy feeling bone-chilling fear.

Removing his underwear and flinging it into the water, aware of the trickle of blood running down from his scalp, he dipped into the river and began to wash his nethers with the ice cold water, all the while throwing up at the sky apologies to great Arduenna and her spirits. After all, if she could control bats, what was she truly capable of?

Chapter Ten

Samarobriva - Caesar's camp

The days had passed for Priscus in an increasingly irritating haze. Already, mere days after Fronto and his party had left, the tribal leaders had begun to arrive at Samarobriva for the assembly, and the general had been largely closeted away on his own, leaving the ever-enthusiastic Marcus Antonius at something of a loss.

Antonius seemed to be one of those people who find it almost unbearable to pass the time on their own, and any moment in which he found himself at a loose end, he descended on one of the other officers to socialise. Fronto had been his companion of choice for much of his brief time in Gaul, but now - with Fronto gone - Priscus seemed to have been selected to fill the void.

Every night for the past four nights, Antonius had turned up at his door with an amphora of wine - often with some unintelligible - if shapely - local girl draped on his arm. Priscus had almost forgotten what it felt like to go to sleep sober and to spend a morning without a 'seven horn' hangover. In his more malicious moments, he wondered if this was what it had felt like to be Fronto.

Rubbing his pink eyes and wondering what fresh hell the day would provide, Priscus stepped out from his tent and spotted, with a sinking heart, Antonius striding towards him across the grass.

'Ah shit.'

'Gnaeus?'

'Antonius. You seem agitated.'

And he did. Antonius was almost bouncing as he walked, and his face had creased into a frown of concern, lacking its usual mischievous humour.

'The Aeduan chieftain has turned up, in a small party of warriors, alongside the Sequani and Lingones.'

'That must be nearly the full complement, then,' Priscus said in surprise. 'No assembly's ever been gathered so quickly. 'Who are we missing?'

'The Carnutes and the Senones, apparently,' Antonius replied with a strange tone that Priscus couldn't quite identify.

He frowned. 'But the Carnutes and the Senones are two of the more local tribes - certainly a lot more local than the Sequani and the Aedui. They should have been among the first to arrive.'

Again: that look, as Antonius nodded.

'The two wolves who won't eat with the pack'.

'What?'

'Hercules speaks to me plainly on occasion. Suffice it to say, the Carnutes and the Senones won't be attending. Nor the Treveri, Nervii, Eburones or Menapii, of course, but Caesar didn't bother sending messengers there, given the situation.'

'What has the general to say on the matter?'

'I'm about to go see him. I thought you might like to accompany me.'

'*Like* is a strong word,' Priscus grumbled. 'Come on, then.'

The two officers strode across the damp, dewy grass. While spring was officially upon the land, the weather Gods had apparently failed to notice and were gripping tight to winter, unwilling to see it leave. Ingenuus' Praetorian cavalrymen stood at attention by the tent, but did not deign to question the approach of two such senior officers. By the time Priscus and Antonius had reached the command tent, one of the guards had already ducked inside and announced them, returning to his place and holding aside the tent flap for them to enter.

'Morning, Gaius,' Antonius said conversationally as he stepped inside. Priscus had long-since become accustomed to the casual, familial relationship between the two men and simply saluted and waited to one side as Caesar acknowledged them with an idle wave of the hand without looking up from his work.

'I think we have a problem with the assembly.' Antonius scratched his chin.

The general paused in his scratching of marks onto his tablet and looked up. 'Oh?'

'The Senones and the Carnutes have not sent deputations.'

Caesar's brow creased for a moment, but he shook his head. 'Perhaps they are delayed. The experience of repeated councils at this time of year has allowed the tribes to send their ambassadors with unusual alacrity, yet we cannot expect every tribe to be so prompt. My couriers were fast, and the chieftains will have been awaiting the summons, but still, it is inclement and early. We have to allow a little leeway.'

Antonius shook his head. 'They're not coming, Caesar… trust me on that. You hold to your consultations of Venus and you know that I do so with Hercules. The great club-bearer himself tells me they are not coming.'

Caesar's brow continued to lower. 'What would you have me do, Antonius?'

Priscus cleared his throat with a quick glance at Antonius. 'It might be prudent to bide our time and be certain, General. For all the wisdom of the Gods, I would prefer to trust the word of our scouts and the evidence of my own eyes. When your couriers return we will know for certain whether those tribes are refusing the summons.'

He held his breath. A delay in the council would buy Fronto a few extra days, and could make a great deal of difference to him. There was a leaden pause in the room. Antonius had agreed that they should do what they could to grant Fronto the space to work, but Priscus was coming to realise that the new senior officer was as unpredictable as he was cunning. He had back-flipped on more than one decision since Priscus had got to know him.

'No.' Caesar straightened and stretched. 'The Carnutes have been troublesome before, which is why we garrisoned a legion on them last year. And the Senones are local enough that they should have been here by now if they had any intention of attending. Your demi-God is correct, Antonius. These two tribes have refused my summons. So the question now is what to do about it?'

'I think the answer to that is fairly clear,' Antonius replied with a firm, hard edge to his voice.

'Dispatch the legions?' Caesar enquired.

'Send them against these two tribes. Do unto them what you did to the Nervii.'

Priscus narrowed his eyes as he glanced at Antonius. Was the man attempting to buy Fronto more time or simply moving to slake his thirst for battle? Such an action would certainly delay the council, but Fronto would hardly approve of the method. To utterly wipe out two tribes just to buy Fronto time was hardly appropriate.

The general frowned. 'I do not like the idea of moving the entire army further west, while my main objective lies east.'

Priscus cleared his throat again. 'And with respect, General, we do not have the details yet. It is somewhat premature to order the extermination of tribes without being fully aware of why we are doing so.'

Caesar nodded and Antonius cast a momentary irritated look at the prefect.

'Very well...' the general said, leaning on his desk. 'There is a supply depot two days south of here at the Parisii capital: Lutetia. That's on the border of both Carnute and Senone lands. I will move two legions there and reconvene the assembly. You,' he pointed at Antonius, 'will take three legions south immediately. Strip them of kit so that they can travel fast and move against these two tribes. Be quick and either bring them to the assembly or find out why they have not attended and chastise them appropriately. The rest of the army can stay here and wait for us to return.'

Antonius nodded his approval.

'And you, Priscus... I shall put the camps in the hands of my lieutenants for the time being. You go with Antonius. He is new to Gaul, but you know the tribes and their ways well enough now. Antonius? You have a tendency to leap in with both feet before you test the water's temperature. Priscus knows the Gauls. Listen to him, and if he advises you to do something, I strongly suggest you do it.'

The prefect saluted. He had attempted to slow things, but it seemed Caesar was set on putting things in order quickly before he moved on. At least with Priscus along for the ride and with Caesar's given authority, he might be able to nudge Antonius' hand and keep him on the right path. Caesar's friend and senior officer gave Priscus a sour look and the prefect sighed. What Caesar saw as sensible advice, Antonius likely saw as emasculation.

Reaching out, Caesar drew his tablets and stylus across the table, ready to return to his work. He looked up at them briefly.

'Are you still here? Go. You have your orders.'

Priscus and Antonius saluted and turned, striding from the tent. As soon as the flap had fallen back into place and they were past the protective cordon of Ingenuus' guards, the younger - yet more senior - of the two men turned, grasping Priscus by the shoulder and jarring him to a halt.

'What the fuck was that about?'

Priscus sighed.

'What?'

'You wanted to buy Fronto time. I bought him a whole damn campaign's worth. Now we delay matters long enough to kick seven shades of shit out of the Carnutes and the Senones. Fronto will be grateful. And instead of giving me a hand, you start throwing around all this rubbish about waiting just in case and being sure they deserve a beating. I thought you were Fronto's friend?'

The prefect bridled and turned, wrenching his shoulder from Antonius' powerful grip.

'The whole reason that Fronto is *doing this* is to prevent the unnecessary ravaging, enslaving and burning of whole tribes. We should be working on making allies and subjects out of them, not corpses and slaves. You really think the best way to aid Fronto is by further perpetrating exactly what he's trying to stop? For the love of Mars, Antonius! What if the Senones and the Carnutes aren't attending because they're falling foul of other rebellious tribes? It's happened before!'

'Then we'll find out while our nailed boots are poised over their throats,' Antonius snapped. 'Better to negotiate from a position of strength, I'd say.'

'Well we're set now' Priscus sighed. 'We lead three legions against them and deal with whatever we find. The big problem we have is timing. It would benefit Fronto if we took as long as possible in the task, but two things weigh against that.'

'Caesar's orders to move fast,' agreed Antonius, nodding.

'And the fact that, if these tribes *are* planning on rebelling, every extra day we give them allows them more time to prepare. Sadly for Fronto, I think we need to do as Caesar commanded and move as fast as possible.'

Antonius tapped his chin in thought. 'We take the most veteran, trained and experienced legions. They'll move faster and work better together.'

'That would be the Seventh, Ninth and Tenth, I'd say,' Priscus agreed. 'The Eighth are as long-standing, but despite years under Plancus' rotting command, the Seventh were posted in Carnute territory over winter, so they might be more use.'

'Then I'll leave you to pass the news to them. What's our first move? You know these people, as Caesar says.'

'The Senones, I'd say,' Priscus replied. 'They're closer, smaller, and easily reached along the river valley. We move south. The nearest Senone oppidum of any size is Melodunon, but the bigger ones of Vellaunodunon and Agedincum are not far south of that. We take Melodunon and hopefully we'll resolve what's happening. If we need to move further, from there we can move to either of the larger settlements along the river, as the Sequana forks and each lies on one branch.'

'You know the land that well?' Antonius asked in surprise.

'Never been there. But I've studied the maps and spoken to the officers who have. Come on. Let's get things ready. Sooner we leave, sooner we can sort this mess out.'

* * * * *

194

Priscus reined in his horse as Antonius held up his hand to stop the advancing column.

'Well?'

The prefect took a deep breath and glanced at the two scouts who had accompanied him as they moved back into position with the cavalry escort. 'I think we're in luck.'

'Explain.'

'Melodunon would be a nightmare to take unless we have naval support. There's three islands strung out in the middle of the river, and the town's on the big one in the middle. It's connected to both banks by wooden bridges. Got good solid walls, too.'

'Doesn't sound that lucky to me.'

'Lucky, because we're not going to *have* to assault it. Looks like the place is undefended. Gates are open and no one on the walls. Hearth smoke and general noise says the town's occupied, but not defended.'

'So we intimidate them with numbers? No fight required?'

'My thoughts precisely. Have the three legions move in full formation to the river bank near the bridge and look deadly. Then you and me - as well as the legates and tribunes - ride up to the gates and find out what we need to know.'

'Fanfares and everything. Good.' Antonius turned to the knot of officers following him.

'Plancus, Trebonius and Crassus: have your senior centurions send the legions to the shore and form up facing the island, then bring your tribunes, eagles, standards and musicians forward to the bridge.'

The three legates saluted and returned to their legions, issuing the commands. Priscus and Antonius waited for the army to begin moving in concert, the Ninth and Tenth manoeuvring out to the sides to flank the Seventh and moving three legions abreast towards the low bump in the land and the woods around the edge of which the road to Melodunon passed.

By the time the army reached the treeline and approached the bend, the officers had all ridden forward to join the commanders and, accompanied by the pomp and fanfare of a Roman command unit, they rounded the bend and began the gentle descent to the river bank.

As Priscus had described, Melodunon was a long, narrow settlement, nestled on an island some half a mile long, yet only a hundred and fifty paces wide. Its heavy, high walls looked down on strong timber bridges that connected it to both banks, and onto the small, reed-swamped islands that sat at either end - a haven for birds and other wildlife.

Still no warriors stood watch on the ramparts, and dozens of tendrils of smoke wound up through the pale grey air into the sky. Melodunon seemed peaceful... passive. No hive of rebellion.

'Doesn't look like much of a prize,' Antonius noted.

'We're not here for conquest,' Priscus reminded him quietly. 'Just for information, right now.'

As the legions moved into position at the river's edge, a gleaming mass of silver and red, the officers walked their horses out onto the bridge. At Antonius' cue the musicians began to intone a repetitive rising scale in harmony, which echoed out across the water and back from the walls of the small oppidum.

'Still no one on the walls,' Antonius noted. 'If it weren't for the background noise and the smoke I'd say the place was deserted.'

Priscus nodded, his own curiosity piqued.

Slowly and purposefully, in time with the blasts of the cornicen, the officers' horses rapped across the heavy timbers of the bridge. Still, the gates stood open. Finally, when they were perhaps two thirds of the way across the bridge, a figure stepped out from behind the walls and into the centre of the gate.

'Go!' it commanded in an old, reedy voice, the Latin heavily thickened with Gallic harshness.

'Could this be the leader of the town?' Antonius asked Priscus incredulously.

The two men looked at the warrior. He was not a young man - clearly more than a decade older than Antonius, but his arm rings denoted a martial past of some merit. As they watched, two younger, though less decorated, warriors stepped out to flank him.

'The Senones,' Antonius announced loudly and with the booming depth of a skilled orator, 'have not sent a deputation to the Gaulish assembly called by Caesar. At this time, the Proconsul's courier, who carried the summons, has also not returned, and nor has his escort.'

'Go!' repeated the old man. Though he stood with his sword still sheathed, the younger men to his sides pulled out their blades and hefted them.

'Why was no deputation sent?' Antonius demanded.

'Go!'

196

'Or you and your two trained apes will fight off twenty thousand soldiers? Do not make me laugh, old man. Answer my question.'

The old man reached out to one of his companions, who handed him something. With a contemptuous flick, the man cast the object forwards and it hit the wooden surface of the bridge and bounced to rest near the front hooves of Antonius' horse. It was a roll of parchment in a bronze ring, sealed with red wax. The beige parchment was dotted with other crimson marks that clearly were *not* wax. Though no one could see the seal from this distance, there could be no doubt that this was the document borne by the courier sent to the Senones.

'Your answer is duly noted,' Antonius growled.

'Send in a century of men and secure the gate,' Priscus barked to the nearest tribune - he wasn't sure what legion the young man was from, but he looked excited.

'Hold that command,' Antonius raised his hand. 'I'll deal with this.'

Lifting himself over the horns of the saddle, the officer slid from the horse's back and down to the bridge, where he stooped to collect the scroll. The blood was long dried. Turning it to confirm Caesar's Taurus seal, he walked steadily forward towards the three men in the gateway.

'What the hell is he doing?' muttered Priscus, mostly to himself, and then leaned back to Trebonius. 'Have a century of men brought forward ready anyway. Just in case.'

Trebonius nodded and relayed the order as they watched the scene before them. Antonius stopped half a dozen paces from the old man. The Gaul's two companions, hefting their swords menacingly, stepped slightly forward as the commander raised the scroll and held it forth.

'In the name of the Proconsul of Gaul and the ongoing Pax Romana, I offer you once again Caesar's summons, that you send your emissary to the assembly.'

The old man spat, missing the scroll by several feet, but conveying his meaning well nonetheless.

Slowly and with deliberate menace, Antonius drew his sword, the rasp as it left the scabbard cutting through the background noise with a bone-chilling sound. The two younger men stepped forward again.

'Go!' shouted the older one.

197

Antonius took another step forward, and the two younger warriors moved to intercept. His arm low and the blade down by his side, the Roman commander looked casual, as though he were moving in for an informal chat.

The warrior to his left was the first to make his move. His long, Gallic blade came up to his shoulder, where he now grasped the hilt with both hands, and then he swung, the sword coming down in an unstoppable arc towards Antonius' shoulder.

The Roman officer took an extra, nimble, half-step to the left - dropping the scroll - and, as the sword fell past his shoulder, he lashed out like an uncoiling cobra, smashing the point of his expensive, decorative gladius into the man's throat-apple, slamming it in hard enough that it completely severed the spine and the man's neck gave way with a loud crack, the head lolling and flopping to the side. The sudden lack of bone support aided Antonius in retrieving his blade, which he ripped out in a single movement, swiping it round just in time to block the second attacker's sword, the blades meeting with a clang and then scraping and rasping along one another in an attempt to break the lock in which they found themselves.

Priscus watched in surprise. He'd seen many sides of Antonius in the short time the man had been serving with the army in Gaul, but he'd never for a moment expected a natural-born killer, too.

The second warrior was concentrating on the blade and on gaining control of the struggle, but Antonius had different ideas: keeping the struggle deadlocked with his right arm, he reached up with his left and with simple, violent economy of movement, put out the Gaul's eye with his finger.

The warrior screamed. The sudden agony and blindness and shock devoured him and the struggle for the blades was forgotten. Not by Antonius, though. As the man's strength went from the blade, Antonius turned slightly and allowed the big Gallic sword to slide past, flicking his gladius up and across and opening up a second mouth below the young warrior's chin.

It had all taken maybe five heartbeats.

One young Gaul lay on the timber, his head at the most astoundingly odd angle, a spreading pool of blood beneath him, dripping between the timbers and into the river below. The other sank to his knees, the arterial spray coating the bridge before him as he collapsed dead onto his face.

The old man, shocked into sudden action, reached down to the hilt of his sword and grasped it.

'Uh, uh,' Antonius denied him, raising the tip of his gleaming red blade and resting the sharp point on the man's neck where his collar bones met. 'Leave the sword.'

'No kill!' shouted a female from somewhere behind. Keeping the sword exactly where it was, Antonius looked up over the old man's shoulder. Three women had scurried into the gateway. One was white as a sheet, another blubbering uncontrollably. The third - the older one - was watching with hopeless dismay. She spoke again. 'No kill!'

'Where are the warriors of Melodunon? Why have you not attended the summons to assembly?'

The old man tried to motion the old woman to silence, but Antonius applied a little pressure and the blade broke skin, stopping him.

'Men go Agedincum. Go for chief.'

Antonius nodded. 'Good.' He turned his head. 'Hear that, Priscus? Agedincum. The chief's gathered the warriors.'

Priscus nodded. 'Might have a fight after all, then.'

'Perhaps. Perhaps not.' Antonius kicked the old man in the knee and the 'protector of Melodunon' fell back with a hiss of pain as the Roman sheathed his blade. 'Look after him, old woman. He's got balls of iron, this one.'

With a carefree laugh, Antonius turned and walked back across the bridge towards the army, pausing only to pick up the scroll he had discarded during the fight. He tucked it away into the large pouch at his belt and produced - Priscus couldn't even imagine from where - a small wineskin, which he lifted and began to pour into his mouth as he walked.

The man was one constant surprise.

* * * * *

Agedincum was something of a different prospect.

The ramparts of the oppidum were more impressive than those of Melodunon, but its positioning less so. Instead of a commanding island position mid-stream, Agedincum sat on a low mound in an area of damp marshy ground, apparently constantly affected by the river and which would present a horrible danger to attacking troops. Its walls were as packed with warriors as

199

Melodunon's had been empty, and the very prospect of taking the oppidum soured the soul of every Roman present.

'What's the plan?' Priscus asked Antonius wearily.

'I thought Caesar sent *you* along as the 'plan man'?'

'Caesar sent me along to help guide things, and I did just that by directing you to Melodunon first. *You're* supposed to be the tactical genius here. I'm still just a glorified centurion with a superiority complex.'

Antonius laughed. 'Actually, I have no intention of launching an assault.'

'Oh really?'

'No. You saw at Melodunon how easily these people capitulate with the appropriate encouragement. I have no desire to lose a legion's worth of men in these festering marshes in order to storm a well-defended town of little or no long-term strategic value.'

'So what do you plan to do?'

'Your knowledge of the area sounded pretty thorough when you were planning this little pleasure jaunt. Just how well *do* you know it?'

'Better than most Romans, I guess.'

'Then when I give you the cue, I want you to supply a few nice rural or peaceful places. Fishing villages, small unwalled towns or religious sanctuaries. That sort of thing.'

'Alright,' consented Priscus with a suspicious frown.

'Come on. Just you and me.'

Priscus blinked in surprise as Antonius started walking his horse forwards. The marsh was traversed by means of a number of tracks created using timbers sunk into submerged causeways that provided a relatively solid surface, though even these were often hard to spot and occasionally vanished from sight.

'This is clearly insane, Antonius,' he grunted as he caught up and followed the senior commander, watching the swampy ground nervously and keeping the slimy timbers in sight as much as possible.

'I thought you were all in favour of solutions that did not involve endless bloodshed and burning?'

'Not if it means riding on my own up to the enemy walls and baring my arse at them while they try to loose arrows up it!'

Antonius laughed and drew out his mysterious wineskin, taking a swig.

'We've got the upper hand. Don't worry about it. Have some wine and try to resist the urge to bare your buttocks to anyone.' He held out the skin and Priscus took it gratefully, sucking down several mouthfuls of apparently unwatered wine before he handed it back.

'Smooth,' he rasped though his battered throat. 'What's it made from: sheep or thistles?'

'Probably both. It's made by the Gauls. Bet you didn't even know they made wine.'

'They don't. Whatever that is, it doesn't deserve that name. It's probably good for searing the rust off armour, mind.'

Again Antonius let out a mirthful burst of laughter.

'Truthfully…' Priscus urged, 'what are we going to do? We'll have to stay outside arrow range. The opportunity to stick feathered shafts in two well-dressed Romans is not something any rebellious Gaul is going to pass up.'

'They won't loose arrows at us, Gnaeus. They'll be too intrigued to see what we've got to say. That's why it's only two of us and not a hundred. More, and they'd have to kill us, just in case.'

'And when they've heard you out and laugh from their walls and call their archers forward? What then?'

'Not going to happen. Watch and learn, my cantankerous friend. Watch and learn.'

Priscus rode on behind, grunting and grumbling about officers with more balls than brains, occasionally throwing Fronto's name into the cauldron of spite just for cussedness. Slowly, carefully, with Antonius paying close attention to the wooden walkways, the pair closed on the walls of Agedincum. The large towers to either side of the heavy oaken gate - which remained firmly shut - were packed with native warriors armed with swords, spears and bows, as well as a few bearing the traditional stylised animal standards of the Gauls and the odd unshapely carnyx among them.

'This looks shittier with every step,' Priscus grumbled.

'Just play your part and watch with wonder,' smiled Antonius as he drew his steed to a halt in a nice clear area close to the gates and well within range of the archers. Priscus pulled alongside as close as he dare, given the terrain.

'Nobles and leaders of Agedincum… I am here to offer you a last opportunity to send ambassadors to the Gaulish assembly and pledge your loyalty to Rome with a further donation of auxiliary cavalry and, shall we say a hundred, noble hostages?'

There was a prolonged silence which suddenly erupted in laughter. A second wave of mirth issued forth - much louder - a few heartbeats later as the words were translated for the benefit of the non-Latin speakers. Finally a man wearing a bronze helmet that appeared to be topped by a bronzed dead rabbit stepped to the parapet.

'You make us laugh, Roman. We safe behind strong walls of oppidum. Swamp keep legions out. No tunnels. No towers. No ballista. No way you come in. We safe.'

Antonius laughed loudly and turned to Priscus.

'What was the name of that picturesque little village back along the river towards Melodunon?' he asked loudly enough to be heard in the towers.

Priscus' mind raced as he tried to remember the detail of the maps he'd scoured for hours on end.

'Brixi, I think, sir.'

'Brixi. Lovely place. Buxom women. Happy children. Not much industry, since all the menfolk are here inside these walls. No one to defend them, either. Shame for them.'

Priscus felt a cold thrill run through him as he realised what they were doing.

'Don't forget that shrine on the hill west of Melodunon,' he chipped in. 'I presume the druids are busily raging around holed up behind these walls too. Bet their precious nemeton is in the hands of a young, inexperienced apprentice?'

'Indeed,' Antonius sighed as he turned back to the walls. 'Such a shame. You see, if you were allies of Rome as you'd always claimed to be, Rome would be duty bound to protect these places and their delicate occupants as though they were our own. But if you refuse Caesar's summons and stand defiant against us, shattering your oaths... well, that means we're effectively at war. And I'm sure I don't need to explain to you people just how good we are at war. It's practically our national pastime.'

Priscus laughed at his fellow officer's audacity.

'So you can sit here in Agedincum, all defiant and mighty behind your walls and marshes. But remember that we'll leave a legion to keep you sealed in. We can spare one, you see. We've just raised another especially for the task. And soon your food will run out and you'll have to eat the pets. And then the rats. And then, in the end, each other. It's happened before when Rome sets herself to a purpose.'

Antonius straightened in the saddle.

'But there is one bright side to your fate: those of you who starve to death or become too weak to defend yourself and are eaten by your neighbours will not have to live with that moment when you finally break and surrender and have to see what we've done to your tribe while the warriors starve in there. The burned cities and homes. No living soul for a hundred miles, as they're all in the slave pens at Massilia. You won't join them, of course. Near death, weakened and half-starved, you won't be worth enslaving. You wouldn't make it to the coast.'

He straightened. 'I think that pretty much concludes my announcement. Anything you'd like to add, Priscus?'

'I don't think so,' the prefect shrugged. 'Think you've covered it.'

'Farewell then, warriors of the Senones. Enjoy your voluntary captivity. We'll enjoy your women.'

He turned his horse and started to walk her back towards the army. Priscus quickly joined him.

'Dangerous way to end, that. They might have stuck us full of arrows just out of spite.'

'But they didn't,' smiled Antonius. 'Any moment now…'

The horses took a few steps further, carefully, between the marshes.

'Wait!' cried a desperate, panicked voice from the battlements.

Antonius turned an insufferably smug smile on his companion.

* * * * *

'A welcoming party?' Antonius muttered to Priscus, as the army tramped at a steady pace through the fine, soak-you-to-the-bone drizzle. The prefect widened the viewing hole in the hood of his cloak in which he had almost cocooned himself for the last day of the journey. It had been less than a week in total since their three legions had left the very gate through which their 'welcoming party' now emerged: the west gate of the massive camp of Samarobriva.

'Not a good sign.' Priscus shifted his sore rump as the bony nag beneath him bounced up and down.

Over the past three days, returning from the borders of Carnute lands, the weather had turned inclement again, this time

203

warmer, but considerably wetter than the late winter had been. Complaints and grumbles had become the norm among the three legions - as well as their officers. All everyone wanted to do was get into that camp, drop their armour to the ground, peel off the soaked wool and bathe, change into something dry and then go to sleep, inside and warm.

The small knot of mounted officers converging on their column from the gate suggested that such a dream was a way off as yet.

'It's Rufio,' Antonius frowned. 'Him and a few lessers. What in the name of Juno's bony arse is he doing coming out to meet us?'

'We'll find out soon enough,' Priscus muttered and turned to the rider behind him, who sagged under the weight of his cornu. 'Sound the halt.'

The man extricated himself from the enclosing circle of the horn and tipped it upside down to empty the collected rainwater before blowing a somewhat soggy call through it. The column came to a halt as the order was repeated back through the Tenth, the Ninth and the Seventh. The legates of the three legions, riding alongside to stay out of the press and the mud, kicked their horses forward to meet the commanders at the fore.

Waiting, rained-upon and tired, the returning victors - such as they were, having fought a grand total of two men - waited for the approaching riders. Rufio reined in his steed as they met on the low ground before the camp.

'Miserable day you've brought back with you.'

'Cut to the point, Rufio,' grunted Priscus. 'I'm cold.'

'We've been waiting for your return. Caesar's convened the assembly, but he's also announced our next move to the staff. As soon as matters are settled with the natives, we're moving against the Menapii in force.'

'Surely he plans to let us settle in and get dry first?' Priscus snapped.

Rufio chuckled. 'Some of you. The Tenth are to return to quarters and stand down until after the assembly, but the Seventh and the Ninth have been redirected. Trebonius and Plancus are to take their men and make immediately for Labienus' camp, along with the entire army's baggage train. Labienus is being given overall command of three legions in order to crush the Treveri, while we squeeze the tribes from the north, starting with the Menapii.'

204

Priscus sagged slightly. 'What about Fronto? He's right in the middle.'

'The general seems to think that Fronto will find his task easier if we can drive the enemy to him, working from the edges.'

The recently-arrived staff officer peered at the damp legions before him, noting the sour, less than happy looks on the faces of the two legates who would not tonight find the comfort of a warm room and a hot dinner. 'Sorry, gentlemen. Caesar's already had the support wagons and the baggage train readied for you at the east gate, so that there's no delay. You'll be slowed badly by the baggage, so you'd best get moving immediately. Your specific orders are with the prefect in charge of the wagons.'

'What news of the assembly?' Antonius asked pointedly.

'Caesar's drawing new oaths and new levies of cavalry from all the states that can still afford to do so. What happened with the recalcitrant tribes you went after?'

Antonius thumbed in the direction of the column behind him.

'The deputation from the Senones was delayed by stupidity. They're with us at the back, as are a number of hostages from their tribe. The Carnutes apparently panicked when they heard we were approaching, and their deputation found us, almost falling over themselves fawning and simpering, wanting to attend.'

Priscus gave a hard smile.

'I suspect that had something to do with what you told the Senones. Word of things like that spreads fast through the tribes. The Carnutes' King probably shat a brick when he heard what you told his neighbours.'

Antonius chuckled as Rufio raised a questioning eyebrow.

'Suffice it to say,' added Priscus, 'I think Antonius frightened the tribes into submission. They took the oaths again in a hurry and followed us like sheep. The west is settled, for now.'

'Good. As soon as this council's over, the Fourteenth and the Fifteenth will take on garrison duties here and the other five legions march on the Menapii.'

Priscus glanced at Antonius.

'Great. More swamps.'

Antonius shrugged, droplets of water showering from his shoulders.

'I'd rather be in a swamp with five legions than in the Eburones' sacred forest with just a dozen men,' the officer replied pointedly.

Chapter Eleven

Divonanto in the lands of the Condrusi

Fronto ground his teeth as he hiked up the last few feet of the near-vertical slope, his breath coming in gasps and puffs.

'Would they... really be... offended if... we didn't bother?'

Samognatos shook his head. 'They know we... are coming. They... always know.'

'But... we know where... to look next... anyway.'

The Condrusi scout flashed him a look that illustrated his feelings on the notion of bypassing the sacred nemeton of Divonanto. Fronto had been in two minds all morning. As far as his direct mission was concerned, he was unlikely to get any better directions to Ambiorix's current location than the council had given him last night. And whatever the scout said, Fronto had his suspicions as to how helpful the druids were likely to be. He'd as soon stand knee deep in the sea, wearing copper armour and calling Jupiter a spiteful prick as trust a druid, but Samognatos seemed convinced they had to visit, and in these lands, Fronto was to some extent reliant upon the man's continued help and goodwill.

The pair reached the top of the interminable and evil slope and Fronto reached down, gripping his trembling knees and heaving in breaths, watching the singulares labouring up the mountainside behind them. The 'easiest' route to the nemeton without circling round a few miles involved heading to the side of town away from the river, nestled up against the slope, and coming at the cliff outcropping from an oblique angle. Easiest: maybe. Easy: no. The slope was still one of the steepest he had ever climbed, and certainly one of the highest. His legs may never stop shaking, and he knew just how badly his calves and shins were going to hurt tomorrow.

'I'm not leaving anyone outside... you know.'

Samognatos simply widened that infernal grin. 'Won't you want to leave someone to guard the weapons?'

Fronto blinked. 'If you think for one... moment I'm going in there unarmed...'

'That is the only option, I'm afraid, sir.'

'Screw that.'

'Respectfully, Romans do not approve of bearing arms in their temples. Indeed, the whole of Rome is weapon free I understand?'

'That's because Rome isn't home to a bunch of savage...'
He stopped short, not for fear of insulting Samognatos' druids, but
rather because he was about to claim that Rome was safer and more
civilised, but a quick mental run through his past few visits silenced
that notion.

'I give you my word that you will be unharmed.'

Fronto sighed. 'I'm not impugning you, my friend, but I
could give you my word that up is down. Would that make it so?'

'Come on... Let's get inside,' coughed Palmatus, clambering
over the edge onto the grass.

'Samognatos here tells me we have to leave our weapons.'

'Fair enough.'

Fronto frowned. 'You approve?'

'Not really, but we've come all this way, and they're only
old grey-beards with sticks. We're legionaries, with Masgava too.'

'Grey-beards? You'd not say that if you'd met the bastard
with the crown over in Britannia that tried to carve me a new
arsehole on the front!'

Samognatos cleared his throat meaningfully and Fronto
turned to him, and then followed his gaze to see two men in white
robes standing in the open gateway in the wicker fence.

'Arduenna tells us that Romans are coming and that we are
to open our arms to them.'

Fronto narrowed his eyes. 'Experience tells me that one of
those arms will hold a dagger.'

The druid held his arms out to the sides. 'Please enter. You
will come to no harm.'

Again, Fronto maintained his steely stare, but Masgava was
suddenly next to him, striding towards the gate. As he approached,
he drew his sword and three knives from various places about his
body and, removing his cloak, placed them on the ground, on the
thick wool for protection from the damp grass.

'Masgava?'

'Come on, sir.'

Fronto sighed and stepped forward, unsheathing his blade
and dropping it onto Masgava's cloak with the others. He gestured to
the men behind him to do so. 'Pontius and Quietus? You two stay
out here with the weapons.'

'We were led to believe there were twenty of you?' the druid
enquired, performing a second quick headcount and eyeing the
seventeen visitors with interest.

Fronto paused as he approached. 'Our three Remi riders are bringing the horses and gear the long way round. They'll wait for us at the main road. You are surprisingly well-informed?'

'You travel within the Goddess' lair. She sees all.'

'Comforting.'

The druid gave a smile that did nothing to ease Fronto's tension and ushered the Roman party inside. As they passed into the sacred nemeton, Masgava and Palmatus took a surreptitious opportunity to wink at Fronto and indicate the location of their hidden knives.

The Divonanto grove consisted of three rings of trees regularly spaced and offset so as to almost create a barrier that one had to pass through at an angle. Consequently, the centre of the grove was not visible until the three rings had been negotiated. As far as Fronto was concerned, it was a terrible waste of what must be an astounding view, but with a shrug he followed the druids through the trees into the centre.

Within, a circular area consisted of well-tended turf and a ring of small jagged standing stones. At the centre was a wide, flat slab of blue-grey rock, four felled trunks surrounding it, forming benches. A veritable banquet lay on the slab, including platters of fruit and meat, bread and cheese, and jugs of what looked to be water.

Two druids sat at the slab opposite and raised their hands in welcome. Fronto approached the feast cautiously and sat on one of the logs, as far away from the druids as he could. As the others took their seats, his eyes strayed across the table, surveying the food. He also saw, with no surprise, a purple stain on the stone beneath.

'A new use for your stone?'

The druids frowned in incomprehension.

'I note the stains. Telling ones, those are. Fruit's not the only thing that gets laid open on this stone, eh?'

The man who had escorted them through the gate and had first spoken to them arched an eyebrow and smiled knowingly.

'Many sacrifices on this stone. Goats, sheep, bulls, chickens and more.' He laughed. 'And fruit.'

'I'm sure.'

The silence that fell was cold and uncomfortable, and Masgava, in his usual easy manner, broke the spell by reaching out and laying a slice of pink meat on the white bread, stuffing it into his mouth with a happy sigh.

The druids nodded approvingly at him, and then one turned to Fronto. 'You hunt Ambiorix of the Eburones.'

Fronto nodded. 'I am a little uncertain how the druids stand on this matter. Traditionally, none of your sect has spoken civilly to a Roman and I am having a great deal of difficulty in believing that you mean us anything less than harm. Tell me why you would aid us.'

There were shared glances between the four robed men, and finally one of the pair who had already been seated at the table leaned forward, pouring himself a cup of crystal clear water and cleared his throat.

'Do not be mistaken, commander. We are no friend of yours. It simply suits our purpose to supply you with what you need to accomplish your goals at this particular time. When your task is complete, we will have no further business with you.'

The druid next to him nodded. 'It is a troublesome matter for us and has created divisions in our society. Some would happily cast their blessings upon Ambiorix for what he has done and what he continues to attempt. I have to say that even I toasted his success when he destroyed your legion in the winter.'

Fronto's eyes darkened dangerously, and the legionaries around stopped reaching for the food, suddenly on their guard. Masgava shrugged and stuffed a plum into his mouth.

'Let us not fall to argument,' the first druid said, soothingly. 'This nemeton is home to seven shepherds of the people. Three disagree with our stand and have left in support of Ambiorix and the enemies of Rome. We four remain as we have no interest in perpetuating the Eburone king's campaign of resistance.'

'You still give us no reason. Why this divide?'

'It is a matter of deciding where the best path lies for our people. Those of us you call 'druids' are not an army, but a caste of wise men, each with our own free will. And as wise men, we each believe we hold more wisdom than others. Perhaps *true* wisdom would be trying to knit all possibilities into one garment.'

'So some of you think Ambiorix is bad for Gaul? I tend to agree. Alright... for now let us assume that you are hiding nothing and that we can trust you, although the very idea makes me twitch. Have you any helpful information for us?'

The fourth druid, who so far had not spoken, cleared his throat. He was an old man - older than the rest, anyway - and his voice was reedy and quiet. 'Ambiorix has only a small following of his own, but enjoys the favour of kings and councils. He is welcome anywhere from the sea to the mountains, except in Condrusi lands.'

'That's not particularly helpful.'

'Where he is now is of no use to you. By the time you get there, he will be gone. I offer you the greater solution: where he will be.'

Fronto narrowed his eyes. 'Now you're talking. Go on.'

'Ambiorix has finished treating with all the eastern tribes and gained their favour. The Treveri are already making war on your general, and the Nervii are all-but destroyed, yet he has hopes to build an army from the rest before your forces reach them. He will not look to us, as the Condrusi have consistently refused to deal with him. So only one path remains to him: to return home. He still needs the Eburones, as they are the centre position of his tribal alliance. And the Eburones that still thrive are loyal to his opposite number, King Cativolcus. To complete his army, he must wrest the land from his brother king. Find Cativolcus, and in time Ambiorix will find you.'

Fronto nodded. 'As much as it irks me that I'll be aiding druids towards their goals, thank you for this. Needless to say, if we make our way to Cativolcus' court and find that we have been sold out and that the entire Eburone nation is waiting for us with sharpened blades, I will find a way to come back here and nail you to your sacred trees, even if it is my larva - my vengeful spirit - that has to do it. I trust we have an understanding?'

The druids simply smiled indulgently, as though they fully expected and accepted his threat.

'I have one further matter to discuss.'

He picked up an apple from the table, inspected it as though expecting it to be rotten, rubbed it on his tunic, bit and chewed for a long moment.

'Where did the Arverni go?'

His companions turned frowns upon him, and Fronto ignored them, watching the faces of the four druids. Just as he expected, two of them immediately displayed expressions of guilty surprise before plastering innocence across the top. The other two were instantly guarded.

'There are no Arverni in the north.'

'Now you and I both know that for the lie it is. How do you expect me to trust your information on Ambiorix when you lie so plainly about your visitors?'

The man who had first accompanied them, and who Fronto had begun to think of as the headman, leaned forward and steepled his fingers.

'The Arverni are no concern of yours. They are about on the business of our brothers from the south, and not in connection with your hunt for Ambiorix.'

Fronto narrowed his eyes and took a deep breath.

'Bear in mind that I am an eminently practical man. Even my undead spirit will be able to handle a hammer and nails. Keep uppermost in your mind an image of the four of you hanging from your trees while your precious sacred stone is stood upright and carved into a statue of Nemesis. I do not like to be lied to or crossed.' With a grunt, he dropped the part-chewed apple back to the platter and rose. 'I think we're done here.'

Masgava gave him a quick glance and grabbed a handful of meat and bread before rising with the others. Samognatos looked distinctly uncomfortable. For the first time his odd smile had slid to an almost straight line.

The druids rose together and bowed their heads, the 'leader' speaking for them once more. 'I cannot say I am surprised at your attitude, and if our own circumstances were not so troubled, we would be a great deal happier to watch you from the far side of a battlefield, but the fact remains that we both desire Ambiorix's swift death, and so we will ask great Arduenna to shelter, protect and guide you within her demesne until your task is complete.'

Fronto nodded his head in a curt acknowledgement.

'I pray your information leads to a swift resolution, and that we never meet again.'

Turning, he strode from the laden stone, back between the trees and towards the gate in the fence without waiting to be escorted by the druids. His men marched along behind purposefully, Masgava still stuffing meat and bread into his face as though destined to starve. A chill breeze rose and ruffled the trees, sending a shiver up everyone's spine as they exited the nemeton. Spring was here now, with flowers bursting into colourful life and the trees budding green, but the air still held a morning chill. At least, Fronto chose to believe it was a purely natural, seasonal thing, and nothing to do with the sacred site of the druids.

Outside, the Roman party paused to collect their weapons and pass on the information to the two soldiers waiting by the pile,

212

after which Masgava slung his cloak over his shoulders and shivered into the cold material.

'Alright, Samognatos.' Fronto sighed. 'Lead us down to the main road. The other three should be there now with the horses.'

The small force traipsed down the grassy slope without looking back at the nemeton they had left and when they reached what appeared to be a regularly-used path, Fronto cleared his throat. 'Palmatus? Are they watching us?'

The former legionary turned his head slightly to look out of the corner of his eye. 'No sign. They must have gone back inside. They'll be out of earshot anyway.'

Fronto nodded. 'What did you pick up there?'

'That they want Ambiorix dead. That they have some secret business with the Arverni that they won't share, and they don't like us any more than we like them.'

Fronto nodded. 'More than that. They assume that we want Ambiorix dead and that is what joins our goal to theirs. What they don't know is that I *don't* want him dead. I want that bastard alive to answer a few questions. I get the impression that the druids wouldn't like that one bit, and noted that they expected a 'swift death'. And they carefully told us that the Arverni were on their business, and not connected with our *hunt* for Ambiorix. They did not say they weren't connected with Ambiorix, and that leads me to suspect that they are. The druids are trying to use us to put Ambiorix down - or at least some of them are. And I believe that these are the same druids who are allied with the Arverni and therefore that big warrior back in Bibracte who also had a low opinion of our quarry. We're being played, but we haven't much choice at this point but to go along with it. No one is to put a blade through Ambiorix's neck before I've had a chance to talk with him. Got that?'

The men nodded their agreement, a number of them with hard expressions. The party strode on in silence towards the wide defile that rose east from the river and along which the road deep into the forest of Arduenna ran from Divonanto. For more than a quarter of an hour they descended until they saw the main road tracking through the trees ahead.

The Remi seemed to have located the junction successfully as the party could hear the many horses whickering and snorting nearby. With a sense of relief, they strode out onto the road, and it took only a matter of heartbeats for Fronto to realise that something was wrong. The atmosphere was charged with a nervous energy. The two Remi standing among the horses wore unpleasant expressions, Magurix's big, muscular, handsome features darkened by a worried frown, and Brannogenos' dark, bearded face scowling as he fiddled with one of the multitudinous sigils hanging from his person.

Two!

'What happened?' Fronto cast his glance back and forth, looking for the third Remi, but only two men were present. He was trying desperately to remember the other man's name. He was an older man. A grey-bearded warrior. Seemed to be sensible. Gaul-something.

The dark, strange Brannogenos gestured back along the track. 'Galatos has gone. No sign of him.'

'He was with us this morning before we left,' Fronto said, suspiciously.

'Aye. Magurix went to rope the horses, while I went to settle up with the innkeeper. Galatos stayed in the hayloft, packing away the last of the gear, and when we got back, there was no sign of him or his kit. Vanished. No blood or sign of a scuffle, either.'

Palmatus scratched his chin. 'You think he was spying on us?'

Fronto shrugged. 'Could be. If so, whoever he's passed his information on to only knows that we're heading for the lands of the Segni, from what the ordo of elders told us. They don't know that we're heading for Cativolcus now. In a way, I'm hoping he was a spy. It could be very useful if he's given inaccurate information to whoever he works for.' He sighed. 'There is, of course, another explanation. We know the Arverni have been here. What if they still are and Galatos bumped into them somehow? Unless we find him or his body we'll not know.'

'Do we go back to the town and see what we can find?' Masgava muttered.

'No. We're unlikely to discover anything of use and it'll cost us valuable time. We need to get deep into the forest and look for Cativolcus.'

One of the legionaries was making warding signs against evil and muttering something. Fronto glanced irritably at him. 'What are you babbling about, Aurelius?'

'Arduenna's bats, sir. That's what got him. The bats.'

Fronto rolled his eyes as Aurelius shuddered, reaching up and rubbing his head. 'A bat cannot kill a man, Aurelius. Don't let

214

your fears carry you away with them. Come on. Mount up. We have a long way to go and time gets ever tighter.'

* * * * *

Fronto reined in the column yet again on the interminable journey deep into the forest. Celer was cantering back along the track towards them. Sensing danger, Masgava and Palmatus joined Fronto with Samognatos at the front, waiting for Celer, who halted inexpertly, his horse dancing and stomping, his breathing heavy.

'What is it?'

'Company,' Celer pointed back down the road, where it curved sharply to the left. 'I found the side track Samognatos was talking about and was just looking at it when I heard the sound of armoured men in the distance. They were quite a bit further down the main road and moving quite slowly so I went and had a look. There must be two dozen of them, and they're well armed Gauls. Local ones too, from the colouring.'

'Well done.' Fronto looked around and then to Samognatos. 'We're out of Condrusi lands now?'

'Yes. This is Segni territory.'

'Then we can't assume they're friendly, given that Ambiorix has been in their lands and they're apparently tooled up for war. Equally, I'd rather not have to fight them, given that they probably outnumber us slightly, and we'd suffer a number of casualties. But... it doesn't look like there's anywhere here we can get out of sight with so many horses.'

He turned to Celer. 'Can we all make it into that side track before they get here?'

'There's a good chance, sir.'

'Then we'll do that. The road's mostly turf and mud here, so the horses aren't making much noise. Everyone secure their mail, scabbards and helms. Try not to clank. If Celer heard their armour they could hear ours. We ride fast, get into that side track and then stop and wait, quietly.'

Without waiting for confirmation, Fronto kicked Bucephalus into action and they rode off to the bend in the road, the rest following close behind. Around the bend, the road ran straight for some distance before disappearing over a ridge and into a dip.

'Where's this track?'

215

'Just there,' Celer said, riding alongside and pointing ahead. Fronto peered into the gloom and spotted the dark opening into the forest on their left, which would take them away from Segni lands and towards the heart of the forest and the Eburones.

Fronto strained his ear, but couldn't hear the approaching Belgae over the sounds of his own hooves and those of the men beside and behind him. Pushing the big black animal for an extra turn of speed, he raced down the track and, with a sigh of relief, veered off into the narrow path that led into the deeper woodland.

'There!' Samognatos indicated a clearing off to one side of the narrow path and Fronto nodded, nudging Bucephalus into it. Behind him, the rest of his mismatched band arrived and moved off the path into the handy clearing, sliding from their horses and holding the reins to keep the beasts quiet.

Fronto looked around the clearing and noted with some distaste the large rock standing at the farthest edge - the reason for the clearing's existence. The huge stone, some two feet taller than him, was of rough granite, but the side facing the clearing had been sheared off and chiselled to a frieze of a bare-breasted, squat, malformed woman with a bow, a huge hound to one side, a stag by the other.

'Isn't that Artemis?' Masgava muttered. 'Diana to you?'

'I think you'll find that's Arduenna. If Diana was really that shape she'd have been cast from Olympus centuries ago for upping the ugly-quotient of the divine. Let's hope she listened to her druid friends, anyway.'

'Shhhh!' hissed Samognatos, who had crawled into the undergrowth near the stone. Fronto glanced across and realised that where the man lurked, the clearing went back almost as far as the main road, affording a view of the approaching Gauls between the bushes. Taking a deep breath, he gestured for everyone to be quiet and crossed the clearing, ducking into the undergrowth and joining the Condrusi scout where he crouched.

The itinerant Belgic warriors were close now, approaching along the main road, their armour clinking, swishing and jingling as they made jokes among themselves and laughed in their guttural voices. Fronto peered through the foliage. Celer had been right: they were northerners. Locals, though of what tribe he could not tell. Not Arverni, though. One thing was certain: they meant business, their torsos covered in heavy mail shirts, helms and shields in evidence and swords at their sides. It was tempting to see them as a border

216

patrol, since they were just leaving Segni territory, but clearly that was not the case. The Gauls did not do such things, did not think in such rigid terms. Moreover, these men were moving with purpose. They were taking a fight somewhere, either into Segni or Condrusi lands.

Behind him a horse neighed loudly. Fronto's head whipped round to see Luxinio looking panicked and embarrassed, trying to calm his steed, who was dancing around. He froze at the sound of Gallic voices raised in alarm, and slowly turned his head to peer through the greenery once more.

The warriors had halted and were pointing at the trees and talking animatedly.

'Ah, shit,' Fronto exclaimed under his breath as he saw one of the warriors drawing his sword. Moving back just far enough to be able to make out the figures through the leaves but provide a less ready target for them, Fronto noted with interest that they were starting to move towards the undergrowth at the side of the road. Not locals, then, if they didn't know about the side track ahead. Turning, he gestured to Masgava, made a 'five' sign with an open hand and pointed to the track. The big Numidian nodded and pointed to five of the men, making his way back onto the path.

'Arm up!' Fronto bellowed. 'On me!'

Ripping his glorious blade from its utilitarian scabbard, he stepped back to a more open position, waiting for the enemy to push through the undergrowth. Beside him, Samognatos had moved into a better position, while eleven men rushed across the clearing, drawing their swords and hefting their unfamiliar Gaulish shields.

Almost comically, the first of the warriors appeared through the undergrowth face-first, his broad, ruddy features framed with greenery like the mane of a strange floral lion. Even as the image sank into Fronto's consciousness, he was lashing out with his blade, which smashed, point-first, into the man's cheek, scattering shattered teeth and rasping across bone, tearing through muscle and tendon and sliding into the man's brain.

The eyes widened, but Fronto had no time to pay any further attention, as the man was rudely elbowed aside by a companion, almost ripping Fronto's sword from his grasp.

The second man leapt for him, blade glinting in the bushes and Fronto ducked to the side, shieldless and unable to parry until he'd withdrawn his blade from his last victim. It was a near thing, the Gaul's blade whispering past his shoulder, only to meet the sword of

Iuvenalis, who had fallen into position on Fronto's left, hampered a little by the plant life. A grunt drew Fronto's attention and his head whipped to his right to see a blade ripping towards him through the undergrowth. For a heart-stopping moment, he realised there was nothing he could do. His sword was not yet free of the falling body and he had thrown his weight to the right, out of the way of the previous strike, straight into the path of this one. Samognatos was at his side, but already busily engaged with another Gaul.

Fronto braced himself for the blow and then blinked in surprise.

The sword had stopped. He stared at the tip, only a hand-span from his eye and then looked back along the blade. The Gaul gripping it seemed equally surprised, and their eyes both dropped to the sword, where the hilt had snagged on a bramble. Frantically, the warrior waggled the hilt, trying to free it for a second strike or push it on through the greenery. Spurred into desperate action, Fronto tore his blade from the face of the fallen man and leaned back to afford himself room. Unable to bring his blade round in time, the Gaul having forced his own sword free, Fronto settled for smashing the glittering orichalcum pommel into the man's face.

The warrior fell back among the greenery, blood spattering the leaves, and Fronto was annoyed to realise, as he moved back and righted his blade, that a small dent had been left in the smooth pommel by the Gaul's hard head.

Bastard!

Now, more Gauls were pushing through the undergrowth, and the rest of the men were with them, lunging and stabbing into the green, shields to the fore. It was by far the best position to fight from, the enemy hampered by the tangles, while the Roman party fought mostly in the open, dealing with them as they appeared and preventing them from coming in force.

Again, Fronto had to bring his sword round and knock aside a strike from the bushes. Turning his parry into a swing, he brought the blade down through the wrist of the attacker, lopping off the hand, which fell to the earth still clutching its sword. The gladius was designed for thrusting, but a sensible soldier always kept the edges razor-sharp to allow for every eventuality.

A sudden cry from beyond the bushes announced that Masgava and his men had fallen upon the rear of the Gauls. What had been a mad push into the greenery to get to Fronto and his men suddenly became a desperate, panicked fight for survival. The men coming through thinned out as they turned and tried to deal with the new threat and Fronto, grinning, launched himself forward, crawling across the Gauls' bodies as he pushed on towards the enemy survivors.

A quick mental count led him to the conclusion that there couldn't be more than half a dozen of them left.

'Masgava! Prisoners!'

Pushing himself from the bushes out onto the main road once more, Fronto took in the scene as he righted himself and brought up his sword.

Eight enemy warriors remained, two busy to either side of him, trying to halt the advance of the Romans who were now pushing through the greenery after Fronto. The other six were engaged with Masgava and his men. A legionary - Pontius, he believed - was lying on the ground with a spear protruding from his chest, wavering in the air as he shuddered, and Magurix the Gaul was still fighting, but clutched his chest with his shield hand, where a jagged rent had been torn through his mail shirt and blood had begun to stain the broken links.

The Belgae clearly had no intention of halting the fight, and despite Masgava's best efforts to bellow an order for surrender over the din, they continued to fight like men possessed, even to the last.

With a sigh, almost casually, Fronto stepped up behind the man struggling with Masgava and brought the pommel of his sword down on the man's head with a 'crack' driving the wits from him as he sank to the ground unconscious.

Giving the man a quick kick, partly to be certain of his condition, but partly through sheer irritation, Fronto turned and drove the point of his gladius between the shoulder blades of the man fighting Magurix. Now, others were at his side again, and the last of the Gauls were being hewn down like saplings.

'Get this pissflap tied to a tree. I want to know who they are.'

The last enemy collapsing, clutching his torn gut, his men began the grisly task of going among the fallen and driving their blades into necks to be sure of the kill, then piling the bodies to the side of the road. Masgava and Iuvenalis dragged the unconscious Gaul back to the clearing and tied him up. Other soldiers appeared, dragging the form of Myron the archer from the bushes, a huge crimson bloom on his mail where the death blow had been dealt. Pontius and Numisius also seemed to be down, though the latter was still grumbling about being badly manhandled. Pontius, however, was clearly moments from the boatman's journey.

'Any more wounded?'

A few men shouted out, but a quick count suggested that the archer and the legionary were the only two complete losses. A few scratches and scrapes and bruises, along with Magurix, who was swearing and trying to tie his bloodied mail shirt together with leather thongs, and Numisius who seemed to have lost the use of his left arm, broken when his shield had given to a blow.

Two gone and two injured. More casualties, but not at all too bad a showing against a larger force. And all the enemy dead, barring one prisoner.

'Luxinio, try and keep your damned horse quiet in future!'

The Hispanic slinger's face was thunderous as he turned to Fronto. 'Not my fault, sir,' he snapped in his thick accent. 'Some pisser kicked my horse and set him off. There's bloodied stud-marks in his leg from a boot!'

Fronto frowned. 'Did you see who it was?'

'No sir. Too busy keeping the poor sod from bolting.'

Fronto's glare passed around the clearing, falling on every man as it passed. It *had* to have been accidental. Who would kick a horse in that situation... unless someone here wanted them to be caught? The very idea set his teeth on edge. He would have to be very observant in the coming days and keep his guard up at all times. Palmatus and Masgava would need to be told. Other than them, only Biorix and Damionis made it to his 'trustworthy' list. He would have to make sure that one of them was on watch at all times. Irritating, given that all four had specific duties that could not be replaced: command, engineering and medical, and they should be excused things like watch duty.

Damnit!

A commotion drew his attention and he turned angrily to see Damionis yelling up at Magurix, his neck craned, the latter a good foot and a half taller and still trying to tie up his mail.

'What is the problem?' the commander snapped angrily.

'This man will not let me look at his wound,' the capsarius grumbled, fishing in his leather satchel.

'I have had worse wounds shaving,' Magurix snapped as he tied a thong off.

'You're bleeding profusely, man. Get somewhere soft and quiet, get that mail off and let the capsarius tend your wound.' He pointed at the medic. 'Anyone more urgent?'

'No,' Damionis shook his head. 'Lots of minor abrasions, two men beyond my help, and a broken arm that needs splinting, but who's not bleeding and in no immediate danger.'

'Right. Get Magurix seen to, then deal with the arm.'

'That was my plan, sir.'

Fronto turned his attention to the enemy warrior tied to the tree, slumped unconscious.

'Wake him up.'

Striding across the clearing and uncorking his canteen, Palmatus threw a splash of water into the Gaul's face and, when he failed to respond, stepped forward and gave him several slaps in the face. Gradually, the native came to, groaning.

'What tribe are you?'

The Gaul stared at Fronto, groggily, and then spat blood and saliva at him.

'Oh good. Someone to take my bad mood out on! Tend the wounded, bury the dead and set pickets. We camp here tonight.'

* * * * *

The flames danced and crackled in the small fire as Palmatus took a swig from his wineskin, watered three parts water to one wine, and then passed it to Fronto.

'The Segni? So we can now assume that they are part of Ambiorix's 'great uprising'?'

'Safe to say. But they're a small tribe, and we're almost out of their lands now, so I'm not going to lend too much thought to this. I put it down to an unfortunate chance meeting. Samognatos is still insistent that the Segni are loyal, and if he's right, they might be split the way the druids seem to be. However it pans out, we're moving away into Eburone territory anyway. Hopefully without further incident.'

'Hopefully. We've lost three now. Three out of twenty. First Galatos back in Divonanto and now Pontius and Myron. Both from my bloody contubernium too, they are. As is Numisius with his broken arm.'

Masgava's brilliant white teeth glittered in a smile in the dark. 'I lost Galatos. And Magurix has a flesh wound.'

221

'Which he barely notices,' Palmatus snorted. 'That lunk is almost entirely muscle. Probably most of his head is too.'

Fronto smacked his hand on one of the flat stones upon which they'd prepared their dinner. 'Can you two save this kind of pointless one-upmanship for another time? We're three men down and two wounded and we're not even officially in enemy territory yet. And you might argue about how many are down in each of your contubernia, but I'm missing *all* of them!'

The two officers fell into an awkward silence.

'You're convinced we have a traitor with us?' Palmatus asked in little more than a whisper.

'Someone set Luxinio's horse off on purpose.'

'Could it not have been an accident?'

Masgava shook his head. 'I saw the stud-marks. They were about two feet up. No one kicks that high accidentally. I think he might have been trying to break its leg. Nearly succeeded, too.'

'I'd hoped the traitor was Galatos,' Fronto sighed. 'Then we'd have lost him and he'd have passed on misinformation. No such luck. So I think we have to assume that Galatos either fell foul of the Arverni in the town, or one of his companions did away with him. That means either Brannogenos or Magurix would have to be the one we seek.'

'We could just get rid of them both?' Masgava muttered.

'I'm not about to dispatch two Remi on the off-chance one of them is not what he seems. Galronus might be a little pissed at me. Besides, when we find him, I want to have a few choice words with this traitor.'

'So we keep an eye on the two Remi from now on,' Masgava muttered. 'Never leave them alone?'

'Got to be the most sensible course of action,' Fronto agreed. 'Think it's time I got some shut-eye. We've a long ride in the morning. Which one of you is on next watch?'

Masgava stretched. 'That would be me. I'll go and relieve Damionis now. The poor bastard spent every moment tending the injuries and then went straight on watch. He'll be exhausted.'

'Send him back to the fire for a warm up.'

Masgava nodded and rose, disappearing off into the night.

'Have you given any thought to what we're going to do when we find the other king?' Palmatus asked quietly, pulling his blanket round him and settling to the ground uncomfortably.

'Depends on whether he's feeling cooperative. If so, we'll camp down with him and his men and wait for Ambiorix to show up. Cativolcus is well known to hate the man, so we might be in luck. If not, then we'll take the bugger hostage and wait anyway. The details we can hammer out as we go.'

'I think we'll have to get the plan set well in advance if we...'

Palmatus fell silent at the sound of Masgava's voice raised in alarm. A heartbeat later both he and Fronto were up, their blankets dropping to the ground, drawing their swords and sharing a look before they ran off in the direction of the shout.

Around the clearing, the men of the singulares were coming rudely awake, blinking and lurching from their beds, some alert enough already to be scrambling for their swords. Past the rising men Fronto and Palmatus ran, towards the figure of Masgava, standing at the watch position where the main road and the small track could both be easily observed from the same point.

'What is it?' Fronto yelled as he closed on the man, but then added 'Shit!' as he saw the shape of Damionis the capsarius splayed out on the ground, soaked in glistening dark liquid.

'Damn it!' Palmatus snapped. 'We should already have been watching them!'

Fronto's eyes widened as Palmatus turned and raced back into the clearing, the other two officers at his heels. Despite the unity of the singulares, its constituent members were still new enough that they tended to separate off into their national or professional cliques at night. Arcadios had camped down with Myron and Luxinio, Biorix and Iuvenalis tended to talk late into the night in the way engineers seemed to need to, and the Remi habitually camped together.

Fronto's heart sank as he came to a halt with the others at the edge of the clearing, looking down at the two sleeping blanket/cloak piles. Brannogenos, with his charms and sigils, his dark hair and darker eyes, had gone, and all his kit with him. Magurix lay wrapped in his cloak, snoring like a boar with a sinus condition.

'Shit, shit, shit!' snapped Fronto.

Masgava stared down at the sleeping Gaul as the rest of the group began to assemble near them, barring the few who had spread out to search the edges of the clearing. 'How can he still be asleep through this racket?'

Palmatus shrugged in defeat. 'Damionis had given him some concoction of poppy juice for his chest. He'd probably sleep through another stabbing, the lucky bastard.'

'Well I guess that answers one question for us,' Fronto snapped. 'Unlucky old Galatos must have been onto him back in Divonanto, so Brannogenos did away with him before following. I guess he realised now that after wounding the horse he'd be watched, so he did a runner. I wonder what the piece of shit has in store for us. He knows where we're going, too, so there's a damn good chance Cativolcus will know we're coming.'

'We still have an advantage,' Samognatos announced, strolling up behind them. 'The horses were all corralled and roped close together near me and they're all still accounted for. Wherever Brannogenos has gone, he's on foot. We can beat him there.'

'I hope so,' Fronto grumbled, picturing the dark, sour-looking Remi with his various sigils. Was one of them a symbol of Arduenna? He should have looked when he had the chance. Now the man would be out and about preparing to cause them endless trouble.

'Everyone get back to sleep. Masgava, get on watch, but now I want three men on watch every time we stop. Always in sight of one another, too. It's time we got this situation under control.'

Turning, Fronto spotted Aurelius climbing back into his blankets, his eyes nervously scanning the branches above that blotted out the stars and moon even in the clearing, courtesy of trees that had been left growing here and there to add to the leafy canopy. He remembered hearing the story of the legionary and the bat that had been entangled in his hair as he went for a late-night piss. Drusus had roared with laughter as he told the tale under the sullen gaze of Aurelius.

Fronto had dutifully chuckled along, but his mind had furnished him with a question. How had the bat got entangled in the first place? He'd encountered endless clouds of the vermin in the caves below the villa in Puteoli and the one thing he knew about them was they never, ever, collided with you.

Arduenna.

'You'd better have listened to those druids, you ugly, untrustworthy bitch.'

224

Chapter Twelve

Delta of the Rhenus River

Priscus stood at the water's edge and watched debris floating out towards the cold northern sea from the heart of Gaul and Germania. His gaze took in the variety of humps of land that sat defiantly out in the sluggish flow and then strayed back to the near bank and the Menapi town. No one knew what it was called - even the native scouts from other Belgic tribes. It was a miscellaneous, unlabelled town. It was also a ghost-town, the latest in a long line.

'How many does that make?' Antonius sighed as he skipped a flat stone across the wide waterway.

'Twelve, by my count, plus endless tiny villages and farmsteads.'

'All deserted.'

Priscus took a deep breath. 'I told you before we marched north that these bastards flee into the swamps and islands at the first sign of real danger and feel safe as anything. Largely because they are.'

Antonius nodded dejectedly, his eyes scouring the deserted, empty town as though for a solution. 'So you think they're out in that estuary, on those islands?'

'Yes. And beyond, spread over about fifty miles of marsh, fen, swamp and river.'

'Is this the Rhenus I keep hearing about?'

'Not really. But it's connected... everything's connected here. The delta and its rivers cover an area half the size of Latium. It's enormous, and impregnable.'

'I swear some of those islands are actually moving!'

'Probably. This place is the worst place to campaign in the world. I'd rather drive a wedge up mount Olympus against the Titans. I'd rather fight a battle underwater. Looking at this place, that might actually happen!'

The army, five legions strong, had pushed north after the Gallic assembly, marching on the Menapii in the same fashion as they had against the Nervii, swiftly, but with considerably less success. While surprise and the early season had been on their side against that other tribe, it was now high spring and word seemed to have leaked out in advance, so that the forces of Rome met nothing throughout Menapii territory but empty buildings and deserted

225

towns. Finally, this afternoon, they had reached the first of the wide, marshy delta areas. So far, the ground had been reasonably solid, though with a sogginess that would see foot-rot rife within the army. This wide stretch of water with its islands and reed beds marked the beginning of the Menapii's place of refuge. From here to the north, scouts had confirmed over the past few years that at least fifty miles of territory would yield nothing other than wide channels, swampy areas, reed beds, treacherous sucking muck, fens and cold, wet, rotting death.

Priscus grumbled and Antonius smiled mirthlessly at him before skipping out another flat stone towards the nearest of the islands.

'I think I saw something move. Something glinted in the sun.'

'Probably one of the occupants from this town.'

A tell-tale noise attracted their attention and the two officers turned to see Caesar striding across the squelching grass towards them, half a dozen of the more senior men behind him.

'How long would it take to bring the fleet from Gesoriacum, Brutus?' the general enquired, coming to a halt by the water, and nodding a greeting to the others.

'Five or six days at the very least, General, and that's using fast couriers and relying on the fleet being ready to sail, as well as conditions being right and the captains and crews willing to sail every hour the Gods give them. But it's a moot point. Even with the shallow draught of most of our vessels, they're too wide, deep and cumbersome to risk in most of these conditions. The locals don't take anything bigger than a four-man trader anywhere in this delta.'

'The main channel looks wide and deep,' Caesar noted with a frown.

'That it is, sir, but that would only give you access to the centre of the main channels, and the ships cannot reach the shore in the delta to embark men; only out at the coast or inland some thirty miles. Anywhere else and they'll be mired or holed. It would be endless trouble, and would only give us access to the larger islands at the centre, not the endless swamps beyond.'

'What about using the local vessels?' Gaius Fabius, legate of the Eighth, asked, scratching his chin.

'All gone, like the people,' Priscus cut in. 'They took them to their refuges with them. Besides, sending a legion against one of these island havens four men at a time would take forever and put the army at too much risk from missiles. Not feasible even if it were possible. It's difficulties like these that's kept the Menapii out of our reach for years.'

'No longer,' Caesar said with a fierce glare. 'They ally with Ambiorix and defy us. They will share the fate of the Nervii.'

'But how?' Antonius sighed. 'Without ships or boats.'

The general rubbed his forehead and turned to the cadre of officers behind him. 'Mamurra? Causeways: are they feasible?'

The engineer stepped forward for a better look, nodding to himself.

'Not an easy job, General. There's no local source for quarrying, so it'll have to be brought a good distance. We could take a lot of the weight of the men with timber lashed together, mind. If we did that, we'd cut down on the stone needed, and they could be dismantled quickly and moved to the next causeway. It's feasible, but difficult.'

Caesar nodded. 'Then that is the way we shall proceed. Each of the islands we can see from here will play host to whole settlements of Menapii. We have five legions. Have one legion assigned to each of three of the larger islands and begin the causeways. The other two will work on supplying the resources. We begin today.'

Priscus pinched the bridge of his nose and winced. 'General, there are literally thousands of islands in this dreadful place. If we have to build a causeway to each, we'll be here for years.'

'You are not thinking it through, Priscus,' the general smiled. 'Watch the local Menapii tribes fall to our swords within sight of the others and imagine the word spreading among their people. Once these islands have fallen, we will move upriver to where we can cross and then begin to assault the islands on the far side in the same manner. I anticipate a matter of weeks at most before the Menapii come to us on their knees begging for clemency.'

'I hope you're right, General,' Priscus sighed. 'I really do'.

* * * * *

Lucius Vorenus, second most senior centurion of the Eleventh legion, gave a legionary a sound 'ding' around the side of the helmet with his vine staff. The man spun in shock.

'You drop another nail in the water and I will use the few we have left to nail you to a fucking cross. Do you understand?'

The legionary recoiled with a muttered apology. Vorenus shook his head and left the man - who'd dropped six into the water even as he watched - striding to the head of the causeway. There, Titus Pullo, the legion's Primus Pilus, stood, overseeing the work with the expression of a man who is less than impressed with his lot, but is damn well not going to let it interfere with his duty. Here, men were busy tipping endless buckets of earth into the water, within the edges of the wooden frame they had constructed and ahead to form the submerged bank upon which it was built. Pullo was looking back along the six hundred paces of four-man-wide causeway, where the Eleventh and the Thirteenth constantly ferried goods to the front to advance the ramp. Two days. It had taken two days for ten thousand men to move six hundred paces.

And since dawn this morning, the missiles had started coming. The Menapii on the island apparently included some fairly competent slingers and archers. The causeway was now only perhaps fifty paces from the island, and only ten from the reeds that marked the shallow water. Consequently, half a century of men were now standing in the knee deep torrent at the business end of the causeway, creating a shieldwall - almost a half-testudo, in fact - to protect the workers from the attacks. Despite the efficiency of all involved - and both Pullo and Vorenus had to concede that their men and those of the Thirteenth had excelled beyond all expectations in the awful task and horrible conditions - they had lost more than a score of men to missiles already.

'How long, sir?' Vorenus queried

'At this rate another three or four hours.'

'By then it'll be starting to get dark. We'll have to protect the bloody ramp 'til morning, and then launch the assault. Can't do it in the dark.'

Pullo nodded his agreement. He was itching to get stuck into the cowardly Menapii, but the idea of running through this treacherous terrain in pitch black under attack by arrows didn't bear thinking about. But then they'd already lost so many men to stray hits, and would lose a number more during the night protecting the finished causeway.

'Tell me you're not thinking what I'm thinking, sir,' Vorenus smiled wickedly.

'Legatus Cicero was quite plain. Finish the causeway. Let him examine it and the island and decide on the plan of action, consult with Legatus Roscius, and then give the order. *Then* we take the Menapii.'

'So you're not thinking what I'm thinking?' grinned Vorenus.

'Of course I am. I'm just weighing it up against the possibility of being broken for disobeying orders.'

'We've both served long enough, sir, to know that that only happens when you lose. If you succeed, no one will break you.'

Pullo took a deep breath and craned his neck to look over the shield wall. An arrow whicked past him for his efforts, plunging into the water nearby.

'Get those bloody shields higher. I know your arms are tiring, but men are relying on you.'

He turned back to Vorenus. 'We don't know how deep it is in the reeds. The amount of muck we've dumped means we'll get to the greenery without getting our balls wet, but those reeds could be sat in twelve feet of water.'

'They look like the reeds in the lagoon near Altinum. I'd put money on there being only a few feet of water at most, and some nasty, silty muck.'

Pullo narrowed his eyes. 'You want the honours?'

'If there's a wager on it?'

Pullo shrugged. 'Jar of wine. Only if you lose no one to the water, though.'

'And Cicero?'

'You said it yourself: only losers get disciplined. Win for me.'

Vorenus grinned and turned to the cornicen a few paces back. 'Sound the advance.'

Pullo raised his eyebrows. 'You're ready?'

'Knew what you'd say.' Behind him, four centuries of men were busy tramping along the causeway before even the call went up from the curved horn. 'Best clear the way, sir.'

Pullo shook his head in exasperation at his incorrigible second and started yelling orders to down tools and pull back. Last of all, as the men ran back along the causeway, sidestepping around the advancing centuries, he gave the call to the shieldwall, who broke up, keeping their shields presented to the enemy as they withdrew.

A moment later, ignoring the missiles coming surprisingly close to him, Pullo stepped away from the end of the causeway, nodding as he passed Vorenus. 'Be safe, Lucius.' Walking until he decided he was out of immediate missile danger, he stopped, the advancing centuries shuffling aside as they passed him like water round an island.

Vorenus paused only long enough to fall in at the head of his century, the musician moving to the rear. 'Fast and hard. Shields up. Don't stop at dry land, but keep going until there's room for a legion behind you.'

The men laughed and Vorenus took a deep breath. 'Alright men, at the signal... Charge!'

Three hundred men broke into a run as they neared the end of the causeway. Not a few faces fell in dismay as they reached the tip of the wood-framed, compacted-earth causeway, looking out over some twenty feet or more of water to the reeds beyond.

With a war-cry to Mars, Vorenus plunged into the torrent, hoping he was right. His feet touched sucking dirt just beneath the surface where the buckets of mud had already been dumped. He had been fairly sure that the slope the man made ramp had caused ahead would meet up with the natural slope afforded by the island's shore and leave nowhere on the run more than a few feet deep. His heart lurched for a moment as he sank quickly to his thighs in the icy torrent, but then his feet found higher purchase once again. The muck was sucking and deadly, trying to pull him to his doom, but sheer speed and momentum kept him on the surface of the treacherous submerged dirt.

Next to him, a legionary shrieked, disappearing backwards with an arrow protruding from his face.

Something whipped against his legs and he peered down, half expecting to see a red line drawn by a near-miss, but instead he saw green reeds. They'd crossed the open water!

The uneven wet ground in the reeds almost tripped him and he was forced to right himself more than once. A few of the legionaries next to him or following in his wake fell foul of the terrain and disappeared with a cry of pain, falling amongst the green forest of reeds. More were struck by arrows or sling stones, but dozens more were with him and solid ground was but a few paces away. He could see the pale figures of the Menapii in the trees, desperately loosing missiles at them. No defences. No ditch or mound because of the terrain, and no palisade. After all, who needed to defend an unreachable island from infantry?

Vorenus laughed as he chose a target and ran, sword out and ready. Legionaries were now shouting their challenges at the enemy.

On the causeway, Pullo laughed loud: a deep belly laugh.

'Something amusing, centurion?'

He turned to see Cicero and came to attention automatically, with a salute. The legate was livid, his face an unattractive puce colour. Behind him, legate Roscius looked considerably more appreciative, nodding his head as he watched the action out on the island.

'Is there a reason my forces are launching an attack, despite my express orders?'

'Expediency, sir. An opportunity suddenly arose, and a good officer does not allow such an opportunity for victory to pass ungrasped, sir. So I grasped it.'

Cicero's face changed colour again at the veiled insult. 'There will be a reckoning for this, centurion.'

'Yes sir. Shall I order them back, sir?'

Roscius stifled a laugh behind Cicero.

'Don't be idiotic, centurion,' Cicero snapped. 'Sound the general advance. Since we're committed, we might as well go the whole distance.'

'My pleasure, sir,' Pullo nodded at his commander, as Cicero turned and stomped angrily away back along the causeway. Roscius grinned. 'Don't worry, centurion. I'll talk to him. He'll calm down when he realises he'll get the credit. Will you require the Thirteenth?'

'I think a couple of cohorts will take the island convincingly, sir, but thank you.'

Roscius nodded again and turned to leave. Pullo glanced once more at the island. Briefly he caught sight of Vorenus whooping as he leapt over a large rock, sword in hand, coming down on top of an archer who was desperately trying to nock another arrow.

It would be over within the half hour.

* * * * *

'Almost two weeks into Menapii lands and still no sign of an end, each day up to the knees in water, mud, shit and blood, and yet every bloody group we take seems no less rabid than the last!' Priscus grumbled as he watched the wounded being stretchered or

231

helped back along the latest in a long list of causeways which led to the latest in a long line of pointless, unpleasant island havens.

'Look on the bright side,' Antonius rolled his shoulders wearily. 'Every day we spend out here is another day for Fronto. I thought that was what you wanted?'

'Happy to buy the old bugger time, but I'd rather not do it up to my knees in a barbarian latrine.'

The enslaved Menapii were next to follow the wounded, escorted by a group of legionaries who looked as tired as Priscus felt. They were former Pompeians of the First Legion, their tunics no longer a plain off-white wool, but more of a drab brown-grey, the colour of damp silt. The colour of dysentery. The colour of Gaul, mused Priscus sourly. Every passing season made him wish this whole damned campaign was over and that the army could return to the healthier, warmer climes around the Mare Nostrum.

'I know you think this is going to go on forever,' Antonius muttered into the face of Priscus' bleakness, 'but they're breaking. They still fight as hard, but there's something in the atmosphere now. I've felt it before, on campaign in the east. When that supercilious prick Aristobulus caused trouble in Aegyptus, and Gabinius and I went down to Judea and beyond to kick ten shades of shit out of him, we had to take fortress after fortress. They were all big brown places with big brown walls built on big brown hills, and if you think Gauls are rabid, you should see the Jews and the Nabateans and the rest of those desert-dwelling lunatics. But gradually, as we razed the places and enslaved them, you could see the fight begin to go out of them, even while they struggled on. They knew they'd lost, but wouldn't admit it. This Menapii lot are the same. Sometime soon, a chief or a holy man is going to decide that their lot is better served coming to terms with us than fighting on.

'Perhaps. Though it looks more like they intend to fight to the last man to me. But if they offer terms, you know what Caesar will do?'

'He'll accept the terms, so long as they're favourable - which they will be.'

'I'm not so sure,' Priscus grumbled. 'I've seen him press on in the face of utter madness just because his blood's up.'

'You forget his overriding desire to punish Ambiorix, though. He only sees the Menapii as a tool of Ambiorix and if he can break the link between them, and they bow to him, he'll leave them alone so he can concentrate on the rebel.'

232

'You're probably right. Let's go get a drink.'

Behind the two officers as they turned to leave, a hundred Menapii were herded off the causeway and roped up for transport.

* * * * *

Lucius Fabius, Tribune of the Tenth Legion, turned to his long-time compatriot, Tullus Furius, and sighed as they watched the legates of both the Tenth and Eighth giving the orders for the disposition of the men.

'Every time someone shouts 'Fabius', I look around. It's starting to piss me off. I'll be glad when the Eighth depart.'

Furius grinned. Lucius Fabius: Tribune and son of a grizzled centurion who'd died in the siege of Aesernia and a whore from that same city who'd passed of the flux a few years later. Lucius Fabius: dyed-in-the-wool soldier and rough countryman. And not ten paces from him stood Gaius Fabius Pictor, descendant of one of Rome's most illustrious lines, former magistrate, patron of many and commander of a legion. The two could hardly be less alike if they tried, and yet any time either of their names were called, they both turned and then shared a despairing glance. It was infuriating for them, for certain, but it gave Furius plenty of laugh-fodder. No one, of course, called the legate 'Pictor' - 'the painter' hardly did his nobility justice, no matter the name's illustrious origins.

'You only *half* look around,' Furius grinned, gesturing at the external, painted-clay false eye than never moved or blinked on Fabius' face. 'Anyway, perhaps we need to assign you a cognomen? Something truly individual? How about 'Porculus'?'

He ducked the slap just before it struck, Fabius' enraged face suddenly distracted as his namesake gave the last command and the standards began to dip and wave, the musicians honking their calls for the men to move. The eagles of the two legions stuttered into life and then bounced along at the front, a few paces from where the two tribunes stood. Crassus had tried to persuade them that the place for tribunes was at the rear with the rest of the command. Such was probably sensible for those tribunes who were still barely in the toga virilis and whose voice had only just broken. For veterans in the most unlikely of roles, Fabius and Furius knew their place was in the thick of it, near the front. Fronto would have been there with them, though the young Crassus was more cautious in his role. Furius laughed at himself. Before associating with Fronto he would have

233

thought such a thing the right and proper way for a legate to conduct himself.

In deference to Carbo's wishes, they had settled to one side of the column, close to the first century but not quite at the front. The Primus Pilus had his system, and they did not quite figure in it. And despite the senior centurion's smiling, pink, boyish face, he was a man with an iron will and brooked no argument, even from his supposed superiors, when it came to his command.

As the two legions moved off in columns eight men wide, the Tenth on the left and the Eighth on the right, the two legates, most of their tribunes and the musicians and various hangers-on remained motionless, letting the army progress before falling into position some way back along the line, away from the 'business end'.

Even over the squelching of thousands of boots and the jingle and rustle of armour and equipment, the pair could just hear all the crashes, thumps, splashes and cursing of the engineers who had tried to transport a ballista and an onager across the causeway and had ended up sinking into the mire near the island-end, damaging the walkway in the process. A tremendous splosh announced the demise of one of the war engines as it disappeared into the swampy fens that formed part of the great Rhenus delta.

Still, two thirds of the two legions had made it across before the pig-headed engineers had blocked the route, and four scorpion bolt throwers had reached the large island.

It would have been nice to be able to name the island. Furius felt curiously lost and disconnected in a place where they didn't even have the names of most of the settlements, let alone the natural features.

Two weeks into the campaign against the Menapii, captured and enslaved warriors had revealed under 'coercion' the location of a particularly large island in one of the most unpleasant swampy areas, where the leaders and the most senior druids had taken shelter. Upon learning of this, Caesar had shifted the focus of his campaign to that area of swamp, ignoring the endless small hideaways and preparing to strike at the heart of the tribe. It had taken four days to build the enormous causeway out across the sucking bogs and squelching fens to the long, low, ship-like island.

The legions had then mustered on the open ground at the causeway's end. It had seemed odd that no missiles had been cast at them while they built, but the plumes of smoke rising from the forested island centre confirmed that the place was home to a sizeable population, and carefully-placed lookouts and patrols from the First legion kept an eye out for any attempts to flee the island by boat, which had not occurred.

The first scouts sent into the island centre woodlands had not returned, and so second forays had been ordered with heavier-armoured scouts in larger parties. They had also come under attack, but had confirmed that the island's population were protected by a strange hedge-and-palisade arrangement that would be difficult to assault in force, especially within the trees.

Caesar was in no way deterred, of course. His other two legions were recuperating from the business of constructing the causeway, leaving the Eighth and Tenth to make the main assault. 'Should be more than enough,' was the common opinion, shared by both tribunes.

The men squished through the wet grass and silty earth towards the defences within the woods.

'Feels good to be launching a proper attack again, eh?'

Fabius sucked in moist, fetid air and nodded. 'Make the most of it, though. I overheard the legates this morning. They reckon Caesar's thinking of heading south to flatten the Treveri after the Menapii cave in.'

'So we get to fight endless little actions south of the great forest, then?'

'Sounds like it.'

'Then we'd best kick the shit out of this lot quickly, eh?'

A squawk announced the first casualty. As the legions approached the trees an arrow whipped out of the foliage and struck a standard bearer from the Eighth, who fell, clutching his neck, a legionary behind leaping forward and grasping the standard from his falling hand, discarding his own blade in favour of the honour of the legion.

'That came from the branches,' Furius said sharply, then turned and raised his voice, bellowing 'they're in the trees! Testudo! Testudo!'

Carbo had apparently spotted the same thing, and the front ranks of the Tenth were forming into an armoured box of shields even as the tribune spoke. As the legions reformed for their better protection, more and more arrows and stones whipped and thrummed out of the green canopy and into the advancing army. Here and there a legionary who was too slow to react fell, an arrow jutting from his leg, his arm, or his torso. The sheer number of missiles was staggering, given their source. They must have been putting half the population up in those branches all the time they watched the legions crossing. That, of course, was why they had not been struck on the causeway.

It was horribly effective against a column of men.

Against a testudo of interlocked shields it was about as effective as a hail of beans. The Menapii had never had to field an army against Rome. They had supplied men to various revolts and attacks, but had responded to Roman incursions by simply retreating into their impregnable swamps. And now those swamps were no longer impregnable, and the unprepared Menapii had no idea what to do about it. They had responded with the best, most innovative method of defence they could manage. It would have served them well against a disorganised horde of other Belgae, but they had committed their bulk to the first attack, which had been quickly negated by the shield configuration.

Unless they had more surprises at the palisade...

Fabius counted under his breath each and every footstep that brought them closer to the trees. Not part of a century of men, the two tribunes were not enclosed by a testudo, keeping the large body shields they had requisitioned facing forward and hunched down behind them, making sure that the only body parts they presented to the attack were feet and the narrow slice of face between the shield's rim and the brow of their decorative officers' helmets.

Thirty seven paces and the first leaves brushed across Fabius' plume. He had also noted half a dozen yelps of men struck by well-placed arrows or sling-shots during the advance, and there would have been many more he couldn't hear over the din, but now they were at the trees.

'Break!' Carbo yelled from the front. 'Pila!'

Like an anthill splitting open, the testudo formations exploded into individual activity, each legionary immediately looking up into the canopy above them and readying their pila. Most of the trees were oak and beech, the former lower to the ground, but with wider, heavier branches and therefore favoured by the Menapii archers and slingers sitting there. Their favouring of those branches was their instant undoing, most of the branches being within easy reach of the legionaries' pila.

Men stabbed upwards with their javelins, skewering the natives and ripping through arms, legs and bodies. Many pila were lost to the men as their victims fell from the branches, smashing the shafts as they tumbled to the earth. The woodland resounded to the noise of bodies crashing through twigs and foliage. A few of the more accurate legionaries began to cast their pila up into the branches, aiming for the men out of reach of simple thrusts.

Fabius found himself wishing they had sent the archers of Decius' auxiliary unit across first, for now they would have had an effective force to remove the more difficult figures among the greenery. Alongside the crashes and cries of the dying Menapii, the occasional shriek or Latin curse confirmed that the legions were still suffering casualties to the missiles even at this more difficult range.

'Get those four scorpions into this clearing!' Furius yelled. 'Have them set up and take out the bastards in the trees. Carbo! Get a century to each machine and make sure they're shielded while they work.'

The pink-faced centurion turned and waved his understanding as he gestured for his men to move on towards the heart of the island. His orders began to ring out, melding with those of the officers of the Eighth, who were bringing their two scorpions forward.

Fabius and Furius shared a three-eyed glance and nodded, leaving the clearing up of the archers in the trees to the scorpion crews and their defenders as they moved on to the island's heart with the bulk of the legions.

As they moved between the wide boles of oak and the narrower, taller beech, the trees began to close up, growing tighter together, the ways between hindered by thick undergrowth. Fortunately, years of using these havens in times of need had led to the natives keeping them well-maintained, and the approaches to the settlement were clear and wide enough that there were gaps in the green canopy above. The legions had lost their neat formations during the first encounters in the woodland, and had now broken up into individual centuries, the Eighth and Tenth largely intermixed, and yet working in concert with the efficiency that was indicative of veteran centurions. Centuries moved four men abreast towards the defences ahead.

Furius stared in surprise. This place must have been settled for a long time. The trees and plants had been trained to grow together, interlinked like a giant wattle fence, branches curling around one another like some strange chain of brown and green, and wherever nature could not be trained to form a wall, the Menapii had inserted a solid palisade.

The scouts were right: it would be troublesome to assault. Far from impossible, though. For all the oddity of the system, there was no ditch - the land was too low-lying and swampy to permit such a defence, and for similar reasons there was no rampart.

The lead centuries, at the orders of their commanders, roared out a challenge and broke into a run, leaping at the strange, knotted defence system, hacking at anything that protruded and attempting to clamber up the root systems and grasp the palisade to haul themselves over.

A guttural shout from within echoed across the island and without warning several hundred spears - simple wooden affairs formed of beech shafts with sharpened ends - lanced out between the defences through every crack.

The unprepared legionaries of the lead centuries took appalling casualties in that first strike and Fabius and Furius, delayed at the first encounter, watched from a dozen paces back as men were impaled and skewered all along the line of attack, some being lifted off their feet as they slid down the tilting shafts towards the wielders, leaving a trail of wet red along the wood.

'Shields, you miserable dogs!' bellowed centurion Atenos from somewhere off to the left. The scant survivors of the first assault staggered back from the defences, amid the groaning wounded and dying, readying their shields and falling in with the next group of centuries.

More cautiously this time, the men moved forward, shields held forth to deflect the spear thrusts. Furius and Fabius looked at one another and the pair nodded. As the legionaries reached the defences and the wooden shafts lanced out again, this time the majority of them being turned aside by the heavy body shields, the two tribunes leapt into the fray, swords coming down and shearing off the wooden spears where they protruded from the wall before clambering up onto the lower twisting limbs of the tree-fence. Fabius glanced off to his right briefly and saw his friend disappearing into a knot of legionaries who were already at the top of the knotted defence and attempting to clear away enough defenders to drop down within.

Gritting his teeth, aware that Furius would rib him endlessly if he failed to bloody his sword, Fabius let go his shield and reached up, gripping the top of a short section of palisade and pulling himself up. As his face came to the upper edge, sword in hand at the same level, a rabid Menapii woman appeared before him, rising over the palisade tip, dagger readied.

For a brief moment, Fabius baulked. In all his years of fighting with the legions, he'd never been presented with the necessity of doing away with a woman in mid-battle. It was the slightest of pauses, but it was enough. With a snarled imprecation in her unpleasant tongue, the dirty, dishevelled farmer's wife stabbed down with her dagger, the blade sinking into the back of Fabius' hand where he grasped the wall top. He heard the delicate bones smash as the blade drove deep enough to pin him to the timber.

Shock flowed through him, though decades of war experience drove his actions even as his brain filled with blinding pain-light. He never even thought about or saw what he did as his sword hand swept forward, driving the tip of the gladius into the snarling woman's eye, slamming though liquid and brain.

And then the flesh of his hand gave way, the pinned limb the only thing holding him up at the top of the palisade. The flesh and blood ripped around the dagger's edge and tore free, and he fell back to the ground, his hand split down the centre, sword lost to him, stuck in the dead woman's face beyond the wall.

Fabius gasped in agony and looked down at his ruined hand as he landed heavily on his discarded shield. With a grimace, he used his free hand to unknot his scarf and rip it free of his neck, winding it round and round his wounded one and pulling it tight, tying it to slow the blood loss.

Wincing against the pain, Fabius grasped the shield in his good hand and held it up against the possibility of stray missiles as he staggered away from the fight. He'd seen enough wounds in his career to know that this wasn't deadly - though it could be debilitating - but if he left it to bleed too long, that would all change. He needed to find a capsarius with a good, steady sewing hand as soon as possible.

Shield raised, he passed the centuries marching into the fight, and spotted a medicus in a white robe, surrounded by half a dozen orderlies and capsarii, close to the legates and their tribunes, setting up in a clearing. Turning, he made his way towards them.

'Ah, tribune,' Crassus greeted him with an enthusiastic voice, 'all goes well?'

'Apart from this, sir,' he raised his wool-scarf-wrapped wounded hand. 'I think we'll have the place secured in about a quarter hour.'

'Good.'

'Let me look at that, Fabius,' called the medicus, spotting the wound, and the tribune and the legate of the Eighth both turned at the name, then shared another glance and shook their heads. Tribune Fabius stepped across towards the medicus and something caught his attention. It was a slight creaking noise, almost lost in the din of the battle, but he knew it for what it was. His gaze was moving around the branches and boles of the trees for the source even as he heard the release and the whisper of the arrow in flight.

His sharp eye caught the airborne missile as it shot towards its target and he leapt forward, knowing he would not make it. Legate Fabius was unaware, concentrating on the minutia of command. The arrow would take him in the neck - an instant and definite kill.

Fabius threw himself forward, shield extended as far as possible.

The arrow passed him, not stopped by the shield. He'd not been quick enough to prevent the strike. But the feathers of the missile brushed the shield's bronze edge as they passed, and the course of its flight changed at the last moment, the shaft plunging off-course into Fabius' shoulder, some of the force of the blow dampened by the leather strops hanging from his cuirass. Legate Fabius gasped in pain as his tribune namesake fell to the ground at the end of his dive, shield falling away.

'Get that archer!' bellowed Crassus to the nearest optio, who drove his men into the woods at the arrow's source.

'It would appear I owe you a life,' the legate of the Eighth said, his eyes wild as the wounded tribune slowly and painfully climbed back to his feet.

'My pleasure, sir,' he answered with a weary smile.

'No,' the legate replied, chuckling. '*That* is a pleasure.' He stopped and cupped his hand to his ear. Fabius listened. The sounds of fighting had subsided, and the cacophony of the Gallic carnyx lowed its injured bovine call across the island, indicating the end of the fight and a desire to parlay.

'We appear to have won, sir.'

'It appears so.'

Fabius sighed as the medicus began to slowly and carefully unwrap his tightly-wound bandage. Maybe he would be able to go find his sword if it was over. He would need it if Caesar was planning to turn on the Treveri.

* * * * *

Priscus watched the dejected Menapii leaders as they were escorted from Caesar's headquarters by the implacable horsemen of Ingenuus' Praetorian cavalry. They had attempted to bargain with the general, even knowing that they had lost everything. They had tried to seek favourable terms, and Caesar had simply ignored them and laid out his own conditions which, after an hour of bluster and wheedling, they had found no alternative but to accept.

Commius - chieftain of the Atrebates and long-time loyal supporter of Caesar - would be given overall control of the Menapii, who would submit to his every command. The Atrebates would station their own men in Menapii territory to be certain of their ongoing submission. The usual hostages given, slaves taken, reparations, donations, and the like had followed. Already, before negotiations had even begun, all the druids had been forced to announce themselves and step forward, and without delay or pause for thought, Caesar had ordered the strange Gallic priests crucified along the causeway. Priscus had, of course, argued against it, but the general was not to be halted in the matter. Shame, since they undoubtedly had information that Priscus felt they could very much do with.

'Come inside, Priscus. You're letting in the damp and cold.'

The prefect turned to the interior once more, where a few of the more senior officers had remained after the negotiations at the general's request. Dropping the tent flap back into place, Priscus returned to his seat.

'I am of a mind to travel with my hammer of five legions and crush the Treveri against the anvil of Labienus,' the general said thoughtfully, peering at the map on the tent's dividing wall. 'I sent him three legions and the baggage on the basis that we would be moving south after the Menapii fell. Then the army will combine once more in order to deal with the Eburones and their craven leader.' He took a deep, cleansing breath. 'Now, we could travel upriver from here along the Rhenus to the Mosella and then back into Treveri lands. It's a deal further, but faster terrain. Or we could cut directly across the forest of Arduenna. Much shorter, but troublesome going for a full army.

'Faster is better,' Antonius said from the shadowed edge of the room. 'The men are weary after two months of endless raids and sieges against these two northern tribes. If you give them too long to ponder before they are committed once again, you may find them indolent or flagging. Added to that is the possibility that the Treveri and their allies might fall on Labienus before we arrive. Better to move fast and combine the army all round.'

'*I*, on the other hand, would *avoid* the forest,' Priscus noted, snapping a glare at Antonius. 'A hundred and fifty-odd miles of stomping through unfamiliar, tough, enemy territory? Not favourable by any stretch of the imagination, and that's if your scouts can find a clear way through that nightmare that allows for legions, cavalry and wagons - Fabius and Furius reported that there's hardly a track big enough in the whole place to take even a horseman unless he ducks a lot. If you travel along the river bank, skirting the great forest and Eburone territory we might learn something of use about Ambiorix in our journey. Are the Treveri enough of a threat? Labienus already crushed them months ago, and now he'll have three legions instead of one.'

Caesar pursed his lips. 'My sources inform me that following his prior victory, Labienus was his usual peaceable self, allowing the tribe to return to their lands with just a hard word and a smack on the behind. Such magnanimity the Belgae simply consider weakness. Mark me: he has not seen the last of the Treveri. And do not forget that, while Labienus may have three legions, and may be able to deal with one tribe, we now know that Ambiorix is not in the north. If he is not among Nervii and Menapii lands, then he is south - close to the Treveri. That being the case, Labienus could be facing not only what is left of the Treveri, but also any other combined force the Eburone traitor has managed to raise. With three legions, if the worst happens, he should be able to hold even against the largest force until we arrive to lend a hand, but the Treveri are the remaining powerful ally of Ambiorix, and my focus should naturally fall there next. You would prefer I turn on the Eburones directly and risk Fronto? I have given him ample time, after all.'

Priscus simply sat back wearily. The general spoke sense. Campaigning against the Nervii and Menapii had been hard work, but the two tribes were now certainly unable to support Ambiorix. Where *was* Fronto? The whole reason for his hunt was to provide

242

Caesar with an alternative route to burning the Belgae to ash in his vengeance, but already the general had brought death and destruction to another great tribe, and now he turned to a third. Priscus was unpleasantly aware of the mood among the auxiliary cavalry - many of them Belgae. Desertions among the allies had risen threefold since the start of the Menapii campaign, and things would only deteriorate as the Treveri were crushed.

He nodded.

'And what then, Caesar?' asked Marcus Antonius, sitting over to one side with his ubiquitous flask of wine. 'When you have crushed all the tribes Ambiorix would rely upon?'

The general's brow furrowed and his eyes glinted.

'Then we will trap the fox and tear him to pieces. Fronto will have had far more than the time I offered him, and I will not see this season end with that animal free to cause further trouble. I have vowed his death and I *will* have it.'

Priscus took a deep troubled breath and glanced towards the closed door. A couple more weeks, then. A month at most, before Fronto's hunt was to be consumed by Caesar's vengeance - surgical strike replaced by the mallet of the general's wrath.

He turned back to the general, who was moving on with his briefing.

Fortuna be with you, Fronto.

Chapter Thirteen

Deep in the forest of Arduenna

'Where the hell are we now?' Fronto gave Samognatos a dark stare, and Masgava and Palmatus shared a look and braced themselves for the latest attack of Fronto's bad mood.

'The oppidum of Atuatuca.'

Fronto shook his head. For the past week or more, they had moved back and forth through the more major tracks in the oppressive forest of Arduenna, even to the point where the hill regions ended and they looked down to the north over Menapii territory, where Fronto had almost expected to see Belgic armies massing against them. They had maintained a steady easterly direction, but roved a great deal at a nerve-gratingly slow pace in the process, covering Eburone territory and the heart of the great forest. Rarely had they come across any real settlement, and when they had, Fronto had kept the main force with him, while Samognatos and Magurix had gone ahead along with Biorix, the Gallic engineer, to investigate and pick up any information.

News was scant. Apart from the rumours that Caesar was now laying waste to the Menapii - near where they had been five days ago, Fronto noted with irritation - they had picked up precious little of Cativolcus. Rumour suggested that the second king of the Eburones was trying to obfuscate and keep himself as far from worldly events as possible, still harbouring a deep-in-the-bone loathing of his brother king, along with a very real fear that Rome would soon rage through his lands like a forest fire, destroying all in its path.

It was a very accurate fear, and Fronto could hardly blame the man for hiding himself, but the fact remained that as well as keeping him from harm's way, it also kept him out of reach of those who would provide any kind of aid, such as seeing his hated brother removed from the world.

During more than a week of travel, only twice had they heard rumours of the old king's whereabouts. The last had proved to be complete fiction, and they had arrived at Avendura to find it dull, lifeless and miserable, the few occupants eking out a hard life after the death of many of the working menfolk in the previous year's rebellion. Though the inhabitants were approached by what had appeared to be three natives, the townsfolk were hardly forthcoming, apart from snarling that Ambiorix had ruined them by taking their men off on a pointless uprising and that the old Cativolcus was no better and, no, he had not set foot in Avendura within living memory.

And so they'd moved on in search of more useful information. Fronto had argued forcefully that this was a fool's errand that they'd been sent on by druids, of all people, and so it should hardly be a surprise that they were finding nothing of use, wandering endlessly and slowly in a dangerous forest. He'd even advocated returning to Condrusi lands and skinning a few of the druid bastards to find out where the old King and his young brother might actually be - after all, the bloody druids had failed to mention in their grand suggestion for Fronto's journey that the old king might be hiding and could be harder to find than Ambiorix himself.

Samognatos had patiently reminded him that the locals they were speaking to were genuinely displaying no love of either Eburone king, and that whatever trouble they were having finding Cativolcus, Ambiorix would likely be having just as much difficulty, if not more. And while Brannogenos was out there somewhere, they'd heard nothing of him and experienced no difficulties other than a few minor scuffles with bandits. What his objectives were was anybody's guess, but it seemed unlikely he was connected to Cativolcus. Instead, he had probably gone in search of Ambiorix.

Searching this damned endless mountain forest with its taciturn, recalcitrant occupants for two men was like searching the Mare Nostrum in a rowing boat for two particular flatfish. Fronto's mood had been on the descent for many days now, and his two officers had stopped voluntarily conversing with him some time ago.

And now here they were, at the second location rumour held to be the hiding place of Cativolcus.

Or rather, as far as Fronto could see, they weren't.

'This,' Fronto said with an exaggerated patience that they all knew was not a true representation of his mood, 'is not Atuatuca. I've *been* to Atuatuca. It's a big walled place where the Sambre and the Mosa rivers meet. And if we were there, I'd be able to see the lumps and bumps of all our camps and ramparts from when we besieged the place, burned it to ashes and enslaved the entire population.'

He took a deep breath as something he should have thought of before occurred to him for the first time. 'Anyway, Atuatuca is the oppidum of the Aduatuci! Nothing to do with the Eburones. Why are we going there? We're outside Eburone lands, then? Samognatos, what the hell is going on?'

The Condrusi scout hoisted up his perpetual smile to contain a notch of genuine humour.

'Aduatuca of the Aduatuci. Atuatuca of the Eburones. It is a fine distinction, certainly, but an important one, for they are different places.' As Fronto opened his mouth to shout yet again, Samognatos shrugged. 'The Aduatuci were linked to the Eburones. They were...' he searched for an explanation that might suit Fronto. 'Think of them as cousins to the Eburones. Both tribes descend from the blood across the Rhenus, which separates their whole race from ours. Aduatuca - or Atuatuca equally - is a Germanic term for a 'fortress'. The Aduatuci were the 'fortress' people and, as you can see, this oppidum of the Eburones deserves just such a term.'

Fronto sagged. Samognatos certainly knew his stuff, though his explanations tended to go off on tangents occasionally or spill over into rambling accounts of tribal history and politics. Instead of continuing the debate, he looked up at the great ridge that ran north-south to a spur which looked particularly unassailable.

'We're *all* going in, then,' Fronto said flatly.

'Sir?'

'Look, we've visited numerous of these places and everything Roman that might put them off talking has stayed out of sight with me. I think we've now agreed that the locals have no love of their kings. So if neither Cativolcus nor Ambiorix are there, we shouldn't have any trouble. And if he is there, then I want to speak to the old goat anyway. Now how do we get in?'

Samognatos shrugged and pointed to the western side of the huge ridge with a plateaued top. 'There is a path you can see from here that winds to the top.'

'Come on, then.'

Fronto started to walk his tired horse across the wide valley, the rest of the singulares falling in behind. The mountain loomed as they approached, and Fronto had to admit to a startling geographical similarity in some respects to that other 'Aduatuca' where Priscus had almost died four years ago. Throw in an approach road at the narrow end and heavy walls and the place would be horribly familiar. In fact, where he was riding right now was about where he'd stood with Tetricus and learned how to measure a cliff's height. Strange - this year seemed filled with startling reminders of times long gone and people he'd lost.

246

He was still musing on the matter, which did nothing to lighten his already subterranean mood, when they began up the slope towards the oppidum of the Eburones. The climb was long and slow, much like everything he'd experienced so far in Arduenna's unpleasant forest. The relief he felt as they began to level out at the plateau was quickly demolished as he took in the welcoming committee.

The defences of Atuatuca were of the usual construction: stone-faced, with a lattice of timbers betrayed by the visible ends along the length of the wall, all packed with earth and backed with a bank. The gates were of timber, heavy and well-protected, set back slightly from the walls to provide a killing area. The gates, in this particular case, stood open.

And in that killing zone stood a nobleman with his entourage of half a dozen bodyguards, the usual druid with a sour expression and a beard you could lose a bear in, and several dozen warriors standing about armed to the teeth as though expecting trouble.

'You are not welcome here.'

'You don't know who we are, yet,' Fronto replied with low menace.

'You are Roman. You may not be dressed like one, but you have the stench. And your pets from tribes who betray the Goddess are no more welcome than you.'

'Believe it or not,' Fronto said quietly, 'that is not the coldest welcome I've yet had. We are not here to cause you any trouble. We seek only information.'

'Ambiorix is not here,' the man replied quickly. Too quickly, in Fronto's opinion.

'Then it's lucky for you that we're not seeking that pointless rat.' A qualified truth, but a truth nonetheless. He was gratified to see the noble's expression slip for a moment as he was clearly not expecting such an answer.

'You will have nothing from us.'

'Really?' Fronto curved his mouth into the sort of smile people back away from. 'You are Ambiorix's men to the heart; I can tell. As such, I am leaning towards the belief that you will hold no love for the weasel-king Cativolcus? He did, after all, abandon Ambiorix after last year's massacres.'

Again, the noble clearly had not been expecting this, and his face twisted in confusion. He turned to his companions and a quick, hushed conversation took place, along with a lot of animated waving of arms and slapping of fist on hand.

'We owe Cativolcus for his part in the uprising,' Fronto said as they argued. 'Caesar intends to deal with Ambiorix by wiping the world clean of the stain of the Eburones and burning down every timber they ever built.'

The noble and his companions had fallen silent at this and were now peering with suspicion at Fronto again. 'Rest assured that the little turd has his end coming to him soon enough, and Caesar will see to it. You can stand here and cast your spittle at seventy thousand armoured men as they pound your walls to dust and mate with, or murder, every living thing, but right now I seek the whereabouts of Cativolcus.'

He stretched. 'I was led to believe that the old man was hiding from Caesar and Ambiorix both in this very oppidum.' He watched the men's faces and confirmed what he had initially thought. 'But it is clear he is not here and never has been. But...' he took a single step forward, 'it is also clear to me, from your very expressions, that you *do* know of his location. Tell me where to find him and I may consider interceding with Caesar in the manner of your end. After all, there are worse things to experience than simple death, are there not?'

His threat had carried endless layers of potential agony and misery, and the nobleman had clearly spotted a number of them as he turned and had another quick, hurried and muttered conversation with his companions. Finally, he turned back.

'Espaduno.'

Fronto frowned and turned to Samognatos, who nodded. 'It is a town in the south of Eburone lands, almost in Segni lands. If Ambiorix has been in Segni territory, then the two kings are close.'

Fronto nodded. 'Time to get ourselves to this *Espaduno* as fast as we can, then. Seems to me that that Segni warband we came across after we left your lands might not be the last we see.'

He turned back to the nobleman.

'I offer you a piece of advice. Eschew your connections with Ambiorix, and when Caesar comes rapping on your gate, welcome him with open arms. Ambiorix is not the man to throw your support behind, this summer. And if you feel the need to hold to your vows with your king, make sure your walls are a sight higher and thicker than they are now. But most of all, do not pin all your hopes on that little shitbag Ambiorix, and don't expect to ever see him at your gate again.'

The nobleman, clearly shaken by the whole exchange, simply watched in consternation as the Roman party turned and began the descent back to the valley below. As soon as they were out of both sight and hearing of the Eburones on the plateau, Masgava pulled ahead to walk beside Fronto.

'Do you think they told us the truth?'

'I do. The location's too convenient. The old king hides himself at the very edge of his lands, close to the Segni, where Ambiorix was last thought to be. I wouldn't be surprised if the two of them are already together. Certainly he's not been to *this* place for a long time. I would say from what I saw of them that these locals are desperately hoping Ambiorix will hove into view with an army of Rome-hating Gauls and Germans before Caesar arrives.'

A thought occurred to him and he turned to view the column of men behind him, wondering who he could spare. The answer, obviously, was: no one. Numisius, however, still nursed his broken arm as he rode, and nights wrapped in his cloak were bothering him with the cold and damp.

'Numisius? I have a task for you... and Biorix. Sorry about this, lads, but we need to get a message to Caesar. He's somewhere up around the Rhenus delta stamping on the Menapii, but when he's finished with them he'll turn south, and the last thing we need is for him to then fix his attention on this area. Things could get very busy and dangerous round here if a number of legions start stomping towards us. Get to the general and tell him what we know and that we're closing in on both kings at the Segni border. Tell him to give us more time. You can take two of the pack horses as spare mounts. Head along the Mosa until it meets the Rhenus and then along that until you find word of the army. Ride fast, and be careful. Once you've delivered the message, find Priscus and stay with him until we meet up again - you'll never track us down if you come back south.'

Pausing, he retrieved a small, easily-portable wax tablet from his purse and carved a few hasty lines in the wax with the stylus from the same container. A simple note that took mere moments, and then he snapped it shut and passed it to Biorix.

'This is for Priscus alone. I've no wax to seal it and no time, but if you open it and read it, rest assure, I will know.'

Biorix took the tablet and nodded, and the two legionaries, looking somewhat perturbed at their lot, saluted and dropped back to unrope two of the pack horses. The supplies were now seriously diminished, and so the beasts could easily be spared. The idea of more than one hundred and fifty miles of enemy territory with only hard rations and what they could forage was not enticing, and Fronto could hardly blame them for the mix of nerves and disappointment that showed on their faces. But Numisius was the man most expendable because of his arm, and Biorix was one of the men Fronto trusted most in the unit, and a Gaul by blood, so if any pair could get to Caesar, it was them.

He straightened in his saddle. 'Whatever Ambiorix is up to, I believe Cativolcus is at this Espaduno waiting for him, close to Segni lands. Whether he's changed his tune and is looking to throw in his lot with his brother king or has other ideas in mind, I think we have to hope that they have not yet met and we need to get there first if we can. What do you know of the territory between here and there, Samognatos?'

The scout's brow furrowed slightly.

'It is perhaps forty or fifty miles from here,' he replied, deep in thought. 'The first half of the journey at least will be easy, as we can follow the Mosa as far as Ludico. From there it will be more difficult as we climb and enter the deepest heart of the forest. Travel will be slow and, as well as wandering patrols of Eburones and possibly Segni, the region is notorious for banditry.'

'Sounds delightful. We'd best get going then.'

* * * * *

'How far is Espaduno now?'

Samognatos peered into the dense trees ahead, as though he might be able to see the place. Even had it been visible during clear daylight, it would not show itself through the thick foliage in the middle of the night, and the darkness was near absolute here. Were it not for the dancing flames of their fire, they would not be able to see even the men sleeping across the track.

To call this place a clearing would be to over-exaggerate its space. It was simply an area where the trees and undergrowth were less dense and tangling, with enough grassy area for the dozen men to light a fire and lie down. Perhaps some time in the distant past it had been a proper clearing, but trees had invaded the space and turned it into yet another part of the endless dark forest.

'Perhaps seven more miles,' the scout replied, warming his hands over the fire and reaching for the salted meat that had been heating in the flames for a while.

Fronto's eyes played across the clearing nervously as they had every dozen heartbeats since they'd set up here for the night. Nine stones stood in the 'clearing'. He'd counted them several times. They'd arrived in the inky purple late evening and hurried to make the fire before the last of the light disappeared altogether, the leafy canopy bringing down pitch darkness earlier than the sky intended.

Each stone seemed to be decorated with scenes or figures in that lumpy, misshapen Gallic form when he caught them out of the corner of his eye - especially in the flickering, dancing orange light - but close inspection showed the stones to be plain and unmarked, simply roughly-hewn and with lumps and pits. The whole arrangement made Fronto shudder. The stones looked as though they had been deliberately placed in an oval - an elongated circle reminiscent of a gladiatorial arena. His first thought had been that the place resembled a druidic nemeton, but Samognatos had been adamant that all the features were purely natural and there was nothing sacred about the place.

Fronto still suspected otherwise. An image of the huntress Goddess caught his attention on a granite surface, but had gone when he turned to look at it. He reached up to the figurine of Fortuna hanging around his neck and fondled her repeatedly.

'We should have gone on through the night.'

Samognatos shook his head. 'Better to get there in the light. We do not know what to expect, after all.'

Fronto nodded glumly. He'd still have preferred to camp almost anywhere else, but the scout had been right about this being the best position from a purely geographical point of view. The path sloped down both ahead and behind, to one side a deep gulley with a narrow stream provided adequate defence, and on the other side a steep slope upwards prevented easy access. Added to that the fact that it was the most open area, clear of undergrowth, that they'd seen for hours, and it was obviously the place to camp.

It still put the shits up Fronto.

His only consolation was Aurelius, who lay on his blankets close by, his eyes wide and staring as he continually scanned the area for... something. Every time they heard the squeak of a bat - which was remarkably often in this place - the big, tough legionary stiffened and his eyes rolled wildly. He seemed to be more of a nervous wreck than Fronto.

'How are you intending to play it when we approach?' Palmatus asked from nearby, where he gnawed on a meaty bone.

'Diplomatically, I think. I've been pondering the problem. There are only thirteen of us now, and Espaduno being an Eburone oppidum and current home to one of their kings, I think we can assume a reasonable population. We'll be outnumbered and they have every advantage.'

'How can we be diplomatic, though? What can we offer?'

'That depends on what they want. Is Cativolcus here to make a deal with Ambiorix, or for less amiable purposes. If it's the former, we have nothing. If the latter, we can offer a helping hand. Either way, we have no standing orders against Cativolcus, and we can deal with him on a fair and straight level. I think we go in, hands up and honest, telling him that we're after Ambiorix's head but we have no interest in him, and might even be able to broker a deal between him and Caesar if it plays out right.'

'Caesar may be concentrating on Ambiorix,' Palmatus said, shaking his head, 'but Cativolcus led his men in that same revolt. Caesar won't countenance peace with him, and he'll know that.'

'Perhaps. But I think diplomacy and offering of aid is the way to go. We cannot take on a whole oppidum of the Eburones with thirteen men, after all.'

Palmatus nodded his agreement.

'What is this place like?' Fronto asked Samognatos.

The scout shrugged. 'I have only visited once, and that was many years ago. Espaduno is not a fortress, but a sacred site. It lies in a valley in the deepest of Arduenna's woods. Its defences are meagre, if I remember correctly - none of our people would ever attack such a sacred site in the heart of Arduenna's realm, so defences are hardly necessary. There are sacred springs and more than one nemeton.'

'Great,' muttered Aurelius close by. 'The bat-witch Goddess' home, eh?'

Fronto shot him a warning look, though could only admit to sharing the man's trepidation. Samognatos shook his head. 'Arduenna lives everywhere in these forests. It is *all* her home, and you need not fear her. Our druids have interceded with her on your behalf. If you had not the goodwill of the Goddess, we would all have been dead long before this.'

'Somehow that does not provide me with a deep, warm feeling of comfort, Samognatos.'

'What was that?' yelped Aurelius.

'It was a bloody bat, man. Stop panicking at every squeak.'

'That wasn't a bat.' The legionary threw off his cloak and reached for the sheathed sword lying nearby. 'I've heard a million million bats this past few weeks. That's *not* a bat.'

Fronto had heard nothing unusual, yet something in Aurelius' voice had triggered action, and now he stood, reaching for his own blade and hissing it from the sheath.

'Did you hear it *that* time?' Aurelius asked quietly.

'No.' Fronto shook his head and began to relax. 'You're hearing things, you big superstitious lump.'

'No. I heard...'

He was cut off by a blood-curdling wail a matter of mere paces away from them. Fronto, Palmatus, Samognatos and Aurelius' heads all whipped around to peer off into the darkness, but the fire that lay between them and the scream ruined their night vision. Stooping, Fronto grasped one of the flaming branches from the fire by the dry, cold end and tossed it as hard as he could towards the big stone that loomed in the rough direction of the shriek. None of the men had chosen to sleep too close to the stones, so he was reasonably assured of not setting fire to a man in his blankets if he aimed for one.

Sparks flew from the branch in a spray as it bounced off the stone and landed in the grass, instantly illuminating the far side of the 'clearing'.

Fronto stared in horror at Luxinio's face. His eyes were wide with shock, his mouth open in a scream that had died away as his head rose, while the rest of him fell away to the earth, severed at the throat-apple.

The head, strings of crimson gore hanging from its ragged neck, was gripped by the dark, tightly-curled Greek hair. The orange glow faintly illuminated his killer, who stood behind him, glistening pink sword blade still raised. Fronto felt his bowels loosen slightly as he realised the creature had a wolf's head on a human body.

'Fuck me!' shouted Aurelius in a panicked voice. 'Shit, shit, shit, shit, shit!'

'Get a hold of yourself, man!' snapped Palmatus, showing a great deal more control than Fronto currently felt. All around the clearing, the men were now rising from their blankets, swords in hand. The wolf-thing cast the severed head into the fire, where the hair caught and the burning object rolled through the flames towards Fronto, who stepped aside as it passed. Figures began to loom in the darkness behind the wolf-creature, each one a horrible animal parody. A man-thing with a stag's head, antlers sawn off close to prevent snagging on the branches. A bear-man. Others, too indistinct in the darkness.

'The Goddess!' yelled Aurelius. 'It's Arduenna!'

'It's not Arduenna!' Fronto snapped angrily. 'She's a woman, and she's on our side!'

The horrible creatures stepped out of the woods and into the clearing and, as if from nowhere, Masgava suddenly appeared beside the wolf-man. One hand went up to the creature's chin, illuminated orange in the firelight, and yanked the head to one side as the other struck, driving a thick, long knife into the creature's jugular, spraying dark liquid out into the night.

As the creature jerked and fell away, Masgava's hand slipped, grasping at the wolf's hair, and the wolf-mask slid off in his hand, hanging limp as the man who'd worn it collapsed to the ground, clutching at his neck, bleeding out his life.

Masgava was visible largely from the brilliance of his white grin in the dark as he cast the wolf's head away and turned to face the rest of the animal-masked attackers. As the men leapt forward, Fronto turned to Aurelius. 'Get a grip on yourself, you daft sod!' he snapped as he dashed away to join the fracas, grateful that he'd stopped just short of soiling himself and that Aurelius would never know that.

Now, half a dozen of the men were in the clearing and fighting, though they had lost the element of shock that had accompanied their arrival with the pragmatic Masgava's impressive first kill. Now, the efficiency of Roman-trained soldiers came into play. Fronto ran across and found himself standing facing the stag-man, with Magurix the Remi on his right, fighting off a second wolf-man. Even as he parried a sword strike and delivered a sharp stab to the stag's upper arm, Fronto had a moment to admire the big, muscular Remi warrior's abilities. With a heavy sword in his right hand and bearing no shield, Magurix neatly knocked aside the attacker's blade and delivered a succession of three blows with his left arm: a drive up into the man's kidney, an uppercut to the wolf-muzzled jaw, and then a sharp elbow down onto the cord that connected shoulder to neck as the man fell back. Before he even hit the floor, Magurix had recovered his sword position and drove the blade into the falling chest.

Gods, the man was fast.

Fronto delivered a second and then third stabbing strike to the stag-man, dancing back out of the way of his desperate counter-stroke, and found himself facing the bear-man beyond, as his previous victim fell to the earth. With a deep breath of smoky, cold night air, he readied himself for the next fight, but paused as the big bear-headed man stiffened and toppled forward to the turf. A neatly-fletched arrow stood proud from the man's back.

Startled, Fronto stepped back, wondering whether he could make a dash for his shield. None of them had had the time to retrieve their shields, so sudden was the attack.

'Hold still, Roman,' the archer said in passable Latin, stepping forth from the darker trees beyond. He was clearly a local, in a yellow-brown tunic and grey checked trousers, his white-blond hair braided at the temples and moustaches drooping below his lips. A second arrow was nocked on the man's bow. Even as Fronto lowered his sword, he saw shafts plunge into the remaining animal-headed attackers, killing them quickly and cleanly.

Fronto stepped back, sheathed his sword and raised his hands in a placating manner.

So much for lookouts. One of the pair on duty tonight had been beheaded and the other... well there had been no sign of Valgus during the fight. In truth, these woods were so close and dark and unfamiliar he felt it unlikely he'd have spotted an attacker any more than the others.

'We mean you no harm,' he said sidestepping the fire in his retreat and closing on his shield.

'You said Arduenna was 'on your side'?' the man asked, narrowing his eyes, arrow still trained on Fronto.

'We are here with the Goddess' blessing, on the directions of the druids of Divonanto,' Fronto said, hoping that the blessing of the Goddess and the aid of druids would be enough to offset the mention of a settlement that remained loyal to Caesar.

'The Goddess apparently does not protect you from bandits?' the man said, ironically, nudging the dead bear-man with his toe as he stepped past, bow still raised. Other natives were behind him, also

255

with arrows nocked. Slowly, the men of the singulares stepped back into the clearing, making for their shields at a slow retreat.

'Perhaps she does?' Fronto countered. 'You showed up in a timely manner.'

The archer let out a short barked laugh and let his string loosen, the arrow tipping away from Fronto's chest. 'Well said. A Roman with the blessing of druids and our Goddess is a curious thing. What brings you into the great forest?'

Fronto tried to ignore the real possibility that these very men had been among those who had butchered a legion and a half mere months ago, and forced a smile onto his face. 'We seek Cativolcus, king of the Eburones.'

'A dozen Romans will not slay our king.'

Fronto nodded. 'I am aware of that. I said we sought *him*, not his head.'

'Curious,' the archer replied, his eyes still slitted in suspicion. 'I am Ullio, of Espaduno. And you *must* be favoured of the Goddess. This collection of animals has killed many a strong warrior in the night, and we have been hunting them for two days. Gather your goods and follow. We will take you to Espaduno, but I warn you of this: if the king does not wish to receive you, things will not go so well.'

Fronto nodded. 'Just take us there and we shall see what we shall see.'

As the native hunters, of which there appeared to be the best part of a score, took up guard positions on the periphery, bows still in hand, Fronto and the others gathered their kit and packed everything on their horses, untying the beasts from the branches where they had been tethered for the night. Once they were on the move again, heading south with the Eburone hunters around them, Masgava leaned close.

'When we left, I had a quick look to the north path. I couldn't see Valgus, let alone his body. He's vanished.'

Fronto sighed. 'Great. So now we don't know whether he's alive or dead or possibly even a traitor like Brannogenos, run off to his masters.'

'I think we can discount the latter. He and Celer are close as brothers, and Celer is still here, wearing a mask of grief. I fear they were lovers.'

Fronto blinked. 'What?'

'Lovers. It is not unknown, Fronto, even among gladiators, let alone legionaries.'

'I... I just never knew. Keep your eyes open. I think Valgus is still out there somewhere. The bandits came from the south, and so did our Eburone rescuers, but Valgus was guarding the north approach. He's not the fastest or quietest of men, but if he's out there, he'll be shadowing our party.'

Masgava nodded and moved away again.

Fronto rubbed at his temples. His brain hurt. What had Gaul come to in his absence? When he'd last been here it had been a simple matter of dressing like a Roman, standing in a shieldwall and stabbing Gauls. Now here he was being protected by the Eburones - the most rabid of the tribes Caesar could currently count among his enemies - as he sought an audience with their king at the behest of druids, all with the favour of a Goddess who hated Romans.

It was enough to curdle his gut, let alone make his brain thump.

* * * * *

Espaduno was an impressive sight for its design, rather than its might, even in the dark. This was no oppidum or simple town. It was a collection of holy places visible eerily in the moonlight, linked by houses and shops in neat roads that were betrayed by the orange lights of torches, fires and lamps, all of it surrounded by a low mound surmounted by a palisade fence.

As they reached the edge of the trees and peered down the slope, they took in the settlement, bathed in a silvery glow. Away to their left, along the hillside, stood a collection of grand - for the Gallic peoples, anyway - buildings, surrounded by its own palisade. A neat collection of streets in a tight web below, within the main palisade, connected three different nemeton, each separated from the civic areas by a wattle fence and circle of trees.

'That is the sacred springs of Arduenna,' Samognatos said in a hushed voice, pointing towards the separate area on the hillside.

'That doesn't concern me,' Fronto replied. 'Only Cativolcus and Ambiorix concern me now.'

He turned to address the white-blond hunter who apparently led their escort. 'Ullio? Will you be able to provide us with a place to sleep for the night?'

The man turned in surprise. 'Only if the king tells me so.'

257

'We are to see Cativolcus at this hour? I thought we would likely wait for the morning?'

'The king rarely sleeps.'

Fronto nodded. Neither would he, in the man's precarious position. 'Very well. Will you allow me to take companions in to see him?'

'If he wills it.'

Fronto sighed and followed as the party descended the slope and approached the entrance through the palisade - a simple wooden gate that would hold back a legion for about the time it took to use the latrine. They were held up at the gate for only a moment before Ullio was recognised and they were admitted. The men on guard duty - presumably a reduced number for the night - watched with barely-concealed loathing as they passed, despite the fact that, as far as Fronto was concerned, they bore precious little resemblance to Romans.

Wordlessly, they were led through the dark, packed-earth streets of Espaduno, riding to the end of the settlement that was closest to the sacred springs on the hillside and near to the largest of the three nemeton. Here, the party halted in front of a building of two storeys that looked no different to any other structure in the settlement.

'Wait here,' said Ullio authoritatively, and then rapped once on the heavy timber door and pushed it open, walking inside. Fronto stood and waited with the rest outside, feeling the strangest tension at his surroundings and situation. After a long, odd pause, the door opened, and Ullio reappeared. 'He will see you, and whoever you feel you need to accompany you.'

Fronto felt himself sag with relief. He'd not come up with a viable plan of action if Cativolcus would not see him. 'Palmatus, Masgava and Samognatos: with me. The rest of you be on your guard, but respectful. We are here as guests, strange as that may seem.'

With a nod to Ullio, Fronto stepped to the door.

'Your swords and daggers,' the hunter said, blocking the doorway with his arm. Fronto nodded and drew his sword and pugio, passing them to the blond archer. Behind him the others also removed their weapons. Fronto paused for only a moment, and then turned to his officers. 'All of them,' he noted, raising looks of surprise from the others, but a smile of respect from Ullio.

Entirely disarmed, the four men waited for Ullio, and, passing the pile of weapons to his closest man, he gestured for them to enter, closing the door behind and remaining outside.

The large building was one single room, with a mezzanine floor above. A fire in the room's centre provided most of the heat and a reasonable light, supplemented by a number of braziers. Cupboards and chairs and other furniture lay around the room's periphery, and a large table was covered with bric-a-brac. The room had one single occupant, which surprised Fronto. He had expected the king to have a guard of several on hand, especially if he had agreed to receive Roman visitors.

'Your name, Roman?' The old king's voice was reed-thin and hoarse, like the whisper of a dying man on the wind, and Fronto felt somehow saddened by the tones. Something about the man's voice suggested a once-powerful warlord, now old and frail. Oddly, despite everything, he suddenly found himself feeling a touch of sympathy for the old man.

'Marcus Falerius Fronto, staff officer in the army of Rome under Gaius Julius Caesar, Proconsul of Gaul.'

'Ah,' the old man smiled. 'The 'Proconsul of Gaul'. A title that seems to be contested by many. Not here, though. It is worth remembering that we are Eburones, and not Gauls. Our forefathers came from the great forests beyond the Rhenus, not from the tilled soils of the south. We are the hardened sons of blood-soaked Gods, not smiths and farmers.'

'Very impressive, I'm sure,' Fronto said nonchalantly. 'Shall I laud the Republic of Rome through its history of conquest and violence and its great founding by heroes of Troy? Or shall we stop bullshitting one another and talk straight as men?'

Cativolcus whispered a hoarse laugh. 'I have heard of a Fronto who commanded legions against our peoples. You are he?'

'I am.'

'Very well, killer of Belgae. Tell me why you are here without your legion?'

Fronto gestured to a seat opposite and the old king nodded. As the other three leaned against the table and the wall at the room's edge, Fronto sank into the hard, wooden chair and adjusted himself to a vague semblance of comfort, crossing his legs and folding his arms.

'It is said that you are no lover of your brother king Ambiorix.'

259

'It is said truthfully,' the old man replied, and Fronto felt a flood of relief. That the pair might have been reconciled had been one of his greatest worries.

'You will no doubt be aware of Caesar's wrath towards Ambiorix?'

'All our lands are aware of Caesar's wrath. He burns and levels entire tribes in his anger.'

Fronto nodded. 'He has made a solemn vow to both our people and our most powerful Goddess - as revered as your Arduenna - that he will kill Ambiorix. He will stop at nothing until that comes to pass.'

'And he lays waste to whole lands to do it,' Cativolcus rasped.

'He does. And if you think what he has done to the Nervii and is apparently now doing to the Menapii is unpleasant, it pales to nothing against what he will do to the Eburones, who destroyed an entire Roman army and killed some of our leading citizens.'

'You have chosen a strange way to deliver such a threat, stepping into the bear's jaw, Roman.'

'I am not delivering a threat. I am simply stating Caesar's intentions. He has made an unbreakable vow to a powerful Goddess, and will move the world to see it fulfiled. Fortunately for you and your people, *Ambiorix* is the subject of that vow, and the might of Rome could be turned aside from you and your tribe simply by handing over Ambiorix.'

'An excellent solution,' the old man smiled, '*if* I had him.'

'Ah, but you have come south to the border of the Segni at a time that your counterpart is rumoured to have been among them. A little too convenient to be coincidence. If you have no love for the man, why do you move to intercept him?'

Cativolcus gave a knowing laugh. 'You are shrewd and well-informed, Roman.' He sighed and leaned back. 'Very well. The time has come for the Eburones to unite under one king. Ambiorix wishes it to be him, as he seeks a grand army to lead against Rome in another of his foolish crusades. I am an old man who has seen enough of war and destruction, and I care not at this stage of my life whether I rule all the Eburones, but for the good of what remains of my people, I will do what I must to prevent Ambiorix from doing so.'

Fronto smiled with actual, genuine relief. It was better than he could have hoped for. 'What makes you think Ambiorix will come to you?'

'He must, if he wishes to rule the Eburones. Currently his supporters number small bands of survivors from last winter's war, while much of the surviving tribe are subject to my rule. My scouts tell me Ambiorix waits at this time on the Treveri, who rise once more against your general in the south, and then he will return to Eburone lands.'

'And how do you intend to kill him? With the greatest of respect, he is much younger and stronger than you, and if it comes down to a clash of arms, he will not lead his small band against your larger one. He is not stupid enough for that.'

Again, Cativolcus chuckled. 'One of the benefits of being old is that I have little left to lose. In fact, if it buys peace and security for my people, even my honour is for sale. I have a vial of poison so virulent that a single drop will kill. Ambiorix will parlay with me, as it is our right and duty as leaders of men. He will not walk away from that conversation.'

Fronto nodded slowly, surprised to find the old man so blasé on the use of poison. It seemed anathema to all the Gauls held dear to remove an opponent in such an underhand manner. Still, it suited Fronto perfectly.

'I was about to offer our services in dealing with Ambiorix, but it sounds to me as though you already have things planned out better than I. I would dearly like to ask a few questions of Ambiorix before he dies, though. How fast will your poison work?'

The old man pursed his lips and removed a small earthenware container from his belt, peering at it in the low light. 'That depends entirely upon the quantity. This brew is distilled from the yew tree in methods known only to the druids. It is extremely powerful, and - as I said - a single drop will kill. But slowly. For a quick death, much more must be administered. A single drop would suffice, though, and Ambiorix will linger for some time in exquisite agony. I have seen yew-juice taken before. He will shake like a wild horse, sweat like a running man and gasp like a throat-slashed one. He will have time to tell you what you need.'

'And you have no problem with this interrogation?'

'What care I how many of the rat's secrets he spills to you. I care only for the security of my people.'

261

Fronto smiled and leaned forward, unfolding his arms and legs. 'It would seem, king of the Eburones, that we have an understanding. We are in concord. Have you somewhere that we can stay while we await the inevitable arrival of your enemy?'

Cativolcus slouched into his chair. 'Ullio will see to it. He sees to everything. Strange, the paths down which a man might tread, eh, Roman? That the Goddess deliver a Roman to me and he and I might find common purpose under my roof?'

Fronto smiled as he rose. 'My own Goddess, Nemesis, had no small part in the process, I can assure you. Thank you for your time and your honesty, king of the Eburones. With the help of the Gods and our own strength, perhaps we can see a way through this to preserve the Eburones from the wrath of Rome and leave you as undisputed king with Caesar's blessing.

Cativolcus once more smiled and waved Fronto away, closing his eyes and relaxing back into his seat. Fronto turned and gestured to the other three and they made their way back to the door. As they exited and Fronto closed the portal behind him, Palmatus whispered 'Do you think we can trust him?'

'He certainly seems to want Ambiorix out of the picture as much as we do,' Fronto hissed back.

'Beware just how far you trust,' Masgava added, darkly.

'What?'

'He may have seemed resigned to his fate, but there were at least eight men on the floor above us in the dark, and I heard bow strings loosen as we left. One wrong word in there and we would have been pinned to the wall.'

Fronto nodded. 'A king is allowed his protection. It's expected, but to keep them hidden and secret is unusual, I'll admit. You don't think he was lying, and that Ambiorix is already here?'

Samognatos shook his head. 'He was truthful on that account at least. And he has everything to gain and nothing to lose from Ambiorix's death.'

'Just remember that he might have other agendas too,' added Palmatus.

The four men stepped out to rejoin the rest of the remaining singulares, Ullio standing ahead down the street a little.

'The king would see us quartered for the night.'

Ullio nodded and gestured on down the path. Fronto turned to the others. 'Well, we're closer than ever. Ambiorix is lurking to the south, but is almost in our grasp. Let's just hope Labienus can put the Treveri down first.'

Chapter Fourteen

Hillside in Treveri lands.

Andesaros of the Treveri brushed aside the stray braid that continually hovered on the periphery of his vision and sat on a wide, flat rock, peering down into the valley ahead. Behind him, his warbands took advantage of the pause in the journey to eat, drink, share jokes and boast about what they would do to the Romans when they had overwhelmed them.

Two small groups had broken off from the sizeable army and were making their way forward to him. One of his loyal bodyguards stepped close to him, putting a meaty hand on this hilt of his sword, but Andesaros waved him away negligently. It was only the other two chieftains come to interfere yet again. Besides, what use were these impressive bodyguards? They hadn't done much to save his uncle's life, after all. There was in fact every chance that this big man fondling his sword pommel was one of those who had attempted to claim Roman gold for Indutiomarus' head. Andesaros had long-since decided to keep such men at a good distance, relying on his own solitude, wits and reflexes rather than the muscle of others.

'Why have we stopped?' snapped Dunohorix of the Mediomatrici, sliding from the back of his horse angrily. 'Every hour we stop for something. You promised us Roman blood and Roman spoils!'

Behind him, also dismounting, Solemnis of the Tribocci was nodding his agreement. Solemnis was a weasel who simply agreed with whichever greater man stood next to him at the time, but Dunohorix was a necessity. Without him, the army would halve.

'My scouts ride back at speed, see? I would know what spurs them to such pace before I walk into it.'

The Mediomatrici chieftain harrumphed, but fell silent and stood poised. Unity was needed and they all knew it. Soon, the tribes from across the Rhenus would join them, and their ranks would swell immensely, but the three chieftains would have to work in close consort or risk losing control of the army to the madmen of the Suevi and their battle-crazed allies. Once or twice, Andesaros had regretted accepting that lunatic Ambiorix's advice and making pacts with the dogs from across the river. He had almost ten thousand men right now, with the elements of the other two tribes added to his own. He should be able to destroy that one legion easily without the aid of the

Germanic lunatics, but Ambiorix had been cautious and talked him into a treaty that would seriously diminish potential spoils and glory, but would treble the size of his army. Whatever it took. His uncle would be avenged. This 'Labienus' - a womanish peace-lover' they said - would pay for the dishonourable demise of Indutiomarus, beheaded in a ford by traitors with a lust for Roman coin.

'How far are we from the legion?' Solemnis asked, betraying what sounded like a hint of nerves to Andesaros.

'Four hours,' he replied calmly. 'Across the river on a rise.'

The men fell silent once more, waiting as the four scouts galloped across the open grassland and up the slope towards the leaders of the army. Andesaros stood and smoothed his clothes, making sure his torc and arm rings were in clear view.

'My lord,' the lead scout greeted him, bowing his head in the saddle. The other three followed suit, breathing heavily from their ride.

'What news do you bring me?' he demanded of the men.

'The crows gather, my lord.' The scout gestured off to the west. 'More legions approach, along with artillery, supply wagons and their traitorous Gaul allies.'

Andesaros closed his eyes for a moment.

'What now?' demanded Solemnis of the Tribocci in a voice edged with panic.

'Yes,' sneered Dunohorix. 'What now, leader of warriors?'

Andesaros sighed. 'How far away are these new legions?'

'A day, lord, maybe two.'

The chieftain pinched the bridge of his nose. 'An estimate of numbers?'

'Fifteen thousand at a guess, with support.'

'Too many for us,' Solemnis trembled.

'Without the tribes beyond the Rhenus,' nodded Dunohorix. How far away are your Germanic friends?'

'Who can say? Who can ever predict the Suevi? They could be beyond that rise or still by the river.' He sighed and straightened. 'But the Romans do not know we are coming, so we are not pressed for time. We cannot run the risk of being overwhelmed, and we are still a good distance from the Roman camp, so we shall wait here for our allies before we commit.' He gestured to the scouts. 'Keep track of the Roman reinforcements, but send out men to the east and north. I want to know where the Suevi are and how soon they will be here.'

As the scouts nodded again and turned their mounts to carry out the orders, Dunohorix narrowed his eyes at Andesaros. 'We could destroy the Romans and leave before their reinforcements arrive. And they might already be aware of us. They seem to know *everything*.'

'Calm yourself,' the Treveri's new leader smiled. 'With only a small advantage in numbers we could end up mired in a siege like my uncle did, and would then be at the mercy of their new legions. They do not know of us, my friend. I have men among the horse in their camp. I know their thoughts and moves before they do. We stay here, wait for the Suevi, and then we wipe this Labienus from the land forever.

* * * * *

'I am giving serious thought to having you strapped into your cot,' snapped Labienus, watching the grey face of Baculus as he stumped across the mud towards them.

'I heard a commotion, sir. Horses too.'

Labienus nodded wearily. 'Scouts have arrived with news.'

'Important news. It sounds to me, sir, like you're mobilising the legion for war.'

'I am, Baculus. But I am not mobilising the hospital. Your presence will not be required.'

'But...'

'Stay here, centurion. That is an order which I will not see disobeyed.'

Baculus sagged, only partially intentionally. 'The Treveri?'

'Yes, centurion. The Treveri.'

'I warned against leniency.'

'Yes, thank you, Baculus. I stand by my decision. Because it failed in this instance does not necessarily make it the wrong decision.'

'We can beat them?' Baculus enquired, assuming this was the case, given the legion's mobilisation.

'I very much hope so, centurion. My spies in their camp tell me they are but fifteen miles from here and they outnumber us by perhaps two-to-one.'

'Sounds like a dangerous option to me, sir,' Baculus muttered.

266

'It is an informed decision, centurion. My scouts also tell me that two legions - the Seventh under Plancus and the Ninth under Trebonius - are perhaps a matter of hours away to the west, but other scouts also tell me that a force of Germanic warriors that outnumber them are also hours away to the northeast. Thus it becomes something of a race. I am working on the assumption that the Germanic tribes are coming at the behest of the Treveri, and if I can remove those Treveri from this equation before they get here, I can perhaps prevent a bloodbath on a scale none of us really want to witness. I face twice my number now, or at best we end up besieged in camp by nightfall, with three legions against fifty thousand men - that's at best. At the worst the Germans get here first and we end up trapped, with the other legions unable to reach us. You see? My decision is rather made for me. We march out to defeat the Treveri while we can and send out riders to the reinforcement legions to join us with all haste.'

Baculus nodded unhappily. 'The odds are still not good. You would be better with a few veteran centurions among your number, sir.'

'I have them, Baculus. Just get back to your cot and get better. You still look like the recently-excavated dead.'

Baculus shook his head miserably and turned, tottering a little, to head back towards his sick bed, listening to the sounds of the legion and their support and auxilia preparing for the march. The idea of them moving into battle without him was unbearable.

Labienus had better flatten the whole damn tribe this time.

* * * * *

Quadratus peered off into the distance, watching the hillside beyond the river, where several thousand Gallic warriors were encamped. They were perhaps half a mile away, with the deep, fast river cutting through the land half way between them, creating a dangerous barrier, with its steep slopes on both banks and the torrent at the bottom. Even though it was *officially* a ford, he wouldn't want to try crossing it on foot, especially within range of the enemy. Any attempt to cross in sight of the opposition was doomed to heavy casualties, which was why both armies were arrayed within plain sight, and yet neither moved.

Around him, the army was still manoeuvring, preparing for battle. The legion had settled into cohorts in preparation, standing in ordered rows with gleaming mail and bright shields presented towards an enemy who showed no signs of movement. The auxiliary cavalry were in position, Quadratus among them, to one side and near the front of a field with a gentle slope the river, bounded by trees and scrub and a low rise behind.

Quadratus was nervous. From what he heard, there were many thousands of blood-hungry Suevi bearing down on them, and two legions somewhere close by. Labienus had sent riders out to the Seventh and Ninth and Quadratus has assumed the others were to join them here for the attack. And yet there had been no sign of the reinforcements, though they'd had ample time to meet up. Had they been directed to the camp instead, in case the Suevi hit there while the army was absent? He had asked Labienus, but the commander had simply smiled knowingly and tapped the side of his nose in a conspiratorial manner as was his wont.

'I don't like this.'

The cavalry decurion close by frowned. 'Sir?'

'We're outnumbered and our reinforcements have disappeared into thin air. Half the Germanic nations are descending on us and we prepare for battle here. The Treveri won't attack across that river. They'd have to be insane to try it. So what do we do? Sit here and wait until the Suevi arrive to carve us into small pieces?'

The decurion nodded nervously.

'And this terrain?' Quadratus grumbled. 'Facing the river on a slope towards the enemy, but with the hill and the woods at our rear. It's almost as though Labienus is trying to sacrifice us all.'

'The commander always knows what he's doing, sir.'

'I certainly hope so. We've been here over an hour. If the Treveri were going to attack, they'd have done so by now, while we were still manoeuvring into position and setting up. With the Suevi closing every moment, the situation is getting untenable. We're going to have to decamp soon and return to the fort, else we'll be butchered here.'

'Here he comes, sir.'

Quadratus straightened as he saw Labienus walking his horse forward to where the cavalry sat on the periphery of the army. 'Sir,' he saluted as the senior commander approached.

'What do you think?' Labienus asked, his voice clear and unshaken.

Quadratus could almost have kicked the man. To display apparent indecision in front of the ordinary soldiers was never a good move for morale, but in front of the native horse, it could lead to mass desertion.

'Sir?'

'What do you think? I am thinking that they will not come for us?'

Quadratus, teeth grinding, nodded. 'Could have told you that earlier, sir. They have no reason to. Our reinforcements are nowhere to be seen, but the Suevi cannot be more than an hour or two away. All the Treveri have to do is sit tight on that hill and watch us die.'

Labienus took a deep breath and turned it into a sigh. 'I am beginning to think you are right. We are endangering ourselves with every breath we wait here. Time to return to the fort and hope the other legions join us before the Treveri and their Germanic allies.'

He raised his hand in defeat.

'Very well, give the orders. We fall back.'

Quadratus, his eyes burning with irritation, nodded and began to give the orders. As his signifers, musicians and decurions relayed the commands, Labienus waved to him.

'Walk with me, Quadratus.'

The cavalry prefect walked his horse forward as the commander began to amble gently back across the field, the legions already responding to signals and turning, marching back across the slope towards the rise and the woods, beyond which, at some fourteen miles distance, lay their fort. What a disastrous waste of effort. Quadratus could almost scream with frustration.

'You disapprove of my decisions, prefect?'

'Never, sir.' *Yes... yes I do!*

'And despite having served under my command for more than a season, you do not think to question why I push for such pointless advances only to abandon my position and retreat without forcing the issue?'

'Sir?'

'Quadratus, I never do anything uninformed or without serious contemplation of all possible results first. Unfortunately, I cannot always make my intentions clear, even to such as yourself.'

Quadratus frowned again as they approached the rear edge of the field, where the army was already moving away from the river, across the ridge and back towards the fort.

'Respectfully, sir, if you're going to metaphorically pull a dove out of my arse, I would appreciate enough warning to metaphorically drop my underwear first.'

Labienus barked out a laugh and kicked his horse into a slightly faster pace as he rose to the crest of the hill. Grumbling, Quadratus joined him, and stopped suddenly at the hill top.

'What? Where?'

'Your next questions, I think, will be *when* and *how*, since the *who* is plain?' Labienus chuckled as the pair looked down upon the bulk of the Seventh and Ninth legions arrayed for battle, safely out of sight of the Treveri beyond the river, the ridge keeping them obscured. 'The 'what' is fifteen cohorts drawn from the Seventh and Ninth, along with their artillery hidden in the treeline. The auxilia and five more cohorts have returned to secure our fort and accompany the whole of Caesar's baggage train that is now entrusted to us. The 'where' is safely out of sight of the Treveri. The 'when' is all the time we've been setting up, they have already been ready to fall into place. They arrived immediately after us from the south, unnoticed. And the 'how'? Well, I think that's obvious. Dispatch riders organised everything. Now the Twelfth will fall into position with them, and three legions will await the Treveri attack.'

'What attack?' bumbled Quadratus, feeling as though a rug had been whipped out from under his feet.

'That, my friend, is why I could not inform you of my plans. Just as I have my spies and scouts among the Treveri and the Mediomatrici, this new king has his spies among our Gallic auxilia under your command. Everything had to look natural to them, so I relied upon your fury and irritation at my decisions translating nicely to them. Even now, half a dozen of your riders will have slipped away from your units and taken news of the authenticity of our fearful retreat to the Treveri. They will, of course, want to deal with us before we can get safely behind fort walls.'

'A feint? This whole thing has been a giant feint?'

'Indeed. I wondered over the past few weeks whether to weed out the spies in our ranks. My own spies have identified a number of theirs, of course. But it struck me that misinformation could be more useful than securing our own information.' He smiled at the exasperated prefect. 'Now. If you would be so good, Quadratus, perhaps you can reform your cavalry in the space we have left over to the right side of the slope. But signals only. No horns or whistles. Let's keep the Treveri completely in the dark, eh?'

Quadratus shook his head in wonder and let out a relieved laugh.

'It'll be my pleasure, sir.'

270

* * * * *

Andesaros gave a satisfied smile.

'You hear that, Dunohorix? Solemnis? The Roman commander retires to his fort in defeat. Our Suevi allies close on him and he finds himself in grave danger. Now he must seek the safety of his walls and the legions that are likely converging there.'

'If they reach the fort, we will have to dig them out,' Dunohorix grumbled. 'It will be hard. Like opening a stubborn oyster with one hand. And all the glory and loot will fall to the Suevi. We will have nothing to show for throwing our support behind you. Ambiorix continues to steer us wrong.'

'Not if we take them now,' Andesaros said calmly.

'What?' Solemnis looked more nervous than ever.

'The weather is good. It has been dry for some time so the ground is good. We have hours 'til dark. The river banks will be solid, for all they are steep, and the river is lower than it has been for many months. The Romans are in disarray and on the retreat. My spies tell me that their morale is poor and their belief in their commander is waning. We will fall upon their retreating numbers. Even if they manage to reach the safety of their walls, they will have lost half their number by then, including...' he smiled and stressed the last part as he scoured the eyes of his fellow chieftains, 'their support wagons and supplies, which are always at the rear, slower than the rest.'

'We could crush them,' Dunohorix smiled grimly.

'We can. Rouse your men. Promise them Roman blood and Roman treasure once more. Then join us. We charge at once. We must move fast to catch them while they are far from safety.'

He watched the two chieftains run back to their men. Revenge was in his grasp. His uncle's ignominious death would be paid back ten thousand-fold. And the Treveri, over whom he still had only the most tenuous grasp, could be made to accept him as their true and only king, forged in battle against Rome.

Today was a fine day for the kin of Indutiomarus and the nation of the Treveri.

* * * * *

271

Ianuarius hauled on the wheel, turning it despite the massive resistance it put up. His arms had grown muscular in the two years he had served with the Ninth, and there was little weight he could not manage when required. With a grunt, he gave another half-turn and his fellow artillerist snicked the lock into place.

'Which one?'

The young fellow, more of an assistant than a companion engineer, sounded enthusiastic as he peered between the branches.

With a roar, the Treveri force had seethed across the river mere moments earlier. Ianuarius' ballista had been the last to be settled into position, and he had worried that he wouldn't have time to set it up before the volleys began. It had been a near thing.

'No one if you don't put the bloody bolt in the groove!'

The young recruit flushed in embarrassment and dropped the heavy iron projectile into the slot, wedging it up against the mechanism.

'So which one?'

'Always make the first shot count, Marcius. It's the only shot you'll get where you have the luxury of aiming and the opportunity to be careful. Subsequent shots can just be ploughed into the bulk of the men, but the first one should always be a good one. First choice will always be an officer for preference. If one doesn't present itself, then a good warrior. You can always identify them by the quality of their armour. Look for a lot of bronze or iron and some sort of decorative helmet crest. Horsemen are easiest, of course, but sometimes a great warrior on foot is more important than an ordinary horseman. So be choosy. At first.'

Ianuarius lifted the heavy artillery piece and swivelled it, sighting down the timber and estimating distance.

'See him, there?' he pointed.

The young soldier shook his head and shrugged.

'Him with the bronze helmet. There's a boar standard near him and he's well-dressed. A leader, he is. Good first choice. About three hundred paces. Difficult, but quite achievable.' His tongue poked from the corner of his mouth as he made minute adjustments that would look virtually invisible to the young engineer next to him.

'Now. Get it locked in.'

The assistant locked the ballista into place vertically and Ianuarius swivelled it a couple of finger widths left and right, and then squinted between the leaves and aimed.

The enemy had almost reached the crest of the ridge when the single horn blast echoed out through the afternoon air.

Ianuarius released the bolt and was already beginning to winch the tension back into the machine while the bolt was in the air, nodding to the assistant to select a second missile.

* * * * *

Andesaros of the Treveri urged his men on up to the ridge with imprecations and exhortations to battle and glory, citing the womanly cowardice of Rome and the fear with which they carried themselves from battle with the glorious warriors of the Treveri.

With a thrill of battle-hunger and the golden glow of vengeance fulfiled, he crested the rise across which the fleeing legionaries had passed mere heartbeats earlier.

And his future changed before his very eyes.

Rank after rank after rank of Romans stood implacable and immobile, their shields presented in a solid line, their dreadful javelins already raised and held at the shoulder, awaiting the command. There were so many of them that Andesaros simply could not wrap his thoughts around their presence, let alone how quickly they had reformed to meet him and his tribe.

One thing was instantly clear:

They had lost before the first blow was struck.

He gave a shout to his signallers, and the carnyxes began to wail out the retreat, standards waving to direct the Treveri back to the river. As he turned to take in the whole, disastrous scene, he saw Dunohorix of the Mediomatrici lifted from his horse, a Roman artillery bolt tearing a wide hole through his chest and casting him aside like a child's raggy doll, the missile's momentum hardly slowed as it carried on and passed into the shoulder of a warrior behind him.

Andesaros blinked.

More and more bolts and stones were whipping out of the bushes and trees to either side, the clatter of releasing ballistae joined by the thump of loosing catapults. He knew the sounds well from many previous battles. He knew what they would do.

A huge warrior clad in bronze and iron rushed towards the fallen Mediomatrici leader, and then suddenly he was gone. Or at least half of him was, the onager shot - a shaped rock more than a hand-span wide - striking him in the back, smashing the spine to

273

fragments and neatly separating the body in two halves, the top of which disappeared off into the mass of panicked warriors.

Andesaros turned to the far side, confirming that more hidden artillery were releasing from the treeline to that edge of the field. His eyes picked out the panicked shouts of Solemnis of the Tribocci, shrieking at his men to flee the field. Briefly, he caught the young chieftain's eyes and recoiled at the accusation they launched at him. Then, Solemnis too was gone, an iron bolt smashing through him and driving him from his horse.

'Retreat!' he bellowed.

A sound behind him made his blood run cold. Though he could not translate the Latin words, he knew it for what it was, given that it was repeated along the line by every officer of the legions and followed by the noise of a thousand men tensing.

He turned and dived from his horse, using the men around him and his own steed as cover from the horrible, deadly rain of pila that arced up into the air, seemed to hang there for dreadful heartbeats, and then plunged down among the panicked, pushing and shouting mob.

Andesaros struggled to his feet, and then found himself tumbling to the ground once more when a disgruntled warrior of his own distant kin snarled and gave him a hard punch to the jaw. As he floundered on the floor, the warrior spat on him and ran for the river.

This would be a difficult loss to recover his position from.

There would have to be a lot of casting of blame elsewhere. Fortunately, both other leaders were dead, and Ambiorix gone north somewhere, saying he sought the Segni for his alliance. Blame would be easy to apportion with such little of it falling upon his own shoulders. As long as he could leave the field safely, he could rally those who survived.

Again, he picked himself up and dusted down his muddied tunic, casting a brief glance back at the legions, now marching on the Treveri at an unstoppable pace.

His world went crimson, then black, and ended.

* * * * *

'See that?' Ianuarius grinned at his assistant. 'Two nobles in one fight. And that one through the neck. Bet you couldn't match that in a month of trying.' He turned and bellowed to his equal, aiming the next ballista along. 'See that, Petreius? Two! You owe me two jars of wine, you old cheapskate.'

* * * * *

Quadratus sat ahorse expectantly, his eyes on Labienus, waiting for the command. The legions had crossed the ridge, driving the Treveri before them in panic, their leaders dead already. The cavalry would likely be required for mopping up - chasing down the survivors and bringing them back, but with the narrowness of the ford area, they would not be expected to move until the infantry were not blocking the field.

The legate of the Twelfth, lieutenant of Caesar and commander of the southern forces in Gaul, smiled and walked his horse over casually.

'Prefect?'

'Sir.'

'Would you be so good as to take your horse and harry the enemy for a good few miles? Make them regret their decision. No need to bend over backwards to give them quarter - they've had their chance. If they surrender, have them guarded, then roped and enslaved. If not, run them down until you're within sight of their walls, then return to us.'

Quadratus grinned.

'It would be a pleasure, sir.'

The commander turned to his signifers and musicians. 'Sound the halt. I don't want the legions racing across Gaul after the Treveri. They're beaten and the cavalry will finish the job.' He turned to the tribunes sitting nearby along with the other two legates. Plancus looked satisfied, and Trebonius stretched and rolled his shoulders.

'Congratulations, Labienus. It seems you are turning smashing the Treveri into something of a habit. Caesar is planning to come and crush the Treveri against your forces. He will start to worry that you're outshining him.'

Labienus laughed. 'Hardly, I fear. I just lead them. They're still Caesar's men, and they know it. Let's start moving the legions back to the fort. We're going to have to create a sizeable annexe, given the growing size of the army here.'

'Only a temporary one,' Trebonius said, wearily, reaching into his cloak and withdrawing a sealed scroll case, which he passed

275

over to the commander. 'Caesar is planning to come here as soon as he's dealt with the Menapii and combine the forces against the Treveri, but then we'll all be moving on to deal with the Eburones. That you've managed to crush the Treveri before he arrives will just hasten our departure, I'm sure.'

Labienus nodded as he broke the seal and scanned the lines of neat handwriting. 'Then we had best send riders north to inform Caesar of recent events. Since he no longer needs to aid us against the Treveri, he may wish us to march north and meet him.'

'I hope not,' Trebonius gave a tired smile. 'I'm a little sick of marching.'

'Let's get back to the fort, and then we can discuss it all in comfort.'

'Do you not want to speak to their leaders and set terms for their surrender?' Plancus frowned.

'I shall send a deputation to their capital, which is less than ten miles from here.' He laughed. 'Given the fact that I saw all three standards taken and all their leaders fall in the attack, I wouldn't know who to threaten, anyway! We'll give them a few days for the tribe to take out their anger on the rest of Indutiomarus' relatives and decide who might lead them better and then we'll talk to this new king. The Treveri are unlikely to support any further rebellion now.'

He smiled a tired smile at the other legates. 'In the meantime, we need to get you gentlemen and your forces settled in.'

He turned his horse to see three riders approaching, escorted by a centurion and a contubernium of men.

'Sir,' the officer saluted and gestured to his charges. 'Scouts from the northeast.'

'What news of the Suevi?' Labienus asked pensively. Were five cohorts enough to protect the camp?

The rider, clearly worn out from his ride, gave a weary salute. 'Sir, the Germans have halted. We spotted other riders, and it seems they have their own scouts ranging out ahead of them. I can only assume they have learned of the battle, since as soon as the riders spoke to the Suevi chiefs, the whole lot of them turned and started to walk back towards the Rhenus.'

Labienus sagged and Trebonius chuckled, slapping him on the shoulder. 'How does it feel to frighten off the whole Germanic nation?'

'A bit of a relief, to be honest,' Labienus smiled. 'I was still half-convinced that the Suevi would ignore the death of their allies and come for us anyway. They're not a people to be easily put off.'

'Is there any chance of us catching them before they reach the Rhenus?' Trebonius mused.

'Little,' Labienus said. 'They travel light, living off forage and pillage, so they can move faster than us. Besides, they likely still outnumber us, even without the Treveri, so I'm not sure it would be a wise plan of action. Let us return to camp and thank Minerva for turning them back.'

Plancus nodded. 'It's been a long journey to travel straight into a battle. I for one could do with a bath, a meal, and a lie down.'

* * * * *

Publius Sextius Baculus, Primus Pilus of the Twelfth Legion, eyed the wagon suspiciously.

'I shall ride a horse.'

'No you shall not,' announced the medicus, who, without warning, snatched away the vine staff of office upon which Baculus was resting most of his weight. Relieved of its support, the centurion staggered and fell into the waiting arms of the medical orderly. 'You cannot stand unaided. You quite clearly should not be riding. You also seem unable to grasp the simple concept of rest and recovery. Had you stayed in bed and rested as you were ordered and not poured every vial of medicine the staff gave you onto the ground when they weren't looking, you would be almost back to full health by now. Instead, you continually push yourself to the limit and consequently you are still months from well.'

'You said the infection was cleared up?'

'The infection has gone. What you have now is exhaustion, and atrophied muscles due to your protracted stay in my care. You, Baculus, are your own worst enemy. There is nothing that impedes your full healing but your own inability to rest. Now get in that cart and sit still until we reach tonight's camp site.'

Again, Baculus eyed the cart. The hospital was being evacuated for the journey and the wounded and sick who were incapable of walking or riding had been assigned to the carts - eight men to a cart, except for this one, which held four officers.

'Perhaps I could join one of the ordinary soldiers' carts?' he asked hopefully. Aboard this vehicle were Clemens, standard bearer for the Third Cohort, Second Century of the Twelfth, who Baculus knew well enough to know he was prone to travel sickness, an optio from the Seventh suffering from a gut wound after the Treveri fight and who smelled like he might pass away on the journey, and Dentio, a prefect that was suffering from foot-rot and was delirious much of the time. A worse set of travelling companions he could not imagine. 'When we get there I'll be covered in vomit and innards and have a headache.'

'In the cart.'

'Problem?' asked Labienus, passing by on his horse on a brief inspection of the column.

'Just the usual, sir,' muttered the medicus, gesturing at Baculus with the purloined vine staff.

'Get in the cart, centurion,' ordered Labienus.

Grumbling, Baculus snatched back his staff and clambered with some difficulty aboard the cart.

Four days had passed since the defeat of the Treveri and scouts had brought overtures of peace from the new Treveri leader. It had pleased the officer corps to discover that the man who had risen to rule the Treveri once more was Cingetorix, a long-time supporter of Caesar who had been deposed and exiled by Indutiomarus. The tribe's anger at their recent leaders' foolish decisions had driven them back to the loyalty of Roman client kings.

As soon as Labienus had confirmed that the tribe were settled and there was little likelihood of further trouble, he had made the decision to march north with the entire army and follow the river to the Rhenus, since Caesar's army would be moving south along that course. En route, the army would make a stop at the Oppidum of Vindunaco, where Cingetorix now held court, in order to receive the renewed vows of the Treveri.

It would be a long, slow journey, and Baculus was dreading every moment of it.

* * * * *

Ambiorix placed his prized helmet on the table and dusted the silver boar atop it with his fingers. A helmet made for a Roman general, it had once belonged to Sabinus, one of Caesar's top men before Ambiorix had taken it, with the man's head still inside. He had ripped off the red crest, replacing it with something more appropriate and now it was a masterpiece of propaganda. The helmet

278

announced to every warrior who saw it 'here is a man who beat the best Rome had to offer'.

If only he could repeat his success, but that damned Caesar was in the way at every turn. He had almost had Cicero's head last winter, straight after the first legion's demise, and he'd almost crushed that man's army, but for Caesar's untimely arrival on the scene.

Then he'd set about rebuilding his army, knowing that, if he'd done it once, he could do it again, but Caesar had pre-empted him and launched campaigns against everyone who would speak to him before the winter was out.

The Nervii had been eager to join him once more, and had agreed to marshal their forces and meet him at the site of his greatest victory in the spring, but Caesar had taken his men north while the winter's chill was still in the air and had torn the Nervii apart and burned what was left. Then the Menapii, who had been hesitant at first. They had managed to stay free of Roman interference for years by hiding in their infernal swamps. But shown what Caesar was doing to Gaul, and with a great deal of persuasion and wheedling, they had finally agreed to commit to his cause at the appointed place and time.

And then Caesar had shown up there yet again, like a bad smell in a small hut, and had bridged the rivers and swamps of the Mosa and the Rhenus and reduced the Menapii to a gaggle of blubbering women, effectively tearing out another of Ambiorix's greater allies.

The Treveri had been a true hope, too. Indutiomarus had taken control of the tribe and despite a number of their most powerful men professing continued loyalty to Rome, had committed them to the cause. That Rome-lover Cingetorix had been exiled and powerless. If *Ambiorix* had risen to lead them, he'd have killed the man rather than exiling him, but the Treveri were a divided and uncertain tribe and his execution might have turned much of the tribe against Indutiomarus.

In the end, they had proved unequal to the task. That fool had managed to lose a battle against one single legion, a battle he should have won with little difficulty. And his nephew had risen to seek revenge for him and managed to fail yet again. This Labienus was beginning to become as troublesome as Caesar himself.

Allies were hard to find in these days, and Caesar was removing them as fast as Ambiorix could secure them. Damn the druids and their pet Arvernian chief. Vercingetorix counselled caution and delay and because he had the druids tucked in his purse, most of Gaul and the Belgae would not even speak to Ambiorix, busying themselves with preparations for Vercingetorix's grand scheme. A few druids had flocked to his cause, bringing with them small tribes and a few dissenters, but he was on the edge and increasingly abandoned by the people, while that grinning Arverni lunatic secured a huge army that milled around deep in Gaul doing nothing.

Could they not see that in preparing for a war in months to come they were missing the opportunity of winning one now?

Ambiorix ground his yellowed teeth and took a deep breath. The knowledge that the Treveri were even now swearing a new oath to Rome and that Caesar was marching south to recombine his army did little to calm his mood, but he must appear calm now. In control.

The two men seated to his left had the distinct appearance of men unsure as to whether they were doing the right thing. Bolgios, nobleman and warrior, master of hundreds, cousin to the chieftain of the Segni, fiddled nervously with his braid. Should his cousin discover how deeply Bolgios plotted to overthrow him, the nervous weasel would now be decorating a wooden stake, his head scooped out for a cup. The druid beside him looked less nervous, but his face still displayed unease.

The knock came at the door.

'Come in.'

A burly warrior pushed open the door and a dozen men followed him into the gloom, each of them bulky and prepared for war. Each wearing an arm ring with the snake of Arvernus. Each wearing a face of stone. In their presence, even Ambiorix felt a momentary thrill of nerves. Behind them came another druid, this one tooled for war like his companions. His large sword at his side complemented a staff of oak which had been shod with iron and sharpened to a point. The man even had the audacity to wear a coronet, as though he were some sort of king.

'You have no place here, Arverni,' Ambiorix announced with fire in his tone.

'We have a place wherever trouble risks our plans,' replied the warrior-druid in a thick, southern accent. 'The one we call Esus has a careful schedule for the coming months. Events in Rome itself are falling into place to aid our cause, and soon - as omens and prophecies have foretold - Caesar's grip on this land will falter as he struggles to retain his place in his own country.'

Ambiorix narrowed his eyes at the druid, noting with interest how the Arverni warriors were moving around the walls of the room, making to surround him. Such an expected, easily-anticipated manoeuvre.

'And I am ruining these plans, so now you mean to kill me?'

The druid smiled coldly, and Ambiorix felt the panic in the Segni rebels next to him. Bolgios' hand went to the hilt of the knife at his belt, as though the short blade could stop a dozen swords.

'You have lived all winter and spring, king of the Eburones, because your faltering, insignificant rebellion has served to keep Roman eyes on the north-east and distracted them from the greater events taking place elsewhere. Sadly, all your allies have failed you and now you are all-but alone. Even your would-be German supporters are fleeing back across the river to their wild lands. All you have left is the Eburones, and your brother king Cativolcus is with us, so we cannot, sadly, allow you to wrest control of them from him.'

'I am not an easy man to kill, Arverni,' Ambiorix snarled.

'Perhaps so. But die, you must. Caesar and his hounds are on your scent, and now you have no army to hide behind. You know too much about the cause to allow you to live long enough to fall into Roman hands.'

Ambiorix leaned back in the chair and crossed his arms. 'You may find that I am more resourceful yet than you believe.'

The druid frowned at him, but it was already too late. The thin cord loop that had lowered from the darkness above slipped around the neck, dragging the old man's white beard against his throat as it tightened. The druid gagged and panicked, his fingers coming up to the cord that was throttling the life out of him, but the two men lying on the beam above simply hauled hard enough to lift him from the floor. There was a crunch as cartilage gave way and the druid's eyes bulged.

Bolgios and his own druid were on their feet now in surprise, but Ambiorix waved them back to their seats nonchalantly.

All around the edge of the room, Arverni warriors were shaking with death-twitches as spears thrust down from the shadowed rafters above them drove through the space between neck and collar bone, driving down through their bodies and emerging near the hip to pin them to the floor.

Ambiorix scanned the room to make sure that none of the Arvernian assassin party had escaped his own killers, but they were all busy shaking and leaking out their lives. He rose slowly, casually, and strode over to the hanging druid, who was gasping his last, peering at him with interest.

'Rest assured, old man, that I have a long way to go yet before I am done. Despite Treveri idiocy, with the help of my friends here, the Segni will soon be ours, and Cativolcus is old and feeble and will present no impediment to my seizing back my tribe. As soon as I have those two, the Suevi can be persuaded to cross again and join us, and I will find more allies among those who hate your slow indolence almost as much as they hate Rome.'

He prodded the druid, who swung back and forth as he dangled, the last of his life flickering and dying in his eyes.

'Stupid, stupid man. And go to the Gods knowing that should the day come that I do fall to our enemy, I will do everything in my power to make sure they know all about Vercingetorix and your Arverni revolt.'

He turned to Bolgios and the living druid.

'Time to deal with your dog of a cousin and put the crown upon your head. Time rolls on, my friends.'

Chapter Fifteen

By the Rhenus River, a day's march north of the confluence with the Mosella.

'Any news of the Suevi, General?'

Priscus fell into position next to Marcus Antonius, a few paces from Caesar, who peered out across the wide, fast-flowing Rhenus with an unreadable expression.

'They are gone east, but so recently that their wake is almost still visible on the water's surface.' Caesar huffed irritably.

'Perhaps this is a good thing?' Antonius asked quietly. 'We've a lot to concentrate on this side of the river, and I hear the Suevi have more warriors than their land has trees.'

Caesar turned his irritation on his senior commander. 'We do not flinch from chastising our enemies, even be they ten feet tall and breathe fire, Marcus, which the Suevi most certainly do not, for all the rumours.'

Priscus nodded to himself. He had no doubt whatsoever that Caesar would march his legions through the river and to the edge of the world if he had a grudge with the Suevi. It had been a long journey up the Rhenus, punctuated by visits from couriers along the way. Firstly, two men from Fronto's party had reached them with tidings that were both hopeful and unpleasant. The deaths of several of his men and the knowledge that a spy and betrayer had been among them and escaped unharmed was bad enough. To hear that the Segni were likely rising against them and that Ambiorix was still uncaptured had been enough to plunge Caesar's mood into unplumbed depths. But at least the treacherous Eburone king was almost in Fronto's grasp by the sound of it.

Labienus' riders had reached them only two days ago, and the news that the inventive commander had yet again trounced the Treveri, invested a trustworthy figure as their leader and taken their sworn oaths as well as the heads of the lead conspirators and over a thousand slaves had lifted the mood of every officer in the column. Except Caesar. All the general had been able to say about the matter was that Labienus should have dug in and waited for the rest of the army. Priscus had privately formed the opinion that jealousy over Labienus' success was suppurating in Caesar's head, and doing no good there.

Labienus was on his way north, apparently, and not far away. The two armies would meet, probably at the confluence of the rivers they were both following and after that, Caesar would turn his attentions to the Eburones and the hunt for Ambiorix would begin in earnest. But if the general set his eyes on the Suevi for a while, it might buy Fronto the time he needed to bring Ambiorix to justice.

To some extent the whole purpose of Fronto's hunt had become moot now. An attempt to halt the destruction of the Belgae was largely pointless, with the Nervii all-but gone, the Menapii thoroughly beaten down and their lands ravaged, the Treveri smashed and installed under a pro-Roman king, and only the Eburones and the small tribes like the Segni and the Condrusi left untouched.

And yet Fronto had continued, doggedly. The wax tablet Biorix had borne, apparently unread, though Priscus could not confirm that in the legionary's inscrutable eyes, had briefly and succinctly informed him that, although he had heard of Caesar's deprivations, his friend was not about to give in. He was moments away from Ambiorix and, regardless of any agenda of Caesar's, Fronto believed him to have a connection to, or knowledge of, the Arverni and this 'Esus' character, and he would capture and interrogate him if it cost every last man.

Yes, a good thing: chasing down the Suevi and buying Fronto the time. Priscus would give his right arm to know the identity of Esus. Well, *Antonius'* right arm, anyway.

'The Ubii in this area are as loyal as any tribe can be,' Priscus noted. 'We've never had cause to face them yet. We can cross the river in their boats at leisure and then move against the Suevi.'

Caesar shook his head. 'We bridged this river years ago and beat back the tribes beyond, showing them how easily we could get to them should we have the need, just as we did to the Menapii with our causeways. But it seems the Suevi have forgotten this. They have retreated into their forest and think themselves safe. I will have another bridge here, and this one will stay, this time.'

'Is that a good idea?' Antonius frowned.

'The Ubii here will not attack us as we build it,' Caesar replied. 'Last time, such a venture was considered impractical and too difficult, and the enemy on the far bank did their best to prevent us completing it. This time we have a peaceful locale and prior experience. I expect construction to be speedy and trouble-free.'

'And what of Ambiorix?' asked Antonius, drawing his infernal wine flask from his cloak.

Priscus could have strangled the man at that moment.

Caesar simply tapped his lip in thought. 'Yes, an extra delay could be trouble.'

'But the Suevi?' nudged Priscus, glaring at Antonius, who seemed entirely oblivious.

Again, Caesar turned. 'Yes. We will concentrate the bulk of our forces on the bridge and the Suevi beyond, while Labienus makes his way here - along the 'victory clivus',' he added with a trace of bitterness, 'and joins us. But we can spare most of the cavalry. They are of little use in the German forests, after all.'

His gaze played across the heads of the staff and legates gathered by the river and fell upon a small, eagle-nosed man with unruly hair growing in a circle around a bald pate, like a hill rising from a forest. 'Basilus?'

The officer, a cavalry prefect with little time in Gaul, turned in surprise. 'General?'

'I want Varus and Antonius with me across the river. You have command of the cavalry, barring the few units I will keep in support here. Take them into the Eburone lands and start ravaging. Without infantry support you will be able to do little to oppida, towns and fortresses, so steer clear of them, and avoid pitched battles with only horse at your command. But you will be able to start the process for me. Burn their crops, kill their livestock, and destroy farms and villages as you find them.'

Basilus saluted, looking slightly stunned at his sudden acquisition of an important command, but Caesar had already returned his attention to the others and the river.

'The Suevi, and then, once Basilus has the Eburones starving and at the peak of despair, we move on Ambiorix.'

Priscus shivered at the thought of what such deprivations might mean for the small party of Romans busily hunting the man deep in Eburone lands.

* * * * *

Lucius Minucius Basilus peered through the foliage at the point where the track passed over the crest of the hill and descended into the wide, shallow valley. Behind him, the cavalry of Caesar's army still poured into position, making their way between the tall,

285

narrow trees, winding across the cold, fast stream filled with large, jagged rocks and forming up within the forest as best the tightly-packed trees allowed.

'What do you think, sir?' the prefect beside him asked, smoothing the ruffled mane of his mare.

Basilus frowned at the settlement below. The fields were beginning to glow with healthy grain, marking the clear approach of summer at last, and farmers and peasants moved about the crops tending them and weeding. In the centre of the valley, the settlement itself sat peaceful and quiet.

'I'm in two minds, Catilo.' He sighed and pursed his lips. Caesar had been quite specific. They were to avoid anything that might lead to a siege or a pitched battle. Small farms and villages were fair game to his depredations, but towns and fortresses were out of the question. Clearly this *was* a town, but it was surrounded by extremely weak defences, and the cavalry would have little difficulty overrunning the place. The defenders on the low ramparts were few and far between and the populace worked the fields, the gates of the place standing wide open. 'I think we will take the place with precious few casualties, and this could be one of the greatest symbolic victories of the campaign, causing consternation and fear among the Eburones as word spreads. How fast could you get to those gates?'

Catilo grinned. 'If we keep to the trees and move stealthily, we can get damn close before we move out into open ground. We can be on them before they have time to shit themselves, sir.'

'Right. We'll take the place, then. Take two alae down to the closest treeline and as soon as you're in position, head for the nearest gate. I don't care what you have to do, I want you to be sure you take that gate and hold it until the rest of us get there.'

Catilo nodded, and Basilus turned to the other prefect approaching at the far side.

'Portius? Catilo's going to take and hold the gate. I'm going to take half the cavalry straight for the settlement as soon as he's there. The moment we break cover for the town, you take the other half and ravage the fields. Kill everyone you find and chase any survivors off into the woods. Once you've done that we'll fire the crops.'

Portius nodded and turned to give the orders to the decurions as Basilus once more regarded the town below.

'You poor unsuspecting barbarians. I'm about to turn your world upside down and then set fire to it.'

* * * * *

'What do you mean, he's here?' Fronto snapped angrily.

Ullio, standing in the doorway and blocking the morning sunlight, shrugged. 'He arrived last night, late at night.'

'Well where is he then?'

'He was escorted to one of the houses outside the walls. He has a large number of armed men with him. Segni as well as Eburones, so the king thought it prudent to keep him outside until morning.'

Fronto ground his teeth. The knowledge that he was a matter of moments away from Ambiorix set his pulse pounding with possibilities, but with Cativolcus in charge here, there was nothing he could do until the king had made his move.

'What happens now, then?'

Ullio leaned against the door frame casually. 'Once the sun is suitably high and Ambiorix has been forced to wait for a while, he will be invited into the town with only a small guard, to visit the king.'

'Why wait?'

'Ambiorix is not a patient man, and is given to imprudent and precipitous action if he is pushed. The longer we make him wait, the more likely he is to make a mistake, and the king wants him angry and off-balance enough to take the tainted drink without having one of his men taste it first.'

'He may not be stupid enough to do so anyway.'

Again, Ullio shrugged, arms folded. 'You do not know Ambiorix. He is a man given to displays of his own power. He would not accept a drink proffered by the king, but if the king has an expensive wine open on his table and a cup of it in front of him, Ambiorix will not be able to resist taking the drink. He will want to make it clear that whatever Cativolcus owns, he can take. The poisoned wine will be present, but not offered.'

'You've thought all this through very carefully,' Fronto noted with satisfaction. 'What happens if you've misjudged Ambiorix and he doesn't take the wine?'

287

The native hunter straightened in the doorway again. 'Then things will have to be done my way, rather than the king's.' He made a gesture across his throat with a turned thumb.

'Not acceptable,' Fronto said firmly. 'I need him to answer a few questions.'

'I can disable and cripple him without inhibiting his tongue. Ambiorix likely thinks he can remove Cativolcus with the assassins he brings, but the king has plenty of men like me who can protect him and remove the enemy. We are prepared. Ambiorix has seen his last sunrise, but he will sing songs of betrayal to you before his darkness descends.'

'Good,' Fronto nodded. 'I'd remind you that a lot rides on this. If I can question Ambiorix and then take his head to my general, Caesar can be made to see the Eburones as allies. The whole future of your tribe could hang on this morning's events. Remember that, while you play your part. What do *we* do while this is all going on?'

'Stay in the house. If there is any hint of you or your men abroad in Espaduno, Ambiorix will panic and everything will fall apart. Stay out of sight and I will fetch you when Ambiorix is busy shaking and babbling.'

Masgava stepped out into the light from the doorway to the rear room where he and his four men slept. 'It ends today, then?'

Fronto nodded. 'It ends today.'

* * * * *

Ambiorix toyed with the fine captured Roman helmet on his knee and huffed in irritation.

'These delays are irksome, Garo.'

'Cativolcus is a wily one, my lord. He will be surrounding himself with warriors before he deigns to see you. He will not make himself a target willingly.'

'It matters not how many men he surrounds himself with while you are by my side, Garo.'

The second man in the room smiled a chilling smile. A Sicambri by birth, Garo had discovered a love of pain and an affinity with death early in his life. By the time he came of age, he had killed more than a dozen of his fellow tribesmen, women and children. His methods had become increasingly inventive, until one day he had been discovered in the process of dissecting a young girl to see what parts still pulsed after death. Before the wrath of the elders could be

288

brought down on him, he had fled, crossing the Rhenus into Belgae lands and then Gaul, where he had sold his services as a killer to an endless array of nobles and warriors, honing his craft as he went. Finally, two years ago, he had found himself in the service of the Eburone king, back on the doorstep of his own tribe, and Ambiorix was gifted with a wide variety of enemies for Garo to deal with and plenty of coin to pay for it.

Ambiorix was right, of course. Cativolcus could surround himself with warriors, walls, shields and ditches, but it would avail him little. Garo could kill from the doorway, barely moving a muscle. One of the two poison-tipped darts of a Greek design stitched into his cloak clasp would do the trick. Or the small, light axe hanging behind his shoulder and beneath his cloak, which was perfectly weighted for throwing. There were a number of possibilities without even reaching him. If he happened to get close to Cativolcus, the options were endless.

Whatever happened this morning, Garo was certain the day would end with Ambiorix the sole king of the Eburones, and his former brother king greeting the afterlife.

Ambiorix smiled.

'Are the men armed and prepared?'

'And have been for an hour. As soon as the king sends for us we will be ready to move.'

'No delays, Garo. As soon as we're in his presence, do your job. They will almost certainly make us remove our weapons before we enter. There will follow a brief negotiation during which we will argue and I will be allowed to take my weapon for my own protection. I assume you will have weapons they will not notice?'

'Plenty.'

'Good. Then, as soon as...'

He stopped at a shout from the garden outside.

'What was that?'

Garo stepped across and swung open the door of the small house where they had spent the night, to see two of the Segni warriors that accompanied them racing across the small lawn.

'Romans!'

Ambiorix, his face creased into a disbelieving frown, leapt to the door. 'What?'

'Romans, lord king.'

'Here? That's ridiculous!'

But his eyes were already rising past the Segni warrior to the hillside beyond, where hundreds of crimson and glinting steel cavalry were emerging from the treeline and racing towards the valley floor. His eyes wide, Ambiorix turned to take in the whole scene. A few dozen of the riders had broken cover ahead and raced for the settlement's gate, where even now they were forcing back the Eburone guards to secure it. The rest were coming in two huge groups, one for the town and one spreading out and riding into the fields.

'How did they know we were here?' wailed Bolgios, the new king of the Segni, as he ran for the hut's door.

Ambiorix shook his head. 'They didn't. This is simply bad luck. They're attacking Espaduno, not coming for the house. Caesar has turned his fires upon the Eburones.'

He smiled coldly. 'The general has done me a favour, the idiot.'

'What?'

'They will kill Cativolcus for me. Oh we'll lose Espaduno and its people, but it's a small price to pay when you think that the Romans are about to make me undisputed king of the Eburones entirely by mistake!'

He laughed as he slapped Garo on the shoulder. 'Saddle the horses. We must leave this place immediately.'

* * * * *

Basilus raced for the gate. His men were already in the fields, hacking down the Eburones as they attempted to flee, and a quick glance off to his left afforded him a view of a dozen warriors on horseback racing for the woods, surprised somewhere in the valley. It was a shame to let warriors escape, but the grand prize was the town. He would ravage, loot and burn the place to spread fear among the Eburones.

Tribesmen tried desperately to shut the gate in the face of the attacking Romans, but Catilo's alae were there, keeping the entrance clear. With a whoop of victory, Basilus raced into the town, his sword coming down in a wide arc and taking the head of a local who was attempting to flee the scene.

'Second ala to the left and Fifth to the right. Secure the walls and the gates. The rest of you take the town. Kill everyone.'

The roar of a victorious army surged across Espaduno as Basilus' men raced through the streets, hewing tribesmen wherever they found them, chopping down the old and the young, men, women and children alike, without prejudice. This was to be an object lesson in fear for the last tribe on Caesar's list.

Basilus could almost feel the weight of the decorations that would be heaped upon him. Could almost feel the warmth of Caesar's grateful embrace.

With an ululating cry to Mars, he rode for the centre of the town. Barbarians or not, the centre of a town always held the centre of power. Senate, king or thug, men who ruled did so from the middle.

As panicked natives fled before him, Basilus, his best men following on immediately behind, made for the largest houses he could see - not dissimilar to the rest, but for slightly wider frontages and better quality shutters on the windows. His sword rose and fell, a spray of crimson arcing out through the air with every cut, the screams of his victims all-but lost among the general din of agony and panic that filled the settlement. As he burst from a mud-packed street into what appeared to be a village square - or possibly just a wider road, paved with cobbles - he saw two warriors emerge from the door of one of the larger buildings, catch sight of him and disappear back inside, slamming shut the door.

Reining in at the street/square's centre, Basilus pointed at the house with his blood-slicked sword.

'Get that door open. Every man in there is to be spared long enough to crucify them!'

Around him, men slid from their mounts and ran for the building, swords raised and shields held before them. The well-trained horses milled around a little, but made no attempt to leave the square as other cavalrymen arrived and pressed on into all side-alleys and streets, hewing at anybody they found in their path.

Basilus slid from his horse, tying the reins to the open shutter of another building, and caught sight through the window of two of the auxiliary cavalry - Gauls rather than Belgae from their kit - butchering the building's occupants. One of them grabbed a woman who screamed and fought her captors. He shouted something in his native tongue at his companion, who was busy wrenching his sword out of the last victim, and the man rushed over to hold the woman, while the first trooper busily tried to drop his trousers.

291

'Kill her and move on!' Basilus snapped through the window at the surprised Gauls, then turned and strode across the street to the important building with the warriors.

The dismounted soldiers - mostly the rare Roman regular cavalry, with a number of auxiliary Gauls alongside - were shoulder-barging the door, which was shaking and cracking with each thump.

Basilus almost cried out in shock as someone grasped his shoulder and spun him around. His sword came up defensively, and he almost cut into the Belgic auxiliary officer before he realised he was an ally.

'What?' he snapped angrily.

'This is madness!' the cavalry officer spat into his face. 'Stop this mayhem before it gets out of control!'

Basilus narrowed his eyes and pushed the officer off him, raising his sword threateningly. 'You, soldier, are on notice of discipline. As soon as we're finished here, I will deal with you myself. In the meantime, get your filthy barbarian hand off me before I remove it at the wrist.

The officer, who Basilus realised was unusually wearing a Roman-style tunic along with his Gallic trousers, stepped back, though the fury and fire never left his eyes. 'Two alae of your cavalry have just deserted in the face of this madness,' the man said angrily. 'If you don't stop, hundreds more will be gone before you can burn the place. My own Remi have refused to enter the town and are waiting in the woods!'

'Then your own Remi are also disobedient cowards and will face discipline in due course. Now *get away from me*!'

Turning back from the fuming officer he was just in time to see the door splinter and explode inwards, a burly Gaul tumbling in after it. In a matter of heartbeats, a dozen cavalry were inside and the sounds of murder began. Taking a deep breath to calm the anger raging in his blood, Basilus strode across, sword at the ready, and pushed in through the door.

Three native warriors lay in bloodied heaps on the floor, along with three of his own men, though it took a moment for him to separate them out in the gloom, five sixths of the body-count being of Gallic or Belgic stock, regardless of the side for which they fought.

Two more warriors were still fighting doggedly, both wounded, while Basilus' men laid into them.

'Alive, damnit!' he bellowed. 'I've crucifixes to decorate!'

Behind the warriors, he caught sight of an old man with grey-white hair and a straggly beard, his high quality clothes and golden torc marking him out as some sort of nobleman. Basilus grinned evilly.

'You! Surrender and I will consider halting the deaths!' It was a bare-faced lie, but the old man couldn't possibly know that. He was surprised to see the old nobleman smile at him, reach to the table next to him and pick up a flask of wine. The noble raised the flask in salute and took a deep pull at it.

'Enjoy that,' spat Basilus. 'You'll be thirsty on the cross.'

The old man, still grinning, spasmed for a moment and dropped the flask, which shattered on the ground. 'Your general will kill you for this,' the old man smiled as his legs crumpled beneath him and he collapsed to the floor, shaking violently.

'Damn!' Basilus snorted. 'Just kill the lot of them. There'll be no crosses today. Leave no one alive and no stone standing.'

He turned, still furious at this, to see the auxiliary officer who had manhandled him outside standing in the doorway, a look of defiance on his ugly, barbarian face.

'Get out of the way!' he snarled, stomping towards the door.

Without changing his evil expression, the Belgic officer stepped back out of his way, moving to one side not quite enough to clear the door, obliging Basilus to push him out of the way as he exited. His glorious mood at this unexpectedly easy victory was already gone in the face of impertinent natives, disobedient cavalrymen and a failure to take the leaders alive. He would settle his mood by burning the entire place to cinders and throwing any survivors they found onto the flames. The Eburones would hear of the campaign of Basilus and quake in fear. He would...

He almost jumped out of his skin for the second time in the day as once again a hand gripped his shoulder and hauled him around. His sword came up again automatically, but this time he had every intention of using it.

'What the fuck do you think you're doing?' snarled an oldish man in a mail shirt, with a five-day growth of beard, heavy care-lines on his face and salt-and-pepper hair. It took Basilus half a heartbeat to realise it had spoken perfect Latin with a southern - Campanian? - accent. His sword was already on its swing but the man was remarkably fast, a gladius of unsurpassed quality easily knocking aside his own.

293

'I don't know who you are,' Basilus snapped, 'but if you touch me again I will have you torn to pieces, soldier.' It was an assumption that the man was a Roman, but a reasonable one - possibly one of his dismounted cavalrymen. Everyone was being so damn insolent today!

'Fronto?' said the impertinent auxiliary cavalry officer behind him.

'Galronus?' said the scruffy soldier in front with equal surprise.

Basilus, suddenly very confused, was further baffled to see other scruffy soldiers falling in behind this new irritation, one of them a black-skinned Numidian with more scars than there appeared to be room for on a body. A horrible feeling thrummed through Basilus and his blood chilled a little. He'd heard the name Fronto before. Something to do with Caesar and the staff.

'Fronto?' he asked weakly.

''Sir' to you, you pointless moron,' the scruffy soldier snapped, smacking the flat of his glorious blade painfully on Basilus' forehead. 'Declare yourself and your unit, soldier, before I have Masgava here tear off your arms and feed them to you.'

Basilus floundered, trying to understand what was going on, while a bruised lump began to form on his forehead. He found himself weakly announcing 'Lucius Minucius Basilus, vexillatory cavalry commander, ravaging the Eburones on the general's direct orders.' He realised he was saluting like a junior tribune and almost stammering, and yanked his arm back to his side. 'And you are?'

'Marcus Falerius Fronto, former legate of the Tenth Legion, staff officer, commander of a small insurgent force, hunter of Ambiorix, and - most importantly - bloody furious!'

'Sir?' Basilus realised he was shaking, but couldn't stop it.

'What's all this about, Galronus?' Fronto asked, looking straight past Basilus.

The Belgic officer who'd been so insolent stepped past Basilus, eyeing him as though he were something the man had trodden in and would shortly wipe off his boot.

'What he said. But he was told to steer clear of towns. Seems he is as tactically foolish as he is cruel and stupid.'

Basilus felt his ire rise, but he was still shaking with some unidentifiable fear. *Fronto.* He remembered hearing stories of the legate of the Tenth. A man who was usually to be found standing in the line with his men rather than at the back, directing things. A man who'd insulted Caesar and got away with it. A man who fought duels with assassins. Basilus suddenly felt the uncontrollable urge to urinate.

'Well, Lucius Minucius Basilus, commander of whatever-you-said, have you any idea what you just did?'

'Put the fear of the Gods into the Eburones?' he said, weakly, it coming out more as a question than the proud statement he'd intended.

'No, no, no,' Fronto said, his brow lowering as he wagged the forefinger of his free hand in admonishment. 'No, Basilus. What you have just done is ruined a month of my work, disrupted my hunt, laid waste to a settlement that was about to declare loyalty to Caesar and, prize of all your blunders this morning, spooked the traitor king Ambiorix into flight!'

Basilus felt panic set in and his stomach churned unpleasantly. He urinated a little.

'Sir?'

'Ambiorix was here. In my sights. In a matter of hours he would have been in my *hands* and spilling every secret he knew about rebellions in Gaul, while his brother king helped bring the Eburones back into the arms of Rome as an ally. Instead, you and your men blundered in from the forest and Ambiorix turned tail and fled, or so Ullio tells me.'

'Ullio?'

'The Eburone who has played host to my men and I in our sojourn here.' Fronto thumbed a gesture towards a furious local, who was fiddling with the point of a wicked-looking knife. 'Ullio could possibly track the villain, though he might be disinclined to try, given what YOU HAVE JUST DONE TO HIS KINSMEN!' The spray of spittle that accompanied this last hoarse shout spattered across Basilus' face and his bladder finally gave in and let go.

Fronto rolled his eyes and pushed the man aside.

'Galronus, you're now in charge of this debacle. Try and rein the men in and halt the madness. Take this piddling little moron with you and try and keep him out of trouble. I'm going to see Cativolcus and find out if there's any way we can salvage anything from this.'

'I wouldn't bother,' Palmatus said quietly, emerging from the king's house and shaking his head. 'The king's bodyguard are all dead and he appears to have taken the yew-poison meant for Ambiorix.'

Fronto reached up and cradled his forehead in his free hand.

295

'Today just gets better and better.' He gestured at Basilus with his sword. 'Get out of my sight and do whatever Galronus tells you. If I see you again today, I might just gut you myself.'

He turned to Ullio as Galronus led the disconsolate, leaking commander away.

'I cannot adequately express my regret for what happened here, Ullio. Hopefully we can halt the damage before it becomes absolute. I would like to lay the blame at Basilus' feet, but for all his lunacy, he was acting on the general's orders, and Caesar is unaware of what we know. I suspect the only hope for your tribe's peace just evaporated.'

Ullio nodded. 'There is now one undisputed king of the Eburones, and while many might not approve of him, while he has druids on his side, no one is going to challenge him. Perhaps if he were to meet his end, one of my lord Cativolcus' kin would step in to rule us.'

'I know I have no right to ask this of you, Ullio, especially after what just happened, but is there any way I can persuade you to helping us track Ambiorix down?'

The hunter sagged. 'Ask me again later, after we have attended to the dead and the wounded and I have had my fill of beer. And,' he cast an evil look at the retreating form of Basilus, 'after I have looked for my sister-son and learned whether he and his family are alive.'

'Would you like help?'

Ullio shook his head and turned, walking away down the street. Over the top of the chaos, the sound of Galronus' call to muster outside the walls rang from a dozen horns.

'Disaster,' muttered Fronto.

'So close,' added Masgava. 'We should get going and see if we can pick up his trail.'

Fronto shook his head and rubbed his thumping temple. 'We stand virtually no chance in these woods. Our best hope is that Ullio will help us. He knows these lands like no other, but he must have today to recover and mourn before we consider trying to follow.'

'What will happen to Basilus,' asked Palmatus quietly.

Fronto felt the thumping head worsen. 'Knowing Caesar, he'll probably get a bloody decoration!'

Behind him, Aurelius peered off into the forest with a mixture of resignation and fear and made the signs to ward off evil.

* * * * *

Caesar rubbed tired eyes, sagging in his campaign chair as the officers assembled on the low grassy bank beside the Rhenus. The past few days had not been good for the general. Half a week it had taken to bridge the great river - a speed and efficiency that had stunned even those who achieved it. The bridge was every bit as strong and wide and powerful as the one they had both built and dismantled upriver a few years ago, and this one was planned to stay, at least until the season ended.

As soon as the bridge was complete, Caesar had marched across it with his officers and the Tenth Legion's First Cohort and met with the local Ubii leaders, who had gathered there, curious to ask the general why he had once more bridged their river.

The Ubii had confirmed that the Suevi had retreated into their great forest, skirmishing with the locals as they passed, likely frustrated at being cheated of battle, victory and spoils to the south. They had also assured Caesar that Ambiorix had not crossed the Rhenus anywhere in their territory or that of their allies. Caesar had drawn from them renewed oaths and the promise that if Ambiorix appeared anywhere in their lands they would send the general his head. All had seemed to be to the good, especially when that same day the advance scouts of Labienus' army had arrived from the south, the rest of the three legions and the baggage hoving into view during the afternoon.

Then things had begun to decline.

Caesar had avowed his intent to move into the great forest of the Suevi and chastise them for thinking to invade Roman-protected lands, but the Ubii had made their own signs against evil and had warned Caesar in fearful voices not to pursue the Suevi into the great forest of Baceni.

The general had sneered at their superstitious attitude and announced that he held no fear of Gods-protected Germanic forests. If the domain of Arduenna held no fear for him, then neither would *this* forest. The Ubii had shaken their heads and intimated that this had nothing to do with Gods, as the Suevi believed only in blood, death, meat and what they could touch and see. The Baceni forest, they said, was a place haunted by evil things and even the Ubii who lived within its shadow would not go beneath its canopy willingly.

Scoffing, Caesar had dismissed the Ubii and taken three of his legions into the woods, along with a few cavalry scouts and the

297

senior staff. Priscus had seen nothing to suggest the presence of spirits or monsters among the twisted, densely-packed boles of the forest, but something about the oppressive darkness of the woodland and the constant cracks and scuttles of wildlife made it... eerie in some way. The men of the legions had certainly shown their colours beneath its unhallowed boughs, every soldier clutching his luck charm or divine pendant, uttering prayers in an almost constant stream.

When they had come across a wooden frame some twenty feet long, decorated with the disembowelled and charred bodies of the Suevi's latest victims, the general uneasiness among the soldiery had blossomed into genuine fear.

And yet still, even a day's march into the forest, there had been no sign of the Suevi or their settlements. That morning, Caesar had called Priscus and Antonius to his tent, pitched in the widest space between the trees, and had admitted to feeling exceedingly unwell. He had not slept during the night and had become pale and drawn, vomiting up anything he attempted to consume.

That morning, only an hour from camp, the general had passed out in the saddle and only the quick reflexes of Aulus Ingenuus had prevented a bad fall. A brief confab between the officers had resulted in the decision to abandon the Suevi to their endless forest and to turn back to the Rhenus. Even Priscus, wishing to buy Fronto as much time as he could, had been grateful when the general, barely able to lift his head, had finally nodded his assent to their recommendation.

The army had managed to return from the forest in half the time it had taken to push within - a testament to the intense desire among the men to be away from its oppressive darkness and evils.

Rumours were rife among the men that the Suevi had somehow cursed the general and that he had succumbed to the evils of the Baceni forest. Caesar, too weak to walk among the men, tried to assure them that he had succumbed only to a perfectly natural fever brought on by exhaustion and the damp, unhealthy conditions of the lands they had recently traversed. The medicus had confirmed this diagnosis, assuring the officers and men that in a matter of days Caesar would return to full health, and the fact that many of the men were suffering from some form of fever or foot-rot supported the announcement, but soldiers will be soldiers, and they will always be superstitious.

Now, back at the Rhenus, the general was still too weak to walk for long or move among the men, and his colour was still lacking, but his appetite had begun to return, and he had picked at a plain meal that morning. Some of the sparkle had also returned to his eye.

Now, as the staff assembled, he looked almost eager.

'Ah good,' he said in a tired but enthusiastic voice. 'Is everyone here?'

Priscus nodded and Antonius went to help as Caesar struggled from his seat, but the general waved his assistance away and stood, swaying slightly for a moment.

'I am returning to health, gentlemen.'

A slight stagger forced him to grip his chair and force himself upright again.

'I intend to begin moving into the Arduenna forest on the morrow, but I have been thinking about our position. It seems to be the opinion of natives, officers and scouts alike that the great forest is not suitable terrain for the army to move in its traditional form, with horse, baggage carts and artillery.'

Nods all round.

'And the continued threat of the Suevi, who remain unchastised, must not be underestimated.'

More nods. No one wanted to move against the Eburones with the possibility of the Germanic peoples following on their heel.

'This crossing point must therefore be defended against incursions. I intend to garrison the area against continued threat.' He peered around the officers assembled and his gaze settled on a man in the uniform of a senior tribune. Priscus recognised him vaguely as a long-standing tribune of the Ninth. 'Volcatius Tullus?'

The officer, perhaps in his mid to late twenties, neat haired and clean shaven with an old white-line scar that ran from one ear across his cheek and dented his nose, stepped forward. 'General?'

'Tullus. You held that fort in Lusitania for me for weeks against improbable odds. Care to repeat your success?'

The tribune bowed his head with a smile, and Priscus frowned. He didn't know the man particularly, but he had vivid memories of that campaign, only two years before they first came to Gaul, and the stories of the siege of Centum Cellas had been blood-curdling. That this young, fresh faced officer had been the man commanding that fortress seemed ridiculous, and yet it was clearly the case. Priscus found himself looking at the tribune with a great deal of respect.

'I am giving you a vexillatory command of twelve cohorts, drawn from across all the legions, auxiliaries and cavalry present. Dismantle the far end of the bridge and use the materials to fortify the structure. This will be your base of operations, but I would advise further fortlets along the river for perhaps thirty miles in each direction. Spread out your men. If the Suevi come, you will have a hard fight, but history tells me you will be up to the task.'

Tullus nodded his head again. 'If I may, Caesar, why not simply dismantle the whole bridge?'

'Because, Tullus, when I have dealt with the Eburones and their rat-holed king, I may decide to return to the Suevi issue, and then I will need the bridge.'

Again, Tullus nodded.

'Very well,' Caesar paused a moment, wincing as his strength began to falter, seeping out with such an unaccustomed long period on his feet. 'Basilus is priming the lands of the Eburones for our coming. Tullus will protect our back from the Germanic tribes. Cicero? You will take command of the Fourteenth Legion, the artillery, and the baggage train. Take them downriver and then west past the deeper forest. We are only a matter of days away from the site of Sabinus and Cotta's camp where Ambiorix won his great victory. I will have you reoccupy the camp, make use of the existing fortifications and create new ones. That place is a symbol of Ambiorix's success, but *you* are a symbol of *ours*. You are the legate he and his men could not overcome. You will keep all our baggage safe there as a symbol that Rome can come back from any misfortune and will not bow our heads to barbarian power.'

Cicero's expression momentarily faltered, displaying his disappointment at being given such a quiet, inglorious command, but he hid it well and bowed his acceptance.

'You will also take the wounded of all legions with you. They will be better off with the baggage train than defending the Rhenus against Suevi or hacking their way through the deep forest.'

Again, Cicero saluted.

'Labienus?' the general asked, and then smiled as the hero of the Treveri war stepped forward. 'You will take the Tenth, the Eleventh and the newly-raised Fifteenth, pushing ahead of Cicero downriver, but you will then move into the Arduenna forest from the north, seeking Ambiorix, and razing, killing and burning everything in your path.'

Labienus saluted, the distaste at this policy of burning the land sitting badly with him. Ignoring his expression, Caesar gestured to Trebonius.

'You will take the Ninth, the Twelfth and the Thirteenth to the south, where the Condrusi and Segni lie. You will then push into the great forest from the south. Your orders are the same. Hunt, kill, burn.'

Trebonius saluted.

'I will take veteran legions only - the First, the Seventh and the Eighth - and move at a forced march to the Sambre, where we will press into the forest from the west. The three forces will scour the forest and squeeze Ambiorix between us until we have him. It must be a quick campaign, though. To have all our legions out of touch beneath the great forest is tactically dangerous, so we will all return by the kalends of Quintilis, meeting at Cicero's camp. By my reckoning that should give us near two weeks to move into the forest and find the recalcitrant king, allowing Cicero a week to reach camp and then a further week to put things in order, provide extra fortifications, annexes, hospital complexes and the like.'

He sank back gratefully into his chair.

'Additionally, couriers and scouts will spread word of an offer. The Eburones have a history of violence like few others among the Belgae, and consequently many old enemies. Each and every tribe in the region is to be given free license to raid and kill among the Eburones with Rome's blessing. Any tribe that offers information on Ambiorix that proves useful will be rewarded and relieved of their troop supply obligations for the next season. The Eburones will remember this season as the day their Gods abandoned them.'

He smiled and his smile was tired, but cold and dangerous.

'This matter will be brought to a close within the month. Ambiorix's time is up, as is that of his tribe. Are there any questions or comments?'

The officers shook their heads in silence. Caesar's plan was well-founded and timed to a tee. If the army ever stood a chance of rooting out Ambiorix, this would be it.

Priscus cleared his throat. 'While you're all burning and scything your way through the forest, remember to be on the lookout for Fronto and his men. They are still in there somewhere - to the south at the last mention.'

Caesar and Antonius nodded their agreement.

'Very well,' the general said. 'Brief your men and prepare for the off. We will end this Belgic campaigning season early, by the kalends of Quintilis, and then decide whether to press on against the Suevi'

Priscus could not help but picture Fronto and his small band, somewhere deep in that forest as the might of Rome began to squeeze from all sides. He threw up a quick glance to the heavens and formed a mental image of the lady Fortuna.

'You've always looked after him,' he muttered. 'Don't stop now.'

Chapter Sixteen

By the Rhenus River, a day's march north of the confluence with the Mosella.

'Fabulous timing!' Gaius Volcatius Tullus grumbled as he hurriedly strapped on his cuirass with the help of his body slave. The waiting tribune, drawn from the Thirteenth among the cohorts that had remained by the great river, was clearly nervous about rousing his commanding officer, and with good reason. Tullus knew from bitter experience that a defensive position in daily danger of siege by a vastly numerically-superior army could hardly be allowed any leeway in their lives. He knew his reputation was already that of a martinet, and he was aware of some of the names the men had assigned to him, but he also knew that, should the worst happen and the entire Germanic race cross the river in force, the only chance they stood was with rock-hard discipline.

'I do not believe they are here to challenge us sir.'

'Clearly not, tribune. Had they intended violence, they would likely have battered you with rocks and not words. Still, the fact remains that it has been mere days and the fortifications are far from ready. I care not what they wish to discuss, I would rather do it from a position of utmost security, sure that we can hold them off if things turn ugly. You say they are Ubii?'

'They say they are, sir.'

Tullus nodded and followed the tribune out of his command tent, across the muddy, busy camp, filled with work parties and men coming off duty, even at this early hour. Past the duty centurion, who saluted sharply and gestured his men out of the way, along the timber structure - one of the strongest, most stable bridges Tullus had seen constructed in a single campaign, and testament to the skill of Caesar's engineers. The far end of the bridge had been torn up, only the stumps of the piles rising like wooden fangs from the swift torrent, and a gap of some hundred paces lay between the jagged timber bridge-end with its hastily constructed palisade of stakes and planks and the grassy bank upon which stood the ambassadors, for such Tullus had to assume they were.

'Welcome to the Ubii,' Tullus announced, spreading his arms in the style of an orator.

'Greeting, commander,' replied one of the more richly-appointed of the tribesmen. 'I ambassador for friend tribe.'

303

'You have my attention.'

'Chatti wish cross river. Kill Eburones for Caesar.'

Tullus pursed his lips. 'I've heard the name *Chatti.*' He frowned as he dredged his memories of numerous briefings and maps. His eyes narrowed. 'They're from the east. Are they not part of the Suevi people?'

The Ubian ambassador shook his head, but his eyes betrayed the truth. 'Chatti not Suevi. Chatti friend of Ubii.'

Tullus folded his arms. 'No. The Chatti are a sub-tribe of the Suevi. I don't care whether they're close friends, ambassador, no Suevi scum will cross this river while I remain in command. That tribe has a history of violence against Rome; *recent* history, too'

'But Caesar offer war and plunder to tribes against Eburones.'

'Not to the damn Suevi he didn't. The general would refuse, and you know that. Go and tell your Chatti friends to satisfy themselves with raiding in their forests. There will be no crossing for them.'

The Ubian ambassador started trying to wheedle and persuade, but Tullus turned his back on the man and strode away across the bridge. The tribune hurried along at his side. 'Should we be sending out men to chastise the Ubii, sir? For supporting an enemy tribe, I mean.'

Tullus shook his head as he walked. 'The Ubii have been our allies thus far. Did you see the man's eyes? He was nervous. You have to remember, tribune, that he and his people stand between half a million Suevi warriors and this river. He's concerned with self-preservation, that's all. You might perhaps send some scouts out to check the situation and offer him sanctuary on this side of the river for him and his own people. No one else.'

The tribune saluted and scurried off.

'Sir?'

Tullus looked up to see the duty centurion saluting. 'Ah good. It seems the Suevi and their sub-tribes are starting to take an interest. Double the work parties and shorten rest breaks. I want this place able to withstand anything by sunset tomorrow.'

'Yessir. But sir?'

'What is it, centurion?'

'A courier from the Fourth Cohort, Eighth Legion stationed half day downriver, sir.'

'And?' prompted Tullus with exaggerated patience.

'It seems a tribe called the Sugambri are requesting permission to cross the river and take up Caesar's offer, sir.'

'Are they an allied tribe? I seem to remember mention of them before in less than friendly terms.'

'We had a clash with them a few seasons back, sir, but they've been taking oaths of allegiance for the past two years.'

'Your opinion of them, centurion?'

'Germans, sir. Untrustworthy bastards to a man, sir.'

'Your opinion is duly noted, centurion. Unfortunately, Caesar has made an open offer of Eburone plunder and, while I feel sound refusing passage to an unknown quantity subject to an enemy tribe, it would send out entirely the wrong message to refuse the promise of loot to an allied tribe. Tell the courier to allow them passage.'

The centurion nodded and scurried away.

'And Mars keep a wide eye on them.' He smiled wearily at the back of the retreating officer. 'Untrustworthy bastards to a man!'

* * * * *

Furius glanced round at his friend Fabius as he waved the men on towards the centre of the village. 'I'm going to check the headman's hut. Give me a hand.'

He almost collapsed with laughter as Fabius nodded and reached out towards him, remembering only at the last moment that his hand was still bound tightly with linen, a bee-glue wrap splinted to try and heal the knife wound, hopefully with the bones straight. It was agony in cold or wet weather already and Fabius had given serious consideration to lopping the damn thing off at the wrist.

'Oh you are such a bloody comedian.'

Furius grinned as he slapped his friend on the shoulder. With one useless hand and one fake eyeball, jokes were beginning to circulate among the men about which body part the veteran tribune would lose next. Some were even saying he deserved the name 'Felix' - the lucky - more than Mittius of the Eleventh, who had borne the nickname for a decade.

'You can check the hut yourself,' Fabius snapped irritably. 'There's no one here. Just like the last ten places, the tribe have fled at the news of the approaching force. Can't really blame the bastards. Everyone knows what Caesar has in store for them.'

'Caesar's not in charge here.'

305

'But Labienus is following the general's orders.'

It was true. Despite the senior commander's well-reported leanings towards conciliation with the tribes, he was taking his duty very seriously. For three days now they had scoured the great forest and each settlement they had come across had been recently deserted. And yet at each one, Labienus had paused the advance long enough for his scouts to seek out the hidden population. They had then been questioned by force and then executed. The commander had been conspicuously absent during the mass deaths, but had not once baulked at ordering them.

The Seventh, Tenth and Fifteenth Legions had continued to move deeper into the forest, all the time keeping in mind that they needed to leave the northern treeline and return to Cicero's camp by the appointed date.

'Hey, Furius?'

'What?' replied his friend as they began to move to the centre of the village, legionaries all about them ducking into hut doors to check for occupants and failing to find them, gathering anything combustible and throwing it into the huts to add to the conflagration that would take hold as soon as the commander gave the order.

'I know this place.'

'It looks the same as every other, mud-and-shit-soaked village in this Godsawful forest.'

'Not quite. We've been here.'

Furius frowned and peered around. 'No idea.'

'Picture it deep in snow. Picture the headman hanging by his thumbs from that doorframe over there.'

Furius followed his gesture and his eyes widened. 'Jove, you're right. Best part of - what? - two years ago now.'

'Bet I know where the people are hiding.'

His friend grinned and then turned to see Labienus striding across the dirt of the village centre, the legates Plancus, Crassus and Reginus at his heel. 'Sir?'

'Yes, tribune?'

'I believe I know where the populace are, sir. It's only about a quarter of a mile, but through thick forest. Fabius and I have been here before.'

Labienus failed to mask his surprise, but nodded without further question. 'Take a couple of centuries of men and see if you're right,' the commander ordered. Beside him, young Crassus held up a hand to halt them. 'I shall join you.'

The two tribunes shared a look and rolled their eyes, unseen by the senior officers. The youngest of the Crassus dynasty was open to his officers' advice and certainly an easy man to serve, but he yet lacked the hardness that made a legion commander so efficient and feared. Despite Labienus' humanitarian leanings, it was noted that he had that hardness in spades when it was required. As they crossed the village, Furius gestured to Atenos and Carbo, who were busy ordering the legionaries around at the centre of the settlement.

'Two centuries with us, Carbo.'

The pink-faced, hairless veteran centurion relayed the orders to his signifer, who waved the standard and directed the two centuries to form up and follow.

'Lead on, tribunes,' Crassus nodded professionally, falling in somewhere halfway along the line, still on his horse and protected by the two centuries of men.

'You won't get through on a horse, sir,' Fabius said, and Crassus frowned. 'Got to push through deep woodland, sir,' Furius added. Crassus took a deep breath, apparently weighing up the situation. To the pair's surprise, and some disappointment, the legate nodded and slid from his horse, gesturing for a legionary to take the reins and lead it away.

As Crassus gestured for them to move off, Carbo and Atenos fell in alongside the two tribunes.

'Where are we going, sir?' Carbo asked quietly.

'There's a deep river gulley about a quarter mile from here. It'll be where the villagers are hiding.'

'And why is the legate coming with us?' Atenos grumbled under his breath.

'Because it's his prerogative. Fronto would have done, too.'

'Fronto's more use than a wet flannel.'

'I'd advise you to stow that attitude,' Fabius hissed, though his face bore a smile. The four officers turned to peer back at Crassus, who was striding forward as though out for a summer stroll, the legionaries giving him plenty of space.

'Give the lad a bit of support,' Furius sighed. 'Look at his family. He's got a bit of a reputation to live up to. His dad owns half of Rome and his brother's a war hero.'

'Worth noting though,' Atenos grumbled, 'that since Fronto left and we got Crassus, the Tenth have rarely been fielded in a worthwhile action, and not won any renown.'

'You Gauls and your bloody renown,' grinned Carbo.

'Anyway,' Furius said, his voice lowering even further, to hide beneath the crunch of boots on rock, 'I hear through the grapevine that Fronto is in line to retrieve his command. Crassus will be going back to Rome at the end of the season, and his father will have secured some big-nob post in the city for him.'

'That's just rumour,' Fabius snorted. 'His old man's out in the desert, kicking Parthians about. He's hardly going to stop in the middle of a big campaign and organise a sinecure for his youngest.'

'Big word for you, that.'

'Shut up,' Fabius snapped, starting to get sick of his friend's jibes. 'Simple fact is: the only reason Crassus is here and with the Tenth is that his father didn't know what to do with him, so he sent him to Caesar to mollycoddle.'

He paused, aware that his voice had risen, and turned, grateful to note that Crassus was paying no attention, instead passing the time of day conversationally with a legionary who looked thoroughly uncomfortable at the attention.

'It'd be nice to get Fronto back,' Atenos shrugged, and Carbo nodded. 'He needs us. Needs looking after, he does.'

'The poor bastard's somewhere out here. Wonder how he's getting on?' Fabius mused.

'Come on. Quiet for now,' his friend urged, and they moved out of the village clearing, into the deeper woodland, stepping over fallen timber, circling around brambles and small thickets and snapping branches where necessary to facilitate their passage. Behind them the legionaries followed suit, staying in formation as best they could, and Crassus in the centre smiled as though enjoying the jaunt.

'Off that way,' Furius pointed to their left, and Fabius nodded, working their way off at an angle. A few moments later there was a cry of alarm from one of the legionaries as he slipped on loose earth and had to grasp a branch to prevent himself slipping down a slope off into the trees.

'Watch your footing,' Furius ordered. 'There's a bitch of a drop down there to the river. Anyone slips down there and you won't be coming back.'

As the two centuries of men moved to the side to allow a wide berth around the area where the ground fell away, Fabius and Furius led the column to the gulley that ran down at a steep angle towards the ravine, along which they could now hear the roar of the river.

'*This* is a way down?' Carbo said, eyeing the treacherous rocky slope warily.

'The only one we found. Valley narrows at the far end, but to a steep waterfall. This gulley goes all the way down. Everywhere else it's a drop down a sheer cliff face. Which would you prefer?'

The Primus Pilus grinned. 'To send the men down and sit at the top with a cup of wine, waiting, frankly. Still, let's get it over with, eh sir?'

Furius laughed and began to clamber down the slope. Above, the legionaries jammed their pila into the ground or stacked them in bunches to collect later, slinging their shields round onto their backs on the carrying straps before attempting the descent, using both hands to steady and guide.

The gulley was difficult, but the men handled it stoically. Pausing after a few moments of climbing, Furius looked up to see Crassus beginning the descent, his white cloak already grubby and torn at the hem as he scooped it up to prevent it tangling his feet and draped it over his upper arm like a toga, struggling to keep it in position as he descended. Furius rolled his eyes.

The scene was so familiar as the two tribunes finally dropped the last few feet to the ravine's lush grass: the icy, fast river, strewn with large rocks and boulders. Furius could see the body of the fallen Gaul in his mind's eye, splayed across one of the boulders, broken and bloody. He shook away the memory, hearing something on the periphery of his senses. His eyes tracked it to the trees further upriver as they nestled beside the river

'Come out,' he shouted. 'We know you're here.'

There was a long silence.

'Are you sure they're here?' Crassus said, landing on the grass with a thump and arraying his cloak once more.

'We searched the area thoroughly a couple of years ago. Without going miles from their village, this would be the obvious place to hide. We chased a rebel courier out here and he fell from the cliff. He paused. 'Fabius? You remember any of the names from the place.'

'Of course I don't. Do you?'

Furius grinned. 'Lugius of the Eburones. Surrender yourselves to us and we will spare the women and the children. You've heard of the general's orders for your tribe, I'm sure, so you'll know you won't get a better offer than that. Refuse us and everyone dies.'

Fabius frowned. 'Lugius? He was the druid, yes?'

'Indeed.'

There was another long pause, but off along the ravine, among the stand of leafy trees, there was a shuffling and a few heartbeats later a figure emerged, hands raised in supplication. He was no druid, clearly - more a farmer, albeit a wealthy one.

'And the rest of your people.'

'We just farmer, Roman. Poor person. Not warrior.'

'*All* the Belgae are warriors,' replied Carbo with a raised brow. 'We've experienced that a few times.'

'What do you know of Ambiorix?' Furius said clearly.

'King disappear,' the man replied. Furius peered intently at the farmer, but his face betrayed no subterfuge. 'And have you heard any news of our officer Fronto, who hunts him?'

The man shook his head. 'Other tribe hunt us. Your Caesar offer our land to German monster and they scour land, loot and rape.'

The two tribunes shared a look, and then nodded. 'He's telling the truth as far as he knows.'

Carbo waved an arm at his men. 'Get into that thicket and round them up. Take them back to the village and then commander Labienus can decide what to do with them. He'll stand by your offer, sir,' he added, nodding to Furius.

'Hold.'

They turned to see Crassus stepping across the grass. 'How do you intend to herd dozens of prisoners up that slope? Besides, their fate is already decided by the standing orders of the general. Labienus will simply have them executed when they arrive.'

'What are you suggesting, sir?' Fabius frowned.

'I'm suggesting nothing, tribune. I'm giving an order. I assume this ravine is sealed?'

'We certainly couldn't find any other way in.'

'Then fire the woods and let us return to the top.'

'Sir?'

'It hasn't rained for weeks, tribune. The trees and undergrowth will be like tinder. Fire the woods and we can get back up top and report the task complete.'

'Sir, I gave my word...'

'That you would spare the women and children if they surrendered. You've seen only one man. They have not surrendered. Burn the woodland and report back to the village.'

Furius watched in surprise as the legate took a deep breath and turned, hoisting up his cloak again and making for the narrow gulley that led back up towards the village above. 'Don't fall down and break anything, sir,' he advised with an underlying current of desire.

As the legate disappeared along the crevasse towards the narrow sloping climb, Furius and Fabius turned to find Carbo and Atenos looking at them expectantly, the two centuries of men silent and pensive.

'Well? You heard the legate: burn it.'

As Carbo, frowning his disapproval, set about giving his men their orders, and the panicked head-farmer dashed back into the woodland screaming warnings in his native tongue, Fabius and Furius strode back across the grass, away from everything.

'If that little sod doesn't get called back to Rome, he might find one night that he enters a latrine and never leaves.'

'Careful what you say,' Fabius hissed, but his expression sympathised with the sentiment. Frankly, he couldn't wait for the season to end. The way the Eburones constantly melted into hiding in these woodlands, it could be months, rather than days before they brought the tribe to heel, and months longer serving under Crassus was starting to look unpleasant. He appeared to be turning into his brother.

* * * * *

Quadratus felt his nerves pinch at his courage as his cohort moved into the narrow river valley, jammed in a space barely a contubernium of men wide, between the pitted and holed sandstone cliff and the fast torrent of the unnamed mountain river. Despite the summer sun that had now been warming the lands of the Belgae for weeks, he shivered in this narrow defile. Somewhere down here the warriors of the oppidum known as Durolito were in hiding, crowded in the belief that they had escaped the might of Rome - the latest in a

311

line of settlements that had been left as corpse-strewn charred ruins to attest to the wrath of Caesar, albeit carried out in his name by commander Trebonius.

The three legions under the commander - the Ninth, Twelfth and Thirteenth - had quickly discovered that the particular terrain they had been assigned was hopelessly unsuitable for moving such a large army in force, and Trebonius had given the order to split into three separate legions and stay close but to operate individually. It had been a sensible enough move, but sadly, a matter of hours later, the terrain had become yet denser and more tangled and undulating, and finally, Caninius, who now commanded the Twelfth, had ordered his legion to split into cohort-sized groups and move independently within a set area.

Cavalry being of little use in the woods, Quadratus had been placed in command of one cohort, with orders to take, interrogate, execute and burn Durolito - a small, eyrie-like fortress oppidum rising out of the forest like an island in a sea of whispering green. As with every other shithole they had encountered, the place had been deserted with the exception of lame livestock and starving stray animals picking through the town's carcass.

One of the native trackers had quickly picked up the trail of the fled warriors and followed it down to the river valley, where it had been lost in the lush grass, but clearly they travelled downriver to the north. Or was it the west? Honestly, in these endless tracts of identical forest, Quadratus could not tell one place from another, and with the sun usually hidden by the leafy canopy, a sense of direction was hard to maintain.

'Another mile and I'm going to sound the recall,' he announced to the senior centurion. 'We must have come too far from the oppidum now. Either we've missed them somehow or they're fled to another oppidum or tribe.'

The centurion nodded his agreement - he had been just as unimpressed with the terrain as Quadratus. The commander felt nervous with his lot for a number of reasons, not the least of which was the change in command. He had become used to serving under Labienus and, although the infuriating man always kept him in the dark until the last moment, no man in the Treveri wars could say that Labienus was anything other than a tactical genius - to rival, or even surpass, Caesar, no less. No matter what the situation, the commander's army always felt that Labienus would be able to pull them out of it intact and snatch victory from the jaws of defeat.

Trebonius was an unknown quantity to all.

And as for this Caninius, who was all-but new to Caesar's army? Well, no one knew what to expect. Still, now everything was down to him - Quadratus. If only these damned Eburone warriors would show up.

'Centurion? Sound unit recalls for half the men. I want the Fourth, Fifth and Sixth centuries to start pulling back and secure the entrance to the valley. The First, Second and Third can move on for another half mile or so, and then turn back and rejoin the rest. We're chasing shadows here.

The unit musicians blasted out on their cornus and buccinas, directing the different centuries and Quadratus sighed deeply. This damned forest was killing him by degrees. It had started with his sense of humour, then abraded his enthusiasm, finally chipping at the veneer of his confidence, and was starting to work on hollowing out his will to live. Eight days the army had been assigned to the forest, and he was only on the morning of day five. There would be another three days of this nightmare before they returned to legate Cicero's camp. And unless someone else was having a lot more luck than Quadratus, all they'd have to show for it was a lot of dead farmers and burned huts, and still no lead on the lunatic Ambiorix. Which meant, of course, given what everyone knew of Caesar's vow to kill the man, that the legions would almost certainly be given only a momentary breather and then sent back into the forest for a second shift.

'Bollocks!' he said to himself, with feeling. The senior centurion smiled knowingly at him.

A strange honk turned into a squeak in the middle of the chaos of musical calls and centurions' whistles, and Quadratus scanned the various musicians to identify the discordant culprit. As his eyes fell upon the cornicen responsible, he was already reaching out to grab the centurion's shoulder.

'Ambush!' he bellowed, watching as the musician fell, his long, curved instrument tipped and a stream of blood pouring from the end, choked through the mouthpiece while the arrow through his neck pumped blood into his throat.

Now other missiles were thrumming from the various hollows and cave mouths in the sandstone valley walls.

'Ambush!' he yelled again, the senior centurion taking up the call to arms. Other centurions and optios began to issue orders and within a matter of heartbeats the centuries were reforming into testudos, their shields forming boxes to protect them from the arrows and sling stones.

Quadratus scanned the cliffs and threw himself urgently to one side as an arrow whipped past.

'Move! Each century make for the nearest cave or the cliff edge. Get inside under cover if you can!'

The call was repeated and Quadratus' cohort split into six groups, the various native scouts and officers straggling along, not part of the defensive formations. Taking advantage of the fact that he carried no pilum or shield, Quadratus ducked nimbly behind a tree and then, keeping his eyes on the cliff, moved from bole to bole towards the sheer red-brown valley wall, keeping pace with the armoured units further along. Behind him there was a cry of agony and he turned to see the senior centurion, already sporting two feathered shafts, lifted by a third and hurled into the river, where he disappeared from sight.

This would never have happened under Labienus' command, he grunted through gritted teeth while he scurried to the edge of the valley. As the centuries reached the cliff, their shields went above their heads, creating a solid roof, worrying less about the possibility of ground shots as their assailants began to drop rocks from the cliff entrances. Some of the luckier units managed to find wide cave entrances and moved into them.

Quadratus ducked along the edge of the cliff, eyeing the pitted surface with interest, until he reached another group of soldiers. 'Did you notice how many caves?' he asked as he ducked under the shield roof.

'Several dozen, sir,' the optio answered, 'but only maybe ten that were wide enough for a man.'

Above Quadratus, rocks, stones and arrows pounded the shelter, and a narrow iron arrowhead punched through, emerging a few finger widths from his nose. He tried to stop shaking.

'There are handholds carved in the rock,' he said quietly. 'I ran past two sets between here and those trees. That's the only way in to the higher ones.'

'We could starve them out?' the optio asked hopefully.

'Unlikely. This is a bolt-hole, so it's probably well-stocked, and we have nothing. They'd have us dead to hunger before they emerged. We've only got one option as I see it, since we've no missile troops with us.'

314

The optio listened nervously, blinking occasionally as Quadratus outlined his thoughts.

'Alright, sir. We'll have to be quick, though.'

'Give the preparatory order,' the commander said quietly. The optio turned and passed on the orders, seeing them repeated down the lines, so that each man in each century knew what they were doing.

'Let's hope *I* do', thought Quadratus, eyeing the score of dead legionaries out across the narrow grass strip of the valley. Above, yet more rocks pounded the shield roof, the occasional squawk announcing where they had penetrated the defence. Under the shield-shelter, every other man passed his pilum to a tent mate and, as soon as all six centuries had called their readiness, the optio looked at Quadratus.

'Do it!'

Like the ground parting in an earthquake, the shield roof split in half, three centuries' worth of legionaries taking half a dozen sharp steps back and pulling back their arms, pilum readied. Without waiting for an order, they each released, every man having picked a target from among the wide, weathered holes in the sandstone wall.

With a clatter and crash, accompanied by a surprisingly - and satisfyingly - high number of pained shrieks, the pila arced up and into the cave mouths. Even before they struck, though, the rest of the men, abandoning their shields to the ground, began to clamber quickly up the handholds towards the caves above, other soldiers crowding around the bottom, eagerly awaiting their turn.

The legionaries out on the grass hurriedly extricated the extra pilum from their spare hand, where it was held behind the shield, and readied it for a second wave. Quadratus was kicking himself for having agreed to leaving the spare pila back with the supplies for ease of movement in the woods, but at least they'd brought one each. Some of the cohorts had elected to travel without pila at all for speed.

Pausing, Quadratus counted to six. No good aiming the second volley too quickly - targets would be fewer and the climbing soldiers in more danger. On six, he gave the wave to the centurion out with the lines of men, who dropped his arm. The second wave of two hundred pila rose into the air just as - satisfyingly - the heads of the defenders emerged once again, preparing to drop more rocks. The pila wreaked a terrifying toll on the Eburones, and Quadratus smiled in relief as he saw the first legionary haul himself up into the mouth

315

of a cave and realised he had time to draw his sword before moving in.

Devoid of further pila, the men back across the grass ran forward. Raising their shields, they formed a roof over the legionaries who waited to climb as the Belgic missile attack began again, though much lighter and in dribs and drabs. A number of the cave mouths were now being contested by angry legionaries.

Quadratus sighed and stepped back as he watched an Eburone archer, bow still in hand, suddenly appear from a cave mouth, mid-fight, stumbling backwards into the abyss, the legionaries below opening up their shield roof to allow him the room to plunge to the ground and land in a crack of splintering bones.

All along the cliffs men were spidering up the red rock and disappearing into the caves, swords and daggers in hands and looks of sheer bloody murder on their faces.

It would be over in a matter of heartbeats. Quadratus' shoulders sagged, and he leaned back against a thick sapling. A veteran cavalry commander, he had been dubious about being given command of an infantry force, but Caninius had been insistent. He'd not had enough senior officers to assign to the various separate cohorts in this action, and Quadratus had been needed.

One thing was certain: when they turned back north to Cicero's camp, and the senior command decided to admit that Ambiorix was gone, he would be damn well returning to a cavalry command. Screw this walking lark!

Somewhere above, a legionary shouted some joke about Icarus with a raucous belly laugh, and a shrieking Eburone warrior emerged at speed from the cave mouth, plunging to his doom.

* * * * *

Venitoutos was proud. Generations of his family had borne the pride of the Belgae in their blood, defending their lands from their ancient ancestors across the Rhenus or from Gaulish incursions or, of course, the interminable internecine wars the Eburones fell prey to with their neighbour tribes.

He was no king or noble. He was no druid or warrior with an arm full of rings and a glittering blade. He was a farmer, and a father, and a grandfather. But he was Eburone, and any time his king or his people had called, he had hauled on his grandfather's torn mail shirt and hefted the spear resting in the corner of his hut, bade the women

316

farewell and marched off to teach the enemy what it meant to be Belgae.

Venitoutos was proud.

Four years previously, he had been at the Sabis River when the great Belgic alliance had stood firm in the face of Caesar's army, and had almost stopped the general. The scar all down his left arm was a daily reminder of that almost-victory. Last winter, he had been called on by his King to wipe out the Roman forces who had the gall to winter in Eburone lands. His lack of hearing in his left ear and the ache in his left knuckles hearkened back to that battle.

The Romans had learned time and again what it meant to face the Belgae.

Yes, Venitoutos was proud.

But he was also a father. And a grandfather. And heartily sick of death. It was one thing to bring war to Rome or a belligerent neighbour, in defence of his people. It was another to provoke the Roman bull that stomped around their lands, grinding the people beneath its hooves. That would be inviting Caesar's war machine to murder his family, and the twins and the others deserved better.

For while Venitoutos was proud, he was also willing to see reason. The Eburones had lost all, no matter what their most noble leaders believed. Now all the ordinary folk could do was stay out of sight of the armoured monster crunching across their land, protect their loved ones, and wait for everything to settle down and Caesar to turn his sights elsewhere.

If he'd known anything about King Ambiorix or his location, he would gladly have given it to the Romans in return for his family's ongoing safety. But even that was no use. He knew nothing.

And so he and his kin hid, in a manner most unfitting of the Eburones.

The Romans had passed through here three days ago in force, their steel and crimson ranks laying waste, executing every Eburone they found and burning the farms and villages. In this very valley three other farms had been fired, the bodies of their owners cast into the flames. And the settlement at the river head had gone the same way. Venitoutos had crouched in the bushes near the main road with his wife and children keeping the grandchildren quiet with hands over their mouths as he watched old Aneunos die miserably and their general - Labienus, apparently - ordering the death of his children with a detached coldness.

317

Somehow the Romans had moved down the valley quite thoroughly, burning and killing, but had missed two farms, one of them being Venitoutos'. He had given thanks to Arduenna for her shelter and protection and had promised to carve a stone to her when this was all over.

Then, yesterday, the Romans had returned. He'd found it hard to credit such bad luck, but listening in from a hiding place close to the main track, he'd heard the Remi scouts talking - he had not a word of Latin, but the Romans employed so many of his own people that he needed none. The scouts had talked about crossing the path of Labienus' army and the fact that they'd found only one intact farm in the valley. Caesar, who himself seemed to command this second army, had burned that other farm and crucified the family, leaving them to die at the beaks and claws of the birds or the growling hollowness of starvation, their limbs gradually dislocating as they hung. The scouts had muttered about the other two Roman forces in the forest and about turning north again to the cursed camp of Sabinus and Cotta, where the wagons waited, and Venitoutos had felt a small thrill at the memory of his tribe's victory over that camp.

Venitoutos had waited until the army had moved on, offered up yet more prayers to the great Goddess, passed his farm - now the only one surviving in the valley - and painstakingly took down the crucified family. Only the old man and one of the children would survive, and Venitoutos had taken care to deal with the dead in the old way.

Three armies.

Romans everywhere!

It was hard to credit, and it certainly sounded the death knell for the Eburones.

And this morning, as he stood in the doorway of his hut and breathed in the warm summer air of the forest, Venitoutos found himself wondering what he had done that had so angered the unseen powers? For all Arduenna's protection, the valley had succumbed to two Roman armies and now he watched his family scurry down the bank to their last-ditch hiding place by the stream and closed his eyes.

This army was making straight for him. Though they were likely bound for some unknown location, they would be unable to pass without spotting the farm.

That they were not Roman hardly mattered.

Venitoutos had seen them at dawn, two miles from here where they had stopped to check out a burned farm and had felt a surge of hope at the sight of his fellow warriors, gathered together into a warband. He had almost rushed from the trees to welcome them when he had spotted the differences. These were not Eburones. Not even Belgae. They were the Germans from beyond the great river.

And that meant, if anything, more danger than the Romans.

It was common knowledge, spread by word of mouth in a matter of days, that the Romans had offered up the Eburones' throats and purses to any tribe who wished to take them, with Caesar's blessing. The tribes beyond the river had generations of hate and strife in common with the Eburones and being offered their carcass to pick over would be more than tempting for them. For all the Germans hated Rome, they were not above performing her dirty work for her if it meant loot and murder and a little revenge on an age-old enemy.

And what they would do to the Eburones would make crucifixion look like mercy. The gut post, the burning rack, the skinning knife. And, of course, raping all the women regardless of age, and often the men and boys too. It would make a clean Roman death look like paradise.

And so here they went once more, hiding in the woods.

Even as he heard the first sounds of the approaching warband, he gave his hut a regretful glance, wishing he could have preserved more, had there been time, and scurried off down the bank towards the stream and the copse where their few prized possessions were stored.

Sliding down into the undergrowth, he kissed his wife's head and pulled the inquisitive twins down from the upper foliage and into better cover. The family held their breath.

The raiders burst from the far side of the farmstead's clearing like water from a shattered dam. Hundreds of men, tattooed and painted, decorated with torcs and arm rings, mostly bare-chested, but occasionally clad in mail, poured from the trees and into the hut and the barn and the store house and even the hen coup. Their sounds of disappointment were audible even from this distance as they found the farm deserted and poor. One or two took out their anger on the few remaining chickens, smashing them against the wall of the hut and even tearing at their feathered flesh with jagged teeth.

Would they burn the hut? Venitoutos cast yet another prayer up to the great Goddess Arduenna that his farm might escape this latest deprivation. The wind rustled the leaves in noncommittal answer. The Goddess was known to be fickle and easily enraged. Having admitted - if only to himself - to his wish to see an end to it all, would she still shelter him? Arduenna had a dangerous sense of humour and was quick to anger.

And those two traits were never more in evidence than now, as the tribesmen turned their attention from the hut, leaving it unburned, unbroken and entirely intact, only to focus on the footprints left in the soft, dewy morning grass.

Venitoutos cursed under his breath. He'd sent the others around across the tree roots and down the scree slope to avoid leaving just such a trail, yet in his haste to join them, he'd forgotten to do so himself and had left a line from the hut to their hideout.

'Come out!' snarled a voice in harsh, Germanic tones.

Venitoutos remained silent, though he could hear the faint crying of the children beneath their mother's hands and her own muttered panic.

'The Sugambri are here now, little man,' a huge, blond creature with a broken nose bellowed from the slope, slowing as he approached the copse. 'No need to fear the Romans now!'

No, Venitoutos thought to himself. *Now I need to fear the Sugambri.*

But the sad truth remained that they were trapped. Before them stood the farm clearing full of Germans. Behind them was the narrow stream gulley that was treacherous and would slow them in full sight of the enemy. And the copse was small. It would not take the Sugambri long to root them out. Now, their only hope was negotiation.

But he'd been thinking about this all morning, ever since he'd seen the Germanic raiders. In bringing the Roman armies so close to the farm that he could smell their wine-soaked breath, Arduenna had given him a gift. She had placed in his hands the one thing that might buy off the Sugambri.

With a deep breath, he gestured to the family to remain silent and hidden and clambered up out of the undergrowth, staggering into plain sight. On shaking legs, holding his arms out in a gesture of supplication, he walked a few paces and stopped before the Sugambri war leader.

'Greetings great chief.'

'Where are your goods,' the man replied absently, peering past him at the copse.

'I am a poor farmer with no wealth,' he replied. 'I have nothing to adorn such great men. Just a few tools and some rat-eaten grain.'

'You have warm and comfortable women, I'll wager,' leered the German, still looking past him.

'And if I could offer you riches and glory and easy victory, what would its value be to you?'

For the first time, the Sugambri leader's eyes slid back towards Venitoutos and settled on his face, the big brow creasing into a frown.

'Riddles?'

'No riddles, great chief. We have nothing. We are beneath your attention. But only a day north of here - two at the most - is the camp at the Fortress Valley, where the Eburones slaughtered their legion in the winter.'

'A place of corpses and ghosts,' spat the German.

'More than that,' smiled Venitoutos. 'The Roman general has placed all his army's wealth and supplies there while he raids this forest. Think of the plunder from *ten legions*, great chief. Think of the glory in slaughtering the small guard and taking from Caesar everything of value. More than that: think what damage you will do to Rome! You could cripple their army.'

The Sugambri leader was clearly interested, his lip working away in silent calculation. His eyes widened momentarily as he estimated the goods that would be required to support such an army.

Venitoutos smiled. He had the man. It was a prize no raiding chief could ever pass up.

'You are sure of this?

'I heard if from the scouts of Caesar's army, though they knew not that I was listening. Lead the Sugambri to greater glory than pillaging a simple farmstead.'

Two other war leaders were now making their way across the damp grass, one of them tall and powerful on a horse, his wire-haired chest bared and marked with patterns that protected him from earthly harm and from divine magics.

'Why do you delay, Adelmar?'

'This farmer knows of the Roman baggage train.'

'So?'

'Think on it, Gerwulf! All the supplies for ten legions. With only a small guard. And the whole Roman army in this stupid forest looking for their coward king. We could take it all and be across the river back in our own land before Caesar even hears we have been there!'

The mounted chieftain nodded, with a smile.

'It would be a good raid, I am thinking.'

His nod was echoed by the third chief. 'I agree.'

'Then we will abandon this pointless journey, picking over a carcass already stripped by Caesar and we will find this baggage train and take it for our own. Send out riders to draw the other warbands to us.'

Venitoutos smiled. Arduenna protected her own and this time, even despite his failing courage, she had continued to do so, with no cruel joke.

He was still smiling as his head bounced down the grass leaving a fine red spray, coming to rest a few feet from the copse, from which issued a chorus of screams.

Adelmar turned and smiled at Gerwulf, wiping his bloodied sword on a pelt hanging from his belt.

'Kill the men,' he ordered one of the nearby warriors. 'But fetch the women. I have needs to sate before we leave.'

High in the treetops, a woodpecker laughed hard and long above the untouched farm buildings.

Chapter Seventeen

Deep in the forest of Arduenna.

'He has to be heading for the Rhenus,' Fronto said, rubbing his scalp absently as he leaned against a tree trunk and emptied his water canteen over his face.

'The Eburones are not universally accepted by our cousins across the river,' Ullio replied with a slight shake of his head. Our history of war with many of them goes back to long before we even knew the name of Rome. Ambiorix will find few potential allies there, especially close to the river where all the tribes have given their oath to Caesar. The king would have to be *truly* desperate to try such a thing.'

Fronto frowned at Ullio's use of such a title for Ambiorix, but said nothing. For all the hunter might hate Ambiorix and all he stood for, he still recognised him as the now-undisputed king of the Eburones and accorded him the appropriate honours, if not the allegiance.

'The wily bastard must be getting desperate. Bear in mind the rumours rushing through the forest. Three Roman armies! Nine legions scouring the lands of the Eburones for him, crushing him from three sides, along with every other nation who fancies a try at your tribe's pickings. The whole forest is alive with his enemies. There are more enemies hunting the Eburones in their lands than there are of their own people! And unless he dares try slip between those armies and tribes, the only way open to him is the river. And let's face it, we've been turned east for three days. We can't be a long way from the river now.'

Ullio nodded. What Ambiorix hoped to do was still the big question, and what he would do when he finally reached the river was beyond any of them. In addition to nine legions, Caesar's offer had brought every tribe in on the hunt. Even the shattered Nervii had sent what few warriors they could gather in a band to hunt the fugitive king, as had the crushed Menapii, both more intent on securing Caesar's favour and forgiveness than the potential loot. But the Condrusi and the Treveri were also coming through the forest from the south. Even the Segni, having declared their usurper king and his pet druid enemies of the tribe, were on the hunt. There were even faint rumours that the Germanic peoples had crossed the torrent to help, not that any sign of them had shown up this far into the woods yet.

'You're still troubled, Ullio.'

It was a statement rather than a question, and a stupid one, though neither acknowledged it as such. Of course he was troubled. His tribe was being systematically exterminated and here he was trying to stop it, but in doing so, finding himself teamed up with the very people doing the exterminating. How it sat with his conscience, Fronto could only wonder. One thing was certain: when this was all over, he would find some way to make things right with Ullio. After all, if Basilus had not interrupted Ullio and his lord, Ambiorix would have been interrogated and dead for days now and all would be well.

His blood thumped and his vision darkened at the memory of the stupid, blind, block-headed idiocy of that cavalry lunatic. The last time he'd seen the man he'd been following Galronus dejectedly as the Remi officer led the cavalry back towards the Rhenus with an aim to meeting up once more with Caesar's army. He'd heard nothing about his friend since, but he felt with some certainty that Galronus would be fine. Basilus, hopefully, less so.

He, on the other hand, was starting to despair of ever finding the fugitive, and the Belgae were burning and dying by the thousand because the little rat continued to evade capture.

'I'm sorry, Ullio. Every time we hear of another strike, it's a punch to my gut, so I can only guess how bad it must be for you. As soon as we find Ambiorix, I will personally deliver the man's head to Caesar and make sure this all ends and that the general knows some of the Eburones have been instrumental in his capture.'

The hunter, his face set into a permanent scowl, whittled at the end of a stick with a small knife and paused for a moment, looking up at Fronto.

'I am at war with myself.'

'Sorry?'

'My mind tells me that Ambiorix must be caught, and soon, if we are to end the slaughter. My mind tells me that the only men that can do it are yours, not those of your general. My mind also tells me that you cannot do it without my help. A dozen times these past days you would have fallen foul of the Goddess without my aid. Samognatos is a good man, but we are far from his lands now, and he does not know this forest as well as I.'

'I agree entirely, Ullio. I've said as much.'

324

'But my heart tells me that I am being too longsighted. I am concentrating on the events that could change my world, but while I do so, my family and my kin are in daily danger. Without my bow and my arm and my hunter's senses, my sister-son and his family - who are all I have left - could be crucified by one of your armies or tortured and burned by the Treveri or the Germans. My heart tells me that I should be with them, to look after them.'

Around them, the meagre remains of the singulares nodded their sympathy, unable to even pretend not to hear in such close circumstances. Ten men, in addition to Fronto and Ullio, and of course Drusus and Magurix, who scouted ahead, towards the settlement that lay half a mile away by the river while the rest waited impatiently.

And of course, Valgus.

The legionary who had vanished during the night they had been attacked by animal-headed bandits had yet to put in a re-appearance. Masgava persisted in the belief that the man lived and was somewhere about, but then somewhere out there was also Brannogenos, plotting their downfall. Perhaps the traitor Remi had already done away with Valgus.

Whatever the case, they had gone on working on the basis of his permanent absence.

'I do sympathise with your plight,' Fronto sighed. 'If it were my family, I doubt I would have had the strength of spirit and presence of mind to do as you have done and put your entire people first. For all that my people call yours 'barbarians', the putting of the good of state above the good of oneself is the most Roman of values and defines what we like to think of as a 'good man'. You, Ullio, are a good man. And when things are done with, I will turn Gaul over to make sure your family are safe. But for now I can do nothing but plead with you to stay with us until we have completed our task.'

Ullio sighed and began to whittle again.

'I will think on it. In time, Arduenna will give me her advice.'

Out of the corner of his eye, Fronto saw Aurelius glance around nervously at the name and reach up to clutch the Minerva figurine that sat on a thong around his neck. That man was getting more superstitious by the day. Something would have to be done soon, before he put the whole party in danger.

'Sir?'

He turned to see the two scouts strolling back into the clearing wearily. Magurix unbuckled his sword belt and carried it by his side, while Drusus knuckled his eyes, a nervous energy about him.

'Any news?'

'Best yet, sir,' Magurix smiled. 'This settlement has not yet been touched by the armies of the general, and they were remarkably talkative to one of their own - or the closest I could manage.'

'Well?'

'Ambiorix has been here recently. He passed through yesterday. Better yet, he indicated his intention to the druid there to head south again, for the oppidum of Atuatuca. We're snapping at his heels, now, sir.'

Fronto felt a deep sense of relief flood through him. Even with Ullio's aid, they had heard only rumour, and even that to the effect that they were a couple of days behind him. This was the first confirmed sighting, and to hear that they were a day closer than previously was heartening.

'Well done the pair of you. We'll move on before first light, but I suggest you both take a little wine to celebrate and recover first.'

Magurix grinned, his enormous muscles bulging as he cast his sword belt off to his pile of gear and went in search of one of the few, rare wine skins they'd brought with them. Fronto turned back to Ullio, who still looked intensely troubled.

'We're so close, my friend. Please don't abandon it now. We've almost got him, but without your aid, I fear he will slip through our grasp again.'

He felt a tap on his shoulder and turned in surprise. Drusus stood behind him, looking uncomfortable. Fronto frowned. Such familiarity was unusual among his singulares, even including the officers. It was almost like being back in the Tenth.

'What?'

'Sir, I need to speak to you. Quietly. Alone.'

Fronto frowned and glanced back at Ullio, seeing the man's eyes cloud with doubt and guilt. He felt dreadful. There was nothing he would like more than to let the man go, even to go help him. But duty and sense required him to make the man's life that much more difficult and leave his remaining kin in danger. If he lost Ullio, Samognatos alone might not be able to help them. They needed him.

'Ullio?'

326

'Sir?' muttered the legionary behind him.

'Not now, Drusus. I'll come find you later.'

With a slightly disrespectful huff Drusus frowned, pursed his lips, gave a curt nod and went off in search of his wine ration.

'What can I do to persuade you to stay, Ullio?'

But looking at the man's expression, he was fairly sure that only Ullio would decide and that nothing Fronto could say would influence him.

* * * * *

The firelight played across the boughs and boles of the trees around the clearing, and Fronto slapped Masgava on the shoulder, throwing a weary grin at Palmatus.

'Get some rest. We move on in the morning, whether he's with us or not.'

Two hours of conversation and consolation had done little to change Ullio's mind. He had not yet avowed an intention to leave, but his eyes continued to betray his unease at continuing his journey with the Roman *fugitivarii*, while his kin remained in constant danger.

In the end, Fronto had given in, left things in the capable hands of his two officers, and walked off a short way into the shadowed forest as the last, golden glinting rays of the sun played off its canopy and the shades of its ghosts began to move between the trunks.

In a rare moment of openness, he had stood alone beneath the great forest and uttered a small prayer to Arduenna. She may not be a God of Rome, but she was clearly a powerful Goddess, nonetheless, and he was in her lands and at her mercy. Sometimes, for all their guiding power, Nemesis and Fortuna could not cover every angle of every situation.

He had implored the Lady of the Forest - great huntress and mistress of beasts - to aid him. He'd desperately tried not to think of her as the hairy, bulbous, lop-sided thing she seemed to appear as on stone carvings, but as a Belgic Diana with her bow.

Help us to trap and deal with Ambiorix, he had asked her. *For though he is a son of yours, so are all the rest of the Eburones and the Segni, and the Condrusi, and even the Treveri, and they will all continue to suffer at the hands of Caesar if Ambiorix is not caugh*t. He had felt tiny, attempting to bargain with an alien

327

Goddess, but his need was too great not to try. *Turn Ullio back to us, so that he might help us complete our hunt, in your role as the lady of hunters.*

It was a small thing, but it was all he could do. He had finished by taking the wine flask from his belt pouch and - after a quick swig of the neat stuff just to make sure it was worthy of divine attention - had cast his libation onto the rock that looked as though it might once have been carved, emptying the whole thing in a desperate attempt to draw her attention to a Roman supplicant.

By the time he'd returned to the circle of men it was fully dark and the fire had been lit, food prepared and the men were arranging their sleeping rolls for the night. Celer and Drusus had been sent out north and south, close by, on watch, and the rest of the men had taken them food and drink when it had been prepared. Fronto had settled into conversation about their plans, devolving into general discussion after a while, and every now and then he had glanced across to see Ullio peering into the dancing flames as though his tortured heart might find the answer within them.

Ignoring the urge to speak to him again, Fronto rose and left the two officers, stepping lightly across the clearing.

Aurelius sat wrapped in his mottled brown cloak, fondling his Minerva and carving something into a small lead disc with the tip of his pugio.

'What's that?' Fronto asked quietly, crouching beside him.

'Curse tablet, sir. Brannogenos used to carry several. Gave one to me after Divonanto.'

'If it came from that backstabbing bastard, it probably *is* cursed. I'd throw it away if I were you.'

'Planning to, sir. Soon as I find a nice sacred spring somewhere to drop it in.'

Fronto frowned. 'Who are you cursing? Ambiorix? Or Brannogenos?'

'No, sir. That devious bat-loving bitch Arduenna.'

Fronto reached out sharply and grabbed the lead disc from the legionary, who looked up in surprise, almost scarring a line across the commander's fingers with his dagger. 'Sir?'

'Aurelius, we're in her forest. At her mercy. It is very possible only she can help us find Ambiorix. Some say none of the other Gods can hear a prayer in here, such is her power. And you want to *curse* her? Are you *mad*?'

'She's wicked, sir. The wicked should be cursed.'

'And you should be locked away in a small room where you can't hurt yourself. I'm confiscating this.' He peered at the disc, seeing the half-formed name of the Goddess, and resolved to slash and batter the tablet until the name had gone as soon as he had a few moments free.

'Grip your Minerva and concentrate on her.'

'Sir.' The legionary looked less than convinced... and less than impressed.

'Now, Drusus said earlier that he needed a quiet word with me. Where is he?'

'About a hundred paces out, sir, behind a big tree and next to a square rock.'

Fronto peered into the impenetrable darkness beneath the trees and shuddered. There was the distinct possibility that even with those instructions, he would be hopelessly lost within fifty paces, and shouting could attract attention of the unwanted sort.

'You care to take me there?'

Aurelius peered into the forest with heightened nerves and nodded reluctantly. 'Alright, sir.'

'Come on.'

Pausing only to draw one of the flaming branches from the fire, Aurelius took one of the lengths of shredded blanket they kept for torches and wrapped it round the tip to enhance its flammability. Once it was convincingly bright and durable, he nodded to Fronto and ducked into the darkness beyond the clearing's edge, stepping carefully among the sticks and undergrowth.

Fronto appreciated Aurelius' speed and surprising silence as the legionary moved through the forest with barely a crack, creak or shuffle, while Fronto came along behind with his traditional level of stealth, sounding more like a bull dancing on grain husks and nut shells.

Deeper into the forest they moved, the light from the campfire soon lost to them, their only source of illumination the branch in the legionary's hands. Fronto smiled. Had he been on his own, he'd have been a long way off-course by now.

After a short walk, Aurelius pointed to a pile of large rocks close to a tree. Even in this almost non-light Fronto could see how the ground fell away beyond. An excellent viewpoint.

He nodded and the pair moved on.

Rounding the larger of the rocks, they could see Drusus sitting wrapped in his cloak peering out across the slope, shield propped next to him and pilum jammed into the ground nearby. Fronto moved closer, his footsteps crunching on the forest floor. Strange? The lookout didn't turn at the noise.

Fronto felt that old familiar cold ball of fear forming in the pit of his stomach. He waved Aurelius closer and the pair hurried over, Fronto clearing his throat.

'Drusus?'

No answer, not that he'd expected one. Drusus' eyes were open and he sat comfortable, huddled against the cold. Fronto approached, feeling the fear emanating from the legionary at his shoulder. Close, now, he reached out towards Drusus and snapped his fingers. The man's eyes remained open, glassy.

'Oh shit. She's killed Drusus. *The bitch has killed Drusus!*'

'Get a hold of yourself!' snapped Fronto angrily, reaching out and pulling aside the seated watchman's cloak, expecting to see a sword hilt standing proud of the man's chest.

What he hadn't expected was bats.

As he pulled the cloak away there was a chorus of sharp squeaks, and three flapping black shapes emerged from the shadows around Drusus' seated form, fluttering up into the night air, sweeping a mere foot above their heads.

Aurelius let out a blood-curdling shriek that almost deafened Fronto and turned, pounding off into the woods, shouting curses at the forest's matron Goddess and screaming for the others. Fronto shook his head and rubbed his temples. The legionary had at least, in his panic, dropped the torch, which burned on the forest floor, sparks smouldering dangerously among the fallen leaves and sticks. Sweeping the burning branch up, he stamped on the glowing embers until they went dark, and then leaned over Drusus with the torch, examining him.

He paused, putting his hand in front of the legionary's mouth and then feeling his neck. He was quite definitely dead. But there was no spray of blood anywhere and no obvious wounds. His brow furrowed, Fronto leaned the man forward and searched his back, lifting his tunic to his armpits to examine his torso. Nothing. His legs were unharmed, and Fronto was hardly going to peer into the man's underwear. Whatever had killed him it had been subtle. Perhaps he'd had a heart attack?

After all, *he'd* nearly had one when Aurelius shrieked next to his ear, and the superstitious lunatic was heading that way himself. It wasn't unknown for a man to die of natural causes, after all. Even a healthy, robust one like Drusus.

And yet he was failing to fool himself. He knew Drusus had been killed somehow.

Brannogenos was still out there somewhere. And so was Valgus. And, of course, Ambiorix and all his followers, and probably a bunch of Arverni. Hell, it could be *anyone*! Or no one.

But with Aurelius shouting about Arduenna and running to his mates, Fronto was fairly sure that shortly the entire unit would be blaming the huntress Goddess for this.

With a sigh, he lowered the body back, spoke a few words over him and withdrew a coin from his purse, pushing it under the tongue and closing the mouth again. Turning, he made a rough estimate of where the camp site would be, based on the commotion he could hear in the distance. Now he needed to get back before Aurelius did too much damage to the unit's morale.

Holding the burning branch aloft and slightly to one side so as not to ruin his night vision too much, Fronto began to pick his way back through the woodland as fast as he dared.

His heart almost exploded from his chest as he rounded a tree and the dancing orange glow of his torch was suddenly reflected back to him in two wide, black, glassy orbs. He skittered to a halt and stared as the huge, grey boar peered at him intensely. The damn thing was enormous!

Fronto tried to remember any tale he'd been told about boars and how you dealt with them, but his lifetime's experience with the creatures was entirely limited to what sauce you added to them, and what wine went best. He *did* know that they were extremely dangerous, especially when startled, and bloody hard to stop without a ballista and a nice wall to hide behind. Alone against one, in the dark, in the forest, lost and - he cursed as his hand touched his hip - unarmed, he was likely in some serious kind of trouble.

The beast huffed and a cloud of steam boiled from its snout. Fronto felt a chill run through him at the sight and the sound.

'Erm... shoo!'

The boar remained motionless, huffing again.

Fronto, panic beginning to blind him to sense, waved his arms at it in a dismissing motion.

'Shoo! Go on. Piss off!'

Again, the boar remained.

At a pinch, he could wield the torch both offensively and defensively, but he had the sneaking suspicion that such activity would simply annoy the creature and that would likely be a worse situation than having it stare haughtily at him.

'Go on. Go... go find a sow. Go on.' Panic bubbled ever higher. 'Erm... Honey Glaze!' he bellowed. 'Liquamen and apricot sauce!' Idiotic, of course, but recipes were all that flocked to his mind.

'Oh just fuck off!' he snapped, and hurled the lead curse tablet at it. The disc bounced off the creature's shoulder and still it didn't move.

'What, then?'

Slowly, with a strangely human grunt, the boar turned and, flashing him one last, oddly-disappointed glance, ambled off into the darkness.

Fronto exhaled with an explosion of air as the thing disappeared among the trees.

Somehow he couldn't help but feel that he owed his continued ability to draw breath more to a native Goddess than to his divine Fortuna and Nemesis, for all their power and personal connections.

'Wait 'til I tell Ullio about this!'

* * * * *

Atuatuca had changed somewhat since their previous visit. Even from across the valley, Fronto had been able to see the damage that had been wreaked upon the oppidum. Never had it more closely resembled its namesake - the Aduatuca of that eponymous tribe which had been removed entire from the face of history four years ago. The defences were low and crumbled and darkened by ash.

The journey up the sloping path had been carried out in silence. Even the most ardent Roman could not help but be affected by the air of hopeless loss and sadness emanating from Ullio, though his expression remained harsh and grim. Yet another example of Caesar's wrath being visited upon the Eburones. Much more of this and they would see the last of the hunter, Fronto was sure. When Fronto had returned to the camp following the discovery of Drusus' body, and breathlessly revealed what had happened with the boar, even Aurelius' ramblings about the 'demon Goddess' had been shushed by the rest while they listened. Ullio had simply nodded once, sharing a knowing look with Samognatos, and then affirmed his intention to stay with them for now. Though he'd not once explained his reasoning, Fronto was sure he'd seen the incident with the boar as clear sanction from Arduenna.

And so he was still with them, though he spent increasing time with the Condrusi scout away from the Romans - especially Aurelius, who jumped at the slightest thing and continually took the Goddess' name in vain, despite Fronto's orders to the contrary.

Now, the two natives - hunter and scout - crested the rise and moved towards the fallen walls of the Eburone stronghold. Behind them, the singulares and their commander moved towards the defences, eyeing the destruction with shallow breaths. Whichever of the Roman columns had come through here had been thorough. The walls were less than a man high in most places, crumbled and blackened and tumbled inwards or outwards. Through the wide gaps they could see the charred skeletons of houses, ebony timbers pointing accusingly at the Gods from piles of ash and rubble. Even the dust of the streets was black.

The sounds of a thriving settlement were entirely absent. No animal noises, no children. No trade or manufacture. Nothing. Just the noises of the carrion birds feeding and fighting over the choicest morsels and the sound of a shocked few who had survived.

Those handful of Eburones were at work outside the gates. It was a manufacturing process of the most grisly sort. A few soot-stained men were gathering up the dead and placing them on pyres to render down to ash - pyres which were being constructed by another group from the remaining timbers of the town. Blackened patches with piles of ash around the extramural grass marked the sites of burned down pyres, and a number were in various stages of burning and collapse or embers gradually cooling. Womenfolk were gathering up the cold ash from the finished pyres and scooping it into wine jars and earthenware pots. Others were cutting out shallow pits and carefully laying the jars on an easterly alignment, placing a few charred possessions alongside and then filling in the holes. The sheer number of fresh earth-and-turf mounds spoke volumes as to the death-count of the battle.

'Caesar takes his vows seriously,' muttered Palmatus as they moved towards the silent, grisly workers.

'This wasn't Caesar. This was Labienus showing mercy.'

'Mercy?' Masgava said in a tone of disbelief.

'No crucifixions. Quick deaths. Only Labienus would afford the Eburones that mercy.'

They fell silent as they moved among the crow-black funeral workers.

'You,' Fronto said, not unkindly, to one of the men who had paused and straightened to rub his sore back. The man looked at them and Fronto saw no fear and no anger in his eyes. No life, in truth. The man replied in his own language, and the Roman glanced over at his two natives scouts. Paying him no heed, Ullio and Samognatos between them quizzed the weary, hopeless man, their voices heavy with sympathy. Fronto listened in hopefully and caught the name Ambiorix used three separate times by the local. He waited, trying to exude patience and sympathy, though he was twitching to know what they were discussing.

After a long exchange, Ullio stayed with the man and spoke soothingly to him, while Samognatos turned and strode over to Fronto, gesturing for them to move a respectful distance away from the burials. Fronto realised the presence of Romans among their victims was the worst insult they could have perpetrated, albeit entirely unintentionally.

The Condrusi scout's strange, permanent smile - the result, Fronto surmised, of some ancient facial injury - seemed horribly out of place in this mass burial and land of the lost, but despite the grin, the scouts eyes were dark with distaste.

'You know I wish this had worked out another way,' Fronto said quietly.

'I know.'

'And it could have been so much worse. Those in *Caesar's* path will be suffering so much more.'

'I know.'

Fronto sighed. 'What news, then?'

'We close on him,' Samognatos said in hushed tones. 'Two days ago Labienus' legions came here and it took but half a day for them to reduce the place to rubble. The man said the nobles refused to surrender or even speak of Ambiorix. Now those nobles are gone, and with them almost all their people.'

'Go on.'

'The survivors returned to the oppidum yesterday morning, once it was certain that the Roman column had moved safely on, and began the process of gathering and tending to the dead. As the light was failing last night and they were finishing up for the day,

Ambiorix passed through with a small retinue of warriors. Apparently there was a bit of a scuffle. A few of the locals took exception to their king's presence, after what the Romans had done to them for his resistance. They managed to kill one of Ambiorix's men and wound another, but these men were true warriors and half a dozen locals joined their dead kin before Ambiorix moved on.'

Fronto took a deep breath. 'We're only half a day behind him now. He can't be more than ten miles away in these woods. So close I can almost smell his treachery.'

Samognatos nodded. 'I am not familiar with the terrain east of here, but Ullio says there is a valley that runs towards the Rhenus and opens out into wider, flatter land towards the edge of the great forest. That is the direction Ambiorix left, and it is the most direct route to the river. There can be little doubt now that the king is making to escape across the water and seek Germanic aid.'

'Then we have to get to him before he manages to reach that river. We need to speed up our travel.'

Samognatos nodded. 'There's more.'

'About Ambiorix?'

'No. Not more than an hour after Ambiorix passed through to the east, as the last light went, a huge warband of Germans passed through to the north.'

'Germans?'

The man thinks they were Sugambri, from across the Rhenus to the east. They are about the nearest of the tribes.'

Fronto shrugged. 'Caesar gave permission for other tribes to come and raid the Eburones. I don't like it any more than you, but the Sugambri have sworn oaths to Rome, and are here at Caesar's invitation.'

Samognatos shook his head. 'You misunderstand, Fronto. They're not raiding the Eburones. They're going north. North is out of the forest. We're not far from the flat lands now.'

'So where are they headed?' Fronto asked with a furrowed brow.

'There's no way to be certain,' Samognatos said quietly, 'but by my estimation, and Ullio's too, the road north from here leads to the camp where your legion was destroyed in the winter.'

'Sabinus and Cotta's camp?' Fronto frowned. 'What would they be going there for?'

'That's the other thing. Apparently, while nine of the legions are prowling these woods looking for Ambiorix, the other one is at that old camp, protecting all Caesar's baggage and wounded.'

Fronto felt his pulse quicken.

'Who's in command? Do we know?'

'They say it is the man the Eburones could not kill.'

'Cicero, then. You say it was a *huge* warband?'

'The man said they filled the valley from side to side. Must be every warrior the Sugambri could muster.'

'Gods help Cicero, then. Let's hope he's fortified himself.'

'Should we not send warning?' Samognatos asked quietly.

'No point. The Sugambri would probably be there before our man. Besides, he'd have to go round the Germans to get there. Anyway, now that we know Ambiorix has a party of warriors with him, I'm loathe to release any of our men in case we need them. We'll just have to hope the poor bastard's on top form. He's held a camp against an army around here before.'

* * * * *

Baculus sat up in his sick cot. He was still feeling unwell, though his strength was returning daily now, and his flesh was considerably pinker than it had been. The medicus had even sanctioned him going for a twice-daily constitutional, as long as he stuck to gentle exercise and did nothing stupid.

Time for a walk, he decided, listening to the tell-tale sounds of a force preparing to march. Standing, he used his stick to straighten, more from habit than out of necessity, and walked slowly but steadily from the room.

The camp was sizeable. When they'd arrived a week ago, they'd been surprised to find the defences still of good quality. It had been a simple matter of cutting back the nearest woods to rebuild the palisade and the internal buildings. Cicero had also constructed two large enclosures, each surrounded by equally strong defences, effectively quadrupling the size of the fort in preparation for the arrival of the rest of the army.

The hospital complex was a large one, having taken in the wounded from every legion while their healthy comrades campaigned in the great forest, but Baculus was still the most senior officer within the complex, and ruled the roost of the sick and damaged as though they were a working cohort. Nothing happened in the complex without his knowledge and permission, despite the medicus' exasperation.

Striding from the door and between the small orderlies' quarters, he left the hospital zone and emerged in the open space used currently as a parade ground and muster point within the walls. The camp was larger than necessary for its current occupants, and Caesar's orders - given to Cicero in detail on a tablet - had stated with no margin for misinterpretation that he was under no circumstances to place the legion in jeopardy, and that all forces should remain in camp until the army returned by the kalends of Quintilis. A brief exception had been made upon arrival in order to gather the timber for the camp's fortifications, but after that time, even parades had been carried out within the ramparts.

Why, then, Baculus pondered, were there several cohorts of men forming up in full kit?

He briefly ran through his days in the hospital bed, wondering if he'd missed a day or two somewhere? No. The kalends was tomorrow.

His eyes picked out Cicero standing on the raised timber platform at the far side with two tribunes, and, the twitch beneath his left eye starting up once again, Baculus walked slowly around the mustering men, closing on the podium.

Cicero was in deep conversation with the tribunes as he stomped up the steps and stopped in front of them. After a few moments of clearing his throat meaningfully, the legate looked up in surprise.

'Baculus, isn't it? From the Twelfth? Thought you were removed from duties?'

Baculus saluted gingerly and nodded. 'Yes sir. Heard all the commotion and thought I'd come see what was happening?'

'Well, centurion, it appears that our supplies are running dangerously low. I have authorised a forage party to scour the local countryside and settlements and refill our stores.'

'Sir?'

'Hard of hearing, centurion?'

Baculus frowned. Labienus he'd got to know, and would take that kind of comment from, as he knew he still commanded the man's respect. This armoured politician, on the other hand, was looking at him as though he'd crawled out from under a rock.'

'*Respect*fully, sir,' he replied, stressing the syllables as though he might push them through that decorative bronze cuirass

337

and make them part of the legate, 'Caesar's orders were specific. I was there when they were read out. No leaving the fort until the army arrives on the kalends.'

Cicero's face fell stony and the man gave Baculus a hard look.

'Tomorrow *is* the Kalends, centurion.'

'Yes sir. And *respect*fully, today is not.'

Cicero bridled, but the senior, broad-striped tribune beside him looked distinctly uncomfortable and Baculus realised he had an ally there. The man cleared his throat. 'Perhaps, legate, for the sake of one day…?'

Cicero rounded on his officer.

'Yes, tribune, we have the supplies to last 'til the kalends. Possibly even an extra day or more. But think beyond today. The forest of Arduenna is huge. There is every likelihood that the army will be considerably delayed in returning… if they haven't run into trouble and been slaughtered within its mass! We might be sitting here for weeks yet, awaiting their arrival. Just because the general said they'd be back tomorrow does not mean they *will* be. *Anything* might happen. And what do we do if we fail to replenish supplies and then we find ourselves under siege? What if the Belgae take exception to us and try to repeat their successes of last winter? How long do you think we will hold them off with enough supplies to feed the men four meals each?'

The tribune fell silent, though he was clearly still unhappy. Cicero turned to Baculus again.

'And the sick, I might add, are a *huge* drain on supplies and resources.'

'We'll try to be less sick and wounded for you, sir.'

'That's *enough* of that kind of talk!' snapped Cicero. 'I have here Caesar's baggage train and I will not let it or the wounded fall into enemy hands. It's *one* day. We need to be fully stocked with vittles. What use is a supply train of weapons, equipment and booty if we starve protecting it. The forage party will only be going a few miles and will return before dark. Five cohorts can look after themselves without the walls for a few hours. Stop panicking, centurion, and get back to your cot, where you belong.'

Baculus' eyes widened and his twitch jumped more and more below the left lid.

'*Five* cohorts, sir? That's half the bloody legion!'

'Watch your tongue when you address me, centurion,' snapped Cicero.

'There's always the civilian sutlers, sir,' threw in the senior tribune, and shrunk back as the legate cast a look of daggers at him.

'What?' Baculus frowned.

'The natives have set up outside the ditches in the hope of selling us the goods,' Cicero sneered.

'Then *buy* them from them!' Baculus suggested in amazement.

'Their prices are extortionate, and they are merchants from tribes we have already beaten this year in campaigns. I am not about to take the hard-won booty from Caesar's wagons and give it back to the men from whom we took it in the first damn place.'

'We could just *take* it from them, sir?' suggested the junior tribune.

The other tribune, Cicero and Baculus all turned to the young man, shaking their heads. 'It would violate Caesar's peace agreements,' Cicero said quietly. 'But I won't put coin in their pockets,' he added, turning back to Baculus with a flinty gaze.'

'*I'll* stand the damned cost, sir,' Baculus growled, 'if you'll just buy from them.'

'You?' Cicero laughed.

'You might be surprised how much I could scrape up, legate.'

'Get back to your sick bed, centurion,' Cicero glowered at him. 'If you are still here when I have counted to ten, I will give your cot to someone deserving and have you escorted instead to the stockade. That is a final order.'

'Legate...'

'One.'

'This is endangering...'

'Two.'

'Caesar will...'

'Three.'

Throwing a sour look at the legate, Baculus turned with a rough salute and marched off down the steps and around the gathering forces on the parade ground.

'Moron!' he grunted as he strode back to the barracks, wondering where his full kit was stored. He had the horrible feeling it might be needed soon.

* * * * *

Galronus reined in his horse and gestured for the cavalry prefects to join him. Among their number and wearing a bleak, sour face, was Basilus.

'What do you make of that?' he asked. The prefects peered off into the bright landscape.

'Looks like cavalry,' one of them said quietly. Galronus rolled his eyes at the man. 'I too am capable of counting legs and dividing by four. I know *what* they are, but *who* are they, do you think?'

'Natives,' Basilus said quietly, his voice broken and lost.

Galronus nodded. 'Belgae, I would say. But I think I can see Roman banners. Anyone confirm or deny that for me?'

One of the others, squinting, straightened with a nod. 'That's the vexillum of the Twelfth, sir.'

'You've got damn sharp eyes,' Galronus said with a smile. 'But I think you're right. Them or the Thirteenth, anyway. Let's go see what's happening with them.'

The cavalry raised their own Roman vexilla to display their allegiance and began to move down the slope at the woods' edge, on a course to intercept the second column, which was perhaps half the size of Galronus' force. As they descended, the other column paused, taking time to identify them, and then changed heading towards the slope.

Reining in a few hundred paces away, the commander of the second force saluted, and Galronus returned the gesture, coming to a halt alongside him.

'Gaius Volusenus Quadratus, officer commanding cavalry of the Twelfth, Ninth and Thirteenth legions.

'Galronus. Commander of the Second wing and various associated units. Where are you bound, Quadratus.'

'Cicero's camp,' the Roman smiled wearily. 'For the love of Venus, it's good to see you.'

Galronus answered with a frown and an encouraging nod.

'I know: we're heading the wrong way. Problem is, we *were* heading north ahead of the infantry to let the legate know that the army was inbound, when our path was blocked by the biggest force of Germans I've seen in years, all heading north and singing battle songs. Too many for us to take on, so we skirted round them. I was hoping to get to Cicero and warn him they were coming, but they

340

move fast, these buggers, and I'm sure they'll be there well ahead of us.'

'We're on our way to hook up with the army, too,' Galronus nodded. 'Seems like our forces just joined. Let's see if we can get to Cicero before the Germans. Hope his ditches are deep and his walls high.'

Quadratus nodded and turned to his musicians and signifers. 'Send the orders. We move at speed for the camp.'

Chapter Eighteen

Camp of the Fourteenth Legion.

Lucius Primillus yawned and leaned on the palisade top, his eyes locked on the swathe of darkened grass that lay between the fort's multiple ditches and the treeline and its array of dull, dun-coloured tents with braziers and flickering campfires. The intermittent moonlight, dusted by constant drifting shrouds in the night sky, and combined with the sutlers' firelight, played tricks on the eyes. He had become sick of second-checking the shadows that appeared to be moving demons and flitting shapes, but were simply moon or fire light, interrupted and eerie.

He was tired.

By his reckoning, he was not fit for duty. Dragged from his sick cot by the watch centurion, he'd initially been grateful to be away from the miserable, sarcastic Primus Pilus who'd been convalescing next to him seemingly forever, but now he was standing at the wall, he realised just how weak he really still was. And his bowels ached.... Oh *how* his bowels ached!

The legate, Cicero, had sent out half the legion on foraging duty and, because of the manpower limits imposed upon him, had been through the hospital lists like... like... like whatever it was that had been going though Primillus' guts for the past few weeks. He'd selected a large number of the convalescent - some said *two thirds* of the sick list - and overridden the medicus' outrage, splitting the men into two groups to supplement both the forage party and the fort's guards.

The legate had been around the walls an hour ago, at sunset, fuming that his foragers were still out there and should have been back before dark. But Primillus had seen the state of the countryside and its native settlements when they first pulled in, and every sensible man knew the forage party would have their work cut out to find much of use without going a good distance. Primillus didn't expect to see them until the morning at least, but the legate had pushed himself into an unpleasant corner. Tomorrow was when Caesar and the army were set to return, and if the general returned to find only half the legion in residence, there was a general feeling that Cicero's balls might well end up hanging from the gate top.

His watery, weary gaze strayed back towards the ditches and the tents of the civilian sutlers and merchants who had set up their stores outside the defences. Could he persuade the optio at the gate to let him sneak out? He'd smelled the roasted lamb from their tents at sunset and would give not only every coin in his purse for a plate of it, but probably a limb or two. No. The optio was under orders like the rest of them. No trading with the natives when the forage party would return with extra supplies.

Ha!

Still, his bowels would probably make him regret roasted lamb pretty sharply.

His gaze fell upon the flickering shadows cast by the moon's light playing among the trees and civilian tents.

Although tents and trees tended not to move. He frowned and turned. Gemellus, ten paces to his right, looked every bit as bored as he.

'Gaius? Can you see…?'

He blinked, interrupted, as Gaius Gemellus was suddenly lifted from his feet by the force of a spear blow and hurled from the wall down the inner bank, the thrown weapon impaling him and jutting from his chest. Primillus turned, eyes wide, in time to see another spear arcing up towards him and dropped behind the palisade just in time, the shaft passing over him and clattering down inside the camp. He lifted his head so that his gaze peeked through the narrow gap between helmet brim and pointed stake tops.

His wide eyes strained and bulged as he watched the barbarians on their shaggy horses pouring from the forest edge, behind them a sea of men on foot, waving axes, swords and spears. The bulk of the horsemen were making for the decumana gate and its causeway across the ditches, while a few of their confederates rode for the sutlers' tents.

'Shit! To arms!' He cleared his throat and tried to project his voice more. 'Alarm! To arms!'

It was largely unnecessary. Other men on watch had seen them now, and whistles, horns and shouts rang out across the camp. Primillus stared at the mass of men swarming around the camp in both directions. It was like a nightmare.

The call went up from the decumana gate nearby, and Primillus realised he would be more use there than here. Three ditches stood between the enemy and this rampart, but the cavalry were already making their way across the causeway for the gate, and the duty optio was shouting for support.

Turning, shield and pilum in hand, he ran along the wall top, keeping his head as low as possible, though he took the opportunity to peek out and check what was happening as he moved. The scene was horrific. Whoever the attackers were, they clearly were not Nervii, Eburone or Menapii, as the sutlers who had gathered from those tribes were the first to suffer, the horsemen slashing down at tent ropes and collapsing them, then cutting down anyone who attempted to flee. As the footmen arrived behind them, they took torches from the various cooking fires before the tents and used them to ignite the makeshift trade settlement. Poor bastards. The survivors were fleeing into the ditches and for the gate, but they would find no solace there. The watch guard was hardly going to open up the camp in the face of an enemy force to help a few natives.

Already, as Primillus reached the gate, the attackers were pounding on the timbers with axes and hammers, those with spears jabbing up at the parapet, their horses dancing this way and that, guided with inexpert hands. These men were not the natural horsemen that summed up the spirit of Gaul.

Germans, Primillus decided, looking at them. He'd fought Germans on a few occasions over the army's time in Gaul. Finding a couple of feet of unoccupied gate top, Primillus took up position and began to jab down with this pilum into the mass of riders milling without, striking flesh and armour repeatedly, though unsure in the press whether it was man or horse he was striking. The effect of either was equally valuable.

As he fought, his suspicions about his state of health reasserted themselves and his bowels gave liquid way into his woollen underwear. He should not have been out of the damned hospital! Ignoring his medical issues, he continued to jab down again and again, watching horses rearing in agony, throwing their riders into the press to be trampled to death. Men were pierced and run through, some wounded and lucky enough to pull back through the mass and into the open ground beyond. The first rider to do so immediately fell foul of a pilum thrown from one side of the gate.

In a matter of twenty heartbeats it was over.

The riders, unable in their initial rush to overcome the gate guard, pulled back out of danger, where the rest of their army, still arriving from the forest, were spreading out to surround the large, poorly-defended camp. The last few to leave the causeway suffered for their tardiness, pila cast by panicked and angry legionaries taking them in their retreating backs. In fact, pila were being cast with gay abandon. Unlike food, they were one thing the camp had in almost infinite supply!

The churned turf and mud of the causeway beneath the gate thronged with bodies writhing in pain, both men and horses, the screams and cries echoing out through the night. The ditches to either side were filled with enemy men and horses who had toppled in and with native traders, some dead, others wounded, a few still hale and pleading desperately for the legionaries to haul them up onto the walls. Even as Primillus felt the familiar post-fight leaden heaviness settle into his limbs, he watched those poor souls crying for help as they fell one by one to thrown German spears or loosed arrows and sling stones.

'Jove, what happened to you?' the optio hissed as he moved along the gate checking his men and reached Primillus.

'Bowel rot, sir. Brought from hospital for wall duty.'

'For the love of Venus get away from my gate and wash yourself down!'

'Sir,' Primillus sighed with relief, but the officer grasped his shoulder. 'Are you empty now?'

'Damn well hope so, sir.'

'Then as soon as you're washed and stink-free, get to the supply wagons and oversee the distribution of extra pila around the walls.'

Primillus sagged. A momentary image of his sick bed had floated tantalisingly in front of him before being whipped away again.

'And try not to shit yourself on duty again, soldier, or I might decide to plug your arse shut with a hob-nailed boot.'

Primillus saluted and scurried off towards the latrines with their buckets of cleansing water and the sponge sticks. It very much appeared, given the Germanic voices raised around the camp's periphery, that this evening's fight was far from over.

* * * * *

Baculus stomped around the hospital ward angrily.

'Orderly? Where is my vine staff?'

'I've no idea, sir.'

'When I find it I'm going to use it to teach you wastrels a lesson in looking after important property. I left it with the rest of my gear. Help me get this bloody harness on.'

345

The orderly scurried over to the dressed and armoured senior centurion and helped him fasten on the leather harness draped with torcs and phalera. Still pale and unhealthy-looking, Baculus had been forbidden any kind of hard exercise by the medicus, but that hardly mattered now that the man was busy setting up his hospital for the inevitable influx of wounded, the orderlies rushing around obeying the man's commands.

Even from here, if they paused and listened, they could hear the howling and baying of the enemy outside the walls. Baculus drew his gladius, nodding his satisfaction at the oiled hiss as the well-kept blade came free.

'Is this wise, Sir?'

'Just get back to counting bandages,' Baculus snapped and turned, fully equipped and ready, if a little wobbly on his feet, just as the sick ward door opened.

He took a few tottering steps forward as half a dozen legionaries limped in.

'Where are you lot going?'

The man at the front of the small group stopped in surprise, his eyes widening at the sight of the senior centurion before him.

'Sir?'

'I said: where are you lot going, soldier?'

'Sick-listed, sir. We were all consigned to the sick huts and the duty centurion let us go when Trebulus back there threw up on his foot. We're all sick, sir.'

'You seem to have the requisite number of limbs and you're walking a sight easier than me,' Baculus growled. 'I'll give you the count of three to turn on your heel and get back out there to the camp walls before I test just how much strength I have beating the shit out of half a dozen shirkers!'

'But sir?'

'*Now!*' bellowed Baculus glaring at them and underlining the word with a sword-waving gesture.

The legionaries, suddenly finding themselves a lot more hale and hearty than they'd reckoned a moment ago, turned and hurried out of the hospital. Baculus watched them go and glanced over his shoulder at the orderly. 'Anyone else malingering needs to go to the wall. I will hold you responsible if we're undermanned and I later find out there were men here abed who could stand and wield a sword.'

Without waiting for a retort from the medical staff, who were always outspoken and believed they outranked everyone bar the Gods, Baculus stomped out into the camp wishing he had his vine staff for his free hand.

Chaos appeared to be reigning in the fort. With no apparent organisation, men were everywhere, some huddled in the shelter of the granaries, where a small altar to Mars stood, throwing wine and offerings onto the hollowed top and casting up desperate prayers. Others ran back and forth, apparently randomly. A couple of men seemed to be loading a pack animal with bags.

At least the six he'd chastised were now making for the rampart. With a deep grumbling breath, Baculus stomped over to the men with the donkey.

'What, pray, are you two men doing?'

'Preparing to fall back, sir!'

'What? Why?'

'Centurion's orders, sir. They say Caesar's army has been defeated and now the tribes have come to finish us off.'

'Do they indeed?'

'Centurion wants the unit money chests and the standards secured to leave, sir.'

'Does he? Did he tell you how he intended to retreat, given that, from a simple check with my ears, it appears that the camp is surrounded?'

'Dunno, sir. We just…'

Baculus grasped the man by the scruff of the neck, bunched up his tunic in his fist and dragged the man forward until their noses almost touched.

'Get back to the wall and leave the donkey. Draw a sword and shield and kill some of those bastards.'

'But sir…'

'If the enemy don't kill you, I might consider it myself.' His hand went meaningfully to his sword hilt and the two legionaries saluted hurriedly in a panic.

'And when you speak to your centurion, tell that cowardly turd that when this is over, Baculus, Primus Pilus of the Twelfth Legion, would like to see him in the headquarters.'

Ignoring the two men as they ran off, leaving the donkey looking faintly bored and tethered to the wall, Baculus turned and picked out the men at the altar.

'I think Mars is probably honoured enough, now.'

The men turned to see the senior centurion and saluted.

'Well?'

'Sir?'

'Why are you still here?'

'Sir, this place is cursed. We have to invoke Mars continually, because…'

'Cursed?'

'Yessir. Cotta and Sabinus, Sir. The Fourteenth died here to a man, sir, and the place is full of restless spirits. Now it's *our* turn.'

'No one is dying here without my permission!' Baculus snapped.

'The Gods, sir?'

'Mars has been honoured enough, soldier. And no amount of divine favour compares to shields and swords up on that wall, now return to duty before I start laying about me.'

'But sir…'

'*To the walls!*' Baculus yelled, so close and angry that flecks of spittle hit the man in the face. As the men scurried off, Baculus paused. He could hear the sound of a native charge, all 'dying-ox' music and screaming, outside the Praetorian gate. His eyes picked out an optio who seemed to be a man after his own heart, standing in the mud at the camp's centre, grabbing soldiers who ran this way and that in a panic and issuing commands to them.

Striding over, Baculus stopped in front of the officer.

'Good work. I don't want to see a single man in this whole fort who is not busy on an assigned task or at the walls. No shirking or panicking.'

The optio saluted with a professional smile, and Baculus found himself starting to calm down. 'Direct things here, but I need your shield.'

The optio without question handed over the curved shield, emblazoned with Caesar's Taurus and the rearing horse over an 'X' that the Tenth Legion had affected since their arrival in Gaul. The Tenth? Then this optio was also officially on the sick list. Good man, to be out and doing his duty regardless. Grappling the shield, Baculus staggered a little, still weak, under the weight, and then jogged off towards the west gate, where the renewed sounds of battle were rising into the night air.

Rounding the last building and heading for the gate, Baculus found his heart almost in his mouth. Whoever was in charge of manning the walls was doing a poor job. There were maybe a dozen men around the gate top and another half dozen on the walls to either side. His ears strained over the noise and he could hear the tell-tale sounds of scorpion bolts being released up in the towers, but his experienced, professional ear could only pick out two sources, while there were four towers from which the weapons could be brought to bear. Sure enough, as he looked up, approaching the scene, only two of the towers showed any sign of occupancy. A legionary, leaning on his shield, his leg sheeted with blood, was busy giving out orders as though he held rank, and Baculus naturally made for him.

'You in charge here, soldier?'

'Yessir,' the legionary said, bending to pull the tourniquet on his leg tighter, staunching the blood flow.

'Where's your officer?'

'No idea, sir. He muttered something about supplies and pissed off a while ago, sir.'

Baculus shook his head in disbelief.

'Consider this a field promotion, optio. Get runners sent to any barracks where the men are still not engaged. We need a full artillery crew in each tower, with support and any missile troops you can dig up. And I want ten times this number of men up on the wall.'

'Yes sir,' the soldier nodded emphatically. 'If I'd had the authority…'

'You've got it now. Invoke the name Baculus, Primus Pilus of the Twelfth and get everything you need.'

'Yes sir.'

Leaving the soldier to his tasks, Baculus laboured up the steps to the wall, watching the timber gates bowing alarmingly and the locking bar straining as the four men there threw precious grain sacks behind the leaves of the gate to impede the attempts to break in.

Atop the wall things were already becoming desperate. The sparse defenders were fighting off a large force who were jabbing up with spears, the walls to either side of the gate kept clear by an almost constant rain of sling stones and arrows from the enemy, forcing the legionaries to hunker down behind the parapet and their shields. The ditches would protect the wall areas for now, but with the causeways across the gates were weak points, especially while undermanned and with inadequate artillery crews.

Baculus paused, wondering for a moment whether he really was strong enough for this. Taking a deep breath and trying not to shake, he clambered out onto the wall top and hurried to the gate

349

area. A quick glance over the side brought home just how dangerous the situation was. The enemy out there - Germans by both the look and the sound of it - must outnumber the camp's garrison by perhaps five to one, and that was including the absent forage party. More like *ten* to one with them gone. They could be in trouble.

The men outside the gate were infantry, the cavalry having failed in their initial assault and having pulled back to wait out the next hour or two. Men with spears jabbed up at the defenders, forcing the legionaries to duck back out of the way, while others were busy bringing forth the wreckage of what must have been sutlers' stores and using it as a rubble ramp to give them easier access to the walls. Much longer and they'd have a slope up the outside to rival the earth bank on the inside. They had, cunningly, left a narrow gap in their makeshift bank so that their heaviest, hardiest brutes could smash and batter at the gates, in case they could break through that way, forcing the meagre defenders to divide their numbers between top and bottom.

'They'll be on us any moment, sir,' a struggling legionary shouted, seeing the welcome sight of a centurion appear among them.

'They will if that ramp gets any higher.' He turned, looking down on the newly-raised optio with the leg wound. 'Get me four men, a barrel of water, two buckets, a pot of pitch and two torches,' he bellowed.

The man nodded, giving out the orders, and the legionary near Baculus frowned. 'Sir?'

As soon as they get here, if I'm busy, get the gates thoroughly soaked with water and keep soaking them. Tip the pitch on that pile of broken lumber they're building and fire it. Elseways they'll be on the wall top before you'd have time to shit.'

'Dunno about that, sir. Pretty close to shittin' myself now!'

Baculus laughed and stepped to the wall. A spear lanced up at him and he ducked to the side, throwing up the shield and then swiping down, narrowly missing severing the spear's tip. Even as he drew back, another spear danced up at him and a sling stone glanced off his crest holder, jerking his helmet back and ripping out horsehair on its journey.

Despite the fact that each legionary on the gate top was already as busy as possible, fighting off the dancing points of the enemy spears, the attack had suddenly redoubled in strength at the sight of a centurion's crest. Such a prize, for an enemy warrior!

Another spear lanced past and Baculus managed to trap this one against the wall with his shield, leaning his weight on it until he heard the spear shaft snap and saw two feet of ash with an iron leaf-head fall back inside the wall. Taking the opportunity to glance over the parapet, Baculus felt his heart thump as the nearest warrior leapt, the fingers of his left hand catching the wall top as his right came around with an axe. The ramp was almost high enough.

He ducked to one side as the axe swung through the open air above the parapet, and then smashed down with the bronze edging of his shield onto the fingers wrapped around the timber top, smashing them to a pulp. The warrior screamed, falling away from the wall, but there were already other fingers grasping and an increasing number of bodies at the wall. Concentrating on them, Baculus failed to see the next spear thrust which came from his right until it was too late. Abruptly, he turned his head, hoping the wide, flared neck guard of his helmet would catch the blow, but the spear bounced off the steel, beneath the open ear hole, and ripped into the side of his neck, tearing muscle and tendon and spraying the inside of his helmet with hot blood. He staggered backwards, dropping his shield, his hand going up to clutch at his neck even while he swung with his sword, trying to knock that spear away. Barbarians were all over the wall top now, trying to climb.

'Capsarius!' someone shouted helpfully, spotting Baculus staggering, a torrent of blood pouring from his helmet and soaking his mail.

Ignoring them, trying to staunch the arterial flow with his hand pressing his scarf against the huge rent, Baculus moved to the wall again, swinging with his blade and smashing the nose of the first man he saw, cleaving his face horizontally. He could feel himself weakening again; refused to submit.

The legionary off to his right gave a blood-curdling shriek as a spear slammed into his face, driving home until the point cracked the back of his skull from the inside.

A sword swept at Baculus and he cut down with his own blade, severing the attacker's arm at the wrist, but not before the blow had smashed a deep cut into his arm, sending broken mail links and slices of leather pteruge flying through the air. Baculus grunted at the pain, though it was considerably less than the wound in his neck. His body was weakening fast and his reaction time slowing and he knew it. He had moments left, and was a goner after that.

Another man appeared, clambering over the wall and Baculus jabbed at him with his gladius. The blow struck home, but merely knocked the man back off the wall, such was the apparent weakness in the centurion's arm.

He saw death rise from the mass, a large sword held in both hands in an overhead chop aimed at him. It was something of a relief, really, after so long lying in a sick bed, to at least die actively, and he almost thanked the German warrior as the sword came down. The blow was at full reach, even given the height of the ramp, but there would be enough blade and enough force in it to split Baculus' shoulder even if it glanced off his helm. But it would probably cleave straight through the steel and bronze, such was the length and weight of the native swords in the north.

Baculus winced as the blow came, feeling the slowing of the blood at his neck.

Nothing happened.

He opened his eyes in surprise to see the man with the heavy sword hurtling away from him, screaming, sword still raised, and realised belatedly that an artillery bolt had smashed into his would-be-killer's chest. Glancing up and left, Baculus saw the previously empty tower filling with men as the scorpion sought its next target.

He fell, but a legionary was suddenly there grasping him, holding him up. Then another, bearing the leather satchel of a capsarius. 'Hold still, centurion and don't move that neck.'

Feeling faint and weak, Baculus gave a low cackle as he saw the Germans, on the cusp of victory climbing over the wall top, suddenly repulsed by the relief force who now flooded onto the rampart. He could smell the tell-tale acrid odour of pitch and see the glow of orange torches. The sound of a huge barrel of water being hauled up the bank accompanied it.

'I said stay still. This is bad, centurion, and if you want to live to shout at, beat, and belittle legionaries, you need to do exactly as I say.' Too tired to argue, Baculus allowed himself to relax, the sword falling from his fingers. The newly field-promoted optio with the bandaged, bloody leg appeared in front of him.

'All under control now, centurion. Thanks for your timely help.'

Baculus passed out.

* * * * *

Nasica, rare survivor of the Fourteenth Legion's demise under Sabinus and Cotta during the winter, and now proud eagle-bearer of the same, reconstituted legion, leaned in and added his voice to the discussion. He was aware that the aquilifer held a rank that equalled most centurions, but wasn't yet sure just how much he was expected to chip in to officers' confabs.

The simple fact, though, was that not one officer here could hold a candle to any of those he'd served with over the past few years. They seemed to be indecisive and cautious, timid even. Especially the Primus Pilus, an ageing former training centurion from the camp at Cremona who'd not seen active service in almost a decade.

'They will not be expecting an attack from their rear, sir,' he said quietly.

The forage party, led by some of the legion's senior officers, had been exceedingly late and there had been some discussion about the possibility of setting up a temporary camp for the night. It had taken some persuading by the more veteran centurions to get the Primus Pilus to march the wagons through the night rather than waiting for the dawn, and the senior commander had only seemed to be swayed by the notion that Cicero would be extremely unhappy with him if they returned to find Caesar had beaten them to the camp.

And so the five cohorts, with their accompanying wagons tended by the walking wounded, had pushed on back through the dark, past midnight and into black morning in an attempt to reach the camp before the infamous 'kalends deadline'. Then, only half a mile from the camp, they had stopped, the scouts returning wild-eyed to inform them that the camp was surrounded by a huge barbarian force.

The Primus Pilus had dissolved into a mess, displaying the warning signs of panic, and Nasica's already low opinion of his new commander had plummeted to subterranean depths.

'You advocate an attack?' the commander asked him incredulously.

'Not an all-out assault, sir,' Nasica replied patiently. 'We could form into a wedge and break through. A five-cohort wedge is a solid, unstoppable force, sir.' He remembered momentarily how long the centurion had remained idle in Cremona. 'I've seen it done very effectively over the past few years, sir.'

353

'Didn't help you much in the winter, did it?' the man snapped acidly, and Nasica had to fight to maintain his temper. This cowardly idiot was his superior after all - at least in rank!

'Sir, if we do nothing, the camp will fall. The defenders are not numerous enough to cover all the walls. The fort's huge, especially with all its annexes. A whole legion stands a chance, but only if we combine our cohorts with those inside. We have to give a warning to the fort, form up and break through the bastards and make for the walls. The decumana gate is the best, with the widest causeway. I know, sir. I dug the bloody thing myself last year.'

The Primus Pilus glared at him, and Nasica felt hopelessly outnumbered by the armies of incompetence. His eyes strayed, and he could see several of the lesser centurions, as well as a few signifers and musicians nodding their agreement. He had support, just not from the top ranks.

'The rest of the army will be back soon, aquilifer, and then this rabble will die beneath the boots of ten legions.'

'Nine,' Nasica corrected angrily, 'because the Fourteenth will be gone! *Again!*'

'An assault is suicidal,' the commander declared, straightening. 'We will form up on that hill to the west. It is a good, defensive high point. The enemy will have to split their forces and deal with us as well as the camp. Thus we can survive the night and draw some of the heat for the legate.'

Nasica squared up to his commander. 'Respectfully, you will draw the heat from him for about quarter of an hour. After that all you'll do is occupy the carrion birds until the sun's up.'

The Primus Pilus stared at him, eyes bulging and his face turning a faint puce colour. 'You, man, are on a charge, awaiting disciplinary measures. Hand that eagle and your blade to the centurion there.'

'With respect, stick it up your arse, sir. This eagle's almost fallen once and it ain't happening again. This bird will not fall into enemy hands. I am taking the poor bloody thing back to the fort.'

'You will surrender your weapon until this is over!'

'Make me, and I might just find a new fucking sheath for it, sir,' Nasica snapped and stepped a few feet away, to where a cornicen was watching with fiery defiance in his eyes. The man had nodded at every word Nasica said.

'Sound the wedge formation,' he ordered. The musician saluted and put the cornu to his lips.

'Belay that order!' spluttered the Primus Pilus, pointing angrily. 'Arrest that man.'

The cornicen blew the wedge order, and there was a strange pause as every centurion in the knot of officers looked at one another uncertainly.

'Up the hill!' bellowed the commander. 'Now!'

'Come on!' shouted one of the senior centurions, running over to Nasica and beckoning to his standard bearer. 'Get the men fell in for an attack… wedge formation. We'll take the tip.'

The Primus Pilus stared in disbelief, but rose imperious as several centurions flocked to him, shouting orders for their men to assemble and advance up the hill.

Nasica glanced over his shoulder as he began to give out commands to the men around him. A brief headcount gave him about two thirds of the officers, the rest rushing to toady to the Primus Pilus. Three cohorts, then. It would be enough. They would make the camp. 'Cornicen: as soon as we start to move, use that thing and let the legion know we're coming. For the decumana gate if you can. Then as soon as your call's done, fall in at the rear of the wedge as we pass. Once you blow that thing it'll not take long for the enemy to realise what's happening. And you don't want to be left out here for the crows like those poor bastards will be on the hill.'

* * * * *

'What about the carts?'

Nasica shook his head at the centurion.

'Screw the carts.'

'But the low supplies, man! If we're going back to be voluntarily under siege, we'll need all the grain we can get.'

'Look on the bright side,' Nasica sighed, 'a lot of men will die in the next few hours, so supplies will gradually stretch that much further.'

'But can we not…'

'Look: we can't form into a wedge to charge the enemy with ox carts among us. If you're worrying about getting hungry, go join that lot,' Nasica snapped, pointing at the two cohorts climbing the slope to their position on the crest of the hill. 'None of them are going to be worrying about empty bellies. They won't be around long enough.'

The centurion fell quiet and, turning, shouted his men into better order.

'Soon as we round those bushes, we'll be right on them. We're stupidly close. The only reason they've not noticed us behind them so far is that they've been making more noise than us in their attack. Soon as they hear the cornu and see us, they'll turn and try and present a solid wall. They won't have time. We run. No marching. No treble time or crap like that. Run, and run fast. Stay together as best you can, especially towards the front, but anyone who lags, trips, falls and the like will necessarily be left behind. We have to hit them hard and punch through before they have the chance to form up and prevent it.'

He glanced across at the cornicen and nodded. 'Now!'

The cornicen filled his lungs and began to blow calls into his curved horn, directed at the Fourteenth, using their specific commands, announcing a charge in wedge shape. There was little else he could do. There were no calls to demand the gate be opened, or tell them *which* gate, but a wedge call to charge from behind the enemy should indicate what was happening, and they could guess where from the call's direction. Emphatically, he repeated the call again and again as hard as he could.

Simultaneously, the wedge burst into life, haring forward across the shadowed grass, making for the beleaguered fort. They were close, which was a gift from the Gods, since with the pace they were moving at, they wouldn't be able to keep it up for long. A mere dozen footsteps and Nasica began to round the trees and the scrub bushes that poked out from beneath them, the fort lying directly ahead behind a seething mass of Germans.

Some were already facing his way, their attention drawn by the cornu calls, but most were intent on the fort. Moments later, two cohorts appeared from the treeline off to the side, marching up the bald slope to a crest that rose above the entire scene.

Nasica hoped he was right. Was sure he was. *Knew he was.*

Now, they were past the trees and hurtling towards the barbarians, who were starting to respond to this unforeseen threat. The men beside and behind him were pounding across the turf. It was a loose wedge. It had to be for the men to run so fast. But it would tighten automatically any moment now. The cornicen's calls had stopped, meaning that the man had fallen in with the wedge and was charging along with everyone else.

Nasica was not quite at the front, but behind and left of the lead centurion - the one who'd been concerned about the carts. As aquilifer he had only a small round shield, which was strapped to his arm rather than held to allow him the free hands for the eagle. As such, he could reasonably be assumed to be a weak point in the wedge. Except he was anything but. Keeping the eagle clutched tight in his right hand, he prepared for the sudden crushing pressure.

It came soon enough.

The front of the wedge hit the disorganised army of Germanic warriors while many of them were still unaware of the danger. A few had turned and fought hard, swinging swords and axes, lancing out with spears and swords. A few of them, displaying what seemed to Nasica unusually good sense, dived back out of the way, pushing into the throng of their own warriors so as not to be in front of the wedge.

The Germans were knocked aside, battered out of the way and even trampled under hob-nailed feet as the wedge drove deep into the mass with the momentum of running, furious, desperate men.

Nasica's world became a flashing kaleidoscope of scenes, his vision restricted by his helmet and the press of men: a sword swinging. A German's face exploding in carnage, teeth flying up into the air, shattered by a bronze shield boss. The centurion at the front jerking to the side as he stabbed a man and a counter strike took his arm off just below the elbow, his sword skittering away into the press, and yet the man pushing on with the single-mindedness of a centurion in battle. A barbarian looming. A man falling by the wayside, his leg maimed, as the waiting mob fell on him, hacking him to pieces.

But they were still moving well and gaining ground. Having only slowed to a heavy jog, they had covered half the ground to the gate.

'Come on!' he bellowed.

Suddenly hands were clawing at his small round shield, pulling him out of the formation. One of his assailants was afforded a heavy blow by the legionary behind, but the other clung on, snarling at him. Unable to do much else, Nasica let the heavy weight of the eagle pull the top of the staff in his hand to the right, bringing up the butt end to the left, where the shield-struggle was going on.

The two legionaries to his right shouted complaints at almost being brained with the legion's eagle, but he had it at the right angle

357

for a moment and jabbed with the iron spike used to drive the staff into the ground when needed. The point of the staff smashed into the barbarian's face, imploding flesh and bone, and wrapping round the haft. The grip on the shield fell away instantly, and Nasica yanked the weapon free as the ruined German fell back into the mass, righting his shield arm again, all while moving forward with the same momentum. With no little difficulty and a few curses from the legionaries to his right, he pushed the eagle proudly aloft once more.

The walls were so close now... so tantalisingly close. And yet the advance had slowed to a heavy tread at last, the Germans pushing back as best they could. Nasica wondered how many men they'd lost during the push. It didn't bear thinking about, but they'd have lost a lot more any other way.

A barbarian swung at him, lashing out with a blade, and he ducked, the tip swiping the crest holder from the helm of the man behind. And then that warrior was also lost in the chaos. Heartbeats passed with flashing gory blades, screams, the constant, pushing tread of the wedge and the occasional Latin curses of a man falling by the wayside.

And suddenly the world was clear and open. The one-armed centurion leading the wedge almost fell flat on his face as the press against him disappeared, his arm stump leaving a trail of blood behind him. Ahead - a blessed sight across the causeway - the decumana gate of the camp was opening, legionaries swarming around it and cheering them on.

Grinning like a lunatic, Nasica and the one-armed centurion led the reinforcements through and into the fort, the aquilifer coming to a halt next to the centurion, and saluting the optio commanding the gate, almost concussing himself with his small shield.

'Damnedest thing I've seen in a while, sir,' the optio grinned as three cohorts of men threw themselves with relief into the fort's interior.

Nasica sighed. 'Sadly it's not *all* of us.' Frowning, the optio followed Nasica and the wounded centurion as they climbed the bank to the rampart walk. As the Germans surged forward once again in the wake of the cohorts, the gate guards hurriedly pushed the timber leaves closed and dropped the heavy locking bar into place, piling the sacks and crates next to them.

The three men reached the wall top and crossed to the parapet, where Nasica peered out, surveying the landscape until he spotted the high, bald hill top and the mass of men gathered on it in a shield wall. As he frowned into the eye-watering, pre-dawn murk, a capsarius appeared from somewhere and began to work on the centurion, staunching the blood flow and examining the stump to see whether it could be sealed and patch-clipped or would require a more simple yet brutal cauterisation.

The duty optio followed Nasica's gaze and blinked as he saw a huge mass of Germans surging up the hill towards the small Roman defensive formation.

'Who's the poor bugger, sir?'

Nasica sighed and slumped a little. 'That is the Primus Pilus being bloody-minded, short-sighted, and suicidal. Idiot.'

'He'll not last long up there.'

'No.' Nasica straightened. 'But at least now we have in excess of eight cohorts we stand a chance of surviving the night, eh?'

* * * * *

Cicero stood, tired, his hands flat on the table before him, duty lists and sick lists and supply lists. Everything was lists! The senior officers of the legion, along with the Aquilifer of the Fourteenth, who apparently was being hero-worshipped by the men in the wake of his recent action, stood around the headquarters office sagging slightly.

'I need suggestions about the supplies, gentlemen. What are we going to do about food?'

'We've got sacks of bucellatum still on one of the carts. Found them during the night while looking for the scorpion bolts.'

The officers shared a look of distaste at the thought of the hard-tack biscuits used by legions on the march. They were emergency rations, no more. But they would do to keep the men alive for a while. About as nourishing as a horse turd, but filling in the short term.

'Well if that's what we have, then that's what they can eat.'

'Wish we could eat like the damn Germans, sir,' grumbled a centurion, earning himself a hard look. They had all stood at the walls at some point during the darkness and the first rays of the morning light and watched the barbarians outside the camp feasting on the goods they had taken from both the sutlers' stalls and the abandoned legionary forage carts.

Worse still had been watching them parade a grisly line of Roman heads on spear tops as they bounced around the camp. It had taken, as predicted, less than quarter of an hour for the barbarians to overcome the small force. Surrender at the end had gained them nothing, as the bargaining officers and men were beheaded and added to the Roman dead.

'We can last a matter of days, anyway. After that, we will have to look into the problem again. At least we seem to have the measure of them at the walls now.'

The men nodded. With the arrival of the three cohorts to bolster the defences, the enemy had settled into a siege, making only occasional forays to the gates or walls. It seemed the fort was no longer the easy prospect they had expected and sought, and their voracity had quickly faded. The discovery of the forage carts, however, had explained quite clearly the food situation, and now the Germans simply waited for them to starve.

'All the martial supplies are distributed around the walls. We...'

The centurion paused in his report at a hammering on the door. Cicero frowned. Interruptions were not acceptable during briefings, but in the circumstances, it might be important.

'Come!'

The door opened and a legionary scurried in and came to attention with a smart salute.

'Sir!'

'What is it, soldier?'

The legionary broke into a wide grin. 'Relief, sir.'

'The legions?' Cicero frowned.

'Dunno, sir, but there's thousands of Roman and allied Gaulish cavalry at the end of the valley coming this way, and it's put the shi... it's unsettled the Germans, sir. Looks like they're packing to leave in a hurry.'

The tension in the room broke and the officers breathed deep with relief.

'Thank Mars and Minerva,' said the most senior centurion, currently filling in as Primus Pilus. 'I will never be so glad to see the other legions muscling in on our glory!' he grinned.

Cicero nodded, though the sense of relief he felt was tempered with worry. If the army *was* coming, the Fourteenth were saved. But Cicero knew the general well and shuddered at the thought of the interview that loomed in his near future.

Chapter Nineteen

The forest of Arduenna.

The singulares moved down the narrow track, keeping close together. They were not the well-equipped, sizeable unit who had left Caesar's camp what felt like years before. Gone was the pack train, almost all the supplies used up and what was left cartable by the men. Gone were the mounts. The area of forest they were in now was not conducive to easy riding, and the trail only Ullio and Samognatos seemed able to follow led often through terrain that no horse could negotiate. That hardly mattered now, since it seemed that Ambiorix and his men were also on foot. How else could they manage such terrain themselves. Gone also, however, were more than half the men.

Fronto ground his teeth as he did every time he made the calculation. Nine remaining of an original twenty. Arcadios, Quietus, Magurix, Iuvenalis and Celer alone remained of the sixteen chosen men, along with Palmatus, Masgava, Samognatos and Fronto. Ullio, of course, could hardly be counted among their number for all his presence.

And that meant that they had lost too many good men along the way:

Galatos, missing in the druidic town of Divonanto, presumably murdered by the traitor. Myron and Pontius, felled in the woods by Segni warriors. Damionis murdered in his sleep. Brannogenos - not such a good man, of course, fled into the woods to plan further harm. Numisius and Biorix alive - presumably - but sent back to Caesar's army as messengers. Luxinio dead on watch when the animal-headed bandits had attacked, and Valgus also missing since that fight. And finally, Drusus, murdered on watch last night, though no cause of death could be determined without the medical expertise of Damionis. Damn it!

Nine men. Plus Ullio. And rumour suggested that Ambiorix's small party of warriors would be a rough match for them.

It was a touch of a concern, given that they could not be more than half a day behind Ambiorix as the fugitive king made for the great river and likely to freedom across its waters among the enemies of Rome. What if they caught up and Ambiorix managed to best his pursuers? It was a real possibility, given how weary and

361

travel worn they all were, the evenness of numbers, the unfamiliarity of Fronto's men with the terrain and the desperation Ambiorix would be labouring with. Desperation lent strength, as Fronto knew from personal experience.

And yet when he thought deeply on it, Fronto managed each time to convince himself that he would win. Ambiorix may have the strength of a desperate man, but Fronto and his men had determination on a level undreamed of. And the sanction of Arduenna, apparently, added to his own personal deities Fortuna and Nemesis.

If only it weren't for the uncertainty of what Brannogenos, the sigil-draped superstitious traitor, was up to somewhere in the forest.

One way or another it would be settled soon, and Fronto would invoke the name of Nemesis as he took that bastard by the scruff of the neck and bled him for every secret he had, before sending Caesar the head to put a final halt on the destruction, albeit somewhat late in the day.

His reverie swirled in surprise as something clanged off his helmet so hard it almost knocked him over. The small column of men burst into activity as figures poured out of the undergrowth to either side of the narrow track. Fronto reflexively drew his blade and turned. Already, Palmatus and Celer were armed and moving on the ambushers.

Fronto took a step towards them, the familiar rush of adrenaline at the instigation of a fight thrilling through him, but his eyes narrowed, and his feet were already skidding to a halt in the dust as his gaze picked out details.

No mail or helms in evidence. One or two of the more-than-a-dozen attackers bore swords, but even they were ancient, rusted things. Most carried a sickle or a sharpened pole or various farm or craftsman tools. The big brute advancing on Palmatus with furious ire was clearly a smith, the great hammer swinging in his hand no weapon of war, but the tool of an artist.

'Form up!' he yelled. Masgava and Samognatos whirled in confusion, but the rest, trained with the legions to obey commands even before they'd heard them fully, were already back out at the dusty path centre, straightening into a line, weapons drawn and ready, but no longer threatening immediate violence.

Masgava and the scout took only a moment to realise what was happening and quickly back-stepped away from the fight. Ullio was already out front, hands up in a gesture of peace. The big blacksmith kept coming, his hammer pendulous, and Fronto stepped in front of the man, reversing his grip on his blade and using the hilt to push aside the hammer. The smith glared at him and began to raise the weapon, but Fronto simply shook his head silently.

Back at the edge of the path, where two boys too young to shave wielded farm tools threateningly, Ullio raised his voice and threw out a question in his own tongue. The smith, his head cocking to one side, narrowed his eyes at Fronto and stepped back to his people.

'They are refugees,' Ullio announced, waving at Fronto to put his sword away.

'I'd guessed,' the commander replied, nodding meaningfully towards the smith's hammer as he sheathed his blade. The big man still eyed him suspiciously, but slowly upended the hammer and slid it through a leather loop at his side, where it hung easily.

Fronto turned to the rest of his men.

'Sheathe your weapons. These people aren't our enemy.'

The men of the singulares seemed more than happy to put away their swords and settled into an 'at ease' stance. The rest of the refugees, at a word from an old man with a pitted iron sword, pushed their way out onto the path. There were perhaps four dozen of them, mostly old men, women and young children. Barring a farmer and the smith, there was a notable absence of men of fighting age, which brought a lump to Fronto's throat, since everyone present knew what that meant.

The old man rattled off into his own language at Ullio, who nodded, giving him a sympathetic smile, and then replied. After a short exchange, the Eburone hunter turned to Fronto.

'I won't distress you with the details. You can guess the main of it. These are all that remains of the settlement at the head of the white river. It seems one of the Roman forces passed through here almost a week ago, though they don't know who led it. After burying the dead and gathering up what they could find, they are moving west and south, towards the Treveri, hoping to find sanctuary and land to begin again.'

Fronto tried to give them a sympathetic smile. 'For what it's worth, you can give them my apologies that a feud between two men has expanded so much that it's even engulfed their village. I would recommend that you direct them to Atuatuca. The people there seemed to be willing to try and rebuild, and now that that area has

363

already seen devastation, they will be unlikely to see Romans there again in the foreseeable future.'

Ullio nodded and translated his words to the old man. A look of mixed hope and gratitude swept through the refugees at the news that they might still find a home among the Eburones.

Palmatus and Masgava stepped forward to Fronto's side as the native hunter went back to deep conversation with his countrymen.

'This situation is getting out of control,' the big Numidian muttered at him. 'Pretty soon this land won't be worth Rome having. It'll just be a wasteland of ash and misery. Like Carthage,' he added darkly.

Palmatus sighed. 'It's down to us to stop it, my friend. Caesar's not going to halt any time soon.'

'When I find Ambiorix, as soon as I've wrung a few answers out of the prick, I'm going to skin the bugger alive for bringing this on.'

'You might want to consider Caesar's part in it,' nudged Masgava, and Fronto's eyes hardened.

'He's a mile from innocent, but let's not start talking about skinning the general, eh? He has big ears that hear many things.'

'Ambiorix?' muttered a voice.

Fronto frowned. The smith with the big hammer, standing not far from the three of them had narrowed his eyes to slits and was peering intently at Fronto.

'Did you say Ambiorix?' the Roman asked.

The smith immediately started babbling off in his own tongue and turned to the old man, involving him in a conversation. Fronto looked back and forth between them.

'Ullio?'

The hunter was already asking questions, deep in conversation with the two refugees. He turned with bright eyes and a weary smile.

'You're in luck, Fronto. We're closer than we thought.'

Fronto found himself walking over to them urgently, Masgava and Palmatus at his shoulders. The refugees automatically moved back at their approach, but the old man remained, nodding and chattering with Ullio.

'Less than an hour from here,' Ullio said, 'down a side track in a narrow valley.'

'Gods, we're close. We could nail the bastard to a post before the sun goes down if we hurry. We have to catch him.'

'Well your luck holds,' Ullio smiled. 'The reason these people are all so on edge is that a Condrusi warband are ravaging the area on behalf of Caesar. These poor refugees barely got away from them this morning, but their presence has forced Ambiorix and his men to go to ground in a ruined farmstead and wait until they've moved on. These people passed that same farmstead just now and were hurried on by Ambiorix's warriors.'

Fronto grinned. 'You've got the directions?'

Ullio nodded. 'Very close. Fronto?'

'Yes?'

'I cannot go further with you.'

Fronto's smile slipped a little. 'What?'

'You must have known that I was never going to help you torture and kill my king, no matter how much I dislike him? I cannot help you at the end. I have brought you this far, but what Rome must do to my king, she must do without my help.'

A sad smile crept across Fronto's face. He'd never given thought to what would happen when they caught up with Ambiorix, but in retrospect it would be harsh and unrealistic to expect Ullio to take part in Ambiorix's end. He reached out a hand. Ullio looked at it for a long moment, and then responded, clasping forearms in the universal gesture of comradeship.

'Where will you go? Back to Espaduno?'

'Soon. First I will travel to Atuatuca with these people. Perhaps we can all aid one another. The Eburones will need a great deal of strength and unity to come back from the brink of the pit into which your general has driven us.'

He lowered his voice to a whisper. 'Whatever happens in the coming months, I hope you escape it unharmed. Decent Romans are hard to come by.'

Fronto laughed quietly. 'Can't say I disagree with that. But it is equally good to have travelled with a decent Eburone. When we are done, I will make sacrifices to Arduenna for your continued wellbeing.'

Ullio smiled and turned, pointing off down the trail.

'Follow the main track until you find a split oak, which the locals call the Horns of Cernunnos. It's quite striking, so you'll find it hard to miss. It stands at a crossing of paths in the forest. Take the right side, down a steep slope into the narrow valley. After a very short walk you should be able to see the farmstead in the bottom. Approaching will be difficult, the old man says, but there is a stream bed which is dry in the summer, and might afford you a reasonable approach.'

Fronto stood for a moment, committing the directions to memory, and clapped his palm on Ullio's shoulder. 'I think we can take it from here. Good luck with your people, Ullio. I hope your family are well. Perhaps, when things have returned to normal, we will bump into one another again.'

'Don't take it the wrong way, Fronto, but I hope we don't. Arduenna shelter you until your task is complete.'

The Roman stood on the path and watched the refugees file away towards the south-west, Ullio walking with them. None of them spoke to the singulares as they passed, and precious few even spared them a glance. He continued to watch silently until they rounded a corner and were gone from sight, and then cleared his throat and turned to his men.

'This is it, lads. Less than a mile away, our quarry hides in a derelict farm. He hides from the Condrusi, apparently. Let's give him something else to worry about. Everyone ready?'

A chorus of affirmatives greeted him, though unenthusiastically. Despite now being moments away from their goal, the reality that they had lost so many comrades and still faced dangerous odds weighed heavily, given that they had already failed to prevent so much destruction in their extended mission. No one would feel good about it.

Except Fronto. Because he was sure that Ambiorix would be a repository of vital information on the druids and their planned uprisings. And he was going to squeeze every last morsel from the fugitive king before he wrung his neck.

He breathed deeply, his sense of purpose renewed.

'Right. Let's end this.'

* * * * *

The farmstead had been destroyed by Caesar's men in the preceding days, which provided both a hazard and a benefit to the small group of singulares as they moved into the valley. Of the four structures that had formed the farm, only one retained its roof, and even that was damaged in places, and was charred - hardly rainproof. That narrowed down the choice of location and defensive positions, which was a bonus. Caesar's ravaging, however, had destroyed the small field of crops and had burned back the undergrowth and trees, giving the building a good defensive line of sight, which was bad for Fronto.

The ten men crouched among the trees halfway down the dry stream bed - a nature-provided path of gravel and smooth stones that gave easy access through the forest and down the slope.

'See there?' Palmatus pointed, and the rest followed his finger.

'I see them. Three of them, in that ruined building.'

'It was a granary,' Samognatos said quietly. 'If you look carefully you can see the shadows of the stilts upon which it stands.'

Fronto snapped a glance at Masgava, who smiled and nodded, turning to the others. 'Iuvenalis, Celer and Magurix: reckon you could get to the granary without being seen?'

Magurix grinned with what Fronto thought was perhaps a little too much eagerness for comfort. 'With ease!' Celer and Iuvenalis looked at one another for a moment and then both nodded their agreement.

'Alright. You're the first ones in, then. Get underneath that hut and mark your targets. As soon as the rest of us make our move, deal with them as quickly as possible. As quietly as you can, too, but speed will be more important than stealth. Be fast.'

The three men nodded.

'No sign of anyone else, but we reckon from rumour there's a dozen of them. That means nine more. There can't be nine in that one intact hut with any level of comfort. Six or seven at most.'

'Wait!' Masgava whispered. 'There!' he added, pointing out across the valley. The rest tried to pick out what he'd seen, and it did not take long to spot the warrior leaning against a tree, alert but bored, halfway up the far side of the valley.

'Crap. If they've got men out on watch, there's probably more,' Fronto hissed. Every pair of eyes scanned the trees pensively, and Samognatos clicked his fingers and then pointed. The rest peered into the woods and eventually picked out the man not far from their own position, sat on a rock and leaning back sunning himself, eyes closed and almost asleep.

'We're bloody lucky he's not bright. If he'd been looking the right way at the right time, he'd have seen us coming down the stream.'

Palmatus rubbed his neck and sighed. 'If there's one at the valley head and one on the far slope, you can bet there's at least one more somewhere along this side, where the slope lowers, probably.'

'Too many to send men to. If we set a man to each, we might not have sufficient force to take the house,' Fronto sighed. 'It's a problem.'

'I will deal with them.'

Fronto turned a frown on Samognatos and the Condrusi scout shrugged, his strange grin at odds with the seriousness of the situation.

'They are far from alert, and are spaced out. I am the only man here who can move through the woods with any degree of stealth. It makes sense. I will remove the outer watchers one at a time.'

Fronto looked into the man's eyes and, seeing only resolve and confidence, nodded. 'Do it. There is no need for you to come down to the main settlement, then. When you're done, keep watch out here.'

'Which leaves the hut,' Masgava said quietly. Six or seven men at most. You, me and Palmatus, Arcadios, Quietus and Aurelius. Six men. Roughly even… odds I can live with.'

Fronto nodded his agreement. 'With one exception. Arcadios? You once told me your aim was unerringly true. What's the range on that Cretan bow of yours?'

'From here, sir? Pretty much anything in the farmstead with a good degree of accuracy.'

'See that rock the picket's sunning himself on? That's got a lovely view. As soon as Samognatos takes him out, you take his place. You're our last chance. Follow Samognatos with your arrow and if he gets into trouble, help him. Then train down on the farm. The three in the granary. If any of them live through our assault, deal with them. Then concentrate on the main hut. There's only one door and we'll be going in through it. But there's a couple of windows, and anyone that manages to get out of the hut gets an arrow in the leg. Stop them running, but no killing blows. Understood?'

'Yes sir.'

'Good.' Fronto looked around his men. They were not the Tenth Legion. In fact they were a terribly mismatched, non-military bunch. A former gladiator, a retired veteran, three legionaries, an engineer, an auxiliary bowman and two Belgae. But he'd come to think of them as a unit, and they were, frankly, as good a command as he'd ever held. They all bore hard expressions of determination.

'Samognatos. Move out.'

* * * * *

Fronto and his eight companions crouched behind a wind-felled tree, just off to one side of the stream. The undergrowth would crack and rustle, but the area by the stream was mostly grass, so not too bad, whereas their nailed boots would clack and crunch on the stone of the stream bed and would be far too noticeable as they closed on the enemy.

Each man watched tensely as the strange, silent, ghostly shape of Samognatos moved through the woods. Since the man usually travelled with the rest of the singulares he rarely had need for stealth, and none of the others had truly appreciated his skills until they watched him in the valley. He'd barely left the stream bed before he vanished from sight among the trunks, only appearing here and there in brief flitting glimpses. Moreover, while the rest of them would have made a noise like a war elephant crashing through that undergrowth, they heard nothing of his movements, the slightest whisper of his passage concealed beneath the breeze gusting through the leaves.

'Shit, that man's good,' Palmatus hissed as the Condrusi scout vanished once more among the leaves and then suddenly appeared almost from nowhere immediately behind the picket who sat on the rock enjoying the sunshine. They never saw what happened to him… the man simply disappeared from sight behind the rock, Samognatos' arm round his throat. A moment later the scout stood and signalled them before moving off for the watcher at the far side of the valley.

'This is it, then,' Fronto hissed. 'Arcadios, get to that rock and take aim. Magurix, Iuvenalis and Celer, peel off to the left as soon as we reach the bottom and make for the granary. As soon as you're in position, we'll break cover for the main hut door and everything will happen at once. Be ready.'

As the three men nodded and the Cretan archer moved off, Fronto took a deep breath and scanned the woods once more. Brannogenos was still out there somewhere with treason and death on his mind. What if he were here, in this valley? It would not take much to cock this whole thing up.

He reached up and grasped the twin figures of Fortuna and Nemesis who hung on a thong at his neck, the latter a recent addition. They felt cold. Unseasonably, given the summer's warmth. Something was wrong, but there was not a thing he could do about it without knowing what it was.

* * * * *

He never saw the second picket die. One moment, as he descended the rough grass by the stream bed with his men, Fronto had seen the man peering out across the valley. The next moment he was gone and Samognatos was visible only as a distant movement in the leaves, making for the lower valley end and the likely position of a third watcher.

This was it. Praying that Arduenna was still watching over them now that Ullio had left, Fronto gave his favoured Goddesses a last squeeze and gestured left.

Magurix, big and muscular, shieldless and with heavy blade in hand, moved off, with the hardy figures of Celer and Iuvenalis at his heel, using an old, charred fence and hedge to close on the ruined granary where the three Eburones waited. Fronto felt himself shivering with the tension. All he wanted now was to get in that hut and pin Ambiorix to the floor. He'd been so close before now, and to be this near was making him twitch, especially with his strange sixth sense playing up.

The big Remi and his two legionary companions reached the end of the hedge and paused as one of the Eburones moved past a ruined aperture in the wall, taking a moment to peer out but seeing only what he expected: nothing.

Then they were moving again. Fast but careful across lush grass that kept their footsteps quiet. Just as a second warrior appeared at that broken wall with its wide hole, taking a slug from a water-skin and spitting out onto the grass, the three singulares ducked and hid beneath the raised floor of the granary - necessity of design keeping it raised from the ground for healthy air circulation.

They were in position, and now crawling around to get ready for their attack.

Fronto watched as they disappeared into the darkness below, gave them the count of ten to get to their places, and then broke cover, waving the other four along with him - somewhat redundantly, given each man's knowledge of the plan.

370

Such was their stealthy approach down the stream bed and their proximity to the farm that they had covered more than half the intervening space before one of the watchers in the granary managed to get out a brief word in his dialect which was quickly muffled as Iuvenalis appeared immediately in front of him and ran a gladius through his neck, jerking it this way and that to make sure the man died as quickly and quietly as possible.

No other sounds arose from the granary, attesting the speed and success of the other two, and the five singulares reached the main hut without any obvious sign that an alarm had been raised. Masgava was there first. Despite everything. Despite the training regime that Fronto adhered to these days and the speed of the legionaries with them. Masgava was and always would be faster and stronger.

The big Numidian hit the door like a battering ram, sending the wooden portal inwards in several splintered pieces, a single plank remaining to one side, smashed back on the hinges.

Fronto was in behind him, immediately followed by Palmatus, Quietus and Aurelius.

The interior of the hut was dim, especially after being out in the summer sun-dappled woods, and even as they barrelled in, their eyes were adjusting to the shade. The windows were closed, shuttered against discovery, and the hut's occupants seemingly relied on their outside pickets and guards. But all five or six of those guards were gone.

Sure enough, there were seven figures in the hut.

It had never occurred to Fronto until this point how he would identify Ambiorix. He'd never met the man, and the lack of any kind of strategy for this issue displayed the most horrendous lack of foresight. But there was no time to think. Fronto singled out three figures who sat at the far side and who even now were standing and drawing weapons. Ignoring anyone else, those three were the clear leaders. The druid he discounted, hoping that whoever dealt with him would have the presence of mind to take him alive. That left two men who could be Ambiorix. One was clearly a chieftain or king, his gold in plain evidence draped about his body and his mail shirt of extremely high quality Gallic manufacture.

But it wasn't him, whoever he was. The last figure - Ambiorix - had betrayed his identity with the most blasé and obvious of symbols. The helmet he thrust upon his head as he stood was that of a Roman officer, for all the native crest that had been wedged on the tip. Fronto had seen that helmet before many times, with its embossed bronze scene of the battle of the Caudine Forks, on the head of Quintus Titurius Sabinus. Had shared a flask of wine with its owner. Had counted him friend.

Fronto's blood surged. So many deaths and betrayals. So many friends lost, some of them unavenged. The image of poor young Crispus, run through with a Gallic spear flashed past as Fronto dived for Ambiorix, snarling imprecations as he leapt, sword out and ready.

Quietus, off to the left side of the hut, found himself immediately faced down by an Eburone warrior with lank flaxen hair and a short-handled, basic-but-sharp axe in each hand. The man immediately began to whirl them in a strangely hypnotic manner in an almost figure eight fashion. Quietus frowned, bringing his shield round to take any blow that might come from them, while he readied his gladius for that single moment he knew would come, when he would spot the gap in the man's defence.

Aurelius, mirroring him, moved off to the right as he burst in, diving for the first man. His heart was pounding as though he'd run a hundred miles to get here, and his skin prickled cold. He could feel the wrath of the bitch Goddess as he entered, and knew without any need for visual confirmation, that the beamed roof of this dim hut was home to bats. He could almost feel them flitting about him, almost hear them squeaking in the back of his mind.

His preoccupation with the ceiling was almost his undoing as his eyes flicked upwards into the darkness at exactly the wrong moment. The Eburone warrior lurking at the hut's periphery brought his spear around and lunged as Aurelius saw the flicker of disturbed wings in the rafters.

Aurelius was lucky beyond belief. Though Fronto had ordered the singulares to strip their kit of Roman accoutrements, Aurelius had had the foresight to bring along his shoulder-doubling in his pack and, once it had become clear that subterfuge was not required, he had reapplied the extra thickness of mail over his shoulders. Thus it was that the spear point, aiming for the gap between his collar bones, instead glanced off the iron hook that held his shoulder-doubling fastened and smashed into his shoulder, scattering rings as it drove in deep through muscle until it scraped the inside of the shoulder blade.

Aurelius reacted in a manner that surprised him. Despite the intense pain that ripped through his shoulder, despite the bats preparing to deluge him, and the tangible presence of the evil Goddess, something had protected him, turning aside a killing blow and merely wounding him in his shield arm.

Instead of pain-freeze or panic, what suddenly coursed through his veins was pure fury as he lunged forward again, the spear jerking out of the Eburone's hands with the movement, still jutting from the Roman's shoulder. The warrior barely had time to scream before Aurelius set about him with his gladius, taking out on the man every ounce of irritation that had built since he'd entered this damn forest. A second of the hut's occupants stepped forward to try and halt the fury and instead fell in turn to Aurelius' terrifying onslaught.

Catharsis!

Palmatus, beside Fronto, leapt for the decorative, golden chief, noting with satisfaction Masgava beside him, aiming for the druid. His blade held high and shield presented for protection, Palmatus lunged. The 'king' was no warrior, young and uncertain. Despite the quality of his arms and armour, the sword he raised was in defence only, prepared to block Palmatus' own strike. He would be able to deal with this little prick easily enough.

Palmatus felt rather than saw the space opening up beside him as Masgava disappeared from the attack and, as he feinted and lunged beneath the raised defensive royal sword, the singulares' commander was suddenly smashed to one side when the druid slammed the iron-shod heel of his staff at his chest. Staggering, Palmatus righted himself, realising that with Masgava gone he was now facing both king and druid alone. Neither would be a tough concern, but together they might have an edge.

Gritting his teeth he moved in for the fight.

Masgava blinked. He'd had the druid in his sights when his windpipe had suddenly closed and he'd been hauled to one side in a stranglehold. With regret, the result of an instant decision: he dropped both sword and shield, his left hand going up to the cord around his throat and fingers prising beneath it to give him air, while the other arm came forward and then back again, folded to present a sharp elbow behind.

There was an explosion of fetid breath by his ear as his blow stuck home, and the pressure on the cord loosened enough for Masgava to rip the thing free and turn.

The man facing him was a killer. Masgava recognised the type instantly. He'd fought a few in the arena over the years. Not a warrior. Nothing so honourable. And not a murderer. Nothing so base. A killer. An assassin perhaps? Certainly a man who knew his craft and was comfortable with it.

The barbarian let go of the cord and reached into his belt, ripping out two long knives which immediately came for Masgava's face. The big Numidian leaned sharply to the side to avoid the first strike and almost into the path of the second, stepping back sharply to gain some room. The knives whirled in a confusing, blinding cartwheel of shining steel. The killer grinned as the blades flipped out and back in the blink of an eye, scoring two lines on Masgava's arm, then two on his tunic, two on his other arm. Nothing debilitating, but stinging and angry. Not a blow intended to kill - from the whirling to the strike the man couldn't possibly have built up the power to drive a killing blow home - but enough to enrage an opponent... to drive him to foolhardy action and doing something stupid.

Masgava knew better. The man thought he was playing with a legionary: an automaton of drills and manoeuvres whose rigid adherence to tactics and discipline would render him unimaginative and somewhat at a loss against such an unusual opponent. But Masgava was no legionary, and unusual opponents had been his daily fare for years.

As the man prepared for a fourth and fifth strike with the blades, Masgava kept his eyes locked on the killer's hands, but his foot was moving unnoticed in the shadows beneath them, seemingly independent of his calm upper exterior.

He brought the hob-nailed sole down as hard as he could on the killer's foot, aiming to avoid most of the man's boot and concentrate all his weight and pressure on the toes alone. He heard the smashing and cracking of bone and saw the man's eyes widen suddenly at the realisation of what Masgava had done. One of the knives, momentarily mishandled in his realisation, flew from his fingers and skittered across the floor. The man reacted quicker than Masgava expected, dropping all his weight onto his other leg and flicking out with the remaining knife, drawing an angry line up Masgava's forearm. Even as the Eburone struck the blow, his eyes streaming from the pain in his mangled toes, he was reaching up with his spare hand and pulling something from a hiding place on his back. The light steel throwing axe glinted in the gloom as the man hefted it ready to strike.

But Masgava had anticipated each move. He'd crippled the man's left foot and naturally the killer had shifted all his weight to his right. As the axe came up gleaming, Masgava's kick took him in the right knee. There was an unpleasant crack and the killer screamed as his leg gave way, the knee bending in an unaccustomed direction.

The axe, like the blade before it, fell from his fingers and clanged across the floor.

One foot mangled and one knee snapped, the man collapsed, useless, to the ground. Masgava glanced left and right for a moment. Only for a moment, to take in the situation. And suddenly he was on the floor. The man, despite the agony in his legs, had managed to grab his foot and unbalance him. Even as Masgava tried to roll back, the crippled killer was on him, one hand closing on his windpipe while the other reached into the clasp of his cloak and withdrew a slender, short blade from a secret sheath. The blade glistened with something dark running down its length.

Poison!

Masgava's hand flew up and grasped the killer's wrist, halting the downward momentum of the poisoned knife a finger's-breadth from his eye. As the two men remained locked in the deadly embrace, the battle in the hut raging around them, Masgava felt himself becoming light-headed as his oxygen flow failed. One hand round his throat and the other struggling to strike home with the knife, the killer grinned.

'Garo never fails.'

Masgava, keeping the blade steadily away from his eye, reached up with his free hand.

'Assassins, Garo,' Masgava rasped through the restrictive grip, 'never keep blades like that alone. There's always a twin.' His free hand fumbled for only a moment at the killer's cloak clasp before it found the hilt of the other tiny knife. In a fluid motion, he whipped free the second poisoned blade and jammed it into Garo's neck.

The killer stared, his eyes wide as blood began to gout from around the needle-knife. The pressure suddenly loosened on Masgava's throat and the grip on the knife. Masgava casually turned the man's wrist until the blade pointed at Garo's own face and then pushed, driving the blade into his eye.

With a heave, he pushed the killer off him and stood, glancing only once at Garo as he shook spastically and coughed up a black froth from both mouth and nose, as well as from around the knife in his throat.

A quick glance to one side and he noted Celer busily cutting pieces off a warrior who desperately tried to defend himself with an axe in his remaining hand. Similarly at the far side, Aurelius seemed to be having a good time, bathed to the elbows in crimson and spattered with gore and brains as he repeatedly beat a man's shattered head on the floor, yelling something about bats.

Stepping over to the far end of the hut, he found Palmatus busy, too.

The grizzled veteran's left hand, now divested of its shield and wielding his pugio, was fending off the feeble attempts of the young unnamed king, while his right was busy dealing with the druid. The man's white robe was already blossoming red in four places and a steady trickle of blood ran from beneath it down the man's leg, where it pooled on the floor. Yet the druid fought on with only the severed two-foot remains of his staff, hoping to deliver a strong blow to Palmatus whenever his gaze had to flicker to the young king.

With a smile, Masgava stepped forward and reached past his friend. His hands grasped the feeble king's sword arm and he snapped it hard, so that wrist hung at a right angle to the arm. The Segni king screamed and Palmatus glanced at his friend for a moment with irritation.

'I didn't need any help.'

'Just kill him. Always the last to finish, you... even at dinner.'

'The way you eat, that's no surprise,' Palmatus snapped as he turned both weapons on the druid, feinted once and then slammed the larger of the blades through his heart.

'You took your time, anyway,' he snorted as he ripped the gladius free. 'Spot of trouble?'

'I was held up for a moment. Come on.'

They turned to Fronto.

The hut was done. Celer and Aurelius had finished the rest, while Masgava had put down the assassin and Palmatus dispatched the druid. The Segni king was busy clutching his smashed arm and weeping like a young girl.

Fronto appeared to have had a hard fight. Three small wounds bloomed red on his arm and torso, but Ambiorix had come off the worst. The man was battered around the side of the face and slicked with blood, one eye closed and puffed up from repeated pummelling. Ambiorix was a mess. Palmatus almost laughed as he realised that the unpleasant wound in the man's cheek faintly displayed a mirror image of the Caudine Forks battle embossed on the helmet, from where Fronto had hit him with it. Hard.

Ambiorix was done for, though Fronto was still venting some of his frustration on the king's body.

'Fronto, stop!'

'Don't worry. He'll live. He'll live to sing like a little bird and tell us all about his traitorous friends.'

'Mflhr...'

Fronto grabbed the limp king by the shoulders and lifted him closer. 'What?'

'Vthgtras...'

'A little clarity, if you please.'

Ambiorix took a deep breath and formed the word slowly and agonisingly through his ruined mouth and between his shattered teeth.

'Vercingetorix.'

'Never heard of him,' Fronto replied with a raised eyebrow.

'You will do,' whimpered the other king, nursing his broken arm and flooded with tears.

''What?'

Fronto flinched as something whipped past his face, and he stared in surprise as the feeble Segni king slammed back against the wall, a knife standing proud from his chest. The man gurgled and coughed up a wad of blood which spouted down onto his decorative golden torc.

In shock, Fronto turned, along with his companions - barring Aurelius, who was busy smashing up what was left of the warrior who'd apparently offended him somehow, bellowing curses at Goddesses and bats.

Magurix stood in the doorway, almost blocking out the light.

'You daft sod,' Fronto snapped. 'He might have been as useful as Ambiorix!'

'Sadly, yes,' sighed Magurix, and with a deft flick of the hand sent another thrown blade across the room, where it narrowly skimmed past Fronto's nose and slammed into Ambiorix' throat, hammering in so deep that only the hilt projected as the blood began to pump from the king's throat. Ambiorix sighed, apparently with relief, as he began to fade.

Fronto, shocked beyond action, simply let go of the dying fugitive and turned in confusion.

377

'But why?'

'Oh, Fronto. Can you not guess? Have you understood nothing about this great war of yours?'

A horrible realisation sank into Fronto as he stood and stepped forward.

'*My* war?'

'I am Remi, and my tribe serve the general. But I am also Belgae, and the general exterminates *us*. Do you not realise your army is riddled with auxiliaries who hate you? Who hate what you have done? Tribes that call you friend over a peace table plot your death with a dagger beneath it for your extermination of our people. But at last we have a chance. At last our lands can be freed of your menace. Not by that piece of filth over there who barely has the right to call himself Belgae, but by a *Gaul*, of all people. And I will not see all our hope flicker and die at the hasty confession of a petty king like Ambiorix.'

'You? This was you?'

'You're so short-sighted, you Romans. And so trusting. A little misdirection here and a little nudge there and you do exactly as you're told.'

'Vercingetorix.' Fronto said the name flatly, as if trying to commit it into his memory like carved stone.

'Never heard of him,' Magurix shrugged.

'You're a bad liar, Magurix. Despite all the times you've pulled the wool over our eyes, I saw that flicker in your eyes. You know who he is. *He's* your Gaul, isn't he? *He's* your one hope for a Roman-free future? I'd be willing to place a hefty wager that he and this Esus we've heard tales of for two years now are one and the same?' Fronto paused with a frown. 'I'd also be willing to bet he's an Arvernian prince. A tall one.'

Again, a flicker of surprised recognition in Magurix's eyes.

Palmatus, grunting, stepped forward. 'I am going to knock your bloody head off, sonny.'

'No you're not,' Fronto growled. 'He's mine. And I want him alive to answer a few questions!'

* * * * *

Magurix stepped back into the open ground in front of the hut, backing out into the sunshine, as the singulares in the hut followed him out, tensely, their hands on the grips of their weapons.

378

Even Aurelius seemed to have been jolted from his violence and stood with them, slick with blood from head to foot.

Celer and Iuvenalis, standing at guard positions around the other ruined building shells, turned in surprise as the group fanned out around the big Remi traitor.

'What happened?' Iuvenalis shouted over.

'We found the traitor,' snarled Palmatus, 'but not before he did for bloody Ambiorix!'

'I've got a name,' Fronto said, his voice dark with impending violence. 'But I think this bastard knows more yet.'

'What if he just takes his own life?' hissed Palmatus to his side.

'I don't think so. He may be a traitor and a murderer, but he's also a Remi warrior. He prides himself on that, don't you, Magurix?'

The Belgic warrior shrugged as he drew his long blade and hefted the weight.

'And I don't think he'll just off himself when he has a good opportunity to kill me first.'

Again: a shrug.

'So how about it, Magurix? Think you can take me?'

The warrior simply gave his sword a few test swings and set himself in a fighting stance. Fronto drew his own beautiful blade, the orichalcum hilt glittering in the sunlight, the images of Gods watching events unfold.

'See, Aurelius?' Fronto said, taking a few steps forward. 'Arduenna has always been with us. It's *this* twisted turd that's been cursing us all the way. Your Goddess and her bats had nothing to do with it.'

Magurix swung his long sword in a slow figure eight, the blade thrumming through the air, the huge muscles in his arms moving around each other like cats lost in a sack.

'Come on,' Fronto sighed. 'You're boring me.'

The big Remi stepped a couple of paces forward and lunged, at maximum distance, the tip close to Fronto, enticing him to step into range. Fronto simply knocked the tip aside with his gladius. 'Better. Now try and hurt me.'

Magurix back-stepped a single pace, and turned slowly. Fronto smiled as the big man kept turning, changing the move into a huge swing, allowing the weight of the sword to carry him two steps forward with the swipe as it came back full circle on Fronto.

But Fronto wasn't there. As the big man's back had turned, he'd taken three big steps forward, and was *inside* the swing. With almost subconscious precision, he delivered quick jabs with his gladius to the spinning, surprised Remi, one in the belly and the other in the shoulder. Neither penetrated deep enough to ensnare the blade but, as Magurix staggered in shock and Fronto danced back out of reach, the sword arm dropped to his side weakly and a small coil of intestine poked out of the wide hole in his belly.

'See, the problem, Magurix, is that you think of me as an average Roman. I'm *not* an average Roman.'

Magurix frowned as he tried to lift the sword and, realising his arm was useless, changed hand with the blade.

'In fact, I was trained by the best,' Fronto went on conversationally. 'By Masgava over there. And I know a few things about where to hit a man to cause him *real* trouble.'

Magurix snarled, but stayed safely out of reach.

'Also,' Fronto smiled wickedly, 'I have spent years fending off one bastard or another. Rogue tribunes, assassins, murderers, traitors and big Germans. And I'm a little bit sick of always being on the receiving end. When I came back to the army, I decided it wouldn't happen again.'

Without warning, he kicked up dust from the yard with the toe of his boot. The cloud of grit and dust engulfed the Remi warrior's head, and he bent, choking and trying to clear his gaze. Even as the big Belgian attempted to straighten again, blinking away the dust, Fronto was on him like a cat. His left arm went around the big Gaul's neck, while his right brought the tip of his gladius to rest on Magurix's throat-apple.

'The slightest wrong move now, Magurix, and it's going to be agonising. Now I'm going to ask you a few *pointed* questions. If you answer them to my satisfaction, I will give you the benefit of a good, clean, quick warrior's death. If not, I will cause you intense pain and then you will be bound and gagged for the journey back to Caesar, where you will be handed over to the tender ministrations of some extremely skilled men and their collection of hot knives. Do we have an understanding?'

Magurix strained and gave a hoarse rasp.

'Don't nod' Fronto added with a wicked smile.

The Remi's eyes changed for a moment. Fronto frowned at the shift in expression, wondering what he was up to and realised only too late what it was: resignation. *Acceptance!*

380

He tried desperately to pull back his blade, but Magurix had let go of his own sword and grasped Fronto's right hand in his huge, enveloping meaty grip. With a single jerk, the Remi traitor pushed Fronto's hand, driving the glittering gladius through his own throat and deep into his spine, where it crunched.

Magurix went limp with a defiant, unpleasant smile.

Fronto ground his teeth as he let go of the big warrior and the body collapsed to the dust. As he did so, the collar of Magurix's mail shirt shifted, and something caught Fronto's eye. Crouching over the gurgling, dying traitor, he reached beneath the collar and pulled out the leather thong that hung around his neck, gripping the thing that had caught his attention. He peered at the small silver figure. A cloak clasp in the form of a naked girl... Drusus' most prized possession.

What he found came as no surprise as he worked along the thong: an iron-work sigil in the shape of some Gallic spirit - a trophy of Brannogenos, a man sacrificed to be play scapegoat for Magurix's traitorous activity. A beautiful, decorative, copper-and-gold arm ring that had belonged to Galatos, who lay dead in some alleyway back in Divonanto. A surgical hook taken from Damionis' medical satchel. A Medusa-image ring that had lived on Valgus' finger. It was a *catalogue of murder*. Trophy evidence of Magurix's deeds.

Slowly, drained of energy by the violence of the past half hour and the dreadful realisations of treachery that had dogged their every footstep on this hunt, Fronto rose like some Titan of legend, his face a mask of Jupiter' thundery wrath.

'Someone get back inside and take the heads off Ambiorix, that other noble, and the druid. Find a sack for each and then get your gear packed tight. It's time we got back to the army, and there's a fair way to go.'

Palmatus wandered over to him, rubbing his neck wearily.

'It's all been a bit of a waste of time, hasn't it?'

Fronto shrugged. 'Perhaps. We didn't get to stop the destruction of the Belgae, and we didn't get much of an interrogation in, but I do have one prize... a name: Vercingetorix.'

Chapter Twenty

Camp of the legions.

Antonius and Priscus paused at the entrance to the timber headquarters in the camp - formerly Cicero's domain, but now firmly in the grip of Caesar. All around, the camp was flooded with the noises of legions settling in and repairing the damage done by the Germanic warband, burying and burning the dead and gathering the supplies they so badly needed. Ten legions in this one camp was a squeeze, even given the enormity of the place, and two of the legions had been forced to resort to temporary camps outside the ramparts.

With a deep breath and a shared glance, the two officers opened the door and strode inside, having been cleared for admittance by the Praetorian horsemen on guard.

The large main room of the building - simply a wooden recreation of Caesar's command tent on campaign - was empty apart from the general, who sat at his table before the strewn maps and tablets, lists and parchments. Antonius frowned and Priscus felt a moment of concern when he realised that the general, leaning over with his head cradled in his hands, looked unwell in some way. Caesar, realising sharply that he was not alone, sat straight and the pair noticed - again with concern - the froth of spittle at the corners of his mouth and the strained, drawn paleness of his face.

'Are you alright?' Antonius asked quietly.

'Fine. Mostly fine, Marcus. In actual fact what I am is not ill, but rather concerned.'

As admission of worry from the general was so almost unknown that the pair exchanged their own anxious glances.

'Sir?'

'News from Rome.'

Priscus felt his spirits sink. News that travelled all the way from the city to the northern fringes of Gaul was never trivial, and given the general's expression, it was far from good. A pensive silence filled the room and Caesar tapped a scroll case before him. Priscus noted the use of Caesar's 'Taurus' seal in the wax. Very few people in Rome would have the authority to use that seal. Apart from close family, the only one Priscus could name was Publius Clodius Pulcher, Caesar's pet thug and master criminal.

'Our good, stable triumvirate is teetering, prepared to fall.'

Priscus cocked his head in incomprehension, but Antonius stepped forward and placed his palms on the table. 'Pompey? Has he...'

Caesar was shaking his head. 'Crassus.'

'The Parthians?'

A slow nod. 'And not killed in battle like his son Publius. He was captured in ignominious surrender and then executed. The King of Kings made sure to send a detailed account of his end back to Syria and thence to Rome.'

'Then you and Pompey...'

Caesar nodded. 'Since Julia's death we are hardly on the best of terms. And Pompey is busy building a reputation for magnanimity in Rome, garnering support wherever he can. I am faced with a dilemma: to stabilise Rome, or to stay and see Ambiorix finished. Whichever I choose, I damn myself to failure with the other.'

Priscus cleared his throat and stepped forward to join Antonius. 'Have you told young Crassus?'

Caesar shook his head and indicated another sealed scroll on the table, bearing the mark of the Licinii. 'This came to me first. Crassus has been summoned and should be here any moment. Cicero, also.'

The two officers shared a look again. Cicero's meeting with the general had been delayed by the need to settle the legions, and everyone knew the legate had spent almost two days now sitting in his quarters, sweating, awaiting the dreaded interview.

'You'll punish him, of course,' Priscus prompted.

''I will *upbraid* him, of course.'

'*Upbraid*?' snorted Antonius. 'For his stupidity and disobedience, the man should be nailed to a cross and burned.'

'A slight over-reaction, Marcus?'

'Well you'll at least strip him of command and send him back to Rome in shame?'

Caesar shook his head slowly and both officers frowned again. 'Why?'

'With the situation in Rome,' Caesar explained quietly, 'I need to preserve every connection I have there. Cicero's brother is one of the most respected orators in the city and with no small political influence. He has already been outspoken against me in the past, and we have recently settled into a mutual quiet discontent that harms neither of us. If I send this idiot home in disgrace, I most definitely turn his brother against me. The elder Cicero will blacken my name through the senate and beyond. No. We must, for now, mollycoddle our wayward legate.'

With a sigh of understanding, the pair nodded.

'The larger problem is what to do with Rome and Ambiorix. I have pledged to Rome and to Venus herself to remove the man from the face of the world, and I cannot leave such a vow unfulfiled - it would be political suicide. And yet to stay here, concentrating on him, and leave Rome to a few lackeys without the wit to peel an apple unaided would display an incredible lack of foresight.'

Antonius wandered across and sat in one of the chairs at the side, crossing his legs and producing the inevitable wine flask from his belt.

'Not a decision anyone can make for you, Gaius, I'm afraid. We can advise, but nothing more.'

Before Caesar could reply, a knock echoed round the room, and Caesar raised his voice.

'Come!'

Crassus strode into the office in dazzling armour and freshly laundered and pressed tunic and cloak. He looked glorious, for all his youth and inexperience, with his helm tucked beneath his arm - like one of the statues in the forum of generals of old.

'Crassus. Good. Sit.'

'I would rather stand, General.'

'You might regret that decision in a moment, but as you wish. I am the bearer of news, and I am afraid it is not happy news.'

Crassus faltered very slightly, his leg shuffling into a new position to mask a slight shake. Priscus was impressed. 'My father, General?'

Nod.

'The Parthians?'

Another nod. 'And there's more, I'm afraid.'

'Publius?'

'Yes. It seems your father agreed to parlay with the King of Kings when his army was destroyed, and he suffered an ignoble end, but your brother went to Elysium like a true Roman, buying time for his cavalry to leave the field. It saddens me to relay the news, but better, I thought, to come in sympathetic tones than in a cold written missive.' He held out the unopened scroll and Crassus took it and tucked it away without cracking the seal. His arm quivered a little, but Priscus was still surprised at the show of control.

'Your situation in Rome will have changed, General.'

Again, Priscus noted with surprise how suddenly the young, enthusiastic officer was almost gone, subsumed by a shadow of his father and brother. He'd heard of the legate's command in the forest and the burning of the survivors, and marked it as another step down on the ladder to his family's harshness of spirit. Every passing month brought the young man a little closer in resemblance to his brother and now, here, Crassus was speaking to Caesar as something of an equal. Priscus was almost waiting for Caesar to take exception, but the general simply nodded and smiled sympathetically.

'Indeed, but do not let my situation concern you. Your continued command here is assured, should you wish it, but I will also quite understand if you wish to resign that command and return to Rome. There will be much to administer and take care of with your father gone.'

Crassus nodded. 'Thank you. I will - I must - resign my commission, sadly. As you say, Rome will require my presence.'

Caesar nodded. 'I will prepare appropriate communiques to confirm that you have distinguished yourself in command and that your short term was in no way a reflection upon your abilities but rather on family tragedy. Also, rest assured that any help I can provide in Rome, I will. You have but to ask myself or any of my factors or clients.'

Crassus nodded and a small, humourless smile crossed his face.

'Fear not, General... I am your man, not Pompey's. Though I owe you naught but gratitude for my term of service here, I will never align my family with that fat lunatic - my father's shade would haunt me the rest of my days if I did. In return for your support in my endeavours in the city, I will reciprocate and help balance things against Pompey. If that is all, Caesar, I must begin preparations. Rome is a long journey.'

Caesar nodded. 'The Gods go with you, Marcus Licinius Crassus. Be well.'

The young legate saluted, turned on his heel and opened the door to leave, at which Cicero, paused outside, almost comically fell into the room.

'Eavesdropping, Cicero?' Antonius sniped with a malicious grin.

'Hardly,' snapped the legate, nodding professionally as Crassus left the room and closed the door. Cicero saluted, and

Priscus had to stifle a smile as Caesar deliberately turned to the other two and made no sign that he'd even seen Cicero.

'Crassus will be useful in Rome, I think. It eases my concerns a little to know that he hates Pompey so vehemently.'

'Frankly I'll be glad to see the back of him,' admitted Priscus, and Antonius and Caesar both frowned. 'In just one season,' Priscus explained, 'he's gone from being an inexperienced and ineffectual youngster to being an unpredictable martinet. I see a fire growing in him that reminds me greatly of his kin. The Tenth will certainly be better without him.'

Caesar smiled. No matter what role he assigned to Priscus, the man always thought of himself as a member of the Tenth. Cicero, standing in the background, cleared his throat meaningfully. He, they noted, was not wearing freshly pressed tunic and polished armour. In fact he resembled a battle-worn soldier, with mud on his boots. Despite the temptation to see it as a façade, Priscus knew enough of Cicero's past few years to afford him a little leeway. Despite that idiot call while in command of the camp, Cicero had distinguished himself more than once in Gaul, and had earned glory over the winter in his defence against the Eburones.

'Ah, Quintus. Sit, man. You are not on trial.'

Priscus saw Antonius' expression before the man covered it with the mouth of his wine flask. The senior commander clearly thought otherwise. Cicero simply stood, looking tired.

'I'd rather stand, sir.'

'Everyone would stand today. Ah well. Know that I am disappointed in your inability to follow my instructions, Cicero.'

The tired-looking legate opened his mouth, bridling, but Caesar waved his hand and spoke first. 'I gave you specific orders not to split your force and leave the fort, and I gave you my word that we would be there for the kalends.'

'We were facing the danger of legion-wide starvation, General, with many additional wounded sapping the food supplies.'

'When did we return, Cicero?'

The legate stood silent.

'When did we return?' repeated the general, quietly, patiently.

'On the kalends, sir.'

'Would men have starved by then?'

'Well, no, but…'

'So you understand my disappointment.'

Again, Cicero's ire rose and he opened his mouth angrily.

'But, apart from that,' the general said calmly, 'it seems to me that during the siege, you and the Fourteenth comported yourselves appropriately and efficiently. I understand that the only poor decision made in battle was made by your Primus Pilus and he seems to have paid the price for his failures. I also understand that your success was in no small part assured by Baculus, from the Twelfth and among the wounded, as well as the eagle-bearer of the legion?'

Cicero nodded, defeated. 'Aquilifer Nasica will be receiving commendations, and Baculus is sore wounded, Caesar, but the medicus says he will live, so long as we can strap him to a bed and stop him interfering with things.'

Caesar smiled at a few personal memories of the veteran centurion. He had fought alongside Baculus in the press of men when the Belgae had first resisted Roman presence, and the man's indomitable spirit had impressed himself on the general even then.

'We appear to understand one another, Cicero. I am certain you will not disappoint me again.'

'You wish me to retain my command?' Cicero blinked in surprise.

'Five seasons of excellent and strategically sound command deserve to be recognised regardless of any moment of short-sightedness. Of course I wish you to retain your command, Cicero.'

He leaned back and glanced at the room's other two occupants and in that gaze, Priscus realised that Caesar had reached another decision.

'In fact,' the general went on, turning back to Cicero, 'I want you to give the Fourteenth a little action. Ambiorix still evades us despite the devastation we have wrought. Until the season changes and the snows set in, I want all ten legions based here, continually ravaging and destroying until the renegade king is brought to justice. I will remain as commander of the camp garrison. You can take turns with the other legates campaigning around the Belgae lands until you have fulfiled my vow for me.'

Cicero smiled. An opportunity to redeem himself loomed. 'What of Tullus?' he asked.

'Tullus?'

'His command was the Rhenus. To stop the tribes crossing. Had he obeyed your commands, *I* would not have faced *my* problems.'

Caesar frowned in deep thought, but shook his head. 'Tullus used his initiative in interpreting my orders and I cannot condemn the man for that - in fact, he obeyed their spirit above their letter. I had extended an offer of plunder to our allied tribes. Tullus would have been at fault had be prevented an ally from joining the hunt. He cannot be held accountable for the Sugambri's betrayal. But rest assured I will give him the opportunity to explain to them how disappointed I am at their actions.'

Cicero nodded, again wearily. 'Is there anything else, sir.'

'I do not believe so. See to your command. You will want to make some promotions and arrange some transfers I have no doubt. See to it and be at the general briefing tomorrow.'

Cicero turned with a salute and left the room. Caesar looked across to the other two.

'Thoughts?'

'You are too soft on the man,' grumbled Antonius, slugging back his wine.

'You've decided to stay, then?' Priscus asked. 'Despite Rome?'

'To return to Rome having failed to uphold my promises would be a dreadful thing and would play into the hands of my political enemies,' Caesar sighed. 'It seems I am left with little choice.'

The three fell silent for a long moment - a silence broken by a commotion outside the building. Caesar frowned at the others and Priscus stood, stretching. 'I'll have a look.' Leaving Antonius and Caesar arguing over Cicero, Priscus stepped out through the door.

'Better to have Clodius do away with Cicero's brother in an alley and then send the incompetent fool home,' grumbled Antonius.

'A plan with a few merits,' Caesar smiled, 'but a number of drawbacks. No. Cicero is better tamed and sweetened than turned into a martyr by my enemies. We could...'

He paused as the door opened again unannounced, and Priscus returned with a wide grin.

'Prepare yourself, General. Fronto's back. And he's brought you a gift.'

* * * * *

Fronto strode into the general's office with Palmatus and Masgava at his shoulders, the remaining six men of his party remaining outside, crowded at the doorway with Ingenuus' guard. He was aware, as he passed the immaculately turned out cavalry troopers, that he and his men bore a closer resemblance to common countryside bandits than Roman soldiers, and probably smelled more like goatherds after so long in the same clothes with only a fully-dressed dip in chilly rivers to serve as a bath. Certainly Caesar reached up and rubbed his nose as they settled in, Masgava closing the door behind them.

'A gift from the Goddess Arduenna, Caesar, who seems to favour Romans over fugitives.'

With no ceremony, he dropped something bulky and heavy in a dark-brown-stained oiled skin bag on the floor before him. The rounded object hit the boards with a bony clunk and rolled a short way. Caesar fixed the bag with his piercing gaze and then frowned as the other two men dropped a similar bag each.

'Need I ask what that contains?' Caesar prompted, pointing at the bag Fronto had dropped.

'It is exactly what you think, Caesar.'

A nod. 'And the others?'

'What we believe to be the usurper king of the Segni and their chief druid - the pair who were planning to tear their tribe away from you and join Ambiorix. Traitors both. Without them, the Segni are still ours.'

Caesar nodded and a weary smile crept across his face. Fronto turned to his friends. 'Take the rest of the lads and get yourselves bathed, dressed properly, and then fed until even Masgava's fit to burst.' The pair grinned and saluted Fronto and Caesar, then turned and left the room, shutting the door behind them and leaving the two senior officers in the relative gloom.

'You were a long time away, Fronto. Despite everything, I found I worried for you. Especially when we began to campaign around you. Priscus never missed an opportunity to remind me of your proximity and your peril.'

Fronto chuckled and sank unbidden into a seat. 'The forest of Arduenna is a big place to search, as it seems you have learned yourself, sir.'

'And finally, in the end, you have given me the means by which to fulfil my vow.'

Fronto nodded, his eyes darkening. 'There is more, though, Caesar.'

'Oh?'

'My unit was infiltrated by an anti-Roman Remi warrior, who it seems killed half a dozen of my men during the journey and only revealed himself when he was forced to murder Ambiorix to prevent the man spilling his guts to me.'

'You got nothing from him?'

'Almost. Despite the betrayal - which, I must warn you came from the bosom of one of our staunchest allies due to the current policy of devastation against the Belgae - I managed to coax a name from him: *Vercingetorix.*'

'Never heard of the man. Who is he?'

'That remains a subject for investigation, but I am fairly certain that it is the real name of the revolutionary we have been hearing of called Esus. Also that he is a nobleman of the Arverni tribe who I actually spoke to in Bibracte back in spring. He is friend to the druids and from what I saw a man to be reckoned with.'

Caesar sighed. 'I thought for a moment you had brought me the solution to my quandary, but it seems instead that you have simply altered the parameters.' He saw Fronto frown and explained. 'I have been debating whether it was more important to return to Rome and deal with the problems arising there or to continue in my hunt for Ambiorix. You have solved the latter for me, but only by raising another problem in Gaul that will demand our attention, possibly more so than Ambiorix.'

Fronto took a deep breath. 'I've been thinking about this Vercingetorix, Caesar, and I have a few thoughts on the matter for you, but what news from Rome? What demands your attention?'

Caesar's fingers steepled and he leaned forward. 'It seems that the three most powerful men in Rome are now two.'

'Crassus fell to the Parthians.'

'You say that as though you knew?'

'Let's say the Gods gave me a little preview and leave it at that. I've been half expecting the news all year.'

'His son fell in the battle, also. Consequently, the younger Crassus is returning to Rome. The position of legate of the Tenth Legion seems to have opened up somewhat fortuitously for you. Almost as though that damned random Goddess you so favour had a hand in it.'

Fronto nodded, but pursed his lips. 'Caesar, you cannot tell the world you have taken Ambiorix.'

The general paused as he sat back, his eyebrows dancing curiously. 'Pray, why not?'

'It's one of the main conclusions I've drawn, General. The trouble to which the druids and these rebels went to in order to prevent any information falling into our hands is somewhat telling about its value. We have a name. With that name we can learn more, but only as long as they are unaware of the fact that we know of Vercingetorix. As soon as you release the fact that you have Ambiorix's head, the enemy will assume we know things. Their secrets will be closer held... their treachery tighter controlled. This Vercingetorix will, of necessity, go into hiding until the time for action comes. We have an advantage, but only as long as the enemy believe Ambiorix is still free. Vercingetorix must be the pin at the hub of years of Gallic unrest.'

'No matter how true what you say may be, Fronto, I made a vow to Venus Genetrix and to the senate and people of Rome. I have spent the best part of a season hunting the man and I cannot stand in public and admit failure, holding up empty hands. Especially when I have the man's head at my feet.'

'Venus already knows of the vow's fulfilment, and the Goddess is the only one you need fear, General. You know as well as I that the senate and the people are pliable. You have fulfiled the important vow and kept the Gods content. Feed the public a distraction.'

'You suggest I lie somehow to the people of Rome?'

'I suggest that you shift your focus. Take the Roman thirst for vengeance and slake it on another. We've the heads of two more conspirators here,' he added, nudging one of the bags with his toe.

Caesar frowned and tapped his chin. 'It's a dangerous gamble, failing to deliver a wolf and instead trying to hand them a rat.'

'The public are fickle. Have Hirtius release your campaign records again this year, but play down the part of Ambiorix in them. Focus on your destruction of the Belgae and on the smaller rebels whose heads we can deliver *without* spooking the main players in the game. You've always been a master of *leading* the public in their desires rather than simply *satisfying* them.'

'I cannot give them the king of the Segni as a grand traitor. His proximity to Ambiorix puts him in danger of spooking them almost as much as the renegade king - and the senate will know the Segni are a small, almost insignificant tribe. Sadly, Labienus has disposed of Indutiomarus.' He paused. 'Perhaps the culprit behind the earlier potential rising of the Carnutes and the Senones? Antonius

391

and Priscus went and brought them back beneath our heel, but the man responsible was never punished.'

'Then he could be your man,' Fronto noted, 'but be careful how you handle that one. The Belgae are disenamoured with Rome after the events of this year and we don't wish to do the same with western Gaul. Don't push those tribes too far in order to produce a scapegoat.

Caesar nodded. 'Unfortunately, none of this solves my dilemma, regardless. I am somewhat inclined, given the events of the past two years to stay in Gaul over winter and bring this Vercingetorix to heel. Priscus, at least, will be pleased. The man's been urging me to deal with his Gallic revolutionaries for many months. Perhaps Rome can wait.'

A series of real and imagined images flashed through Fronto's head in the blink of an eye: Catullus, fatalistic and sad, relating the prophecy he had been given and then lying twisted and vomit stained on the floor of his villa; Julia, lying lifeless next to her stillborn child, swathed in the blood of the birth bed; Aurelia Cotta rendering down to fat in her burning house; Crassus pinned to the sand with a hundred Parthian arrows; Rome's silver eagle falling in a collapsing building, the banners of crimson on fire. An end to the Republic? Fronto hated temples and prophecies more than he cared to admit, and yet it was difficult to deny the evidence of this one playing out, and the conclusion was a horrifying prospect. He shuddered and dragged his mind's eye back from the images.

Pinching the bridge of his nose, Fronto shook his head. 'Despite everything, I feel that to be unwise, General.' He leaned back and stretched. 'Rome will be unstable following the loss of Crassus. They will be looking for strength and, if you are occupied in darkest Gaul, they will find it in Pompey. No matter how many your clients in Rome, without a sense of your presence, they will not sway the crowd. Crassus was off in a foreign land. You must not be, unless you wish to hand the city to your enemy. The Republic hasn't been in this delicate a state since Sulla and Marius were hitting each other with rocks. The eagle mustn't fall.'

Caesar frowned at that last and the peculiarly intense expression on Fronto's face, and let out an exasperated breath.

'Then it seems that I am plagued with having to place one side of my dilemma or the other in the hands of my subordinates. And forgetting all of these issues, there is also much that requires my attention back in Aquileia with the governing of Cisalpine Gaul.' He rubbed his temples against the threat of a headache. 'I think perhaps Aquileia is the place to go.'

Fronto was nodding. 'Close enough to either Gaul or Rome if you are needed. Makes sense, I suppose. Not showing your face in Rome might be dangerous, though.' *A collapsing building; burning vexilla; a falling eagle.*

'I can visit Rome during the winter,' Caesar sighed, 'but my presence in the city full time would bring matters with Pompey to a head at a stage at which I am ill prepared to deal with him. In Aquileia I am close enough for the people, but not *too* close for Pompey. Clodius will still act as eyes and ears in the city for me. And I have others, in the senate. Young Crassus will play my pieces for me, too. Until I can observe what is happening in Rome after Crassus' demise, I cannot push any more than that without further endangering matters. The big question, then, remains what to do with Gaul.'

'Winter the troops as usual, and place Vercingetorix's fate in the hands of Priscus,' Fronto suggested. 'He's been the one at the forefront of the matter for years anyway, and we both know he's the man to trust with the task.'

Caesar nodded. 'If I winter the troops in a line beneath the Belgae, right across the land, we should be able to react to anything. And in pairs, given what happened last winter.'

Fronto nodded. 'And if you're going to deal with the Carnutes you'll be north of the Aedui and the Arverni. Concentrate the legions to the west and they will be on hand for anything.'

Caesar nodded and leaned back in his chair. 'There are matters here that sit uncomfortably with me - principally the failing to make public Ambiorix's death and the need to keep my wits focused on two fronts of battle. But I agree with your interpretation of the situation.'

The general let out a tired sigh. 'I have missed your counsel these past years, Marcus. It has not escaped my notice that in your absence things seem to have addled, slowed and complicated. I fear Fortuna is as much yours as you are hers, and she departs with you when you leave.'

Fronto shrugged. 'I owe her a great deal. Is it your wish, then, that I take up command of the Tenth when Crassus leaves?'

Caesar nodded slowly. 'I shall have the orders drawn up. I believe I will reconvene the Gaulish assembly at Durocortorum once more before the season ends. The lands of the Remi are the most secure for us in the north, and we will move the legions there and utilise our allies among the tribes to bring the leader of that earlier conspiracy to justice. From there I can disperse the legions to winter quarters easily, and we are close enough to the Carnutes and the Senones to deal with any issues arising.'

'I presume Crassus will be heading for Rome as soon as he can?'

'Yes. He already prepares for the journey and will not come as far as Durocortorum with us. And neither, I fear, will you.'

'Caesar?'

'I am informed that your young wife is with child - by now probably *heavily* with child. I imagine she would be pleased to have her husband present for the child's first days in the world? Women are very sentimental, and events of the past year have somewhat brought home to me the value of family. The rest of our sojourn here will be largely political and ambassadorial, dealing with the chiefs' assembly again and, without wishing to sound too harsh, you are not the world's most natural ambassador, Marcus. The army can cope without you until you return in the spring. You have a few very good officers who will command the legion in your absence. And I would suggest you travel home with Crassus. Given the current state of Gaul, the combined protection of your guards will be sufficient to see off all but the greatest of threats.'

Fronto sat in immobile silence for a long moment, guilt coursing through him. In all the adrenaline and danger and fury of the past week and more, he'd rarely given more than a passing thought to Lucilia, and he had all-but forgotten about the pregnancy, but now that Caesar had brought the subject to mind, he suddenly found himself desperate to see her.

She *would* want him there.

'Thank you, General. And when your business with the assembly is done, I'm sure Lucilia would be disappointed to hear that you had travelled past Massilia without gracing us with a visit?'

Caesar's eye twinkled in a manner that Fronto hadn't seen in years and he realised just how much tension had been dispelled in the last cathartic few months, culminating in this very conversation.

'I am less convinced that a new mother will be so desperate for guests, Marcus, but thank you for the offer. When I travel south, it will likely be the more direct route, across the Alpes Mountains, past Octodurus. But you never can tell... perhaps I will find reason to come by Massilia. Give my regards to your family, including Balbus.'

Fronto smiled and straightened. 'Then if there is nothing more for us to say?'

'No. Go and pack and speak to your officers. Crassus will be ready to leave in the morning, so you would do well to stow your gear tonight.'

* * * * *

Fronto knuckled his eyes wearily. It was now three hours past sunset. His pack was stowed for travelling, he had bathed, shaved and changed into a good, red, officer's tunic and his favourite soft boots. Now, he would have a few hours' proper sleep to prepare for the journey.

After leaving the general's tent he had sought out Carbo and delivered the news of his new command, which had been well received by the smiling pink-faced centurion, and had then looked for Galronus and Priscus, only to discover they had been called to Caesar's headquarters.

It felt somehow deflating to be preparing to leave after such a busy few months, despite what he was travelling back to. With a sigh, he unlaced his boots and collapsed back into the cot, allowing the calm to enfold him in its sleepy embrace.

The rapping on the door of his small quarters woke him in that fuggy, muzzy state that is the result of being only half way deep in sleep before being roused once more, and he blinked a few times, trying to remember where he was before he sat up and hastily pulled his tunic down a little for modesty.

'Come.'

Priscus pushed open the door and grinned. 'Tired? Oh you poor old fart. I'd heard the new commander of the Tenth was in here, but instead I find only an old man.'

Fronto's own grin split his face. 'Piss off, Gnaeus.'

'So you won't be wanting any of this jar then? A rather fine vintage that Cita's men will be furiously trying to locate when he does his inventorying tomorrow.'

Fronto laughed and sat forward.

'And we won't be there to toast the new scion of the Falerii, after all,' grinned Antonius pushing through behind Priscus, fetching

395

a 'you might not, but I will,' from Galronus at the back. As they made themselves comfortable in the temporary officer's quarters, Varus and Carbo fell in behind them, carrying an armful of mugs and a plate of meat cuts, and closed the door.

'Careful,' Fronto grinned. 'I'm a lightweight these days.'

'Shouldn't be a problem,' Priscus rolled his eyes. 'Antonius here more than makes up for that. I swear this man could work through a trireme full of Falernian and still get up for parade detail at dawn!'

Fronto sighed as Varus reached across and grabbed a cup, raising it to be filled. For all he was about to set off on weeks of travel to the south, right here and right now he felt at home for the first time in years.

* * * * *

It was with a sense of tense nervousness that Fronto waved farewell to Crassus and his escort, and he and Galronus turned to the villa on the hillside above Massilia. Unlike the last time he'd been here, this time the windows glowed with a welcoming amber and smoke rose from the flues, suggesting a nice warm interior. Some way beyond, Balbus' villa displayed similar homely signs, and Fronto was surprised to find himself tensing further rather than relaxing.

The small party of singulares who accompanied him, along with the pack beasts at the rear, came to a halt behind their commander.

'Why are we paused?' Palmatus frowned.

'I'm not sure,' muttered Fronto.

'You're nervous?'

'Actually, yes. I've not thought about this moment often, but it occurs to me that my family have never had a lot of luck with childbirth. It's been a touch-and-go process for generations and we never have numerous issue. I was the fourth boy and the first to live past the night.'

'You are a cheerful old sod, you know?' grinned Palmatus.

'Anyway, last I heard it was the women who did that bit, and Lucilia's ten times as strong as you,' laughed Galronus. Fronto gave them a look composed in equal parts of grumpy disapproval and mischievous acceptance, but still his heart felt encased in steel. Cold; defensive.

'Come on,' snorted Galronus and kicked his horse into movement again. Fronto paused for a moment longer and then followed, the singulares behind him. In the early evening air, Massilia's first bad flittered, squeaking, overhead, and from the rear came the sound of Aurelius casting curses at the sky.

Through the gate and into the villa grounds.

The garden had flourished and, though autumn was now pulling in, the care with which it had been planted and tended suggested Balbus' involvement. Rose bushes and flower beds complemented neat green lawns and gravelled paths, with marble benches and a trickling fountain. Even as Fronto and Galronus passed into the courtyard, the front door of the building opened and three slaves scurried out into the dim evening light. The pair reached the wide gravel area before the door and the three men rushed across, heads bowed.

'Welcome, Domine.' The first of the three reached out for the reins of Fronto's horse, while the other two ran off behind to the rest. 'Your men will have to bunk for the night in the outbuildings. We will have proper rooms prepared for them in the morning, but the Domina was not warned of your arrival, and so we are not prepared.'

Fronto looked around at Palmatus and Masgava, who both nodded, dismounting.

'Fine.'

'And master Galronus, I believe?'

The Remi officer nodded his head in answer.

'The Domina bids me tell you that the lady Faleria is at the Villa Balba along the road.'

Fronto frowned at Galronus, who simply shrugged and turned his beast. 'Women have their reasons, Fronto. I will see you in the morning.'

As his friend made his way back out onto the road and the singulares were led by the other two slaves around the villa's side to where a variety of solidly-constructed buildings stood, Fronto found himself alone in the gathering dusk, with only the slave and Bucephalus for company.

'What's your name?'

'Amelgo, Domine.'

'Hispanic?'

' Yes. Sedetani, Domine. You have a sharp ear.'

'Heard the accent a lot in my time. Well, Amelgo… this is Bucephalus and he's been with me a long time. Look after him.'

'Naturally, Domine. I shall see to the stabling myself. If you head into the atrium, Aridolis will take you through.' The Spanish slave gestured to the door and waited patiently for Fronto to dismount before leading the big black steed from the courtyard. Fronto stood silent for a moment, his eyes on the glowing gold rectangle of light, before taking a deep breath and putting one foot mechanically in front of the other until he passed from the evening shade and into the well-lit atrium.

The painters had been here, as had every other type of decorator and fabric salesman. Fronto couldn't even estimate how much the atrium had cost to get it into this warm, wealthy, elegant state. A short, swarthy man with glistening black-blue hair cut to mid-length and held back from his face with thong, bowed his head.

'Follow me, Domine.'

Fronto, his tension refusing to dispel, wandered across the atrium and followed the Greek slave through into a warm and inviting chamber decorated in reds and browns and golds and with deep red drapes. The slave bowed and retreated from the room as Fronto took in the large, comfortable looking bed and the numerous piles of linen and other 'womanly stuff' around the room, which was seemingly partitioned with drapes.

'Shhhhh...'

Fronto's heart jumped at the sibilant hiss in his ear, and a hand landed on his shoulder, gently, like a falling leaf.

'Bloody hell, Lucilia, you nearly scared the shit out of me!'

'Marcus, hush.'

Fronto, his pulse racing, looked at his wife. She wore a large, fairly shapeless gown of thick white wool, voluminous to hide the bump that was not as large as he'd expected, but was clearly there as evidence that so far nothing had gone wrong.

'Lucilia...'

'Hush, Marcus. Come.'

She wrapped his rough soldier's hand in her pale, smooth one and led him across the room, where she pointed down. Fronto frowned and looked in among the piles of linen.

'What's that?'

'That, you big numb ox, is a baby.'

Fronto blinked.

'Your son: Marcus. Named for you in the traditional manner.'

'But...?' Fronto stared, his brow furrowed. Something shuffled behind him, and he turned in surprise to see beside the wide bed a second small cradle stuffed with white linen. He frowned and turned back to Lucilia.

'And that is your second son: Lucius, named for your father. He is a grand quarter hour younger than Marcus but already more mature, which I fear says a great deal.'

Fronto blinked, his mouth flapping open and closed.

'Have you nothing to say?'

'But... bump?' he gestured at her midriff, where it bulged beneath the white cassock.

'Marcus, women do not go from orca back to sylph immediately. It takes time. Especially with twins.'

'But... early?'

'Yes. Definitely a little early, but the obstetrix says they are both fully healthy and all is in order and that I have suffered remarkably little given the healthy size of the pair.'

Fronto shook his head and collapsed onto the side of the bed, looking back and forth between the two.

'When?'

'Three days now. A shame you were not a few days early, though in truth I was not expecting you until the winter. The campaigning season is still in progress?'

Fronto waved it aside as meaningless. 'Just some menial things to sort out. I've got the Tenth again, but not 'til spring.

'That's good. Faleria is intending to seal matters with Galronus before next year, so they might have time over the winter. I assume he travelled with you?'

Fronto simply nodded. Young Marcus suddenly let out a squeak that sounded agonising and the stunned father leapt to his feet in a panic.

'Calm, dear. It's just wind.'

As Lucilia reached down gently for the distressed infant, the boy flapped his small, chubby arms and rapped his knuckles on the basket side, raising a new cry. Lucilia kissed the hand as she picked up the baby and smiled at Fronto. 'He is so definitely *your* son. Accident prone to the limit. We shall have to watch this one. If he follows his father too closely, he will discover the wine cellar as soon as he can walk.'

Fronto simply stared as Lucilia rubbed the child until it issued a reverberating belch and settled with a comfortable smile.

Just when he thought he was getting the hang of things life, as usual, threw at him something new to experience. He shook his head and tried to back away as Lucilia proffered the baby, but she was insistent, moving his arms for him until she could slip the small bundle into them.

His jaw firmed as he looked down at his eldest son and he felt a resolution he'd never experienced before. That eagle would not fall. The building would stand and the fire be extinguished and to Hades with prophecy. His sons would grow up to live in a Rome of peace and security.

Smiling down at Marcus and with a warmth beginning to infuse his chilled body, Fronto made his vow silently, beneath his breath. To Fortuna and Nemesis both. He would move the heavens if he had to, but he would stop the crumbling of the Republic for the sake of his family.

He would do whatever needed to be done.

Epilogue

'Carry out the sentence!'

The centurion in command turned and saluted Priscus and the camp prefect stepped back and took his seat on the benches along with the other officers. Caesar was conspicuous in his absence. Whether or not he had decided to leave for Aquileia this morning to throw further insult at the Carnutes and the Senones, or whether he truly cared so little to see his will done, Priscus did not know, but Antonius sat in the general's chair, watching events unfold with a stony face.

The assembly had lasted for two days, and the Remi and the Aedui, apparently eager to display their loyalty to Rome, had delivered up Acco, the chief of the Senones, as the man behind the rebellious attitude of the tribes, and the chief architect of the troubles. The Carnutes and the Senones had almost come to blows with their old friends over the betrayal, but with ten legions breathing down their necks, they checked their weapons, held their peace, and produced the wretched Acco as requested.

The man was terrified. Priscus had in his mind an image of the architects of Gallic revolt. The Ambiorixes and the Vercingetorixes and the Indutiomaruses of the world.

Acco was not one of them.

As he had been led out into the dusty square before the council of his peers and the senior commanders of Rome, he had been slumped, defeated, broken. As Caesar had listed the crimes of which he was accused and summarily pronounced his judgement without even bothering to seek approval from the Gauls, Acco had stood shaking, with wide, frightened eyes, a pool of warm urine growing at his feet.

Rome needed a villain. Priscus understood. And with the major villains gone or unavailable, this poor sod was being raised as a mastermind, but he could not find it in himself to approve of this or to hate the man. He had nodded when Antonius had requested that he be the officer in charge of the execution of Acco. He'd disliked it, but he'd agreed. And after this brief, unpleasant duty, the legions would be sent to their winter quarters - two on the borders of the repeatedly troublesome Treveri, two with the Lingones, where they were within striking distance of much of the Gallic and Belgae lands, and six in Senone territory, close to what was now being perceived to be the heart of the troubles.

But Priscus would not be going with them. With a few centuries of veterans, Priscus would be making for Aedui lands, where he would continue to pull apart the web of deceit and rebellion and learn what he could of Vercingetorix without alerting the man to his suspicions.

The winter looked like being a difficult, if interesting, time for Priscus.

The centurion startled him back into the present, calling out for the legionaries to perform their tasks. Acco was dragged, screaming like a defiant child, to the wooden 'T', where his wrists were lashed to the horizontal bar. The soldiers stepped back and the punishment officer walked across the dusty ground, his *flagellum* gripped tight. As he reached the mark in the dirt, he set his feet in position and let go of the barbed whip's multiple tips, which fell to the ground and hung there ready, the leather thongs knotted around shards of glass, pottery, bone and iron. It was a brutal weapon. One of the worst ways imaginable to die, and reserved for the worst of criminals.

At the centurion's whistle, the man pulled back his arm, tensed, and delivered the first blow.

Jagged fragments ripped across the man's back, tearing flesh from it in chunks, fracturing bones and flaying the man in excruciating agony.

Acco screamed and his cry echoed around the valley and across the silent spectators. Priscus took a deep breath. It would be over soon. He'd seen a few 'scourgings' in his time, and even hardy condemned soldiers would be dead by the count of thirty. A weak man like Acco might not make it past a dozen. And in the absence of Caesar's specific instructions, Antonius had declared that he be scourged to death, rather than the more common practice of stopping near death and then crucifying him for the end. Priscus knew Antonius well enough to know that this was no showing of weakness or compassion, though. It was simple expediency. He wanted the chiefs to watch Acco die and there to be no doubt as to his fate and no potential that he be saved from the cross by rebellious sympathisers.

No. Acco would die in the next dozen strokes.

He watched as a lung was exposed and then shredded with the third blow, and the man's cries of agony quietened with his inability to draw in enough breath.

Around them, the Gallic council watched. Silent. Angry. Helpless.

* * * * *

Vercingetorix, exiled noble of the Arverni, both master and pawn of druids, pulled the cloak tighter about himself. There was no likelihood of anyone here recognising him, especially at the back and lost among the spectators, surrounded by the equally miscellaneous figures of his men, but there was sense in leaving as little as possible to chance. It seemed that Ambiorix had escaped Roman clutches and fled across the Rhenus to his German friends, and the druids were content with the result, but Vercingetorix's men had not returned nor sent any word, and his suspicions kept him in a heightened sense of awareness of danger. He would not relax now until Rome was naught but a burning hole in the ground.

It was ironic, really. Here he was, standing watching the death of a poor fool who had - like Ambiorix - tipped his hand too early. He was surrounded by an assembly of the same chieftains who had condemned his own father to death for seeking to unite the tribes of Gaul under him. And the druids who had done nothing to help the father were now doing everything in their power to see that very thing happen to the son. Many of his father's judges were now pledging their tribes' swords to his command.

He would have laughed had he not been trying to maintain his anonymity.

'The Senones and the Carnutes are straining at the leash now,' the druid beside him muttered from the depths of his plain brown wool hood.

'They will not move, though, until they are told to do so.'

'They will not wait for long. This humiliation is the final one that they will suffer. Already their nobles plot and plan and gather their men.'

'Tell them that if they move early they will simply follow Acco to the whipping post. If they seek what we all seek, they will wait until I give them the order.'

'You are our figurehead and general, Esus. Remember that. Not our king.'

403

'I am the man who will rid you of Rome and if you wish to succeed in your endeavour, you will do exactly what I tell you, and when I do so. You will tell the Carnutes and the Senones not to move until I give the word. The word will be given before the spring - you know that.'

The druid nodded. 'It is said that their Crassus has died out in the east and that Rome teeters on the brink of disaster. It is said that Caesar will have to concentrate on Rome if he is to survive. The foretelling is that Caesar will be slow to move and mired in the workings of his webs in Rome.'

'We will wait until the legions are settled in for the winter and believe themselves secure and in control. Until Caesar is in his palace and dealing with the failings of his own people. And then, when all is right and our people are ready, straining like the river against the dam, the word will be given, and the Senones can loose the fire arrow that signals the end of Rome.'

They watched the sagging figure of Acco, who must even now be dead.

'Send word to all our friends. There must be no exchange of hostages - no evidence to betray us. Only the oaths of all. Each man must be ready to act when that fire is unleashed.'

The druid let out a slow, controlled breath.

'The time is upon us.'

END

Author's Note

Book six was a tough prospect, and I hope the result is what readers of the series had hoped. In general theme, there was always a plan with this book and the next to pull back from the political and personal troubles in Rome and return to the war in Gaul as a main focus, in anticipation of the coming great events of 52BC. It was, however, simply unfeasible to return to the familiar military dynamic of the first few books. Too many chasms in relationships needed to be bridged following the dramatic events of books four and five, and so book six was naturally destined to be the connection between them, where things are returned to 'normal'.

And it has happened. Now, Fronto will return to command of the Tenth in time for the climax of the war and one of the most dramatic battles in the history of Rome. Priscus is in position, Antonius has joined the fold, Crassus is gone and the stage is set.

The theme of this novel, as you are now well aware, was the hunt for Ambiorix. This is a personal decision. I examined in detail the events of 53BC when planning the book and made a conscious decision to focus on one aspect of the year and push others into the background. It had to be done. For those of you who've not read Caesar's commentaries, I'll try and explain why. To those who have, I suspect it will be self-evident.

Caesar's sixth book (released into the public that same year, we believe) is the weakest, shortest, and least realistic of all his works. It reads partially as a catalogue of failures and half-successes, and partially as a rambling diatribe on the mystical and socio-political nature of the barbarian. It has all the hallmarks of a work that was put together in a hurry, using pointless filler and hearsay to pad out what would otherwise be a tiny work with little merit.

Book 6 of Caesar's commentaries tells us of his punitive campaigns against the Belgae, which are brutal and have long-lasting effects. It is believed that it took over a generation for the region to even remotely recover and achieve a basic liveable sustainability. Caesar systematically works through the tribes, flattening them without any great notable battle or siege, while to the south Labienus achieves victory after victory in his name. Then, Caesar decides to cross the Rhine once more and disappears into the Suevi woodlands.

At this point, Caesar for some obscure reason (simply: it must be to pad out the work and provide a point to his abortive journey) goes off on a rambling description of the Gauls and

405

Germans, their social stratigraphy, their nature and culture, and – most pointlessly – a description of the massive German forest, even including a number of fantastic, mythical creatures. While the information he imparts is extremely valuable in terms of historical information, it has little bearing on the book and sits strangely in the midst of a running diary. In short, in turning this book into a workable Fronto novel, I had to pull the text apart, make some assumptions and, most important of all, ignore large quantities of drivel.

After a short, abortive time in the German forests, Caesar changes his mind, returns across the river and begins the hunt for Ambiorix properly. I have expanded upon this somewhat by making Ambiorix and a vow of Caesar's the main reason behind the punitive campaigns also. Caesar's work tells us that, despite everything, he fails to capture Ambiorix and it is assumed that the fugitive manages to cross the Rhine to the Germans. He disappears from history at this point in a shroud of mystery.

I chose to provide an answer to what happened to the man, as well as a feasible reason why it was not reported.

Fronto's part in this hunt is of course fiction, but at least one scene in it is drawn from record. Basilus and his cavalry really did happen on Ambiorix quite by chance in the Ardennes and really did miss capturing him by a hair's breadth. Cativolcus is noted to have committed suicide by the poison of the yew. That Fronto could have been there was too good an opportunity to miss.

And that leads me neatly to Vercingetorix and the whole conspiracy.

In the original texts, the years leading up to the great revolt see a number of lesser revolutions, some of which were more successful than others. Nowhere does it state that Vercingetorix and the druids had been in league, secretly developing a plan for outright revolt over years. In fact, the obvious conclusion from the text is that the great Gallic hero did not actually arise until between books 6 & 7, largely as a reaction to events that left Caesar in difficulty. It would be a rebellion of convenience.

I chose a few books back to see the 'great revolt' as the climax of an ongoing conspiracy rather than a rash reaction, and I stand by that, regardless of any criticism I may receive for straying from Caesar's words. Vercingetorix is, to France and the Gauls, a great hero. Their Churchill or Joan of Arc… their Robin Hood. And such a man deserves more than: 'Caesar's busy? Right. Get some swords, lads – we're going to kick some Roman bottom!' In fact, Vercingetorix is to some extent my Anti-Caesar. He is a man of no small talent and of huge charisma.

In short, small liberties have been taken in order to provide a novel with a tighter plot and a realistic premise, rather than a bunch of half-arsed village burnings, a holiday in a German forest, some drug-induced hallucinations of mythical beasts, a fruitless hunt, and an almost-accidental revolt.

I have played with some locations, too. There is ongoing discussion about *Aduatuca/Atuatuca*, and its proposed sites, as well as the nature of the Aduatuci in relation to the Eburones. I chose to solve the problem by making there two of them and making Sabinus and Cotta's camp nothing to do with either. After all, *Atuatuca* is a name that means fortress, supposedly, and there is more than one Roman '*Chester*' so why not more than one *Atuatuca*? Some places required their Belgic names to be constructed. Dinant in Belgium is at least presumed to be the sacred valley of *Divo-Nanto*. But *Espaduno*, for instance, is my construction for the ancient name of *Spa* in Belgium. Should you wish to examine the site of Basilus' folly in the book, look for aerial views of *Spa*. The towns of the Nervii that are besieged are Celtic oppida, and *Asadunon* is my creation for the oppidum of *Asse*, while *Avenna* is my creation for *Avesnelles*. We won't even go into the nature of the locations of the Menapii, since they cover the very north of Belgium and into the Netherlands, and the systematic drainage and reclamation of those lands have rendered it impossible to gain a reasonable picture of what it would have been like when it was marshy and swampy.

Last but not least on my list of deviations from the norm are the *singulares*.

A Praetor in times of war would in Republican days have a personal bodyguard (Caesar's cavalry under Ingenuus) and this is the basis for the eventually-notorious Praetorian guard. Generals and emperors are noted to have had 'singulares' bodyguards in later eras and, while there is no direct reference to their existence in the late republic, there is also no definitive work that denies their existence, and there may be (my thanks to the knowledgeable Mike Bishop for producing fragments of texts for me) hints that such a things happened. I have chosen to make it somewhat optional and mutable, as was the case with so many things in this era of change. Fronto needed his singulares to go hunting with, and Masgava and Palmatus needed a job.

And before I metaphorically 'down pen' I will confirm the next step in the saga. Marius' Mules VII is set for roughly a year from this day – give or take – but as you will be aware from the last chapters and the epilogue of this book, there are a number of events that may need a little extra coverage before I get my teeth into the great revolt. As such, I intend in the next few months to release a collection of short tales under the title 'Marius' Mules: Prelude to War'. This will provide a bridge, covering a few of the events of winter 53/52BC in detail. I will, of course, cover the same ground in extremely brief form at the start of the next book, but for those wishing to delve into the detail, I feel it is a project worth the effort.

As usual, thanks for reading thus far and I hope you enjoyed book six with its fights, betrayals, conspiracies, prophecies, hunts and... *and its bats*!. Fronto is an old friend now, and I look on him with immense fondness, all the more so since only a day ago, the great Peter O'Toole passed away, and his Flavius Silva in 'Masada' (1981) is one of the main influences in my portrayal of Fronto. It feels like half of Fronto has just vanished. Dis Manibus Flavius Silva. Enjoy Elysium.

Fronto will be back to confront the Gauls in their greatest moment.

Until then, thank you everyone and have a good year.

Simon Turney

December 2013

Full Glossary of Terms

Ad aciem: military command essentially equivalent to 'Battle stations!'

Amphora (pl. Amphorae): A large pottery storage container, generally used for wine or olive oil.

Aquilifer: a specialised standard bearer that carried a legion's eagle standard.

Aurora: Roman Goddess of the dawn, sister of Sol and Luna.

Bacchanalia: the wild and often drunken festival of Bacchus.

Buccina: A curved horn-like musical instrument used primarily by the military for relaying signals, along with the cornu.

Capsarius: Legionary soldiers trained as combat medics, whose job was to patch men up in the field until they could reach a hospital.

Civitas: Latin name given to a certain class of civil settlement, often the capital of a tribal group or a former military base.

Cloaca Maxima: The great sewer of republican Rome that drained the forum into the Tiber.

Contubernium (pl. Contubernia): the smallest division of unit in the Roman legion, numbering eight men who shared a tent.

Cornu: A G-shaped horn-like musical instrument used primarily by the military for relaying signals, along with the buccina. A trumpeter was called a cornicen.

Corona: Lit: 'Crowns'. Awards given to military officers. The Corona Muralis and Castrensis were awards for storming enemy walls, while the Aurea was for an outstanding single combat.

Curia: the meeting place of the senate in the forum of Rome.

Cursus Honorum: The ladder of political and military positions a noble Roman is expected to ascend.

Decurion: 1) The civil council of a Roman town. 2) Lesser cavalry officer, serving under a cavalry prefect, with command of thirty two men.

Dolabra: entrenching tool, carried by a legionary, which served as a shovel, pick and axe combined.

Duplicarius: A soldier on double the basic pay.

Equestrian: The often wealthier, though less noble mercantile class, known as knights.

Foederati: non-Roman states who held treaties with Rome and gained some rights under Roman law.

Gaesatus: a spearman, usually a mercenary of Gallic origin.

Gladius: the Roman army's standard short, stabbing sword, originally based on a Spanish sword design.

Groma: the chief surveying instrument of a Roman military engineer, used for marking out straight lines and calculating angles.

Haruspex (pl. Haruspices): A religious official who confirms the will of the Gods through signs and by inspecting the entrails of animals.

Immunes: legionary soldiers who possessed specialist skills and were consequently excused the more onerous duties.

Kalends: the first day of the Roman month, based on the new moon with the 'nones' being the half moon around the 5th-7th of the month and the 'ides' being the full moon around the 13th-15th.

Labrum: Large dish on a pedestal filled with fresh water in the hot room of a bath house.

Laconicum: the steam room or sauna in a Roman bath house.

Legatus: Commander of a Roman legion

Liburna: A small, fast moving oar-or-sail based galley-type vessel.

Lilia (Lit. 'Lilies'): defensive pits three feet deep with a sharpened stake at the bottom, disguised with undergrowth, to hamper attackers.

Lupercalia: Festival in Rome, noted for its riotous behaviour.

Mansio and **mutatio**: stopping places on the Roman road network for officials, military staff and couriers to stay or exchange horses if necessary.

Mare Nostrum: Latin name for the Mediterranean Sea (literally 'Our Sea').

Mars Gravidus: an aspect of the Roman war God, 'he who precedes the army in battle', was the God prayed to when an army went to war.

Massilia: Nominally-free Greek port on the south coast of Gaul, allied to Rome, now known as Marseilles.

Miles: the Roman name for a soldier, from which we derive the words military and militia among others.

Optio: A legionary centurion's second in command.

Orichalcum: a lost metal, possibly a mix of gold and silver, or possibly akin to brass.

Pilum (p: Pila) : the army's standard javelin, with a wooden stock and a long, heavy lead point.

Pilus Prior: The most senior centurion of a cohort and one of the more senior in a legion.

Praetor: a title granted to the commander of an army. cf the Praetorian Cohort.

Praetorian Cohort: personal bodyguard of a General.

Proconsul: Former consul and governor of a proconsular province.

Primus Pilus: The chief centurion of a legion. Essentially the second in command of a legion.

Pugio: the standard broad bladed dagger of the Roman military.

Quadriga: a chariot drawn by four horses, such as seen at the great races in the circus of Rome.

Samarobriva: oppidum on the Somme River, now called Amiens.

Scorpion, Ballista & Onager: Siege engines. The Scorpion was a large crossbow on a stand, the Ballista a giant missile throwing crossbow, and the Onager a stone hurling catapult.

Signifer: A century's standard bearer, also responsible for dealing with pay, burial club and much of a unit's bureaucracy.

Subura: a lower-class area of ancient Rome, close to the forum, that was home to the red-light district'.

Testudo: Lit- Tortoise. Military formation in which a century of men closes up in a rectangle and creates four walls and a roof for the unit with their shields.

Triclinium: The dining room of a Roman house or villa.

Trierarch: Commander of a Trireme or other Roman military ship.

Tuba: A Roman musical instrument – a straight horn.

Turma: A small detachment of a cavalry ala consisting of thirty two men led by a decurion.

Vexillum (Pl. Vexilli): The standard or flag of a legion.

Vindunum: later the Roman Civitas Cenomanorum, and now Le Mans in France.

Vineae: moveable wattle and leather wheeled shelters that covered siege works and attacking soldiers from enemy missiles.

If you enjoyed the Marius' Mules series why not also try:

The Thief's Tale by S.J.A. Turney

Istanbul, 1481. The once great city of Constantine that now forms the heart of the Ottoman empire is a strange mix of Christian, Turk and Jew. Despite the benevolent reign of the Sultan Bayezid II, the conquest is still a recent memory, and emotions run high among the inhabitants, with danger never far beneath the surface. Skiouros and Lykaion, the sons of a Greek country farmer, are conscripted into the ranks of the famous Janissary guards and taken to Istanbul where they will play a pivotal, if unsung, role in the history of the new regime. As Skiouros escapes into the Greek quarter and vanishes among its streets to survive on his wits alone, Lykaion remains with the slave chain to fulfil his destiny and become an Islamic convert and a guard of the Imperial palace. Brothers they remain, though standing to either side of an unimaginable divide. On a fateful day in late autumn 1490, Skiouros picks the wrong pocket and begins to unravel a plot that reaches to the very highest peaks of Imperial power. He and his brother are about to be left with the most difficult decision faced by a conquered Greek: whether the rule of the Ottoman Sultan is worth saving.

Legionary by Gordon Doherty

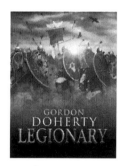

The Roman Empire is crumbling, and a shadow looms in the east. 376 AD: the Eastern Roman Empire is alone against the tide of barbarians swelling on her borders. Emperor Valens juggles the paltry border defences to stave off invasion from the Goths north of the Danube. Meanwhile, in Constantinople, a pact between faith and politics spawns a lethal plot that will bring the dark and massive hordes from the east crashing down on these struggling borders. The fates conspire to see Numerius Vitellius Pavo, enslaved as a boy after the death of his legionary father, thrust into the limitanei, the border legions, just before they are sent to recapture the long-lost eastern Kingdom of Bosporus. He is cast into the jaws of this plot, so twisted that the survival of the entire Roman world hangs in the balance.

Printed in Poland
by Amazon Fulfillment
Poland Sp. z o.o., Wrocław